# WILDERNESS

# WILDERNESS

*A Novel*

Lance Weller

BLOOMSBURY
New York   London   New Delhi   Sydney

Published by Bloomsbury USA, New York

All papers used by Bloomsbury USA are natural, recyclable products made
from wood grown in well-managed forests. The manufacturing processes
conform to the environmental regulations of the country of origin.

LIBRARY OF CONGRESS CATALOGING–IN–PUBLICATION DATA

Weller, Lance.
Wilderness / Lance Weller.—1st U.S. ed.
p. cm.
ISBN 978-1-60819-937-2
I. Title.
PS3623.E4668W55 2012
813'.6—dc23
2011048741

First U.S. edition 2012

1   3   5   7   9   10   8   6   4   2

Typeset by Westchester Book Group
Printed in the U.S.A. by Quad/Graphics, Fairfield, Pennsylvania

*For Kathryn*

# PROLOGUE

## *Rise Again*

### *1965*

SHE COMES AWAKE with an urgency she does not at first understand, surrendering the overbright tidelands of dream to the sightless dark of her waking day. She'd dreamt a campfire upon a shadow-polished beach. A heap of burning driftwood orange with flame. And, out upon the rim of the world, a paring of sun to redden the westward ocean. Burnt swell tips flashing beneath a dark sky touched with a pale light that lit the low bellies of rain clouds. Wet black sand and a jagged chain of yellowy foam to mark the snarl of tide across wavecut stone. Sparks from the fire rose in a spray to fall and lie like bright little jewels upon the shore. They flared and died and flared again in the wild yellow eyes of the wolf that watched her from the forest rising dark and quiet from the low cliffs behind.

This the landscape of dream that she had fled to wake.

Jane Dao-ming Poole stirs early, while it is still cool, while she can still yet feel the night's last darkness sweep slowly over her

1

sleep-becalmed face. Dawn-colored shadows fill soft declivities where once her eyes looked upon the world and took delight in it. She lies all atremble, for it was the howl of a wolf from the forests spilling off Hurricane Ridge far above the rest home that woke her. Gone now, if it ever was at all. She lies quiet a moment more, then sighs and pushes back the covers to let her body's fierce heat seek the upper corners. As though to lend the cool, nondescript room something of her own character. Breathing, she tastes from the cracked-open window the fecund odor of the wilderness beyond the grounds, tastes sunlight and beyond the sunlight bitter cold. And so she wakes completely.

Old now, she has become gray and frail beyond all her childhood reckonings of age. Of necessity she rises slowly, moves carefully into the kitchen space of the little studio apartment. By rote, by touch, by measured pacing from counter to refrigerator to drawer to counter again, Dao-ming moves thoughtlessly through her daily ritual of morning coffee.

Sitting at the Formica table by the window, she waits for the day's light, imagining in the way she was taught to imagine the sun gilding crusts of cloud—high, bright shelves of airy wonder—touching the forest below and sparking like strange fire on the peaks of the mountains east and west. She sees there suncups pressed into high snowfields that never melt, that are laced with watermelon fungus that never moves and feeds on sunlight and is always full. The night retreats beyond the sea, and the landscape's darkness is slowly conquered by degrees of light.

Uncoiling her stiff fingers from around the warm coffee mug, she splays them on the tabletop in a pane of sun. Gradually, warmth sinks through to her palms, eases up around her finger joints to dull the old, cold aches at palmheel and knuckle. Her soft, aubergine eye sockets are uncovered so that she might sense the quality of light and realize the day. And all the while, she shuttles a piece of splayed bullet—long

2

imprinted by shattered bone, crazed by muscle fibers pressed against it where it had burrowed hotly into his living body, dry and light and old as the American Civil War—along one of two cords that hang about her neck.

At seven o'clock every morning, the nurse taps lightly at her door with his foreknuckles, and every morning when he sees Dao-ming at her table with her coffee he lightly scolds her for it. By then she has remembered to put on her dark glasses because she knows how it bothers him to see her naked face, that the old ruins of her mad apple eyes, testimony to the outrageous violence of her youth, offend him. She can still remember the time she forgot and the high, startled pitch of his voice when he saw her. He'd stuttered and stammered, stumbling over himself until he'd found the glasses for her and she covered the soft, wrinkled folds of her wasted lids. Bruised-looking cavities sightless since the winter of 1899, when the world changed. Never to be changed back. The nurse's name is Michael, and she does not know his face or age or race but reckons him a young man and can feel herself blush when he flirts with her.

Beyond the rest-home staff—the daily nurse, one doctor or another once a month, the other occupants restlessly walking the halls— there are not many who come to visit her these days. Her husband, Edward Poole, lost at sea fifty years ago now while whaling in the old Makah way, has begun to fade from her dreams. She knows exactly where his picture is upon the bureau near her bed, and every night before sleep her fingers stray to touch the cool silver frame that sits tilted in the place her imagination puts the moonlight. Dao-Ming was blinded before she ever met him, yet there was a time, later, when she could find him in a crowded room by the certain soft shivering of the air he displaced, a time she could remember with astonishing clarity his voice, his smell, his blunt, tough fingertips tracing patterns of delight upon her upper arms. All that fades and fades away now like the diminishing ripples of a single raindrop fallen

3

into a wide lake, like the silvery cavitation of bubbles flung through seawater by the blade of an oar. Though she speaks of it to no one, it is the great tragedy of her ending days that she is losing him all over again.

There are, of course, children and the children of children. Even great-grandchildren whose names she can never quite manage to remember properly and whom, for the most part, she knows she'll never meet. Most send cards at Christmas and, when they remember, her birthday and wedding anniversary. Perhaps they visit once or twice a year, but they never stay long because no matter what the staff does to decorate, to cheer the place, the home remains a sanitary facility where old folks go to die as cool, dry, and comfortable as possible.

So sometimes, for want of husband or family or friend, Dao-ming will open her mouth as though to speak of things that lie restless upon her mind to the walls themselves, to the hollow void of her own dark world, or even to Michael the nurse when he comes tapping at her door every morning. But on this morning, in this gradual, cool light, she senses a change in things beyond the wolf howl that woke her—a taste in the air, something subtle yet with a metal-hard edge. The coffee smells richer and stronger. The sunlight does not stay long, yet neither is there rain.

When Michael knocks, then lets himself into her kitchen, Dao-ming's dark glasses are in place and the three remaining fingers of her right hand are touching lightly the sweating windowpane. Tilting her face toward him, she asks, "It snowed, didn't it?"

She can hear the soft, moist sound of his lips unsticking with a smile and hears him flip on the overhead light. "Yes," he answers. "Last night. Must've started just before midnight sometime, and now we've got . . . oh, three–four inches of the stuff."

Dao-ming can tell by the creak of his shoes and the rustle of the clothes upon his body that he is leaning over her counter, watching her. "You're pretty damn good, aren't you?"

"You bet," she says, grinning. Then, "I pay attention, is all." She takes her right hand down from the window and covers it with the good, strong fingers of her left.

"Well," says Michael, moving to the refrigerator and opening the door. A pneumatic sigh as the rubber seals part, and she can feel the sudden chill from where she sits. "Let's get you set up. Corn or peas with your dinner?"

"Steak. Whale."

He sighs, and she turns her face toward him. "Venison," she says. "Just slap it on a fire front and back and get it on a plate. I like it good and bloody, always have."

"Jane Dao-ming!" he cries in mock alarm. "You'd be killed! Why, you'd die from the shock of it."

Dao-ming exhales sharply through her nose and crosses her arms. "Jane Dao-ming, Jane Dao-ming," she says mincingly. "Well, aren't you fresh? Using my name like you were courting me."

He takes a moment to breathe and collect himself.

"All right. Fine. Is it creamed corn?"

"Now, now."

"Won't eat it. Baby food."

She hears him sigh again.

"Are you going to stand there and tell me it's not?"

"Yes, I am," he says. "Just like yesterday." He pauses a beat. "And the day before."

"Peas, then."

"Peas," he repeats. She can hear plastic containers being moved about from shelf to shelf, and when the doors sigh shut again, she asks, "Did you say it was a Douglas fir? Outside my window?"

"I don't think I remember saying, but I think so."

"You don't know?" she asks sharply.

"Well, sure. I mean, I think it's a fir—"

"What kind of man can't tell what kind of tree he's looking at?"

"Well . . ."

"It could be a lodgepole pine out there for all you know, couldn't it? My great good God, there could be a weeping willow right out there and you wouldn't know, would you?"

"Mrs. Poole . . ."

"Mrs. Poole now? What happened to 'Jane Dao-ming?'"

He sighs, and Dao-ming follows his example, then says, "You need to find out. For yourself, if not for me. The details. They're important. The smallest things," she says, casting her voice breathless and desperate as a sideshow mystic and wangling her fingers through the air. "They loom."

"All right, I'll find out," he says, then pauses. "How do I . . ."

She sighs again. "First look at the bark," she tells him. "Look for pitch blisters. A Douglas will have them if it's young. They'll be sticky. Hard. Maybe a little warm. Then look at its cones. If it's a Douglas, the needles around it will be pitchfork-shaped. You can feel those too."

"Okay," says Michael. "I'll try and figure it out this afternoon."

"My second father taught me that." Jane Dao-ming's voice softens suddenly, becomes distant and hushed and steeped in memory, and she folds her hands upon her lap as though holding there something precious that is passing or has passed. "He was carrying me through the snow. I remember white. I remember cold. He'd wrapped me in his coat because we were caught out in a storm. In the mountains far from shelter. I was five or six then, and I didn't have two names, let alone three. Just the one. My mother spoke to me in English and called me Dao-ming." She turned her face as though to address the cold, flat winter light cooling the air above the table. "He was trying to find a place to rest. My second father. He had a bad arm, and he was so sick. He was so tired. He told me the branches of the firs were too weak, too slanted and high to keep the snow off us. That it would come down in big clumps and he didn't think he could dig us out if we were buried. He was stumbling along, going down the hill, and I uncovered my face to try and see him in the dark—I wasn't blind then, but my eyes had begun to freeze—and I could just see his silhouette against the falling snow. It was very cold and very white and when the snow touched my face I began to cry because I didn't have the strength to brush it off. Nor the wit to call for him. It was so cold on my eyes and there was already something wrong. They'd been hurting since the night the wolf came to the door. Coming like it was the wind. I remember its eyes and the wet sound of its growl. I remember the dark of its fur like it was a piece of shadow, like it was made all of night. It stood there, watching me through the open door. And then it opened its mouth and its tongue fell out and for just a moment it looked happy, and I saw then that it wore a collar, just a crude, handmade thing of metal, and wondered was it part dog. And then it was gone, and all that was left was the night like the coldest thing there ever was and—"

The nurse gently interrupts to ask if she is all right, then tells her he has to finish his rounds. Tells her that if she wants, he'll come back later and they can talk a while. She turns her old, blind face to him, shuts her mouth, and does not answer. After a few moments she hears the door open and close again, and she is alone once more.

Jane Dao-ming Poole sits at her little table by the window with a cup of coffee cooling near her abbreviate right hand, the fingers lost along with her eyes to frostbite that long-ago winter. Her left hand is fisted around the bullet. Awash in memories deep as the cold, gray sea. For the first time in years she thinks of her first father, but there is little there, little left now, save the image of his sallow complexion and his caved chest by flickering lamplight. The man who was her father for five years and who was killed along with her mother high in the mountains. And Jane Dao-ming sees again her second father, Abel Truman, who found her there and who brought her down and whom she knew for two days and who gave her vision to replace

7

sight. By the window in her studio, her breath comes hot and catches high in her chest to think of him and of her third and final father, who raised her with her second and final mother. This third father, Glenn Makers, who adopted her and taught her what she'd need to know to survive in a sighted world—arithmetic and how an apple feels when ripe and sweet and how the quality of light differs by season and by temperature—and who was hanged by the neck until dead from the branches of a black cottonwood on the banks of the Little Sugar Creek by a man named Farley for the simple reason that he was a black man with a white wife.

The coffee grows cold. Ice slowly scales the window beside her. After a while, the falling snow comes to tap softly at the window and sugar the Douglas fir outside. It falls and falls and shrouds the grounds and coats the town at the bottom of the long hill. The snow gathers upon the fir slowly, branch by branch, until the entire tree becomes a rounded, soft thing that creaks and shivers softly, then finally looses all that cold weight with a long, dry, heavy thudding sound of snow falling onto snow in a breathy rush. Beside Dao-ming, the window rattles softly with the impact.

All the long afternoon, Jane Dao-ming Poole barely moves. The widow of a fisherman, she is well used to waiting. She sits, her iron-colored hair down about her shoulders and one hand lightly touching now a little crucifix—made of bone or something like bone—hanging from a cord around her neck beside the bullet. Two of her second father's, of Abel's, few possessions to survive him, she has kept them close to her all down the long years. Glenn Makers gave her the keep-sakes when she was old enough, when she'd asked him for, and he told her, Abel Truman's story.

She'd been young then, yet old enough to understand a bit about Abel's war, so it had been hard for Dao-ming to grasp how her new parents could speak fondly of a man who'd been on a side meant to keep men like Glenn in bondage. The cause for which he'd fought made what she knew of Abel's life an upsetting mare's nest she could not untangle, and the sound of Glenn's voice, when he'd call her from her warm thoughts of the old man who'd saved her from the cold and fed her hunger with a meat that made him weep to cook, made her hot with a shame she could not understand. And when she finally asked about him, her third father sat down on the porch step beside her and was quiet so long that Dao-ming had to reach and touch his face to know the set of it—feeling the lean dip of his cheeks beneath her nimble fingers and his high, knobby cheekbones, the thoughtful cast of his mouth. Then his work-rough hands took hers up and enclosed them completely while, behind them, her second mother, Ellen, stood from her porch rocker and said, "You go on, tell her, Glenn. But you tell her all of it," then went into the cabin to occupy herself at some small chore. Glenn had sighed then, and Dao-ming felt the soft squeeze of his hands.

"Skin started it," he finally told her. "That war. You know that. Skin started it, but there was more to it than just skin, and even though Abel fought for what he fought for, you can't take a man out of his time then expect to understand him. That's just not something you can do. Like the war, there was more to him than just the side he was on. Why are you crying?"

Beside the window, Jane Dao-ming smiles to remember how he always cupped her face when she cried. She couldn't weep from ruined eyes, so her face convulsed in a hot, dry copy of grief, and when it did, Glenn used his rude thumbs to softly chase down her cheeks as though to wipe away real tears.

"You can love him," he told her. "It's all right, it doesn't betray me, so you can do that."

And when it had eased and she'd gotten control of herself again, he took her on a long walk through the woods around Makers' Acres. There was a fresh and gentle wind that day and they could smell the distant sea and he began to tell her of her second father, Abel Truman.

"One thing about him," Glenn said, and Jane Dao-ming heard the moist clicking of his smile, "is that I've never seen a man who loved his dog like Abel did."

Now, beside the window, Jane Dao-ming is bathed in soft, blue winterlight that smoothes the lines from her face so that, sitting there just so, she looks just a little like the girl she was when she was young. With black hair, long like her first mother's. Staring out the window and seeing nothing but remembering everything. She can conjure the old man, the old soldier, from her memory whenever she wants. For her, he never died. An old man rocking slowly, slowly rocking, watching the gray Pacific rise and fall. And rise again.

# ONE

## *Call These Men Back*

### *1899*

IN THE FALL of that year, an old man walked deeper into the forest and higher into the hills than he had since he was young and his life was still a red thing, filled with violence. He walked longer and farther than he had since he was a soldier, campaigning with the Army of Northern Virginia in the Great War of the Rebellion when the world was not yet changed and his body was not yet shattered.

He began his journey late in the year, when the sky seemed a mirror of the ocean: flat and gray and stretching out to a horizon where darkness presided. The old man did not know he was going until he rose one morning and gathered his things—the old Winchester that had served him so well these long years of exile, his walking stick, his blanket roll and haversack—and set off southward down the dark, wet, cold, and windswept beach.

He lived beside the sea in the far northwest corner of these United States, and in the nights before he left he sat before his tiny shack watching the ocean under the nightblue sky. Seagrass sawed and rustled in a cool, salty wind. A few drops of rain fell upon his face, wetting his beard and softly sizzling in the fire. This light rain but the after-rain of the last night's storm, or perhaps the harbinger of harder rains yet to come. The shack creaked softly with the wind while the tide hissed all along the dark and rocky shore. The moon glowed full from amidst the rain clouds, casting a hard light that slid like grease atop the water. The old man watched ivory curlers far to sea rise and subside noiselessly. Within the bounds of his little cove stood sea stacks weirdly canted from the wind and waves. Tide-gnawed remnants of antediluvian islands and eroded coastal head-lands, the tall stones stood monolithic and forbidding, hoarding the shadows and softly shining purple, ghostblue in the moon- and ocean-colored gloom. Grass and wind-twisted scrub pine stood from the stacks, and on the smaller, flatter, seaward stones lay seals like earthen daubs of paint upon the night's darker canvas. From that wet dark across the bay came the occasional slap of a flipper upon the water that echoed into the round bowl of the cove, and the dog, as it always did, raised its scarred and shapeless ears.

Their shack stood at the edge of the dark forest just above the high-tide line and beside a slow, tannic river. The door, only an opening in one wall covered by an old piece of faded blanket, looked out upon the gray ocean. The old man's tiny house was but one room with a packed earth floor and walls of wind-dried drift-wood of various shapes and thickness. It was bone white and silvery in its coloring and ill suited in every way for providing home or shelter. The leaking roof was fashioned partially from scrap board he had scavenged from the mill outside Forks—he'd towed the boards north up the coast behind his boat back when his boat was sound and had painted his roof red with river mud that had long since faded to a general rust color. The door, when there had been a door, had been nothing more than long pieces of driftwood and chunks of tree bark held together with a craze of baling wire.

Off to one side there had once been a lean-to built from the same lumber, but the old man had fallen through it one night before the dog came, when he was out of his mind with drink and sorrow. He'd knocked the whole shelter over with his weight, chopped it apart in anger, and his carpentry skills were not such that he could later fathom how to set it all right again. The salvaged wood now lay pieced together tilewise on the riverbank, serving as a sort of dock for the old man to clean fish upon and stand free of mud when he washed.

The rocker in which he sat was a found item, having washed ashore one fine spring day five years ago and needing but minor repairs to its caning. The old man sat every evening to face the watery horizon and watch the sun fall, when he could see it for the rain, and to listen to the way the forest behind him hushed as light bled slowly from it.

All along the shore, behind the cabin and down the banks of the river, stood the dark wilderness, tumbling in a jade wave to the shore. Numberless green centuries of storm and tide had stranded massive logs of driftwood against the standing trunks so they lay in long heaps and mounds. Strange quiet citadels of wood, sand, and stone. Natural reliquaries encasing the dried bones of birds and fish, raccoons and seals, and the sad remains of drowned seamen carried by current and tide from as far away as Asia. Seasons of sun over long, weary years had turned the great logs silver, then white. The endless ranks of wood provided the old man's home with a natural windbreak in storm seasons, and he spent many nights awake, listening to the mournful sound of the wind at play in the tangle.

A fire burned from the little stone-lined pit before the cabin the night before he left. Yellow flames danced up into the dark, and the burning wood shivered and popped upon bright embers that shone like tiny, pulsing hearts lit bright. As he sat rocking and watching the flames at their work, the old man did not yet know that he was going, and yet, hunched before his fire, he could feel something within him shift. Beside him, the dog sensed his despair and knew what the old man did not and knew that he would soon try a thing and fail at it and that they would soon be traveling. The dog also knew they would not return. It knew these things the same way a dog knows well the heart of the man it loves and understands it in better ways than the man could ever hope. The old man patted the dog's head absently, and the dog looked up at him a moment before settling its chin upon its forepaws and closing its eyes.

The old man sat and rocked and tried not to remember his younger days when he was a married man and soldiering was the furthest thing from his mind. He tried hard not to see his wife, his infant daughter. After a while, the breath that escaped his bearded lips was hot, and he covered his eyes with his right palm and left it there until it was over.

Far to the west, where the night was fast upon the ocean's rim, the clouds had blown back and the old man could see stars where they dazzled the water. He breathed and rocked before the fire. His thoughts, beyond his control, went from painful recollections of women and family to worse remembrances of war because it had been his experience that one often led to the other—stoking its fires until there was not a man who could resist and, upon yielding, survive as a man still whole.

The old man began to tremble, though the wind was still mild and the rain still warm. He could not help but see, once again, war's sights and hear war's sounds and know, once more, war's hard gifts that are so difficult to live with after war. And then the old man closed his damp eyes again and thought of the blue door he had found on the northward beach that morning.

★ ★ ★

He'd risen midmorning, after a late night spent waiting out the storm, and went downstream to wash. Checking his lines at the river mouth where it fanned darkly into the ocean, he found a single butterfish struggling weakly on his handmade hook. He watched it from the sandy, crumbling bank—a bright little teardrop shape hung quivering in bark-colored water. The old man hauled it in and cleaned it, fried and ate it all, without much thought and with no joy whatsoever. He threw the dog the innards and what he could not himself finish and watched it eat, after which it wandered off into the forest to scare up whatever else it could. The old man carefully washed his plate in the river, dried it on an old rag he kept for that purpose, and replaced it neatly on the table near his cot.

His breakfast finished, he set to doing chores about his home. He used a hand axe to split shingles from likely-shaped chunks of driftwood and used these to mend his roof. He worked slowly, carefully, favoring his crippled left arm that would never straighten from the angle in which it had healed while he lay wounded in the Wilderness of Spotsylvania after battle there in May of 1864. The previous night's storm, though mild, had set the shack to trembling and blown rain sideways through the walls. He patched the walls with mud and handfuls of thick moss, and after finishing the job, the old man took up his rifle and set off north along the beach. The dog appeared out of the forest and ran ahead through the surf where it was shallow and fast and cold, then cut back toward the forest to stand atop a high dune, shaking head-to-tail so water flew from it in sprays of silver. It was part Labrador and part something else, and it stood waiting for the old man—a patch of black and gold and red against the dark forest behind.

Without realizing it, the old man walked soldierwise with his rifle at right shoulder shift, his tough palm cradling the butt plate and his steps measured and even as though to conserve strength for a day's hard marching. He walked a beach lit bright by sudden sunlight

15

escaping the close-packed clouds and felt the hard wind sweeping in off the water. He tasted salt, could feel the wind scouring his flesh and crackling in his beard. He drew his lips back as though such wind, such salt and raw fierceness, might bleach clean his river-stained teeth and kindle heat in the hollow, cold places within him.

With the tide rising, the old man was forced up amidst the tide-stacked driftwood and he picked his way carefully, mindful of the waves and his balance. The great silvery logs lay crosswise and askelter like huge breastworks against the battle line of the ocean, the onrushing attack of the tide. Climbing over and around them got the old man to thinking of battles despite himself. How they'd rush screaming and hollering through some field, some forest or farmer's woodlot, where musket smoke hung from the branches in pale tatters like strange moss. How they'd go down on their knees in fallen leaves or dew-slick grass, firing blindly and fast. No skill to it. No time for aiming. Driving powder and shot down the barrel and pulling free the rammer and fitting the firing caps and raising the pieces to their cramped, bruising shoulders. Kneeling there, sobbing and loading and screaming and firing and loading again, hearing the shouts and cries and sobs of those everywhere around. The great, rolling, throaty percussion of cannon and the sharp crackle of riflefire swelling up and up like an orchestra in the throes of some grand flourish. And that sound rolled together into a single noise, a solitary booming wail of a sound that had no correlation to any other sound the world makes or that a man makes upon it.

Until the Wilderness, he had hardly been touched by battle, and he had seen his share. The old man, who was then a young soldier named Abel Truman, had only been scratched and bruised, had never gotten sick, and was thought by many to be a lucky man. Men took bets on how Abel would fare that day. They shifted their places about to march near him, as though his good luck might shield them. In the end it rarely did. And while other men died everywhere all around him at Malvern Hill, while other men fell rudely shocked into their deaths in the green cornfields at the base of Cedar Mountain and in the cool, piney shade of the West Wood beyond Sharpsburg, Abel Truman was not touched until the Battle of the Wilderness, and then it had been very bad.

The old man sat resting on a silvery log. The tide was falling in the early afternoon and the ocean lay gray and foam-cluttered, touched on the horizon by steel clouds shot through with shafts of pale sunlight that stood like great, clean columns on the heaving swells. In the shallows were otters at their play. The dog padded about, sniffing after the strewn purple dung of raccoons and chasing those gulls that landed nearby. After a time, the old man took out a little sack and from that a brown twist of dried venison. He sat eating in the sun, letting it warm him through. He sat eating and trying to empty his mind to the moment, but once started, he could not turn himself from memories of his war.

Too many times to count he'd felt hot metal go buzzing past. The little winds that followed, sharp and cool. He'd felt them come plucking hard at his sleeves and pants legs as though to gently steer him from his path. Holes blown through his canteen and four good hats lost as though borne back by strong wind. Abel had even seen bullets mid-flight—small and dark and fat as horseflies. He remembered one in particular: how he whipped his head around in time to follow its path into the wide, sunburned forehead of Huntley Foster just behind him. A man who had found his way through Second Manassas and Antietam and Chancellorsville and who had wagered good writing paper on Abel's luck. The moment of Huntley's death in front of Culp's Hill: a sharp, flat crack and a look of bottomless surprise on Huntley's face. His mouth fell open in mute astonishment as though he recognized the moment for what it was, and a silent question formed in his liquid eyes, as though he'd ask of Abel something and would have his answer. Huntley had fallen back with the ball mixed in with the contents of his skull, a wide tongue of blood laid across the bridge of his nose. When Abel made his way back later, he found Huntley in a bank of fallen leaves. The boy's eyes were open, now questioning someone else, and his pockets were all turned out, his shoes and writing paper gone.

Abel had seen many men die just so and worse. Scores of men. Men whose bodies were dashed apart like waves against stone. He thought of Gully Coleman. He thought of David Abernathy and tried hard not to think of poor Ned.

Now, an old man sitting in the sun taking his lunch, Abel thought that if he concentrated hard enough, he could call them all back to memory. Each man who died in his sight and whose face he knew. Recall them and let them live again, even if only for a moment and only in his mind. Abel breathed, feeling the steady work of the cool air within him. He sat thinking that if he could call these men back, he would ask of them many, many things.

Abel Truman sat with his right hand open on his thigh, his left arm cocked tight against his ribcage, and the sun on his face. His crippled arm throbbed, as it often did. He wondered why he was left behind. Why, after his daughter's death and his wife's and all those good men and boys he marched with. Not to become an old man on a beach where no one ever came. Not just to live steeping in pain and memories of pain, he reckoned. Not unless God were even crueler than he'd proved himself to be.

And, because it was a day for such things, Abel conjured an unwanted vision of his daughter, who was when she died still too young for them to have settled on a name for and so went unnamed to her tiny grave. He had risen early that morning and lifted her from the cradle he'd built for her. It was well before the war and he was still whole and he held her in his strong left hand while with his right hand he reached to move the blanket from her face. It was a blue paler than the swaddling. A darker blue around her lips and darker still about her eyes, and she was so cold. Behind him, Elizabeth called his name. He turned, and in so turning dropped the child to the floor.

Even now, sitting in the sun on this dark beach, the gorge rose up Abel's throat to remember the look on his wife's face. The shock of realization and, finally, the pale, outraged blame that darkened like a bruise until it rotted her with hate.

Abel felt the sun against his eyelids, saw heat pounding redly through the thin panes of flesh that separated his eyes from the air and closed him from all the rest of the world. For no reason at all, he suddenly remembered Elizabeth's voice when it still loved him— deep and throaty, not what you'd expect from her small frame—and how she'd sing quietly small, sad songs of her own composition that he sometimes thought might break his heart. He remembered her white skin and her strong fingers and her square face. The brown, sun-dazed hair that stuck to the back of her neck when she sweated, and the way that she stood when she stood next to him.

The old man opened his eyes. Such remembering was hard on him. He blinked wetly, sighed, and looked over at the dog. It sat looking from the venison in Abel's hand to his face and back again. Slowly, deliberately, Abel put the twist into his mouth. The dog cocked its head and popped its jaws. Abel chewed and gave the dog a look and the dog sighed. Drool dripped from its underjaw. After a while, Abel stood. He looked down at the dog. "You are pitiful," he told it. He looked to sea, then reached into the bag and tossed the dog a piece of meat before continuing up the beach.

He walked a long time with the tide falling and the sound of rattling pebbles and the pungent iodine stink of the waves. Bits of fishing net, broken boards, jade-colored glass floats drifted over the ocean from Japan, and a stove-in cooking pot that Abel knelt to examine before tossing away again. At one point, he thought he saw two figures

19

on the beach far to the north. He waved, but if they saw him, they did not show it, and when he looked again they were gone.

By and by, the old man came upon a pale blue door lying abandoned in the sand. It had a rusted knob and a rusted knocker and it lay athwart the high-tide line as though to shut something away beneath the cold black sand. Abel walked around the door while the dog sniffed at it, barked once, and scrambled off to chase gulls.

He squatted beside the door and touched its weathered surface. Flies rose from the wet weeds and went exploring the air around his head. For all the sweet reek of tide and rot, the door, baking in the sudden afternoon sun, put Abel in mind of pitch pine, maple leaves, green trailers. Tree bark.

How the mind works, by what strange paths it pursues memory. The old man smiled, remembering how it had been in his soldiering days to boil any dark liquid and call it coffee. Roasted corn and apple cores and peanut shells. Withered potatoes and crushed acorns. Tree bark. The only requirements were that the drink be dark-unto-black, scalding hot, and ungodly strong. Abel could taste the brew suddenly, so sharp was his memory of it, and he remembered the little pouch of coffee he'd found in the haversack of a dead Union boy in the Wilderness. He remembered how rich and pure and good that real coffee had smelled, and how, on smelling it and then finding amongst the other possibles a wondrous handful of real white sugar, he'd ignored the pain in his newly ruined arm and broken down to cry like a child.

How the mind works when presented, without warning, with sights and sounds and smells and doors.

The old man frowned, staring at the door lying on the sand. He did not see it but saw, instead and for just a moment, the blue front door of the home his wife and he had once made—framed by two little windows lit softly from within by lamplight. And then he was gone from there and stood instead in the dark, cool shadows of the

Wilderness watching a tow-haired boy with both eyes shot away destroy his left arm with a lucky pistol shot. He stood instead on that old, red ground they'd fought and refought for. Ribcage curves stood from the grass like strange plantings while gray skulls grinned eyeless and mute from brown leaves like stones.

Parts of the Wilderness had been afire that night, and the air was thick with the stink of burning sweet woods, scorched hair, and stale powdersmoke. Burning horseflesh raised a pall of greasy black smoke against the starlight. Other flesh burned there too that night to raise a stench more shocking still. And the dark that night was hot and orange.

Abel Truman wandered far behind the army's lines, stumbling through the dark with the soft, mournful cries of the whippoorwill dogging his bloody heels. There was a bullet fast in his upper thigh that had not touched the bone, and another somewhere in the soft part of his trunk—a wound he was afraid to look at in case he was killed without knowing it.

The Union boy, when Abel found him, lay alone in back of the Confederate lines where their afternoon charge had reached its terminus in smoke and leafy green confusion. He lay alone in the deep woods with both eyes shot away and one knee blown redly open so a white, round knob of bone came poking through his trousers. Abel heard the soft, sick creak of the joint when the boy tried to sit up, and as his sack coat fell open, Abel saw a hole in the boy's chest that he couldn't have plugged with his thumb.

On hearing Abel enter the glade where he lay, the boy lifted a pistol from somewhere about his person and fired from his darkness at the greater dark beyond. Abel felt his arm destroyed. He fell, and when he reared back up the boy was dead, and Abel went pawing through his haversack after the smell of coffee.

Two days later, Abel stood before a tiny shack in the Wilderness fronted by another blue door, and this time, he was taken in. The reek of human fear and human hurt, the warm sweetness of mother's milk at the back of his throat—kindnesses he did not deserve.

A wind had risen on the coast. It blew sea foam along the beach and froze the gulls mid-flight, static and quiet, as though hung by threads from the dark clouds. The old man knelt in the wind beside the old door with his hard palm covering his mouth and his rifle crosswise on his lap. Nearby, the dog sat watching. When the old man sat unmoving for a long time, the dog came up, tilted its head to one side, and turned three tight circles before settling onto the sand.

Abel uncovered his face. He took a great, deep breath. The dog stood quickly. The wind set the old man's clothes to snapping and stood the dog's thick fur at strange angles. The old man's crippled arm ached, as it often did in cold wind. He took a long last look at the blue door, then silently gathered his things and set off for home with the dog running off ahead and the wind at his back, making the walking much easier.

Now, Abel Truman sat before his fire in the night with the dog lightly sleeping at his feet. Flames jumped orange and yellow from the shallow pit. He sat watching the water, remembering times gone by. When he reached down to stroke the dog behind its ears, it woke and looked at him, then sighed and settled its head between its paws to lie staring with contentment at the fire.

After a time, the old man stood and went into the dark shack. He held a small, burning stick plucked from the fire and with it lit two candle scraps standing palely from waxy puddles on a rough table. Tossing the stick back out the door onto the fire, Abel stood looking at his cot and, stacked beside it, the few volumes he read from each night before sleep. A dog-eared King James Bible with a worn calf-skin cover. An old *Farmer's Almanac* borrowed from Glenn Makers the year before last. Abel had read bits from the Bible and nearly all the almanac—if for nothing else than to try and anchor himself in the world by staying aware of planting seasons and predicted weathers, now past. He touched with two fingers the covers of these and some few other books of his keeping, then turned to a shelf on the back wall where sat a small pine box.

The old man sniffed deeply and rubbed his cocked left arm. Through his shirt, he felt a thick map of scar tissue—the gristle grown through and around shattered bones that had knit themselves back all wrong. He imagined shriveled tendons embedded with old, cold, corroded flakes of metal that frayed the nerves yet still allowed him some little use of the hand. He thought of Hypatia and the taste of her milk. He thought of the blue door of the cabin she'd occupied in the dark of the Wilderness of Spotsylvania and of another blue door closed upon a home and family long lost. Abel took a breath and set the box on the table in the flickering candlelight.

The first thing he took from it was the Union bullet she had cut from his arm. Its tip was splayed and flattened, and by certain lights you could still see a fine craze where the fibers of his shattered capitulum had engraved the metal while it was still fast and hot. Abel sniffed again and put it in his pocket, then took from the box a little crucifix fashioned from a piece of bone or something like bone. Abel never knew exactly what it was. There was an old bloodstain on the transom, faded now to the color of tree bark that took the shape of a bird wing mid-flight. David Abernathy had died holding the crucifix aloft that day in the Wilderness. How dark the mouth of the cannon. Abel shuddered.

He took a deep breath. Let it out. He held the cross in his palm as though to judge its value, weighing it in the manner of a prospector with a gold-flecked stone who wonders if this be true gold or something false and therefore foolish. The cross hung from a salt-wearied leather thong, and Abel, having reached a careful decision, slipped it around his neck and turned back to the box.

He lifted from it a brass picture frame no bigger than his palm with a hinged brass cover set with a steel Maltese cross. It was, on the whole, as beaten and weather-scoured and tired-looking as the old man's face, his hands, his heart. He opened it carefully and looked upon the tintype within. The frame joints had gone green with age; the thin glass cracked from side to side and turned a smoky yellow, glooming the image behind. But it was all right; the old man did not need to see their faces anymore for he knew them well by his heart's own photogravure.

There hung behind them, mother and child, a painted canvas lush with green valleys and white waterfalls, blue rivers, high clouds. In the far distance, snowy mountains purple under the sun. All this detail reduced to a general, brown fogginess that obscured even their faces and clothes where they sat posed upon an ornate, high-backed settee placed before the backdrop. Their dressfronts starched and their skirts arranged just so about their crossed and folded legs. The mother held the daughter's hand, and their free hands were composed precisely on the armrests. Their faces serious as befitting a moment of high gravity—neither smiled but for their eyes, and the girl was the softened echo of her mother and her mother so very beautiful. In all, a proper keepsake for a soldier gone to war to help him dream of home and hearth, and indeed the Union boy who'd shot Abel wore it on a chain near his heart when Abel found it. And there were long times and many afterward that Abel stared upon the tintype and fancied there his own wife's face, his own daughter's, had they lived and posed thusly for him.

As it often did these past months, the old man's heart fell to beating all wrong. A scrim of sweat broke upon his forehead and his breath whistled in his chest. He shut the frame carefully and reached to grip his knee with his right hand as he leaned to better breathe. He began to cough, hot and harsh and sick and foul tasting, and he coughed a long time. When it was done, Abel spat out the door into the dark so he would not see its color. After he felt right again, and before he could reconsider, he opened the frame once more, pried out the glass, then stepped toward the fire and turned the tintype out into the flames. He watched the bleary image blacken and after a while tossed the frame itself upon the coals. The dog watched him, and he lifted his chin. "It was a poor thing to thieve a thing like that," he said softly.

Abel stood beside the fire and watched the ocean move constantly, restlessly, in the outer dark. He looked at the stars that glistened hard and cold through gaps in the clouds and at the hazy moon behind. He looked at the dog where it lay sleeping by the snapping fire. Older now, it tired easily and slept hard, its long legs moving restlessly as it gave soft little puppy-barks from its dreams. Abel watched it for a time, then shed his clothes and stood naked, pale and ghostly in the shadows.

He started across the wrecked driftwood toward the sand, picking his way along carefully. The tide seethed and rattled along the shore. It sprayed and echoed on the stones in the deeper waters and slapped against itself still farther out, under the moon as it moved beyond the clouds, where men could not dwell nor prosper. Beds of kelp, like inky stains upon the general darkness, bobbed on the swells while mounds of it, beached days past, lay quietly afester with night-becalmed sand fleas near the driftwood bulwarks. Glancing to the little river that cut sharply and dark through the sand, Abel saw the largest wolf he'd ever seen, standing in the current watching him.

The old man stood stock-still. The wolf stared and did not move. Silver, moon-struck water fell from its underjaw and its hackles were raised in a dark ridge somehow reminiscent of other predators, saurian and long-extinct. They were silent together in their separate places on the shore—the old man and the wolf—and when it finally stepped from the river and turned to lope back into the forest, Abel saw the moonlight glint hard and fast off a crude, handmade collar round its neck and wondered how much dog was in it.

"I'll be damned," he said softly, thinking maybe he was or would be. "I'll be goddamned." Then he turned back toward the ocean and walked out into it.

Abel caught his breath as the cold, cold water closed around his bare thighs. He looked down the lean, pale line of his body and felt the ache throb freshly in his ruined elbow and down his forearm to the center of his palm as though the old, violent metal had spread corrosion to those places. The dark water swallowed whole his lower half while moonlight reflected his torso back, pinning and twinning him upon the water as though he faced there some pale, wavering alternate self. A doppelgänger with a history, perhaps, separate from his own but that had been fetched, after all, to the very same place, the very same ending. With all the same hurts and sorrows and ill-healed wounds. "And this is what you get," said Abel, panting and struggling with the cold. "This is what you get."

He breathed deeply, shudderingly. The sharp stones beneath his naked feet made him wish he had worn his boots. The old bits of metal still within him cooled further still in the cold water and set ice points of pain through the meat of his muscles, along the curved piping of his bones. Setting his lips together, he started forward once more with purpose and determination as though he had become, one last time, the soldier of his youth. But no bands played and no banners waved and no comrades marched beside him, for all had died long ago. The only thing to urge him onward was, perhaps, a wolf watching from the deep of the forest behind him. Abel walked until he was a head upon the waves and the waves broke over him. He spat salt and his eyes stung and streamed but he did not weep.

And then he floated. His feet no longer touched stone or sand and his head was no longer exposed to the moon and the night. The old soldier closed his eyes and floated between earth and air with the cold water touching every part of him. He shut his eyes, tasted the sharp flavor of ocean salt and imagined it seeping into him, claiming him back—his poor, ragged flesh—to leave behind bleached and knuckled bones, bits of rusted metal, forever knocking along the floor of the sea.

Beside the fire, the dog raised its head. It stood slowly, stretching and yawning and twisting about to bite after its own haunches where the fur was matted and tangled. Wandering down to the water, it climbed stiffly over the driftwood to sniff the old man's tracks in the sand. And then it smelled another thing—a wild dog-shaped scent beside the river—and whined and paced and turned about a moment with indecision before continuing down toward the sea. And when it came upon the old man where he lay, the dog whined again and licked his face. A wave surged up around them and pushed the old man's body through the sand and the dog danced up out of the cold water, then came sniffing back after it had receded. It nuzzled the old man's neck and licked his ear and the old man began to cough. He sputtered and coughed and sat up with his eyes red and his nose running. After a moment, he leaned to vomit. The saltwater left the back of his throat raw and he sneezed a thick clot of bloody snot into his palm that he wiped off on the sand.

Abel Truman sat staring at the water, trying to will warmth back into his limbs while the dog licked salt from his crooked arm. He looked at it, and then stood. "You just shut up," he said. "Bet if you was to try it, it'd throw you back too." Then he turned to make his slow way back to the shack, where the fire still burned up out of its little stone ring while, for its part, the dog paused beside the little river to stare across it at a dark patch of disturbed sand and the tracks that led from it into the forest. It bristled and growled softly until Abel called to it from beside the fire, "Get over here, you old cuss," he said. "Don't you know there's a wolf about?" The dog huffed its indignation twice, then turned to join the old man in his shack.

That night the old man dreamed a dream terrifying and strange. Buried without a coffin, he clawed the suffocating earth and broke to air with his mouth full of dirt. Around him, campfires burned on a vast and featureless plain. The feminine curve of hills in dark silhouette marked the horizon and there were fires there too, and stars in the sky. The very air was dark as though the dark had become a part of it and it was cold. White flames that shed no heat flapped on twisted black braids of wood.

And there were men that he knew gathered in that place with their hands stretched flameward. Taylor there. And old Hoke who lost his leg to the hip at the base of Culp's Hill and who died in the ambulance two days later. David Abernathy and old Joe and Gully Coleman and Scripture Lewis. Ned was there, breaking Abel's heart forever. And countless others known to him and not. Dark crowds gathered around tiny fires. Their breath smoked palely and all were utterly silent, standing like sentinels or crouching apelike in the glassy cold.

Abel called but no one turned. He stood apart from them and when he stumbled forward he woke with his face wet and his thin blanket bunched up around his neck. He breathed into the dark. After a while he flung an arm out from the cot and called the dog to him and it rose stiffly and came.

The next morning, the old man left the shack while the dog stood beside the firepit with its head raised to sniff the morning breezes. It pawed the ground, turned three tight circles, and settled down in its usual place near where the warmth of the fire should have been.

The old man's steps were loud upon the upriver trail, and the dog's ears stood half cocked with listening. It waited a long time, twice longer than it knew it should take the old man to make his toilet and return. In the distance, it could hear him walking on the forest paths and swearing and coughing up great quantities of phlegm, as was his morning custom. After a time, the dog realized the old man had crossed over the river into the shade of the trees beyond. It stood quickly, shook itself, and sniffed the air once more before it bent its nose to the soil to find the old man's scent upon the earth and follow.

# TWO

## Hell on Clothes

### 1864

DAVID ABERNATHY HAD never had much luck with clothing during the war, and the night he ripped his last good shirt he was walking picket along the Confederate works south of the Rapidan River. He was cold and he was wet and it was well past midnight when all good, God-fearing folk should be to bed when he leaned his rifle against the stout wall of packed earth and felled timber and stepped into the dark brush to piss. His water streamed from him with hot force that set the moss to steaming. When he finished, David crouched in the lee of the low wall where the wind coming off the river was less. Raising hands to face, he blew warmth into the cold cup of his palms.

Sneezing suddenly, he groaned and sniffed it back. His sinuses rattled and he winced as the deep, tight ache seeped through his face. A dull, bottle-green throb that sometimes made him stagger with nausea, sometimes drove him to weary vomiting, the sick headaches had become his constant companions over the long winter. Because of them and because of the everyday privations of war and warring, his idle daydreams were of sun, warmth, food, and the smoky brown taste of real coffee drunk from delicate china cups on some wide porch somewhere where the sounds and sights of war did not come. He ached for parlor rooms with overstuffed chairs and fine-bred young ladies in crisp, clean dresses. The smell of books on shelves in a study and the feel of real writing paper under his fingers, anything but soldiering and headaches.

David blinked hard and blinked again. He removed his spectacles to chase rain from the corners of his eyes with his thumbtips. Standing, he stretched his arms over his head and laced his fingers as if to push back the dark. He stood that way for a long time, tensed as a diver, regarding the depth of the night as though it was the sea.

The old moon that night had run to dark, and the new had not yet come. And still the night was bright and wet and silvery with an exaltation of stars all shimmering brightly in the sky. The very air was electric, all acrackle with the residuum of yesterday's storm. David stood listening to the creaking of the dark trees beneath the cold wind and the constant whispering rush of the river as if it was all a soft music played for his delight alone. He lowered his arms and pushed his hands into his trouser pockets to watch clouds race amongst the stars like funeral bunting on some dark and solemn train traveling slowly westward.

Standing in the gloom, David wondered if the others on picket that night, ranged along the Rapidan's south bank, had such thoughts as his. He wondered if they thought to listen to music such as he heard, such as was orchestrated by the cold wind.

Yesterday's storm had swept in from the north and the west and had covered the Army of Northern Virginia in its camps with a ferocious demonstration of wet sound. Back at the Second Corps camps near

Morton Hall, tents had been blown off their pegs like strange, out-size birds taken to awkward flight. Sucked up on the wind, they had landed, finally, torn and mud-fouled in the shuddering, windwracked brush. Men stampeded this way and that down the narrow, muddy camp streets chasing their meager possessions—their hand-carved pipes, their toothbrushes and sewing thread and housewives. White flashes of lightning and tremendous crashes of thunder lit and shook them, flashing ill-shaped shadows on the wet earth, then echoing them, gone again as though they'd never been.

David had seen bareheaded men chasing windblown hats and men who stood motionless to watch the wind bedevil the branches as though they had been assigned such duty. A small group of fright-ened drummer boys, new to the army and to army life, huddled beneath a wagon and could not be coaxed out, while nearby a single officer stood coolly shaving beside a rain-doused fire. Another sol-dier set out cups, pots, hats, and anything else that would hold water to collect the rain for later drinking.

During the worst of the storm, while the trees clashed and swayed and thunder set horses panicking, David saw one old campaigner with a wild shock of white hair and beard strip away his shirt to kneel fish-pale in the mud beside an emptied wagon. This man closed his eyes and began shouting of the Lord's Own Vengeance come finally upon their heads for transgressions against His Own Dark Children. Ham's folk whom they all had sorely abused. The old man swayed on his knees as the wind buffeted him, the wispy horns of his long beard blown back past either shoulder. David watched him take a deep breath and start in again, warning of the Lord and of Grant and all the Yankees coming south. He shouted to all who would listen of locusts and vermin, of hail for rain and flaming fire upon the land. None paused to listen save David, who stood watch-ing beside an old molasses barrel with loose hoops that rattled like dull sabers in the wind.

"Brothers," called the old man as men rushed past, chasing down their windblown possessions. "Brothers, don't ye know the Host is coming? Cain't ye feel them coming even now? On this wind? In this rain? Ain't they et up all the grains and all the fruits of the land, brothers? Ain't they run the waters red?" The fanatic beat his breast with open palms, leaving handshaped designs in mud upon his pale flesh. "Listen! Does He suffer any man to do them harm? To do Them harm? No, sir! No! He reproved kings of men for them and He taught senators wisdom for them. What's Jeff Davis but a king? And surrounded by senators, brothers." The old man clawed weakly at the air as though it had thickened around him. Men went by, following the muddy thoroughfare with their shoulders hunched and their eyes downcast.

The old man went on, his voice weaker now, his eyes crazed. "He bound princes for them. For their chained feet and the marks upon their flesh and for their turned-out kinfolk. And . . . and for . . . And for their ravished sisters, wives and . . . And for the ravishments of their daughters! Yes. And for their children too! You know the truth of it, brothers. I did not mean to . . ." The old man put a thin, mud-spattered fist before his lips and his eyes went wide as his voice fell to a hoarse croak. "Always her," he said. "That dark, sweet berry."

His head serpentined about and his wild hair streamed in the wind as he pulled himself up beside the wagon. "Listen to me!" he shouted once more. "He sent down darkness and made it dark! He made it dark, I tell ye! Listen to me!" He swung about and his eyes lit on David where he stood and David felt pierced by that wild gaze. "Every mother's son of you's a dead man!" shouted the old fanatic, who then covered his face with his muddy palms and fell down weeping in the camp street.

While the old man was rolling about, three men chased a wild boar from the forest into an open tent standing nearby. David turned to watch as the canvas bulged and shuddered from within, and then swayed dangerously before finally falling in on itself. He grinned to hear the men's shouts and curses joining song with the outraged squeals of the storm-panicked pig. When David turned back, the old man was gone and in his place was a boy stooping to collect a wind-tossed piece of blanket. The blanket was a poor, torn thing of no account, and every time the boy reached for it the wind kicked it farther along so that he moved down the camp street in a series of half-steps, ducks, and failed grabs until he turned a corner and was gone between rain-doused burn-barrels. As for the boar, it escaped, but not before goring one of its pursuers so badly the regimental surgeon had to take the man's leg below the knee (the leg was buried in a shallow trough in the woods beyond the sinks, and after the army moved on this same boar rooted it up—two summers later the boar was finally killed down near Stubb's Mill by a family moved there from Georgia who found in the pig's stomach bits of shoe leather and a number of thin, white flakes and hard little knobs that had once been the small bones of the soldier's left foot).

But now, this night, the wind had calmed enough for David to hear the swollen Rapidan running in the dark beyond a nearby stand of trees. And somewhere, over the river in the shadows beyond, the dim, pale light of the Army of the Potomac in its camps sent faint shivers of yellow up the damp walls of the night. If he held his breath, David thought that he could hear them there—the tired creaking of harness leather and the soft, musical rattle-and-squeal of poorly greased wagon wheels, the low, heavy rumbling of artillery caissons and the impatient stamping of innumerable hooves. Distantly came the drawn-out wails of trains moving in more and more men, more supplies, ammunition, horses, more metal, more blood and sinew and raw material with which to make war.

Sometimes, on these nights walking picket in the cold dark, if the wind was right and the rain soft or quiet or not at all, David fancied he could even hear the Yankee soldiers themselves as they walked their own pickets or smoked or talked around campfires uncountable. Perhaps they drank good whiskey over there, some of them, or maybe wrote letters home on fine Union stationery. Some of them would have guitars and fiddles, fifes and mouth organs for the making of music, while others would sit back and sing themselves softly homesick—singing so their voices and the sweet sounds of instruments mixed with the wind and rain until it was all of a piece and falling on David's side of the river until he too thought of home because there was nothing else for it.

He shook his head; shook the memories of home and the fantasies of homecoming down and away, then shook his thin white hands and tucked them to his armpits for warmth. In so doing, his cold fingers snagged his shirt through his jacket and he heard and felt the shirt give way. Swearing softly, David unbuttoned his sodden, torn shell jacket and lifted his left arm. There was still no moon, nor would there be that night or the next, but the starlight was such that David saw how the sleeve had come free from the body of the shirt and how the seam that ran along his left side had completely unraveled. The shirt entire, which had been stitched and patched and stitched back again, had finally fallen to rot. The shirt that his mother had bought new for him in Resaca and packed for him and which he'd tended carefully until he had no other untattered clothing to wear had finally and at last fallen past the point of ordinary ruination. It was as though he had blinked and found himself clothed by only so many random, faded threads, nor could he blink again to set them right.

His pale ribcage, the ribs themselves where they pressed against the underside of his flesh like tent braces under weary canvas, seemed aglow. As though what he'd always and secretly feared these long years of war had actually come to pass and he had been killed sometime back without knowing or realizing it. As though he had become, suddenly and without warning in the way such things must always happen, the ghost of himself set to haunt forever this damp and lonely picket.

David swore again and a soft moan escaped his lips as he tucked the remnants of the shirt about himself as best he could. Pulling the jacket close, he buttoned it against the chill, but the jacket's previous owner had taken a burst of canister to his spine and most of the back was gone. David made another soft moaning sound, a ghost sound against the dark, and he grinned to hear it echo back softly. He did it again and again, louder, until Virgil answered back from his own place on picket down the river that he'd better hush before the Yankees heard and shot his pecker off.

"You'd have yourself something to moan about then, wouldn't you?" called Virgil with a soft, throaty laugh. David shook his head and retrieved his rifle. He breathed and watched his breath on the air. David grinned. He was alive. Shouldering his rifle, he walked his route wearily through the dark. Under setting stars, he patrolled the works. Grinning at shadows, his teeth white as moonlit stones.

Abel Truman lay bound in the mud beside the intersection of the Morton's Ford and Mountain Creek roads. He lay on his side in an oblique pane of soft yellow light that came flickering without heat through the brush from the Second Corps camps off yonder. From the tent city also came sounds of men moving on muddy camp streets, talking in night-hushed tones, and the soft singing of slow, sad songs and instruments played with skill and with heart. And there was scattered laughter that was softer than the music and thereby sadder, too. Abel heard fires crackling and popping and snapping and smelled cooking smells as soldiers fixed meager suppers and boiled parched corn for coffee.

Abel sniffed and tried to shift his cramped shoulders. His arms were bound tightly to his sides, with his elbows cocked sharply around a broken length of broomstick. His hands were tied at the wrist and his wrists were raw, secured to his ankles by a short cord. An old greasy rag was balled into his mouth and tied off with a leather strap that stank of cattle. The mud beneath him was thick and cold, and the roads were not really roads at all, either of them, but rather old footpaths rudely widened by shovel and axe to accommodate an army corps wintering in its camps. From where he lay, Abel could see the strange silhouettes of old stumps lining the Mountain Creek Road. Lying where they had been levered, pulled and blasted from the tight soil with their pale roots trembling in the light, the stumps squatted like weird gargoyles cast of wood and mud and bits of stone. Other things—bones and fossils, strange hanks of hair and fur and fetishes lost by men when the world was young—lay bound up in their root balls, never to be claimed.

Abel sniffed again and swallowed a thick and foul-tasting grit as he tried to move his jaw around the spit-soaked rag. He swallowed and gagged and squeezed shut his eyes to better force the sting from them, to better concentrate on the beating of his heart, the breath in his tired lungs. When next he looked it was for a greater dark beyond the shadowed canopy, for a cheering glint of stars in the heavens that must be there.

He reckoned them out there, somewhere. Past the concealment of tree branch, vine, and leaf, Abel imagined stars sparkling in the way stars will on certain spring nights after storms wash clean the dusty air. Throwing off icy sparks and glistening at their points. He imagined a high, fine wind to blow back the clouds and suck the campfire smoke down the floor of the night and away so all the heavens would be revealed. He imagined yesterday's storm now moved out to a sea he'd never seen and that sea heaving, gray and monstrous.

Abel had been put out here, beyond the pale of the camp, even before the wind quit blowing. He'd been bound beside the intersection for beating O. W. Brown bloody, and he beat O. W. because O. W. shot the dog.

It had been slinking about the margins of the camp for the better part of a month, just an old mongrel with black wiry fur gone white at the muzzle and a stiff gait that spoke of far too many years. Some of the men fed it scraps when they had scraps to spare, others aimed kicks at it and worse when it came close, but most just ignored it as it sniffed carefully around the sinks and garbage pits. Just an old dog as lean and worn-down and hungry-looking as any man among them.

As the days passed, Abel had tamed it to the point where it would accept crusts of bread and little gobs of burnt dough from his fingers before darting away again. It had been a long time, that spring, since he'd been around a dog, and something he could not name happened to his heart when it was near.

The storm began with a white burst of lightning followed by a cannon's roar of thunder. Men immediately began rushing about, securing tents and calming horses and chasing down hats. The dog, wild with fear, ran fast down the narrow camp streets with Abel running behind, calling after it. It fled past O. W. and into his tent. Swearing mightily over the sound of thunder, O. W. dashed in after. Abel slid to a stop in the deepening mud before the tent. There came three fast pistol shots and three strobic flashes that lit the mud-stained canvas up from within. With an oath, Abel threw back the flap, looked inside, and saw how it was.

Around camp, O. W. wore an old tricorn from his father's Revolutionary War days. It had been worn at Brandywine Creek and Germantown, and O. W. had worn it proudly in his service to the Confederate States at Antietam and Chancellorsville. Now it lay dented and stained on the mud floor of the tent where the dog had knocked it down and trod upon it, and the dog itself lay unmoving beside the hat. Abel backed away from the tent, staring hard at O. W.

as the man came out holding the hat and making small, useless, brushing motions at it.

"Look at that," he said, holding it up for Abel to see. "Would you just look at what that beast done to my granddaddy's hat?" Abel glanced from the tricorn to O. W.'s face to the dog, then turned on the big man, who crumpled to the mud moments after Abel's fist destroyed his nose.

Abel ducked into the tent and lifted the dog in his arms. It was thin and light as a damp sheet. He took a deep breath and stepped back out into the wind. There was an officer nearby helping O. W. to his feet, and he stepped forward to take Abel's arm, but when he saw his face the officer stepped back again and let him go.

Abel did not have far to go to lose sight of the encampment. The woods were close and dark, lit briefly fantastic by white flashes of lightning. Wind set the trees to clashing, but the canopy was thick and the rain did not trouble him much. He carried the dog through the trees for a long time before he found a little clearing ringed by green ash and sweet birch. At one corner an ancient, misshapen scarlet oak sent two long roots, bent, scarred, and arthritic as an old veteran's fingers, through the moss, and its leaves were scattered across the clearing—little withered things holding tiny pockets of deep shadow and trembling little pools of rainwater.

Abel gentled the dog down in the V of the roots. His face was wet. His hands trembled, and he swore softly to himself for being such a fool. He looked at the dog. "I'm so tired," he told it. "I get so goddamned tired." He looked at the dog where it lay in the moss and stroked its cheek with the backs of his fingers. He could smell its wet fur on the close, electric air, and he knelt beside it in the dripping wet, talking to it, telling it things he'd kept quiet within himself for a long time. Finally, Abel wiped his face with one hand and touched the dog's broad chest with the other, and it took a great, deep breath and reared up under his palm.

And then it was gone—running fast through the storm again, through the dark of the woods and away, leaving Abel wide-eyed with one hand still outstretched and the fingers of the other lightly touching his lips.

When he returned to camp, the storm was in the process of blowing itself out and there were three officers gathered around O. W., studying his absurdly bandaged face and staring grimly at Abel as he approached. They passed sentence quickly and efficiently and did not even spare a man to guard him after he'd been bound, since rumor was they would be marching soon and there was much to do. And Abel did not speak out against it. He harbored no ill-will against O. W. and shook the man's hand as they led him to the intersection at the far edge of camp, where no one came save Ned, who only paced nervously about in the underbrush beside the ford road until his feet were fouled with mud. Ned did not say much, just paced and sucked his teeth, and when he did raise his voice it was not above a whisper and was lost on the wind. After a while he went away and did not come back until after the storm had moved off.

Crouching in the wet brush, Ned waited until he was sure no one was about, then scuttled forward with his canteen and tilted it against Abel's mouth, wetting the rag and loosening axle grease and who knew what else from its folds. Thick and foul against the back of his throat, it left a wash of grit on his teeth that set Abel to choking and sputtering against the rag. Which Ned took as a sign Abel wanted more, so he emptied the remainder of the canteen over his face. There was no way to tell the boy to stop or make him understand, so all Abel could do was swallow grimly and retch against the cloth.

Ned stayed an hour. He wept a little to see Abel bound so and spoke to him of nothing at all before, finally, the supper fires were kindled away at camp and he wandered off toward their pale light. Abel watched him go, then closed his eyes. With Ned gone, he could keep his eyes closed and think of nothing and be alone. But no faster had he shut himself from the world than the havoc of memory intruded and he was dreaming of his dead child, his dead wife.

He saw, once more, sky blue paint splashed upon the walls from one end of the house to other. As though Elizabeth would mark her grief the way an animal marks its territory and then dwell forever within that place. It was a month after the child died (and here and suddenly a dream within the dream, a sunshine-bright image of the baby falling falling falling from his weak shocked hand, from the cooled blanket in which she'd died sometime in the night before Abel woke and lifted then dropped her in shock to see her face as it tumbled tumbled tumbled to the hard puncheon floor where the sound of thin bone against wood was such he felt it in his heart—where it echoed still—and Elizabeth who came into the room and saw, who called the doctor, who came, who told them the child had died in the night and said, "But look, here, it's as though her head's been struck," then looked at Abel with expectation and with blame, who looked at his wife who looked back to him with eyes clouded with bottomless hurt, with infinite blame and there, just there, something more . . . ), and it was her idea, after rising from her sickbed, to put a fresh coat of paint on the walls and sashes. To brighten their home as though in such small ways they could begin their accepting and change by degrees the house that housed their thoughts and memories of that tiny death. Thus the soft blue paint for the sashes, to match the blue of the door, and the white for the walls. Abel brought the paint home from the mercantile one evening, and left it with her the next morning when he walked the two miles back to clerk at the store.

She'd begun with a single brush, and when he came home in the afternoon the brush was soaked in blue and streaked, faintly, with red and fouled in the dust of the lane leading to the broad covered porch. No smoke rose from the chimney. There was no sound other than the watery pulse of the lake beyond the woodshed. Perhaps birds called that afternoon. Perhaps frogs sang to an early-risen moon and perhaps the wind set the green world murmuring, but Abel heard nothing but the lake lapping at the shore as though it was a conscious thing and hungry, and he heard it in his dreams ever after.

He found her on the floor beside the cradle with the paint can upended on the floor, the paint thrown in broad splashes against the walls and ceiling. His wife, Elizabeth, crouched naked and alone in a shallow pool of it as though huddled against a backdrop of sky. Her face was turned from him, hidden by her hair. Even then he did not cry out in astonishment, grief, but only stared in dumb amazement before crouching quickly to brush feebly at her legs as though he could sweep the paint from her with a wave of his palm. It was warm from her heat. It slicked his hands, felt heavy on his skin, as if his skin could not breathe. Abel panted. He looked out the window to a daytime moon hanging pale and cool above the trees. He looked at it a long time, fixing it in his mind so that later he would be able to remember clearly, at least, one thing. He did not speak and he did not tremble because he came to the quick realization that this thing, this scene, was only one in a long and mighty chain of events he felt rather than saw stretching so far along the arc of his life he figured the end must meet itself somewhere again to forge a perfect circle of misfortune. A single moment, this. A single event and not even the worst. A little paint. They could stand that.

So Abel Truman feebly brushed sky blue paint from his wife's bare legs and said her name and when she turned to him he reared up, slipped in the paint and fell back, then reared up again. There was paint smeared across Elizabeth's face and there was no way to tell how much she'd drunk. As he stepped back, Abel kicked over the second can, the white paint, and the lid came open. It spilled, thick and slow, into the blue, running it cold and paler than a dead child's face.

She began laughing then. Rocking back and forth on her hard, red heels with her head thrown back and her white, smooth neck exposed. She shook and was utterly silent. Her square, mannish face stood transfigured with grief-dumbed mirth. Abel said her name. He said it again and again and Elizabeth hushed and turned slowly toward him.

He ran. Abel remembered running, nothing else. He must have run back to town through the mill smoke and sawdust and setting springtime sun where someone must have fetched the doctor and the constable. He must have told them about her, perhaps even led them back to her, but he wasn't sure. He couldn't remember any of it clearly, nor could he remember confessing to dropping the child or the doctor assuring him the child had been dead well before then. Abel had stopped remembering when he saw what she'd done to herself and he didn't begin again until First Manassas when he stood on Henry House Hill, watching them come in all their gleaming color and glory. Everything between had been a blur of begging, wandering, of lying in drink. But Abel knew all the while that his wife had died not from grief or madness but from hate. Hate for him and what he had done, and Abel knew her hate was such she'd tried to cover it, then douse it, with paint.

He remembered all this, bound and dreaming there beside the intersection. He remembered thinking before he saw her face that they could bear a little paint. That they could stand it. But it was more than them alone and it was more than paint and it could not be borne. It could not be set right. Not by him and not by her and not by them together. In the end it was the vast, bottomless silence that could not be filled with any sound save rifle fire, save cannon. It was the teapot thrown across the room in outraged frustration and desperate sorrow that could not do what paint or a bullet could. It was scalding water on a puncheon floor when he had found a little spot of blood that he could not clean and that she had found anyway and tried to cover with paint. But it wasn't paint that was needed. Abel wandered for years not knowing what it was and only realized on the Plains of Manassas what she knew all along: that what was wanted, after all, was fire.

## May 4

That morning, on his long, weary way back to camp from picket duty, David Abernathy saw Abel Truman still lying bound and gagged in the mud beside the intersection. His tent-mate had been there for a full day now, and David wondered how much longer they'd leave him. He stood shivering in his torn, wet clothing, trying to decide what to do. O. W. was an ass of a man, and having decided that, David took his knife out and started forward until Abel caught his eye and in so doing warned him off. David knew him well and could tell how it was with him by the lines about his eyes and the set of his chin beneath the filthy beard and the filthier rag. David nodded and put the knife away and Abel closed his eyes, then slowly opened them again. David passed on toward camp.

He found Ned sitting pantsless on a low, sawn-off stump before their common tent, sewing a patch onto the knee of his weather-colored trousers. His bare legs were pink and grimy in the morning light, and as David approached, he looked up blinking. Ned stood and carefully set his sewing down on the stump, touching and smoothing the cloth lightly with the flat of his hand and looking at it there a moment in the careful, fascinated way he did all things.

"Ain't it a pretty mornin'?" Ned asked, waving his hands through the light. "You can't hardly tell no more it rained at all."

"You weren't stuck out in it all night," David said, stacking his rifle with the others, Ned's and Abel's and a few more, off away from the fire. "You can tell."

Ned licked his lips then pursed them and looked back down the street toward the thicker woods. "Abel still out yonder?" he asked.

David nodded. Ned had kept their fire going and he crouched near it to hold his hands toward the flames. Closing his eyes, he felt the skin slacken, begin to itch as alien warmth seeped in.

"I told him he shouldn't start in with O-Dub," said Ned. "Dog or no dog, and that man hates a dog anyways. O-Dub." He looked over at David sadly. "I told him he shouldn't ought to drink like that neither. Path'll lead him straight away from the Lord in no time." Ned sniffed and nodded forcefully to himself, then stood looking at David as he straightened from the fire and began cleaning the panes of his spectacles on his decaying shirttail. "I took him water last night while you was out on picket," Ned went on. "Way he looked at me, 'minded me of my daddy." The boy stared thoughtfully into the middle distance where dark trees hoarded shadows and stood shivering in a cool morning breeze.

David smelled tobacco. Somewhere, distantly, breakfasts cooking. Ned's small fire snapped and growled quietly, and David bent over it again as Ned settled back down to his sewing. After a few minutes silent work he looked up blinking. "There was mail come yesterday," he said. "You was already out when they called you up, so I went on and took it in for you. Little package what I put on your blanket."

David took a quick breath. With the toe of his split-soled shoe he moved a soot-blacked pebble back and forth through the dirt. "Ned," he said softly. "Did you see where it came from?"

Ned looked at him, his hairless face round and vacant. He wet his lips and worked them around. "I can't make words out," he said, lowering his eyes. "You know that."

"I thought Abel was showing you."

Ned looked back up at him, grinning. "That's right," he said, his head bobbing, eyes far away. "I can print my name now and read it back, even if it's someone else what writes it."

David sighed and nodded. "You say it's in the tent?"

"What's that?"

"My mail. The package."

Ned grinned again. "That's right. Come in yesterday. I put it in on your blanket. Come from your homefolks, I reckon."

The day was warming as the sun climbed, and David grinned and shook his head. "All right, Neddy," he said, unbuttoning his coat and turning toward his tent. "You need anything, yell. Otherwise, I'm going to rest up a little."

The package lay in David's corner of the tent atop the messy folds of his moth-chewed blanket. Even in the dim light, he could tell his brother's hand. He sat on the ground beside it. After a few moments, he reached out and touched the brown paper wrapping with his fingertips. A loud crackling under his cold, unsteady palm. David sat for a long time just lightly touching the paper. Finally he picked it up, eased the string to one side, and tore the paper on one corner to look inside.

When he saw the new shirt he began to laugh, but his laughter was silent, and when it was finished it left him gasping for air. Right away, he recognized the material she'd used, and in that moment of recognition he thought his heart would surely break. Would doubtlessly cease beating. David Abernathy shut his eyes and kept them closed for one long moment with the deep, green glass pain jangling fast through his temples. A quick, dark solitude behind thin panes of flesh. When his heart did not stop or fall apart, when it kept to its old, tired schedule, David wondered idly if there was anything at all left that could shock a pause into the rhythm of his blood save fire, cannon, gore.

There was a letter inside—a folded square of pale blue paper that he eased out without opening the package further because he was not yet ready for that. Pursing his lips, he read the letter slowly for his brother's poor penmanship and worse spelling. Halfway through, the hand that held the paper began to shake, and the one that still

touched the package balled into a white fist that squeezed and relaxed and squeezed and relaxed again like a weary bone-and-muscle
heart. When he reached the postscript recounting rumors of Sherman's route through Georgia, David set the letter aside. He lifted the
package with both hands as though it was a holy relic and pressed it
hard against his face to breathe once more and finally his mother's
scent captured in the cloth.

The thin cotton kept within its fiber and its weave something of
the handmade smells of home and home life. Old cooking smells of
buttered corn and boiled cabbage, of great bleeding flank steaks and
potatoes, carrots, onions, all smothered in gravy and served on thick
platters engraved with blue Chinese scenes of cherry blossoms, fog-
wrapped pagodas, strange, umbrella'd maidens. He could smell fresh
blueberries and cold milk. And there was, also, his mother's smell:
matronly, womanish, and as distinct as her florid signature or her
sharp, cool whisper at prayertimes and candlelighting. Her scent was
as though woven into the shirt and now a part of it and never to be
separate from it ever. When he took it away from his face the paper
crackled in the dark of the tent, and through the rip in the corner
David fingered the buttons. They were carved from a wooden dowel
pin, painted sky-blue by her own hand with paint gotten from who
knew where or how, and sewn to the face of the shirt by strands of
her own steel-colored hair for want of proper thread. His mother's
hair served as thread for his soldiering shirt, such was the strength of
the Yankee blockade.

David Abernathy's tired, starved heart fell to aching, and with
one great gulp of air he pressed his face once more to the folds of
paper that still held it and began a hot, rough weeping that set the
rags to flapping restlessly on his thin frame.

"That's a hell of a handkerchief," said Abel as he stooped to crawl
into the tent.

David looked up. Abel crawled over onto his own blankets like a mud man, with his eyes red-rimmed and his stiff hair standing to. He swayed a little on his hands and knees, and after a moment looked back out the tent and spat wetly through the door. Rolling over atop his blankets across from David, he lifted his chin and asked, "What in the hell is all that, anyway?"

"Mama sent it," David said softly. "Brother wrote a letter too." He sniffed and ran the back of his hand under his nose. Green pain washed like a slow, gentle tide behind his eyes. "Says he figures Sherman'll make a try for Atlanta here pretty quick," he said absently, waving the letter through the stale half-dark.

"Let him," said Abel, shrugging, trying to settle onto his blanket and having a difficult time of it for aching joints and cramped muscles. "I don't give a good goddamn anymore." He stretched and winced and finally settled onto his back, then looked over at David again. The younger man's face was thin and pale and blank where it angled toward the mud-spattered canvas wall opposite him. The panes of his spectacles reflected nothing yet did not show his eyes.

Abel flexed his arms about, trying to work feeling down their length. "What else?" he finally asked, motioning toward the letter.

David blinked. "Old Johnston's back in charge over there now, he says," he answered woodenly.

Abel shook his head. "I don't give a good goddamn who's in charge over there, and that ain't what I meant." He filled his cheeks with air and blew. "I mean, what's happened? With your homefolks?" He nodded to the letter again.

David looked up. Abel could see his eyes suddenly behind the round panes of glass as they searched out his face, lingered there a moment, then drifted off to the side once more. "Mama died," he said softly. "Last month, he says."

"Ah, well," Abel said nodding. He said nothing more but shifted around atop his neatly folded blanket until he was partly comfortable. Lying on his back with his fingers laced behind his head, he let out a long, satisfied sigh. After a time, he sniffed and said, "What's the package?"

Again, David's eyes went roving to settle, finally, on the paper bundle. "Give over your knife," he said, sniffing and reaching out. Abel handed him his little knife and he pried the blade open with a dirty, broken thumbnail, then slid it under the string to cut it, refolded the knife, and passed it back.

David shook the shirt from the paper and held it up. It was, generally, the color of cold oatmeal and was chased with bright, swirling designs of scarlet, turquoise, yellow, and orange like something from a Turkish folktale, like some pasha's bright daydream. It made Abel's eyes swim and his head hurt so he looked instead out the open tent flap with a broad grin.

David held the shirt open before him, staring at it gravely. He studied the cloth, bright and garish even in the relative dark of the tent, then looked at Abel where Abel lay smiling and looking away studiously. David turned back to the shirt. "Jesus-by-God," he murmured. "When I first looked, I figured she'd just used it for the collar."

"Your mama?"

"Letter says she passed on just after she finished it."

Abel nodded sagely. "Maybe that's just as well," he said.

David looked sharply at him, and Abel propped himself up on one elbow with a wince. He nodded to the shirt. "Otherwise, she might have gone on and fixed you up some pants to match," he said.

David stared at him. Abel returned the look and held it. After a moment, they began to chuckle softly together and then both began to laugh out loud and were still laughing when Ned ducked into the tent. He was still pantsless and was grinning happily around a mouthful of wet dough.

"What in hell did you find to eat around here?" asked Abel, frowning.

"Ashcake," said Ned around the food. There was a wet gray dollop of tooth-moistened dough clinging to his chin, and the little cake in his hand drooped with teeth marks. "Been in my pocket and I didn't even know it," he said, holding out the biscuit to Abel, who raised a hand palm outward and shook his head. Ned swallowed thickly, then looked over at David where he sat holding the shirt. Ned's eyes widened in his moon face, and his gullet jerked once then twice. "Well," he said, admiringly. "Well, ain't that a pretty thing?" His voice was soft with wonder and he blinked again, an expression not just of his eyes but of his whole face. "We all gettin' new uniforms?" he asked hopefully.

"Just old Abernathy here," said Abel. The other two looked at him and he nodded. "That there shirt makes it official," he said. "Our boy's done gone into politics." Ned stared at him, and David's eyes narrowed. Abel looked at Ned. "He just got word. He's been called to Queen Mab's Court. That there's his uniform of office."

"Jesus, Abel," said David, grinning and shaking his head.

Ned looked back and forth between them, trying to decide, trying to judge them by their expressions. His lips moved soundlessly and his brow wrinkled as though he was trying to recall some fact or bit of trivia to prove or disprove Abel's statement. After a few moments of this he finally pursed his lips and nodded. "That's off crost over the ocean and all, ain't it?"

Abel and David began laughing again, long and loud and uproarious. Ned looked back and forth between them then shook his head disgustedly and ducked to leave the tent. Abel called after him to put some damn pants on before he caught a chill, and Ned waved a hand as he stepped out.

"What was it, anyway?" Abel finally asked, curling a forefinger to the corner of one eye. "Curtains?"

"You think my mama'd keep curtains this damned ugly?" asked

David, lifting up the shirt again. "No sir. This here was the table-cloth."

Abel set in laughing again, and David removed his spectacles, pinched his temples between thumb and middle finger. "It's been in the family for years," he said, gasping with mirth and pain. "Belonged to my grandmother before my mama got it." He filled and emptied his cheeks with air. On the other side of the tent, Abel twisted around on his blankets as laughter set his sore muscles to protesting, which made him laugh all the harder, the weary lines around his eyes deepening as he thrashed about. David looked at him. "When I was just a little chap," he managed haltingly, "I got sick all over it."

Their laughter rose then fell and gradually tapered away. David rubbed the bridge of his nose and knuckled his eyes while Abel sat up, dragged the back of his hand over his mouth, and massaged his wrists where they were rope-burnt. He didn't want to look at his feet or ankles just yet, so he filled his lungs with air, blew, then looked over at David. "You got the headache again?"

David nodded wearily, lifting his hand and letting it fall again. After a moment, he wrapped his spectacles back around his face, careful to tuck the arms in behind his ears. He opened his mouth as though to speak, then shut it again and bent his head to listen, his expression suddenly sharp and alert.

"What?" asked Abel.

David raised his hand again and stared off into the middle distance. Then he got up onto his knees, stripped the old, ruined shirt from his body, and pulled on the new one. The cloth was stiff and uncomfortable, and he rolled his shoulders about to settle into it. "Something's happening," he said. "I reckon we'll be moving out."

Abel opened his mouth. "How the hell . . ." But before he could finish, he heard the long roll sounding out on the camp intersections. Outside, Ned whooped with shock and excitement.

Abel watched as David worked the sky blue buttons. He shook his head wonderingly. "You're really going to wear it?"

David ignored him. "Maybe this'll be it this time," he said. He looked over at Abel, where he still lounged on his blanket. "You think? Maybe they'll give it up."

"Shit," said Abel, shaking his head and waving a dismissive hand through the air. "They got it going good, now. I don't reckon they'd stop it even if they knew how." He looked hard at David, then finally grinned tiredly. "Which means, you want to wear that damned thing, you better keep your ass down."

# THREE

## Inarticulate Hearts

### 1899

ABEL TRUMAN CROSSED the river half a mile inland where the narrow channel was bridged by a rotting nurse log. Green saplings stood in ordered rows along its surface as though planted so, and the old man was careful in crossing not to tread upon them. For its part, the dog, when it caught up, crossed through the water in three long bounds to stand dripping and panting on the opposite side where Abel stood watching. "I don't know what you're grinnin' about," the old man told it. "You'll be fending for your own damned self."

They cut back through the forest to the ocean. Before leaving the brown river behind to start south along the beach, Abel paused to look back at his little shack. His home for twenty years. He could hear the wind whistling softly through the loose planking. Ashes stirred in the fire pit. The empty rocker moved soundless in the wind as though his ghost had returned already.

He carried his rifle and walking stick, and an old blanket slung soldier-style from left shoulder to right hip. He wore a broad-brimmed hat pulled down low on his forehead and a sharp knife at his belt. A few biscuits, a little rubber-stoppered bottle half full with sugar, and another full of salt lay wrapped in a cloth and tucked into his haversack along with Glenn Makers's almanac wrapped in a good India rubber ground cloth. In his pocket was the bullet Hypatia had cut from his arm all those years ago and the crucifix hung from its cord near his heart.

Abel kept his eyes down as he walked, and he breathed evenly. A fit old man, he tried not to think of all the miles ahead of him—all the rolling country filled with people and tilled fields and painted houses, rich barns, cities of vast industry. Roads and lanes and by-ways and rivers and forests uncountable. He tried not to think of what he might find beyond the mountains. Instead, he conjured images of his long-dead wife, her grave site and their child's. After a time of walking, Abel put all this away from him and concentrated on his feet and the immediate world around him.

Thick mist clung to the forest at his left, and a cool wind slowly tattered it. The tide lay far to sea and the sand was crossed and re-crossed with the rolling, wheel-like tracks of hermit crabs and the precise, pencil-thin prints of oystercatchers. The smell of beached kelp and broken shells, of damp sand that had never been dry and rock pools astir with tiny fishes, was as heavy as the sound of crashing surf was constant. And wind never-ending. Abel walked the day long and in the evening, when there was still yet light, made his camp on a narrow shelf of land that was protected on three sides by huge, wind-scarred boulders and on the fourth by the ocean itself. For a time, he squatted to watch the sun sink and set long fingers of cloud orange and red against the sparking dark.

It was warm with no rain and little wind, and he knew this place well enough not to have need or want of fire. Exploring a little around the stones in the fading light, Abel found small petroglyphs

carved here and there upon their ancient surfaces. Old, old fashion-
ings of whales stretched leaping from waves of granite. Crude human faces with mouths yawning in terror, shock, outrage, grief, and
joy. Countless luck-bringing clamshells scratched into the stones,
and little manlike figures crouched and ran and hunted through the
cold, gray rock. All of it quiet evidence of long-dead tribes who
in ages past whaled these waters, hunted these forests, carved these
stones, and who were now as lost as the individual stories told by
these cold, flat scratchings.

The wind rose with the tide and came moaning over the rocks to
fill with sound the pauses between the ceaseless slap of waves on sea
stacks and the quiet, bubbling rush of tidal pools filling and empty-
ing and filling again. The wind set the old man's sleeves to flapping.
He put his good palm against the cold rock face and traced with his
forefinger the chiseled grooves of a leaping orca, wondering what
strength the act of carving had imparted to the whaler. Abel squatted
beside the stone as the sun went down, wondering what he might
carve had he time and strength. What fortune such creation might
bring. Would he trust his heart's own desire to cold rock? Or some
other thing whose shape would remain unclear until the carving was
complete and that would endure until the breaking of the earth?
Finally Abel stood and picked his way back down to his campsite.

The sun sank beyond the quivering rim of the ocean. Sheets of
coppery light trembled up the sky to fix the sea stacks to their sil-
houettes like lonesome picket guards beyond the pale of the campfire. Abel settled down with his back against a stone and wrapped
his blanket around his legs. He breathed the good, tart scent of India
rubber. After a time, the dog came up the beach like a flake of shadow
split from the darker night that gathered in the forest behind them. It
stood in the sand downwind of him and swung its head this way and
that to collect his scent, then, finding it, came up onto the shelf and
sat nearby. Abel smelled the dog's supper on its breath—the thick

scent of heat and blood. "What did you get?" he asked it. "You get yourself a little gull?"

The dog lay down by taking short little steps with its forelegs, and Abel sneered. "Now I suppose you're just going to go on to sleep, ain't you? Never even crossed your mind to bring me nothing." He sighed dramatically and, as the dog watched, reached a twist of venison from his pocket. The dog pricked up its ears as he chewed and Abel shook his head. "Don't even think about it," he said. The dog barked softly, cocked its head, and pawed the ground. The old man took another bite and tossed the remainder to it. "You're pitiful, you know that?" he said as the dog gulped down the dried meat.

Abel settled down and lay on his back to look at the stars. The moon was a silver coin and Mars, just there, a small dot pale as a freckle in the western night. He studied the stars, how their rarefied light glistened. Raising his arm, he traced Orion's belt and outflung arms and touched the dippers as his father had shown him when he was a boy. Abel moved his shoulder so he could reach to touch some few other constellations, but such movement sent ripples of pain through his left arm and he swore softly and settled down again.

The tide rolled slowly in, attended by the rush and clatter of the seabed, but the forest behind was still and quiet. The occasional call of a far-off owl and the creak of the trees in a high, soft wind. Out on the water, algae glowed weirdly green under the moon and stars, the faint band of the Milky Way.

The light that night was such that when Abel looked he could see the shadows individual trees cast along the beach and out onto the water and upon the carved stones at the headland. The solid black shadow of the forest itself, as though the forest was a single thing and not composed of many and much. Abel raised his arm again and his hand seemed strangely aglow, insubstantial so that he wondered was he man or ghost. Wondered for a moment if he, indeed, had fallen dead in the Wilderness and had all these long, blue years since been nothing but a form of dream or dreaming.

Abel lay back. He closed his eyes against the brightness of the night and listened to the constant sound of the ocean at its labors. Underbrush crackled softly as deer explored the slopes above the beach. Abel closed his eyes and tried hard not to see her, to keep seeing her. He tried not to see either of them, but it came back, like it always did, in the fall when the air grew crisp and the leaves began to turn, then die and fall.

His child was dead, his wife followed soon after, and that happy portion of his life in a house beside a lake with a family ended that morning well before the war came because he had to bury his daughter in a grave too small and commit the wife to a sanitarium in upstate New York where her grief was such it finally killed her. Abel locked the house—for all he knew it still stood—and left that place because he could no longer take being there. His own grief was nothing but suffering, then passing through sorrow, rage. A black gall. Nights steeped in drink. Days of hungry wandering. Begging, petty thievery, and a single wretched night of a full moon passed out facedown in some churchyard's grass. And when war did come, Abel Truman found himself in North Carolina with a regiment of Tar Heels for no other reason than that was where he had happened to be. And then all the rest had happened, and finally, ten and twenty years in a one-room shack on the shore of the cold, gray Pacific, and his life was blown. Passed him by like a slow, tannic river easing out to sea. He'd eked out a meager life beside the waters and when he felt he'd finally had enough he'd walked into the ocean and the ocean had cast him back.

The old man woke to the sound of the dog growling softly. It was still dark, and the tide was up like a dreamlike and unsteady floor. Ragged chains of waves curved southward down the beach. The dog was beside him, hackles raised, its growl low, deep in its chest.

Its battered ears stood cocked, and Abel could feel it tense with straining excitement.

"What?" he asked. "What're you—" And then it came again. Far off, miles away and inland, a long, choked howling as of a single wolf in the low country where wolves did not often visit. The old man sat up against the rocks, frowning but with a curious thrill prickling his skin. This was not singing. Even though the moon had risen to hang silver and bright in the cold sky, this was not singing. This was longing and fear and pain such as Abel had never heard from an animal before. It howled again, and the moon fled behind a cloud as though chased. The howl stretched out over the vast, rolling wilderness, echoed along the inland waterways, and fell softly on the dark tide, leaving in its wake a sudden silence slowly filled by ocean sounds and wind. The dog whined and paced round about the old man's sleeping place as though it had heard something that much disturbed it.

Abel sniffed and licked his lips then and suddenly fell into a harsh coughing that went on and on. He swore softly, and when it was over his throat was raw. He listened hard for any other distant sound the wolf might make or for others to answer, but there was nothing, and the night fell quiet once more. Abel spat. A rank taste and hot. The dog settled back beside him. Pulling the blanket close, Abel reached out and unconsciously twisted his fingers into the soft blond fur behind the dog's ears. It sighed quietly and closed its eyes and Abel eventually fell back to sleep and dreamed no more that night.

The next morning was overcast and cold. A wet mist clung to the lower trunks of spruce and pine and cedar and hemlock. Bigleaf and vine maple thrust up from underbrush, colored bright by spikes of brilliant purple foxglove and ghostly, floating blossoms of cow parsnip. False hellebore like stalks of corn in miniature, and occasionally the slender red slashes of madrone trunks stood curved and twisted from the forest understory. The dog went crashing through the thickets and a junco chitted at it from its hiding place and Abel paused to squint into the general, fog-shrouded gloom until he spied it perched upon a spruce branch, half hidden amidst the soft needles. The bird stared at him, its unblinking eye bright in its dark hood, sang once more, then darted back into the forest and was vanished.

The brown trunks of the forest behind him ran to ground straight and orderly as though the whole of it was of a single piece: one great, confusing mosaic of green and shades of green and cool blue darkness that never saw the light of day and never would. A step into that green, and longitude would fall away. Compasses would read strangely or not at all. The Indians would call him a fool. The old man would hunger, he would fall. His body would be torn open by one of the greater predators—wolf or cougar or bear. Tiny creatures living beneath the fallen leaves and needles—beetles, worms, other, smaller things for which Abel had no names—would harvest from his bones the soft parts of his body. They would curl in the shells of his ears and spin webs across his mouth. Abel knew what became of the unburied dead in a wilderness. The particular way that bones became polished over time, yellow-brown like parchment. Ribcage, skull, and leg bone. Abel shuddered and walked more quickly down the beach, head down, wind blowing past his shoulders.

By early afternoon the threatened rain had not yet come, and the sun had burned away the morning fog. The rain clouds drew back to the horizon in luminous gray clumps that promised a hard wind to blow them back. The air still smelled of rain, but now the sun beat down upon wet stones and Abel smelled a soft electricity in the air as the rocks dried and the tide rolled out. He made his way carefully around a rocky headland, stepping slowly from stone to stone to stone and bracing himself with his walking stick. The wind was strong and the dog some distance behind, chasing gulls and splashing in the surf.

When he'd gotten far enough around the rocks to see the next stretch of beach, Abel paused, then stopped and crouched. He glanced back toward the dog, saw it was still making a fool of itself in the water, and then looked about for a smooth, flat boulder. Finding one, Abel crawled onto it and unlimbered his rifle.

The deer clustered around a small creek that ran seeping from the forest onto the wet sand. The sand there was very brown, with the water cutting a shallow trough before running out fanwise across tide-kicked pebbles to the surf. There were some half-dozen black-tailed deer bent drinking from it, and Abel squinted down the barrel at each in its turn until he was satisfied he had found one lamed, or perhaps merely old. It stood apart from the others with a dull pelt and a certain hesitation to its movements as though it ached deeply. Abel pursed his lips, turned his head to spit once for luck, then fired.

The deer's head snapped to the side. It bucked up once, then fell to the sand half in the seep as the others leapt into the dark forest and away. Abel spat again, nodded solemnly as though in silent acknowledgment, then stood and started toward his kill. Behind him, he heard the dog's nails scrambling for purchase on the rocks. As he stepped from the stones onto the beach, Abel called over his shoulder, "You wasn't no kind of help, so don't think you're getting a good goddamned bite."

The deer was dead by the time Abel reached it. Parenthetical tracks were stamped into the wet sand all around. The dead doe was soft-eyed, with a creamy patch of fur at the base of her throat and two old scars along her flanks where the fur had never grown back. Abel wondered what had been at her and how she got away. He wondered was it barbed wire or something that had once hunted her. He sniffed, spat, stopped wondering, and bent to work.

He knew there were any number of things he should be doing, and were he home or bound that way, the old man knew that he would do them. As it was, Abel was loath to waste any part of the deer but knew there was no way to carry all the meat. Shooting the deer had been like an instinct. He'd not fully realized that he had shot and killed it until he began dressing it and felt the warm blood in his palm. He fisted his strong right hand around the blood, squeezed and watched it run out onto the sand as if it were his own. The dog sat to watch. Abel opened his hand and set his tongue to his fingertips. Heat and gamey salt and life but recently faded. He closed his eyes and breathed. The sand was red. The deer's eyes were closed and soft. Abel laid his red hand upon her flank. He closed his eyes again and waited to see if the deer would come alive again. After a while, he sniffed and looked skyward where a fat October moon had risen over the tree line as the sun slid toward the westward wall of ocean. With blood on his hands and the tide murmuring behind him, Abel knelt in the sand and stared at the pale, risen moon like a primeval hunter quick with awe.

Finally, he took off his blanket roll and haversack and dropped them to the sand. The dog circled about with its head down and ears up. Its nose worked furiously, and the old man took up his knife and pointed it at the dog for emphasis. "Don't even think about it," he told it.

In the end, he cut just enough meat from the deer's thigh for his supper and for supper the next evening, then drug the carcass off into the forest. The deer was heavy with death and hard for him to handle with his crippled arm. Abel's legs felt good and strong as they always did, but his chest and shoulders burned with the effort of the last few days. He laid the deer in the forest, covered it with a layer of soft sword fern, and stood over it a long time, trying to think if there was anything else that needed doing. "Goddamn it anyway," he said, wiping his mouth with the back of his hand. He walked out of the trees and stood looking out at the surf where a sea stack resembling a great phallus stood from the waves. Abel sucked a tooth and walked on down the beach.

Later that evening, he built his fire near another creek in a little ring of soot-blacked stone that he had used for that purpose on other trips. Abel put on as much dry wood as he could gather and let it burn down until the coals glowed like orange gemstones in the black sand. Cutting the meat into thin steaks, he laid them sizzling on the coals. The old soldier sat cross-legged, humming a slow, sad song to himself as he watched the fat come bubbling up along gristle lines. Off to sea, the sun slowly slipped behind far distant rain clouds, shedding an even light along the horizon like a soft, dull bruise.

After a time, the dog came out of the woods like it had the first night it had come to Abel. It materialized out of the dark between the trees and came down the beach to sit across the fire from him with a look composed upon its features as though it sat in judgment on the old soldier. After a few long moments, the dog sighed heavily and faced the ocean, seeming to watch the otters out amidst the waves where they floated on their backs or dove beneath the surface for shells and stones.

Abel moved the little deer steaks about on the coals with his bare fingers, quickly touching each to his tongue afterward to ease the heat from them. He cooked the strips on one side and then the other until they were just brown with the blood running from them in watery pink streams that went sizzling onto the coals. The meat smelled rich as it cooked, with tiny, snapping flames coming up all around it, and when it was done to his taste, Abel set the steaks on a flat stone and used his knife and fingers to cut and eat them. Juice ran down into his beard and fell dripping onto his shirt. The old man breathed deeply through his nose as he chewed, grunting softly his satisfaction and enjoyment.

When the cooked meat was half gone, Abel set to it with his knife again, dividing what remained into small cubes. He jerked his chin up to the dog, and it came around the coals to stand nearby. It looked at him as before, and the old man nodded and watched as the dog ate very carefully from the flat of his hand. "You poor, dumb son of a bitch," he said softly.

Their meal finished, Abel threw sand on the remains of the fire before walking with the dog out across the beach into the surf. The massive, dark sea stacks rose from the water like strange teeth from the floor of the ocean's jaw. Occasionally the setting sun would come flaring through the clouds to silhouette a tiny hogsback island farther out to sea. The old man and the dog sat together on a boulder and watched the tide come in all around them.

Here, in the cool evening under a sky of gray cloud behind which the sun was setting, the water was a dark green color. Wisps of dirty foam veined it weirdly, marking the subtle motions of tide and current the way a field of tall grass will mark the shape of the wind passing through it. Farther out, on other, smaller stones, stood cormorants like Old World gargoyles of strange sculpture, wings outstretched to dry fingerwise against the failing light, their eyes black and dull as chips of coal, their faces bright and baboon-gaudy.

All around them were shallow tidal pools cut into stone by ages of oceanic labor. They refilled slowly with the tide, and beetle-sized crabs came scuttling from the shadows to explore what new terrain had been wrought of their sand patches. Orange and red sea stars clasped fast to the undersides of wave-splashed stones, and everywhere were hard clusters of mussel like fat grapes amidst foam and rock and wave. Abel stood and the dog jumped down into the surf to start back up the beach, the rattle, suck, and roar of the ocean loud as he followed the dog into the cold, knee-deep water. Abel kept his eyes down as he waded ashore, and when he did look up it was to the sight of a thin taper of smoke rising from the northward beach.

He stood with the tide push-pulling at his calves and watched the smoke rise and scatter through the forest. Abel reckoned the fire near the spot he and the dog had camped the night just past. After a time, he shrugged and left the beach for his camp, where the dog stood waiting for him.

After nightfall, they sat up to watch the ocean dark under the nightblue sky. Abel and the dog. The rain clouds lay far to sea and they watched a single star fall arcing soundlessly across the heavens and then another and another while myriad others glistened and shined and moved slowly through the heavens like things alive, and who was there that could tell they were not? They were quiet and still together. The old man knew that in the all the world's turning there had been but few moments such as this and so did not speak. And beside him, the dog's strong, inarticulate heart beat softly and together they sat under the bright, spirited stars until sleep overtook them.

He dreamed again that night of his youth and of absent friends, of the land disturbed by war. He woke once, rising up on his elbow to look seaward. The air was clean and cool and he could see forever across the water. The stars astonishing. And the pale band of the Milky Way. His breath appeared and vanished and appeared again in the starlight, and he wondered what had become of the rain clouds. He saw distant lights on the horizon—ships moving silently over the water. Slotted to their trade routes, they spoke among themselves in the cold, lonesome language of flashing lights and low, doleful horns whose notes came rolling slowly over the dark waves. A deep, heavy, lingering sound that spoke to Abel of vast distances, isolation, infinite sadness. But the dog was a soft, warm shape in the dark beside him, and after a while he lay back down and slept once more.

When he woke the next morning, the sun was well up and the dog was nowhere about. Abel looked onto the beach, the broad panorama where the tide had risen and fallen and was yet on the rise once more. The sand was rearranged, and he marked high tide by the softly undulating line of dead link confetti, dulse, and bleach-weed waving north and south along the beach like the hem of a curtain. Sunlight reflected brilliantly in the tidal pools. Long, pencil-straight lines of golden light lay where the light fell on seawater that filled the trenches of tide-cut stone. And light burst off the sea itself—variegate upon the undersides of sea stacks and silvery in the choppy cove—and through this ecstasy of brightness two men walked across the sand toward the dog, which backed away, head lowered, teeth showing.

The smaller of the two held a looped length of rope swinging slowly from his fist while the other, larger man stood behind, holding a rifle in the cradle of his arms as one would hold a sleeping child. Abel heard the small man's voice beneath the wind-and-surf sounds: a thin, wet rattle contrapuntal to the dog's low growl. The hackles were raised along its back and Abel leaned, spat, then snatched up his rifle and walked out onto the beach.

When he saw the old man come clambering with purpose over the sea-tossed driftwood, the small man let the rope fall to the sand. He pulled a handkerchief from somewhere about his person and held it to the side of his head, then moved it before his mouth and held it there as Abel approached. Abel could tell there was something badly wrong, and as he drew closer, he could see dried blood scaling his face and neck. Behind him, his partner turned, still holding the rifle in the same tender fashion. This second man was an Indian of the Haida tribe whose eyes, beneath long, raven-black spikes of hair, were dark and lusterless as gutterfound pennies. Old white scars tatted the brown flesh there as though something had once tried to scratch those eyes from their sockets.

Abel stopped before them and spoke sharply to the dog. It looked his way then sat uneasily, growling still. With slow ceremony, the old soldier set the butt plate of his rifle squarely on the toe of his right boot. He held the barrel lightly with the fingers of his left hand and stood before them in such a way that his body might help hide his withered arm. Putting the fingers of his strong right hand to his back pocket, Abel affected an air of unconcern by squinting at the sky, looking to sea, then, finally, glancing sideways at the two men before looking to sea again. "Mornin'," he said quietly. "Don't appear we got a lick of the rain I thought was comin.'"

The two men looked at each other. Abel saw the side of the smaller man's head; saw that his ear was half gone along with part of his cheek and the wound still angry and seeping. The man turned to face Abel, and when he spoke his voice was strained, wet and hard to listen to, as he pressed the bloodstained handkerchief against his cheek. "That yours?" he gurgled, pointing at the dog.

Abel looked over at it, looked back, and met the little man's eyes. "He travels with me," he said. "I don't reckon I give you my name. It's Abel. Abel Truman."

"Willis," said the small man as the Haida stepped forward to block the sun from his hurt face. Willis glanced up at the Indian, blinked slowly, and looked back at Abel.

"Well," said Abel. He pressed his tongue against the inside of his cheek and nodded to the rope lying on the sand. "What's all this about?"

"Ours got loose," said Willis, his voice a slow torture. Wincing, he swallowed and grimaced. "Big fucker, he was. Went to put a collar on him and he up and got mad about it and run off. Reckon he was more wolf than dog, 'cause when he saw the chain . . . well, there was no holding him." He squinted at Abel and shrugged. "We fight 'em," he went on. "One we lost might could've really been something, but he's gone, so we figured to replace him with this one." He lifted his chin toward the dog where it sat growling, then stared at Abel, his eyes two crescents as though he'd hide a darkness behind them.

Abel looked to the Haida, the man with the gun. "It don't look like this dog is much interested in any of that." He cleared his throat. "Tell you what," he said. "You head north, on back the way you come three, maybe four, days' march if you don't catch the tides right, and you'll come up on a village. Up past the Arches. Makah. You probably know it already. You go on up there, and old Pete'll most likely have a dog or two abouts he'd be proud to trade for." Abel cleared his throat again, swallowed painfully, and felt a hot scrim of sweat break high on his forehead.

Willis clicked his teeth together and hissed as though the action pained him. He shook his head. Said: "The dog we lost we bought from them goddamn nigger-Indians up near the border." He shook his head. "I don't guess I'd be too goddamn eager for another from the like of them. Like I say, thing was about half wolf." Pausing, he looked hard at Abel. "You want to see what that wild fucker done to me? Besides my goddamned ear? I'll show you what that mean, wild fucker done to me."

Willis lowered the damp, red cloth from his face, and Abel saw the man's right cheek had been mostly ripped away, leaving a moist gash studded periodically with teeth stained yellowbrown like rotted pine-wood. His tongue was in constant motion over the edges of the hurt— sliding out across his exposed gums to moisten them and setting pink slobber running in pale streams down over his jaw. Willis scratched his neck and clicked his teeth together like some weird, half-fleshed skull made animate. "You see my goddamned face?" he rasped, swallowing and grimacing as the shreds of his cheek flopped about.

"I see it," said Abel.

"Well, what do you think of that?" Willis leered.

"I think you ought not to swallow anymore of your own nasty blood, else you'll start cramping something fierce."

"Goddamned beast what done this to me is still out there in them woods," said Willis, gesturing toward the quiet green expanse stand-ing at Abel's back. "Done all this without even thinking about it." Willis's hand moved in the air before his torn face like a magician's assistant directing the audience's attention toward the mystery.

Abel nodded. "Makes a man wonder how you were treating it that set it off," he said.

Willis opened his mangled mouth as though to reply, but the Haida spoke first. "How much lead you got in your arm, old soldier?" he asked quietly.

Abel blinked. He blinked and swallowed and winced, then said, "What did you say to me?"

"I asked about your arm," said the Haida, nodding. "You favor it even when you're trying not to." He spat and watched the surf snarling about his ankles suck the white spittle oceanward.

Abel felt a slow heat working his way across his chest, up his throat. He shook his head. "My share," he said. "No more'n that."

The Haida pursed his lips, narrowed his eyes, and studied the old man. "Your share," he said, then nodded with a small smile. "I've heard of you. You were in that war they had. In the olden days?"

Abel nodded. "That's right."

"They talk about you sometimes. People on the coast," the Haida said. "They say that that war broke you." The Haida blinked and cocked his head. "We passed your house a few days ago," he said. "They call that place Broken Man Cove."

Abel was silent. His throat burned.

"Then, of course, you've seen worse than this," the big Indian said, nodding to Willis without taking his eyes from Abel. "You've probably seen everything that can be done to a body to get the life out of it. Shit. You've probably done most of those things to other men and been glad to do it. Ain't that right? You reckon that's what broke you? Inside, I mean?"

Abel didn't answer. He doubled over suddenly with a hot spasm of coughing. Willis stepped back. The rifle slipped from Abel's hand and his body shook. He tasted blood against the backs of his teeth but did not spit onto the sand. When he'd mastered himself, Abel quickly scooped the rifle up and held it awkwardly crosswise before his body.

Neither of them had moved, but when Abel faced them once more, the Haida said, "That's a bad cough. You sound like you're a sick man."

Abel shrugged and sniffed wetly. He moved the rifle to its previous position with the butt on his right boot toe and the fingers of his left hand curled about the barrel.

"Jesus Christ," snarled Willis abruptly. "What'll you take for the goddamned dog?" He leaned and gingerly opened his mouth to let a bloody length of slobber spool off his tongue onto the sand.

The Haida shook his head. "He's not going to take anything for it," he said. "Are you, old soldier?"

Abel shook his head. He stared at the Haida until the big man grinned a wide, malicious grin and tilted his head as though in deference. As he did this, Willis jumped forward with a long-bladed knife that seemed to appear in his fist as though from the air.

The little man made to jab at Abel's face, but with a single motion the old soldier kicked the rifle up into his right hand and shoved the barrel forward into Willis's thin chest. Abel curled his forefinger around the trigger. "You better believe I keep this ready to go," he said quietly.

Willis dropped the knife to the sand.

When Abel made his move, the dog began barking savagely—advancing on the two men with short, jerky steps until Abel shouted it down again. He pushed the rifle barrel forward slowly until Willis rocked back on his heels. Abel looked at the Haida, who looked upon the scene with unconcealed mirth. Two points of light danced in his dead, black eyes.

Finally, the big Indian bowed from the waist with shabby decorum. When he straightened again, he broke open his gun and let the shells fall into the surf, where they disappeared.

Abel nodded and lowered the gun and kicked the knife into the surf, then jerked his chin, and Willis made feeble little brushing

motions at his clothes. He wiped his ragged, bloody mouth, retrieved the knife and started north back up the beach.

For his part, the Haida stayed behind a moment to study Abel.
Then, as if he'd come to some conclusion, the Indian shrugged and
turned to follow the other. Abel saw that he wore a crude pack, and
from the outside dangled a fly-speckled haunch of deer that bumped
against the small of his back as he walked.

Neither man looked back, and Abel did not move until they'd
rounded the next headland and gone into the cove there. Then he
looked to where the dog sat watching him with his mouth open.
"You're some kind of pain in the ass, you know that?" he told it.

The next day was much the same as the previous and the one before
in that the old man and the dog traveled south. As he walked, Abel
stayed alert for signs that the pair had doubled back through the
forest—tracks, traces of campfire, the pale, shivery foam of urine
cupped into dark sand, and the certain, indescribable awareness of
something other than otter or deer or eagle watching after them—
but he found and felt nothing. All the same, he walked slowly and
shouted for the dog whenever it left his sight.

That night Abel was compelled to a simple meal of dried venison
and water, for the meat of gulls was not to his taste. He gathered the
makings for a fire but stopped short of lighting it, preferring, instead, to walk a short distance out upon a long finger of stone jutting
into the sea near his camping place within the forest. The old man
crouched at the end of the stone as the sun sank slowly down the
fading wall of the day. The waves were gentle, slapping softly along
and over the rock so that soon his boots were wet and then his feet
within. The water was cool against his tight, dry flesh. He crouched
as though in deep thought while the dog sat on the beach watching
him with its ears cocked. Abel sat listening for a long time, and his
hearing was very good despite his years, yet he could not hear them.

There were only the ocean-and-wind sounds and the occasional thin, high screams of two mated eagles calling from their aerie somewhere back in the dark forest.

Satisfied, Abel stood to study the northward beach and by and by found a thin taper of smoke rising from a campfire some two miles away. Their smoke rose straight and unblown until it had well cleared the canopy, so Abel figured their campsite to be a little, wind-sheltered hollow he knew well.

Nodding to himself, Abel spat and walked back to his campsite. As he went, he clucked his tongue and the dog barked once and loud, then ran joyously to him. The old man told it hush and the dog sat quietly beside him as he kindled their fire.

When the fire was burning, Abel took from his haversack two small tins that decades past had held a child's candies. He laid one on the pine-needled earth and opened the hinged lid of the second. It was half filled with dry brown coffee beans, and he pinched up a measure between thumb and forefinger, then set them in his hand-kerchief. After beating the beans between two stones, he poured the grounds into a tin cup of water and set it directly on the fire. Abel stood and for a moment feared he might begin a coughing fit, but it did not come, and so he wandered about the margins of his campsite until he found a small, round stone to drop into the boiling coffee. As the grounds swirled and clustered about the stone, the old man opened the second tin, took from it paper and tobacco and rolled a thin cigarette to draw on as he drank his evening coffee.

Despite the mildness of the weather, the dog lay close beside him near the fire. The stars came out over the ocean in fine sprays of light and the moon as well and soon the smooth, dark sea was bright with reflected light. As though there were two skies and two moons, and the old man watched seaward, wondering would he see there some other self rising from the swells and, if so, what would that second self have learned that he had not?

There was no wind for Abel to smell or not smell rain upon, but he could still feel it coming just the same. He stayed up late into the night, long after he'd finished his evening luxuries, watching the stars and picking out the planets among them. Every once in a while a shooting star arced dazzlingly across the night, and he remembered the Leonids when he'd seen them as a child, holding his father's hand.

He was six years old when the stars fell, thirty-nine when they fell a second time, and both times it was as though the sky itself had caught fire. You had to shield your eyes. Wailings and moanings and desperate hymnals singing from the colored church at the edge of the pinewoods near the river. A soft frisson had moved up Abel's spine to see the lights, to hear the cries, to hold his father's hand. His father was a dark silhouette against the brightness—one arm outflung as though to bequeath Abel the busy heavens and all the planets in them. His mother was not two weeks in her grave, and his father himself but six months from his own.

Abel lay drowsy beside the fire, remembering further ahead—after those six months had fled and his father had gone to wherever it was the dead went. A cold, dark plain, windswept and candlelit. On Abel went, past the years of his adolescence in the dull, weary, cold, silent house of his maternal aunt outside Albany. She'd saved his soul for the Lord, then left him to his own devices. On and on, sleepy by the fire, past his daughter and past his wife, past happiness and hope and the first spring of war upon the land. He remembered Fredericksburg for no other reason than the cold night after the battle the sky was lit by the aurora borealis shining southward, sparkling with every color over all the living and all the dead on those icy, gore-strewn fields below Marye's Heights.

And now this still night becalmed beside the starlit waters of the cold, gray Pacific, and all the twists of life that led him there. But it was all gone and had been for years, and as he finally slipped to sleep,

Abel stretched out his arm to curl his fingers into the soft fur along the dog's neck.

His sleep that night was absolute and dreamless as only an old man's sleep can sometimes be. And so quiet and peaceful, so restful, that Abel had no ready explanation for the quick, bright pain he felt from temple to jaw upon waking. It was sharp and ice-cold, followed by a slow warmth that spread along his neck. As his eyes came open, Abel Truman knew he'd been cut.

Willis crouched in the sand beside him. The little man's tongue slid about the torn, red edges of his cheek, and the knife in his hand was streaked with Abel's blood.

The old soldier blinked and took a breath. He rolled up onto his knees, but before he could stand, Willis' boot slammed into the side of his head and Abel went tumbling back into a stand of waxy salal.

As he rolled over onto his hands and knees, Abel spat a single tooth that rolled off into the brush like a tossed pebble. Willis stood watching. Even had he not been mangled, Abel reckoned he'd have the look of being born out of season. When he raised his palms, Willis brought his boot down again. And when Abel fell, the little man began to use his fists.

Abel woke when water touched his face. The sun was gone, the sky dark gray, and the tide was rising around where he lay in the surf. Every so often a wave would splash against his face. The water was very cold, and Abel was thirsty. He thought to call out for the dog but found he did not have the voice for it. He pushed weakly through the wet sand, but such motion brought him spasms of pain, so he quit.

By and by the sound of the tide receded behind the clatter of his heart. Abel's face was cool. He tasted seawater. From somewhere came the sound of water slapping against wood, of men's voices calling, but he still had no words with which to answer.

After a while, he slivered open his eyes. There was a dark shape upon the water. Other shapes separated from it to come wading through the surf. Their shadows were long upon the water. A wave broke over Abel's head, and he sputtered. He heard their voices again, suddenly close. Their long shadows fell over him. Strong hands lifted him. The dark sky opened. Rain began to fall.

# FOUR

## Cyphering

### 1864

*May 4*

THEY STRUCK CAMP four hours later. Men and boys rolled their meager belongings into blankets and hung the blankets from themselves, shoulder-to-hip. They filled canteens with fresh water and threw their playing cards into the dirt. In the full, bright sun of noon-time they swung out onto the road singing "Mister, Where's Your Mule?" and "I Can Whip the Scoundrel." They marched with that noon sun winking off their rifle barrels and bayonet points and browning already their winter-pale arms. The Army of Northern Virginia marched that day to the soft snorting of a hundred, hundred horses, their collective breath softly redolent of forage and the good, strong, clean, earthy smell horses have when they are working. Their hooves were well shod, their coats brushed to a shine, and their thick, kinked veins twitched cheek and flank.

The army marched that day as it had always marched: in song, laughter, talk, and boast. Happy amidst the stamp-tramp-and-creak of worn shoe leather upon the dust, and the hard, fleshy slapping of bare feet upon the same. They marched with bands playing and flags uncased. They marched knowing in their hearts that after this next Big Thing, the war would surely be won, and that Grant was of no account and that the Army of the Potomac was as good as up the spout, Gettysburg notwithstanding. And who was there that couldn't see it that day, by God? Who was there that could not feel it in the very air of springtime?

But the moment passed and the day grew long. Ahead, down the long pale line of the road and the marching men upon it, loomed a darkness. The road ran east into the Wilderness.

Men by their thousands filled the Old Stone Road and raised the dust in white plumes flecked with gold, shot through with sun. Yet still the air seemed fresh, washed by the rains of the storm just passed. The sun was bright in the leafed trees, upon grass slick with caught rain, and the man-filled road was as protean and indomitable as a river flowing seaward.

And the army flowed—two corps down two parallel roads separated by a mile-wide expanse of scrub forest and hard-luck farms with a third corps, Longstreet's, a day's march or more behind as it came out of Bell and Mechanicsville down in Louisa County. It didn't matter. Two corps marched east to occupy the men from the North, to hold them by the nose until Longstreet, as he always did, could come up for the knockout blow. And then they'd turn them and by God drive them.

The Army of Northern Virginia marched east, and by and by it entered the dark of the Wilderness of Spotsylvania County. The men marching—tramping accordion-style now, bunching up when there was a halt somewhere along the line so that the dust came down upon their hat crowns and fouled their beards—quieted a little as they passed into that dark. They spoke softer if they spoke at all. There was no singing. The bands stopped playing and cased their instruments, placing them carefully in the backs of wagons and gripping rifles instead. All along the road the marching men could not see ten yards into the dark, green tangle, and the road seemed to narrow the farther it ran. Officers rode along the line urging the men onward in soft, tight voices as though they feared waking something. The Wilderness absorbed the sound of the army with an ever-diminishing echo and constant fadeaways. Sound, if it returned at all from the dark hollows, came back softened and strange, and the dust did not rise beyond the canopy.

From its dim, vine-choked heart, the Wilderness of Spotsylvania stretched over the county from the Rappahannock to the Rapidan to south of Chancellorsville and close by the county seat itself. Just as wide east-to-west, it was the darkest, gloomiest mess of forest that most of these men had ever seen, and yet they knew it well, for they had marched through it, back and forth and back again, many times these past years of warring. Vines and creepers snaked across its damp floor and great brown mounds of dried leaves went rustling and skittering along overgrown farm roads when winds actually found them. Strange shadows reared monstrously in cruel thickets to set travelers' hearts to beating all wrong.

Toward the end of the day, men by handfuls fell out of column to lie awhile in the cool shade. They quivered from harder exercise than they'd known all winter and were pale and shaky from hunger. And as he marched with a dry throat and a jangle of green pain at his temples, David Abernathy spotted the testifying fanatic lying beside the road in the shade of a big black oak. Sniffing dryly, David left the column to join him.

Balancing his forearms on his knees, he squatted nearby and tugged a long, green shoot of grass from the springwet earth. Meditatively chewing the tip, David let the bitter juice squirt against the back of his tongue and trickle down his throat. The old man watched him with his dark eyes ashine. After a while, David asked, "Well, how about it, old-timer? You feel any better today?"

The old man blinked slowly and jerked his chin toward the marching column. "Dead men," he said. "Every mother's son of them."

David nodded and pursed his lips. "A good many, probably," he agreed. He took the grass from his mouth, looked at the flattened, spitwet end, then replaced it. "What about you?"

The old man nodded, smiling now. "Have ye seen the devil?"

David frowned and shook his head. "I ain't studying no devil," he said.

"It don't take study," the old man answered. "It don't take nothin' but thought. Thought and breath, and our nature's fueled."

"What nature?" asked David, glancing sideways as the old man moved farther back into the shadows of the oak, crouching now on a length of root that knuckled its way through the grass.

"Killing and war," said the old man.

David looked at him sadly. "You're touched," he said. "Some damn thing's got you. What you ought to do is go on back and find you an ambulance. Let those boys fix you up. Shoot. Maybe they'd send you on home, being like you are."

The old man shook his head, white hair waving soft and dazed about his leathern face. "The devil's got him a dual nature," he said.

"That so?"

"Yessir. And a name for each. Can ye guess them?"

"You go on tell me."

"The one goes by Lincoln. And t'other?" The old man grinned again. "He goes by Davis. My opinion? We ought to hang 'em both from a goddamned sour apple tree."

"That sounds like sedition," said David.

"It is what it is."

David took the stem from his mouth and threw it into the road, where it was quickly trod into the dust. He stood. "Well," he said, squinting up and down the line of marching men. "I figure I got a job of work to catch back up with the rest of my outfit," he said. He held out his hand, but it was ignored.

"Can ye cipher?" the old man asked him.

David sniffed and nodded. "I know my numbers," he said.

"Well, cipher ye this, then. Over across the river—hell, probably this side of it by now—they's going on 150,000 Yankees. Soldiers coming straight at us as Grant prefers. And do ye know how many we are?"

"We aren't any 150,000, I know that."

"No sir, not at all." The old man grinned and clapped his hands. "By my guess, in the Second Corps alone old Ewell can only field no more'n 35,000 of us, all told. And we ain't all told. Not by a long shot. Hell, you put in the rest of the army and it's maybe 60,000, maybe a little more. And Longstreet ain't up yet. Shit. You want yourself a job of work, you go on up the road a spell and you're bound to find it. Probably find it tomorrow, 'less I miss my guess."

The old man held his eyes a long moment, then finally stood from his root and took David's hand in a hard, callused grip. "What will you do?" David asked him.

The old man grinned again and winked. "My share," he said. "I got quite a bit of that old devil in me that's wanting out."

They stood with their hands clasped beside the dusty road where the soldiers marched eastward through the sun and slanting shadows. "I'll see you when we get there, then," David said, and the old man touched a finger to the side of his nose and nodded.

In the evening, that portion of the army with which Abel Truman marched encamped itself in the Wilderness around a burnt-out cluster of buildings known locally as Verdiersville but that many of them, remembering the shade trees that once stood there and the cool spring whose waters so sweetly flavored their canteens, called

"My-Dear's-Ville." Night fell quickly, seemed darker and more oppressive in the interior of the Wilderness, and the shadows lay long and thick through the gutted frames of sheds and barns and long-abandoned shacks. Few fires burned, but you could still smell ersatz coffee on the air. Men slept on their arms in the dust, for they knew not what lay ahead nor when they would see it. The weather grew chill and all trace of the day's heat was sucked starward until the earth became a cool ball. And far away, over the tops of black trees that shuddered and clashed in the wind, there came a faint orange glow that faded by gentle degrees into the upper darkness where the planets were hung, and the stars. From where they sat upon a small, treeless knoll Ned asked about the glow and Abel told him it was firelight from Grant's vast army, camped two miles up the road at Wilderness Tavern.

Ned's lips were damp; he licked them compulsively and swallowed. "Abel," he said softly, staring eastward at the shivering orange light.

There was something in his voice, and Abel looked over at the boy. Ned's jaw was firmly set, and Abel could see stars glittering in the panes of his eyes. "Abel," he said again and licked his lips. "I guess I'm pretty scared."

"All right, Ned," he said slowly, carefully. "Nothing you need be ashamed about."

"In the morning, what do you think'll happen?"

"I reckon we'll go on up the road a ways farther and have us a hell of a time, Ned."

"That's what you said in Pennsylvania."

"And didn't we?"

Ned grinned and shook his head. "We sure did," he said. And then his face fell and he pursed his wet lips. "I get to missing old Hoke sometimes."

"We ain't goin' to talk about any of that," said Abel.

They were silent together for a long time after. They listened to the soft crackling of distant campfires and the low murmur of sleepless men who, like themselves, stayed up into the night talking of nothing and hoping for rest. "Hey Abel?" Ned.

"What is it?"

"I ain't ever been with a girl."

Abel opened and shut his mouth. "Well . . . Well, shit, Ned," he finally said.

Ned made a face. "I reckon that must be a pretty sorry thing."

"Shit," said Abel. "What do you want me to say to you? There'll be time enough for all that."

"What's it like?"

"Shit. What's what like?"

Ned picked up a twig and proceeded to break it into a number of smaller pieces. "You know."

"Christ," sighed Abel, rubbing his eyes with his fingertips, then dragging them down his face to scratch his neck through his beard. "I ain't having this talk, Ned," he said. "I just ain't." But when he looked at the boy's face, he swore softly and shook his head.

Abel looked up at the red-sky night. He looked west where the sun had set, and he looked to the stars, where they had risen silent and bright. He thought of Elizabeth's shoulders and the soft pulse of blood at the base of her throat that ticked against his cheek. He did not know how to answer the boy and still be honest, so in the end he lied and said, "There's other things that're better."

Again they fell silent. They watched men settling down for rest, watched them at their prayers and not at their prayers and watched them as they turned this way and that upon the ground, looking for comfort. After a while of this, Ned said, "Hey Abel?"

"Shit. Yeah?"

Ned dug a shallow trough in the dirt with his heel. "I ain't got no family at home to miss me," he said. "I never did know my daddy, and I only just barely 'member my sister."

"Well, that's all right."

Ned shook his head, his thin hair tracing soft, star-dazzled designs through the dark. "No, it ain't. It ain't all right at all." He broke off and sniffed wetly. "I'm just . . . What—what do you think it'll be like? To be dead?"

Abel took a deep breath. The feathery shadows of trees stood in relief against the stars' far distant light "Won't it be good, Ned?" he said. "Look how pretty it all is, the stars and the trees. Even them damn Yankee fires look pretty, don't they?" He looked at Ned until Ned nodded. "Well, then, think about it," Abel went on, speaking quietly but with soft authority, as though revealing ideas long grappled with. "If God could make all this out of this poor stuff"—he pinched the flesh of Ned's upper arm—"just think what He's been able to do in heaven. 'Sides, it'd give us a chance to see Hoke again. Give the old man a ration of shit about lightin' out early like he done."

Ned sniffed and ran the back of his hand beneath his nose. "You really think that?" he asked.

Abel pursed his lips and looked away. He smirked and sighed and said, "Hell, I don't know, Ned." Taking a deep breath, he let it out again. "No," he finally said. "I don't guess I do. Sounded pretty good in my head though." He shrugged and touched Ned's arm with his elbow. "Tell you what though," he said leadingly.

"What?"

"I'll be goddamned if those Yankee campfires don't look mighty pretty anyway."

They sat together watching. Around them, the myriad sounds of an army in its camps gave way to the gentler sounds of slumber. A few stars, unseen by all but them, fell down the bright wall of the night, their brief arcs described in pale lines like scratches on dark glass. After a little while Ned said, "Hey Abel?"

"What, goddamn it?"

"Sing me that song, Abel."

Abel looked around. Beside him, the boy settled down and crossed his arms behind his head, staring up at the busy sky. "Jesus, Ned. I ain't doing that."

Ned looked at him. "Please, Abel? I just know I ain't goin' to get no sleep tonight otherwise."

"No, goddamnit. I ain't doin' it."

"Well, Jesus," said Ned good-naturedly. "First you lie to me about women and fuckin' and now you won't even sing me to goddamned sleep."

Abel stared at the boy. After a moment, he closed his mouth. Squinting hard at him, Abel asked, "You did that just to get my goat, didn't you?"

"Goddamned right I did."

"Well, stop it. Don't sound right. Words like that comin' out your mouth."

"Will you sing me that song?"

"No, I won't. I told you that."

"Well, shit. I guess then I'll goddamned stop it when I'm god-damned good and shittin' ready."

Abel took a deep breath and blew. He looked around to see how many were nearby and if they were listening, then, after swearing under his breath, Abel began to sing softly a little hush-a-bye song he remembered from his youth. Beside him, Ned grinned and shut his eyes. Abel sang softly, his voice deep and soothing, and after a while he too closed his eyes and settled in beside the boy, still singing.

The stars traced their courses and the orange glow gradually faded and was gone. At some point in their sleep Abel put an arm around Ned's shoulders and Ned leaned into him and they slept that way, together, until daybreak, when the army roused itself and moved on.

## May 5, 1864

They spent the morning digging in the loamy, rainwet earth. All around them rose the soft, seductive scents of spring—the spice of old leaves, the perfume of wildflowers, the richness of turned soil. They could smell the sun and imagine long, hot days to come so that the farmers among them pined for home and the lovers for their sweethearts. Steuart's Brigade, of Ewell's Corps, formed a line with two other brigades of the division that threaded north-to-south along the western edge of an old and overgrown cornfield of fifty acres or so, known locally as Saunders'. Whosoever it was that had once owned the land, that had cleared the trash trees and tangles from it and broke the soil, tilled it, sown and reaped and loved it, that had built home and hope upon it, was long gone now. Long gone and leaving behind only stubby, half-wild corn plantings shooting greenly from the yellow, calf-high grass like weird gothic spikes. The old field stretched several hundred yards north and south of the old Orange Turnpike, which slanted eastward through its center and was, in its turn, cut by a deep gully trickling that morning with stale rainwater. A barren yellow patch amidst the darkness and the green. The Wilderness rose around Saunders' Field like a vegetable wall so that walking from the dark of the wood was like passing from night to day in the space of a step, from sleep to dream.

There was a scarcity of shovels in the division, so men were compelled to break the earth with bayonet points and cutlery and the big, swordlike blades of dragoons that some men carried. A long chain of crumbling mounds rose slowly with the sun. Bristling with roots and twigs and old, dry grass, the earthen mounds were striated light and dark and light again so that those of a geologic bent could see plainly the years of industry that had operated in the Wilderness. Branches and small downed trees were drug atop the earthworks, and by noon the men were hunkered down like gnomes or goblins behind their hasty battlements.

They waited. They watched down the road, where occasionally they glimpsed the soldiers of the Army of the Potomac, now Grant's, in their dark uniforms crossing the median, and they listened to them in the brush across the field at much the same work as they themselves had done.

A blue sky day and hot. By midmorning fluttery waves of heat shimmered off the planks and rose from the yellow field itself where David Abernathy, crouched down in the dirt behind the fieldworks close by the road, watched as Union soldiers formed up in lines back in the woods beyond the other side of the field. He blinked and slipped the spectacles from his face. The surrounding Wilderness became a soft, fantasy wood of dark shadows and delight, and he sniffed mournfully and replaced the eyeglasses.

Abel lay stretched out on his back beside him, and when David nudged him, he blinked, grunted, and wet his lips as though coming back from some far-off place he did not want to leave. The corners of his eyes were wet, and Abel quickly wiped his face with his wrist backs, one and then the other. Rubbing his palm briskly up and down his face to chase the sleep from him, he blinked and frowned. "What is it?" he asked, his voice rough and tired.

David gripped his rifle and lifted his chin. "Looks like they're getting ready over there," he said quietly.

Abel rolled onto his belly and tugged his hat brim down over his eyes to shade them. Squinting, he watched for a long time the far side of the field, where they were gathering themselves behind screens of dense brush—small, dark figures intercut with Zouave uniforms, brightly red, you could just make them out standing double-ranked and bristling with flags and bayonets that sparked in the sun like tiny embers thrown from a fire. You could tell the sound of officers' horses breaking up the underbrush, their hooves making that lovely, hollow, clopping sound that can only come from horses walking upon the earth, and you could hear the officers' voices shouting orders and encouragement, readying the working men for the job at hand. Abel's lips moved with silent counting as he picked out flags from the brush. When he looked back at David he opened his mouth as though to speak, then shut it again and looked back across the field to count a second time. "I heard somewhere Grant went and reorganized the whole works," Abel finally said. "Hard to say what-all's over there. How many, I mean. Counted twelve flags 'fore I gave it up." He frowned and wiped his mouth. "There's a whole mess of men over there, anyway."

David pinched his temples with thumb and middle finger, then pressed hard against the lids of his eyes to try and drive the green jangle from his skull. It did not work—it seldom worked—and he let out a sigh. "I did see a Fifth Corps flag back in there not too long ago," he offered.

Abel nodded. "Could be them Maine men, then," he said. "Maybe them good Green Mountain boys or them New Yorkers, maybe. Sickles' old bunch." He looked hard at David. "You goin' to make it?"

David tucked his tongue thoughtfully into his cheek and seemed to ponder the question a moment before answering. "I suppose so," he finally said, gripping his rifle again. He looked at Abel. "I sometimes forget that you come from up that way," he said.

"New York?" asked Abel, waving a hand through the sunstruck air dismissively. "It's just a place, like any other. Don't mean anything more'n what a person wants it to, and the only claim it's got on me is I've got people buried up there." He shrugged. "Aunt," he said. "My mama and daddy're up there. Some others."

David sniffed and curled his lip. "Goddamn Yankee," he said.

"Fuck you," said Abel good-naturedly. "And watch your mouth." He lifted his chin and asked "How're Lee's Miserables?"

David grinned wide. "Like the book says," he said, finishing the joke. "Faintin'."

They chuckled softly together. A stray bullet whizzed overhead, clipping through the greenery to send leaves spiraling through the blue air and sounding for all the world on this fine spring day like a fat bee or horsefly off about its business. A heartbeat later came the sound of the shot and then its attendant echo. Abel reached out to finger the cuff of David's gaudy shirt, whistling as he did so, and David pushed his hand back, then nodded across the field. "What do you think about it? Really?" he asked.

"What? The shirt? I already told you, you look like a god-damned—"

"No," said David quickly. "About what they're doing across the way. You think they're coming?"

Abel snorted. "Hell yes, I think they're coming. I imagine we'll all have a fine time of it here pretty quick."

David stared at him, and Abel met his eye, then, after a moment, said, "It's like I told Ned. I figure they got us by the short hairs, and once they figure that out, it'll get pretty bad." He pursed his lips and considered the backs of his knuckles a moment before glancing off across the field, where the blue ranks murmured and swelled behind screens of green. Abel rolled over onto his back. "You just hang back this morning," he told David. He stared a moment at David's gaudy shirt, then shook his head. "You hang onto that charm of yours and keep your head down," he said. "You'll be all right." Then Abel tilted his hat back over his face, and a few moments later he was sleeping again.

More noise as skirmishers from both sides found each other in the tall grass. Stray shots hissed over the grass tops, peppering the far side of the earthworks and thunking into the trees. He watched for

Ned or some sign of him rising from and firing over the grass with the other skirmishers but saw no one he knew. Finally, David rolled over onto his back and reached down the front of his varicolored shirt for the little crucifix he'd found that morning on the dead cavalryman.

In the early hours of the day, they'd not known how far the Army of the Potomac had come into the Wilderness nor by what roads, so the Army of Northern Virginia moved slowly east down their two roads, separated by over a mile of dank forest. Ewell moved his corps along the old turnpike with pickets well advanced. As they neared the field where they now crouched, the men fanned out into the shadowy green tangle on either side of the road that ran in a white line that disappeared into the gloom beyond the dull yellow grass. Dust rose and went blowing over the field, and the men were pale with it. Over the treetops, they saw other, larger clouds marking the Union progression through the Wilderness as though Ewell's corps was the stem of a T the Yankees were crossing. As he stepped from the road, David wondered would they feel a tremor in the earth as so many countless pounds of flesh and machines trod and rolled across it. He wondered would they hear them coming like a thunderstorm troubling the next valley and moving swiftly toward them.

Birdsong was everywhere that morning, and shafts of pale sunlight tilted through the branches so the light lay bright upon the leaves and the moss steamed softly from the forest floor. And the sun that morning made the dew to shine like tiny beads strung upon the precise, wiredrawn designs of spiderwebs. And the air that morning was redolent of sun and warmth and good, growing things—the thick, fecund odor of the forest where things grew, fell, rotted out, and grew again. A vegetable reek, thought David, an ancient, womanish scent, and under it, the faint acrid stink of kicked-over campfires and the endless clouds of kicked-up dust.

The body of the cavalryman lay just off the road. The men were filing into the deep brush, paying the deadman no mind. When Ned saw him, he whistled softly and nudged David. "Ain't that just about the saddest thing?" he asked, his round pink face bright with sweat.

The rider lay on his back in a bright green spray of grass that should have been lovely. He'd not been dead more than a day yet the beetles had already begun their gleaning. You couldn't tell if he'd been handsome for he was tightening with bloat. He was hatless and beardless and had been shot through the throat; darkened blood wrapped his neck and ran in a trail from him like a scarf knit by someone missing him. His left boot was tangled up in his stirrup, and his horse lay dead beside him, its long snout laying across the rider's thigh. The ground around them was brown and the leaves crackled with life.

David squatted beside the body and rifled through the saddlebags. He sniffed and wiped his nose with the back of his hand, fighting hard against a vomitous swelling at the back of his throat. "I don't reckon this one'll get a proper burial," he told Ned, who stood nearby, shuffling his weight from foot to foot. "Figure, if we can find his name somebody might get word to his people."

But there had been little time for that. Men were filing to either side of the road and bending to digging. Ned shuffled his feet in the dust. David crouched beside the body. Officers called to them, and before standing to move away, David noticed something clutched in the dead rider's palm. A small white cross carved of a single piece of bone or something like bone. Ned went off—a blink, and he was vanished in the dark brush. Frowning, David pried the cross from the rider's stiff hand. He stood looking at it a long time. The cross was light and porous, still cool with the rider's death. David looked at him. You could hardly call it a face any longer. Touching two fingers to the brim of his hat, he slipped the cross into his pocket and moved off into the brush beside the pale road.

Now, as he lay on his back in the early afternoon sun, David examined the little cross fitted to his palm by a thong wrapped about his fingers. There was an old bloodstain on the transom, and he ran a thumb across it, feeling how smooth it was near the stain. As though some other man, farmer or soldier or miner or clerk or railroad man, some sailor or teamster or drifter or husband, brother or son, had worked his thumbpad back and forth and back again upon the cross at prayers. Or more simply hoping against death in the dark places of the world.

David sighed. He worried the cross with his thumb, and when the sky did not crack open for the good Lord's almighty hand to reach down and lift him bodily from this place, he sniffed and closed his eyes. He rubbed his forehead against the old, green pain that flared and cavitated behind his eyes.

There was more rifle fire now—scattered popping sounds like flames working into damp wood. The noise was still individual enough to echo between the trees before diminishing slowly under the sky. David took off his hat and dragged a sleeve across his face. His heart shuddered with each percussion, but this was only the beginning of things, and he knew that after a time it would return to its normal rhythm so paid it little mind.

He ducked as a stray bullet sent a spray of dirt over him, then lowered the cross down the front of his shirt. As he grasped his hat to snug it back onto his head, Gully Coleman leaned over and tapped David's shoulder. "Hey there," he said, his thin lips tilting up one side of his face and his rail-thin body all angles as he hunkered behind the works. "Let me see your hat a minute, bud."

David frowned and silently passed the hat to him. Gully took the hat in hands that seemed in all ways outsized for the rest of him. He had a small head and a large face, and men who did not know his character remarked on his resemblance to the Union president, but this was mainly for his height and beard, for Gully lacked Lincoln's deep, sad eyes and laughing mouth. Gully took the hat, winked at David, and hoisted it up over the earthen ramparts on the point of his bayonet. Before David could protest, Gully was waving the hat back and forth through the sunstruck air.

His challenge was quickly answered by a spattering of bullets. They came slapping hard against the piled dirt and went clipping through the branches overhead. Leaves spiraled with the sun bright on their smooth backs, and men up and down the line hooted, shouted, called, and laughed. Gully lowered his bayonet, plucked David's shredded hat from it, and passed it back. "See, Virdge," he said to the man crouching beside him. "I told you them boys had their eyes on our section. They all's eager on account we're near the road. They know it's a good spot." Gully winked broadly and grinned at David.

David took the hat back. The crown was blown out, and there were too many holes in it to count. He reached inside and poked one thin finger through a hole, wiggled it about, then looked at Gully.

"Why in hell would you do that?" he asked softly.

Gully nodded to Virgil, then toward the Yankee sharpshooters bobbing darkly in the yellow grass near the far tree line. "Old Virdge didn't allow them Yanks was even in the field, let alone watchin' us, and I said they was." He shrugged. "I figured puttin' up a hat would be the most . . . What do you say?—The most expeditious way to prove me out." Gully hooked his thumbs into the tattered lapels of his rotting jacket and pulled in his chin. Behind him, Virgil nodded vigorously, then looked away with laughter.

David gaped. He lifted his hand, the hat still hanging from his finger, and pointed at Gully, the hat shaking like a dead bird. "God damn it," he said. "God damn it to hell. Whyn't you use your own goddamned hat?"

Gully opened his mouth in mock astonishment. He removed his soiled bowler and held it against his chest. "Why, on account of this is MY hat," he said earnestly, then jammed the bowler back down onto his head and grinned. "Anyway, I reckoned seeing as how you're already dressed for the ball in your new finery and whatnot"—he nodded to David's new shirt—"I just figured you might appreciate your hat being as God-awful-ugly as your shirt."

There were some thirty men crouching behind the works up and down the line from them who had been watching this exchange, and to David's ears they all began laughing at once—except for Abel, who still dozed on his back beside him. David scowled and spat and, for spite, slapped hard at the top of Abel's head with the wrecked hat, but Abel slept on. Disgusted, David put the hat on, then rolled onto his stomach to watch for the Yankees they all knew must come soon.

Gully pursed his lips, leaned and spat, then nodded toward David. "Kindly looks like a pope's cap now," he observed.

"Or some kind of piney-apple," offered Virgil. When David turned to glare at them, Virgil shrugged and held his palms up. "I seen 'em at a stand in Charleston oncet," he said. "It don't look bad. On you."

There was more laughing, and David joined them in spite of himself, but it didn't last. From the north end of the field, blowing south, came a soft, freshening wind, and from the woods there came a rider.

An officer dressed in his blue finery came a few rods out into the grass. His carriage on horseback was erect and very proper, and neither was his horse skittish as they halted. He wore a sash of yellow and yellow gloves, and his black boots shone as though he'd prepared himself carefully for this moment. Men murmured this was Grant himself come to inspect their defenses, and though most had seen newspapers and knew better, the rumor went up and down the line. It was not Grant, yet still no man fired. "Goddamn," said Virgil softly. "Goddamn, but that's a splendid man."

For his part, the officer sat his horse and looked over their lines through his field glasses, pausing now and again to jot notes onto a pad balanced on his thigh. And still no one moved until, with a shout that sounded like pain, Gully rose to his knees and fired his piece. Others joined him, and David watched the grass breaking up all around the horse's legs, yet the officer did not flinch and the horse did not sidestep.

Gully had reloaded his musket and was rising to fire again when Virgil grabbed the barrel and, with a snarled curse, forced it down. Across the field, the officer calmly put the pad and pencil away, set his thumb to his nose and waggled his fingers at them all, and then, without hurrying, rode back into the screening brush and was gone.

Men began to hoot softly and craned their necks about to watch as Gully and Virgil wrestled and beat upon each other in the loose soil behind the earthworks. David nudged Abel's shoulder hard enough to wake him, and Abel snorted and opened his eyes. "You'll want to see this," David told him. "Old Gully's about to get himself a beating."

Still on his back, Abel looked over as the two men rolled around on the ground. He drug a palm down his face and shook his head as though to clear it. "Goddamn," he said softly. "But I get so tired sometimes I dream I'm sleeping."

David pushed his tongue into his cheek and nodded. Gully's nose was bloodied, and blood stained the front of his suitcoat. From across the field came the sound of bugles and fifes followed by a chorus of cheers that rang and echoed and did not seem to fade. They looked up over the earthworks. Their pickets were coming in, holding their hats to their heads and running fast—they could see Ned moving through the grass, his legs a blur, a wide, excited grin splitting his face. Across the field, dark figures marched forward in ruler-straight lines dressed for battle. They crossed from the dark of the wood to the bright of the field and the light came splashing brilliantly as it broke upon their rifle barrels and bayonets. Abel leaned and spat.

"Yonder they come," said David softly.

# FIVE

## *The Branches Above Them*

*1899*

WHEN THE WHISTLE blew, Silas pushed the heavy iron door closed with the blade of his shovel and stepped back from the furnace. The boiler rattled as though the heat was something wanting out, while all around the yard and at the outbuildings the machine sounds of the mill at work tapered to stillness. The gray wind was soft, punctuated by the coughs and sighs, the weary soft moans and the low, tired voices, of men coming off shift.

Skimming the sweat-damp gloves from his hands, the boy looked about for the others but did not see them amongst the multitude of flanneled backs moving slowly out into the yard and onward to the rude lane leading to town where taverns and feed stores, barber shops and land offices, rose shabby and mudspattered and sad from the jade forest beside the sea. Silas watched them walk under the trees where leaves hung brightly dying and farther on, past the town and into the forest itself, where their homes waited. Little cabins out in the

green, little shacks on little plots that produced stingy fists of cabbage
and hard little potatoes that tasted all wrong. Filthy children squatted
in the mud while goats held high court on ragged stumps. Tiny dooryard flower gardens withered slowly in the constant forest dark.

Silas walked alone through the bay of the mill and out onto the
sagging dock that thrust into the harbor from the far side of the ware-
house. The sky a metal plate whose color foretold a greater darkness
yet to come. A faint yellow at the seams where they lay joined and
dark over the earth. Night was already falling beyond the Olympics
and the peaks were shadow-drenched, huge. Waves slapped the pil-
ings beneath him. A magnificently mustached bolt puncher crabbed
his skiff across the darkening shallows. He tied it off to an iron ring set
into a log afloat near the conveyor, then stepped with rude grace from
skiff to floating log to floating log to shore and was gone.

The boy walked to the end of the dock and sat with his feet dan-
gling over the water. Fish and oil smells. Sawdust and smoke and the
sweet fragrance of new-cut wood. The spoiled, acrid stink of machine oil. Ocean scents older than time. An exotic reek. Rain plunged
in gray streaks. A foamy scum churned along the shore.

Silas sat with his hands open, palms up, on his thighs as though
he'd catch and hold the falling rain. Scabbed-over burn marks peppered his brown forearms with intricate patterns while a dull brown
fringe tatted his overalls at the bib. He rested his chin on his chest.
The rain was cool, and he smelled its cleanliness and tasted in it the
ocean and the sharp, pitchy, dark flavor of the forest from which it
had risen cloudward days past. Silas sat watching the rain strike the
salty harbor. The shadow of a big coho hovered in the water, its gills
splayed and redly atremble, while it finned against the gray swells to
stand in place over the sunken remains of rusted-out machinery,
dropped tools, and saw-chewed stumps and board ends. And slowly
the fish tilted slightly surfaceward as though to study the boy and
the solid world above where the boy, in turn, sat studying it.

He had just begun to sing himself a little fishing song that Oyster Tom had taught him when he heard them on the dock behind him. He quieted, and the air he'd gathered for the song came streaming from his lips. The salmon jerked like a stabbed muscle and vanished in the dark water. Silas swallowed, stood, and turned.

There were three of them, and they came hooded, faces covered by varicolored sleeves of flannel cut with frayed triangular slits for their eyes. Two of them carried little clubs of the sort used by fishermen to brain dogfish and spiny rock cod, while the third stood unarmed but for a fat ring of turquoise upon his right fist, and Silas knew that it was Farley.

It had grown cooler still. Silas watched their breath come steaming through their hoods, appearing and vanishing and appearing again on the damp air. He smelled whiskey. From somewhere off on the far side of the mill the yard dog began barking.

"You fucking Indian," one of them finally said. Silas thought it was the man with the ring, but it didn't matter. All three came forward together.

When Charley Poole and his son Edward found him, Silas was still on the dock. He lay on his face with his left hand hanging down as though reaching for something lost in the heaving, rain-stippled water below. He lay in a small red pool that spread from his face and dripped between the boards to the harbor. The boy lay with his eyes closed. He lay absolutely still but for the small breaths that troubled his chest.

Charley Poole covered his mouth with his palm to see him lying so while Edward ran out onto the creaking dock. Himself not much more than a boy, he crouched to touch Silas's shoulder. A little bubble of blood filled and emptied repeatedly in his left nostril and a portion of his cheek was laid open to reveal a delicate white line of bone beneath his eye. They'd poured their liquor out onto him, and the boy stank of whiskey and violence and dull animal fear.

Edward was distantly aware of the rain tapping between his shoulders, a soft hiss as it hit the water. He watched for a moment the boy's blood mixing with the rain upon the planking, then, taking a deep breath, Edward carefully lifted the flap of skin with his fingertips and pressed it back. Thick as a drunk man's lip, it flopped open again after but a moment. Silas moaned softly.

Behind them, Charley had fallen to his knees at the end of the ramp, his hands clasped fast beneath his chin, face tilted earthward and his salt-and-pepper hair wet and ropy. His prayers were silent, yet his lips moved quickly in recitation.

Edward touched the boy's shoulder and softly called his name. Silas groaned and Edward glanced back and said, "Father, I need you here," then slowly, carefully rolled Silas onto his back, cradling his head with splayed fingers and gentling it to the worn silver boards.

Charley came up the dock and knelt beside them. He filled his cheeks and blew, then touched his fingertips to that part of Silas's black hair that was matted and gummy with blood. Swallowing, he took a corner of his shirttail to wipe the bubble from his nose. Looking at Edward, he nodded and said, "He's alive. I prayed it so." His voice in hushed harmony with the hissing rain that fell upon the harbor swells. "I saw how he was," Charley said. "Saw him close to death and prayed him back. Praise Jesus." Charley bent his head again in quick and earnest prayer.

Edward looked at his father a long, silent moment. His lips moved, and he finally nodded and said softly, "I know you did, but he's hurt bad, yes? I need you to go to camp. Get Tom. Find Tom and have him bring the boat around. Father? Can you do that?"

Charley Poole opened and closed his mouth and looked at the boy lying so still, so stained by blood and hurt and rain. "Prayed it so, I did," he murmured.

Edward took him by the shoulders and ducked his head to catch his eye. "Father? Can you do that?"

Charley nodded quickly, then took another long look at Silas before running off across the yard and into the mist the rain had chased off the harbor and into the trees. Edward watched him go, then removed his work-thinned shirt and carefully tore a sleeve from it. He sopped blood from the boy's face and ears and neck and Silas groaned softly through torn lips and two broken teeth.

There came a soft splashing and Edward looked to see that the blood hung in an inky cloud in the gray harbor water. A gathering of dogfish swam below them. Silent but for the splashes, they tore at the underside of the water as though they understood it showed them something hateful of the world above. Their ever-open eyes were black, their mouths agape and their backs speckled.

It was fully dark by the time Charley and Oyster Tom arrived with the canoe. Edward had managed to drag Silas to a little stretch of beach not far from the yard, and when he heard their oars, he called into the shadows until their shapes resolved from the liquid dark.

The long, hollowed-out log from which they'd crafted their canoe came rasping onto the sand. Oyster Tom struck a match to light the little hurricane lamp that hung from the great, curved prow. The flame flared briefly orange upon his ancient face, scouring the dark from the old scars that plagued his cheeks and setting his white hair aglow against the darkness round about him. The old man lifted the lamp from its hook and held it aloft to look at Silas lying limp in Edward's arms. Shaking his head, he sucked a tooth and turned away.

Oyster Tom wrapped the boy in an old piece of blanket while Edward and Charley took their places bow and stern. Blowing the light from the lamp, they set off over the dark harbor. Across the water, where the town of Wheelock spread along the shore, were strung electric lights and wavering lamp-flames like signals from another world. The lights winked silently now and again as townsfolk passed before them. The rain had stopped, and thin reflections came across the choppy water like wavering sepia lines upon an old, untrustworthy map. Distantly they heard men at their pleasure laughing and calling from the streets. The hollow stamp of hooves upon packed earth and clattering on the boards. The sad, lonely discordance of a piano man badly playing at a ragtime. The Indians' course was plotted west then north and took them around the lighted town then off again into the darkness past the harbor where the ocean was, and the vast, cloud-struck sky, the forest and the long, stony, unending beach.

But there were also white sand beaches north and south of town, and back from these stood crumbling cliffs of stone and clay that tide and wind destroyed and recreated seasonally. Against the northern cliffs and sprawling off into the black forest there sat a tiny Indian settlement for itinerant workers. Canvas shelters trembling in the wind. Rude shebangs of cast-off planking, of branch and packed moss and fern. Little tents of stained bed linen rife with fleas. Wan cooking fires glittered here in weak reflection of Wheelock's lights, and quietly under the constant grumble of surf and tide, a plaintive, wet coughing as of a weather-colored tribe taken sick from day labor and hunger.

They beached near the picked-clean carcass of a sea lion. Someone had taken the skull to decorate his shelter or to use in what prayers he would pray and left behind a broken cage of ribs that curved with a flourish from the sea foam, sand, and bladderwrack. Footprints uncountable lay about the bones where starving folk had broken off sections to hold over fires, sucking from them what warmed marrow they could and soaking the remainder for soup. They carried Silas to their shelter, three good walls and a leaky roof constructed from bits of broken, saw-ruined scrap board snuck back from the mill. They lay the boy down at the back where it was driest, where the wind came least, then set about their diverse tasks.

Edward left to gather what driftwood he could find for their fire while Oyster Tom undressed the boy to his tattered underclothes and, humming softly an old song he knew about the Two Men Who Changed Things, searched with careful fingertips along the boy's body for broken bones and deeper hurts. For his part, Charley Poole knelt in prayer just outside the shelter where the rain had begun again. He looked to the dark clouds where he knew heaven should be, and rain ran in streams from the cups of his closed eyes. The Haida in the tent across the way cackled through rotten teeth, mimicking Charley and shouting in the coarse aspirates of his mother tongue. But the Haida was weak and foul with dysentery, and Charley paid him no mind. When the Haida finally withdrew to the dark of his tent, Charley set his palms on his thighs to better support his back, closed his eyes again, and began to quickly move his lips in silent devotions.

After the fire was kindled, water was drawn from the seep at the base of the cliff and set to boil in a little pot set upon the live coals. Edward crouched beside Oyster Tom as he ministered to Silas. The boy was awake now, and Tom looked him in the eye and nodded. Silas swallowed. His tongue worked around the inside of his mouth and presently he spat a pair of teeth onto his chin like little forlorn chips of bone. The wound in his cheek would not stay closed—it kept flapping open, shedding blood and showing the bone beneath. When he asked, Oyster Tom told Edward he could find no broken bones but worried for the blood the boy had lost. The old Indian hummed and sang and stroked Silas's hair. Outside, Charley mumbled into the rain. Finally, Oyster Tom bowed his head, nodded to himself, then stood to leave the shelter.

He returned a short while later with a small leather bag retrieved from the bentwood box beneath the seat of their canoe. Oyster Tom took from it several little squares of clean linen and pressed these into the boy's mouth. He bid him bite down as best he could to staunch the bleeding sockets, then took from the bag needle and thread. Passing the tip several times through the flames, he threaded the eye with a steady hand. The thread dark and coarse, fibery as ship's rope. Rain tapped fast and hard against the roof. Oyster Tom looked the boy in the eye again and Silas nodded and Tom pressed the flap of skin to its place beneath the boy's eye and bent to sewing. The boy's hands fisted and opened in the blankets and when Tom had finished he passed the bloody needle back through the flames. Then he bid Edward hold Silas's head and arms, and Edward did so as the old Indian lifted the boy's shirt.

The boy hissed in pain and Edward saw a wound he had not noticed before. A dull, red arc described his left breast, bisecting the nipple and tacky with drying gore. Silas sniffed a wet little boy's sniffle and closed his eyes as Oyster Tom cleaned around the lips of the wound, then rethreaded the needle and sewed the nipple back. The boy moaned and struggled and after a while passed out.

When they'd finally finished, Edward watched Oyster Tom where the old man sat smoking his pipe and staring out at the wavecut ocean. Finally, Edward asked what they should do. Charley's prayers droned from the dark outside the shelter, and Oyster Tom took the pipe from his mouth to study the bowl as though he'd consult the dull glow within. After a few moments, he said that they must go. He said that Charley would not be coaxed from his prayers before morning, and that the boy needed rest at any rate, so they would leave with the sun. And then he stood and walked off alone into the rain, out into the forest where the dark was deepest.

At daybreak they left that place. They loaded their few and paltry possessions into the canoe and pushed off into the muttering surf. Behind them, a fight broke out for their abandoned shelter. Quinault and Tillamook, Nuu-chah-nulth and Haida come south from Canada—all gathered for the dangerous, poor-paying work around the lumber mills here and farther south at Forks and Aberdeen, all rewarded with sickness, fingers and worse lost to saws or crushed by chains, casual beatings—pitched into each other for four pieces of miscut board and a scrap of rotting blanket. Charley saw the Haida who'd mocked him fall face-first to the sand but did not see him rise. After a time, they turned from the scene, faced north, and went their way.

Silas slept to the slap and rock of wave and tide while the others bent to paddling and watched the shore. In the evening, they made their camp upon the beach and Oyster Tom vanished into the forest. He carried no gun, only a little skinning knife, and was gone less than an hour before returning with two fat ground squirrels for their appetites.

The next day was much the same—the long, dark beach, the gray ocean, their propelled momentum across the swells—and as they settled around the fire that night, they heard a long, drawn-out howling that echoed down from the foothills. "Wolf," murmured Edward, and Charley nodded fearfully while Silas slept. Oyster Tom merely looked at them and slowly shook his head. He told them he did not think it was a wolf but maybe something more or something less, and told them it was better not to think on it because the beast might follow their thoughts back to camp and attack them in their dreams.

So it was that two days later on their northward journey home, Edward stood to shade his eyes from the sun and peer shoreward. Frowning, he pointed with a shout, but Oyster Tom had already seen and set his oar to turn them from their course.

The old man had been left to drown in the surf. He was an old soldier who lived alone on the beach, and he was known to them. They carried him on their shoulders to the forest the way that hurt soldiers and dead men have always been carried: with infinite tenderness and careful respect. When they laid him down, the old man sighed but did not wake. His flesh was cold and his face was dark and he looked altogether near his death.

Oyster Tom kept a single coal live in a smooth clay jar. Throughout the day he'd feed the coal twigs and bits of dry moss, slips of bark and pinches of sticky lodgepole pine needles, so that smoke followed them across the water, mixed up in their hair and fragrant upon their skin. Now Tom rested on his knees and baled a little hole in the earth where it was soft beneath the trees, added twigs and leaves, then set the bright, heart-shaped coal upon the kindling. Charley Poole tied off the corners of their tattered tarp to make a shelter while Silas sat resting with his back against a fallen tree, his legs splayed out so as not to crimp his chest.

Rain dripped darkly in the forest and fell upon the ocean. Edward walked a short ways down the beach with a pair of water skins and sank their mouths into a shallow little stream cutting through the sand. The tracks of deer lay pressed into the damp sand all about, and from the blood upon the stones he could plainly tell where the old man had been beaten. The water was cold, but Edward did not clamber from the stream until both skins filled. He crouched in the water, staring at the dark sand. When he finally returned, his father bid him fill their pot and set it on the fire to warm. Edward did this, watching the men as they bent over the old soldier and began to tend his wounds.

They scraped away his beard with their knives to better stitch the savage cut that ran from his temple to his jaw and tossed the hair into the fire where it stank and sizzled mournfully. All their clean cloth was still fouled with Silas's blood, so they used moss soaked in warm water to clean the drying blood from his neck and face. Oyster Tom pinched up a measure of cobwebbing from the low branches and held a few strands under the old soldier's nose to judge the force of his breath. The filmy strings rippled out and settled again leisurely, and Tom grunted his satisfaction, then grasped either side of the man's shirt and spread it open with two quick tugs.

But for the dark of bruises and other hurts, the old soldier's chest and stomach were fish-pale in the flame-colored gloom. Charley leaned to look more closely. He hissed and straightened. "Good God," he said.

Ropy, pallid scars scalloped the old soldier's chest, and here and there about his ribcage the flesh rose whitely in ill-healed little creases. When Oyster Tom lifted him to check his back, they saw the flesh there rippling with yet more scars that lay like wide roseate coins of cooled wax. Edward leaned into the light to look for himself. "He's the one you said fought in the war?" he asked his father.

They settled the old soldier down again. "That's right," Charley answered.

"At Gettysburg?"

"I think he said that once. Plenty of other places too, from the look of him."

"You believe him?" asked Edward.

Charley looked at Oyster Tom, who fixed Edward with a look and asked why the man would lie. He waved his hand over the man's battered flesh as though to ask what more was needed in the way of proof. When Edward did not answer, he was sent into the forest to gather sneezeweed.

Oyster Tom sat for a space of time looking at the injured old man before him. The old wounds and the new. He sat as though trying to find patterns in the coil, flex, and scrawl of scars fretting his body, each telling the tale of a wound, each the endpoint of a ball or shell fragment, of a blade or a surgeon's filthy probe, and each connected to the next by pale, smooth flesh whose sole purpose seemed to be to bind one scar to the next.

The old Indian leaned over the fire. In the stormy dark of the evening, the flames coppered his pocked, timeworn face and his hair glowed whitely. With the stinking beard burned to ash and the driftwood crackling with flame, he moved his hands in the smoke, scooping up great handfuls and laving them against his face to re-fresh himself before further labors. Charley watched him breathe the smoke, drink it and delight in it. He knelt beside the old soldier and scrubbed with dampened moss at the blood gilding his neck. The old man breathed shallowly. His eyes were closed, sunken and brown, and he lay very still but for the breath that flexed his scars and made his bruises rise and fall.

Oyster Tom set his smoky hands to either side of the old soldier's head and turned it so the light lay upon the wound there. He ran the needle through the flames and had the wound stitched in a matter of minutes. And after he had finished, the old soldier groaned to the side and vomited a slick, yellow bile without waking. Charley wiped clean his mouth as Tom settled down and lit his pipe.

After few moments, Charley said, "It's strange. He's took a beating, but he don't seem hurt bad enough to be like this."

Oyster Tom agreed. He said the old soldier seemed much weakened by something other than his wounds. He said that when he peeled back the skin of his eyes and looked there, when he listened to the sound of his heart and of the blood moving within his body, he had seen and heard therein a deeper hurt. He shrugged and said it was too bad, but that the soldier was much like himself, and that sometimes old men could not recover from the smallest things and old wounds long healed sometimes reopened to do them greater harm.

Charley sat thinking about that. He pursed his lips and nodded, then looked at Oyster Tom and raised his chin. "But you ain't even close to being dead," he said with something like tenderness and something like hard pride, and Oyster Tom looked at him and grinned, then returned to the enjoyment of his pipe.

Charley shrugged and went about tugging more moss from the trees nearby and from the skins of boulders. After a moment, he frowned and said, "I can't for the life of me remember his name."

"Abel," said the old soldier, touching his tongue to his dry lips and swallowing painfully. "Abel Truman. And I know this man here from way back. Ain't that right, Tom?"

Oyster Tom nodded without comment, and Abel winced himself to a sitting position. His eyes widened when he touched his jaw. "Well I'll be goddamned if those sons of bitches didn't steal my beard," he whispered.

When Edward stepped from the forest into the flickering camp light, Abel looked at him and asked, "You-all ain't seen my dog anywheres about, have you?"

They mashed the sneezeweed with hot water in Oyster Tom's little clay fire bowl, then folded the steaming mass into two handkerchiefs—one for Silas and the other for Abel. Silas wept a little for the pain of it, while Abel took several long, deep breaths before nodding and winking at Edward.

Later, they lay listening to Abel tell the story of how his dog was stolen and he was beaten, and when he was finished, Oyster Tom rubbed his jaw and nodded. He stood and, without a word, vanished into the forest where the rain was falling and the night was dark. Abel watched him go, then looked at Charley. "I thought he'd died," he said.

Charley nodded. "So did we," he said. He squatted and splayed his fingers flameward. Edward sat to the side, studying the old soldier and looking away when Abel glanced at him. "He didn't take food for a week," Charley went on. "He lay in his house like sleeping but it was not sleep. Something else. You wouldn't know it, looking at him, but he still carries it inside him. Big as my fist. Right near his crotch. We had the doctor come 'round. He said it had to be cut out before it made little ones inside him. All inside him in different places where they'd grow. Along his bones and in his bones. Places like that. Papa said he didn't want to be cut and wouldn't let anyone touch him. Now he wears a fat man's pants just so he has room so it don't bind up when he walks."

Abel winced at the thought of it. He shifted about and put his back against an old pine, then said, "He's a tough old man."

Charley grinned and nodded. "Our grandfather," he said.

Abel smiled back at him as best as he could and winced as his hurts flexed about. "And you've a fine pair of boys, too," he said, nodding to Edward and Silas. "You're a lucky man to have so much family."

Charley's grin spread wider, and he covered it with a palm as was his habit. "Only Edward is my son," he said. "Silas there, I believe to be an angel sent down from our Lord in Heaven."

Abel raised his eyebrows and shot a quick glance to Edward, who set his face and minutely shook his head. For his part, Silas lay on his side staring at the fire, his eyes glassy with reflected flame, his expression a study.

"While Old Tom lay sick," said Charley by way of explanation, "while he lay not sleeping, I prayed to God to make him well or take him quick. One or the other. I prayed two days. But Old Tom just lay in his house. Then someone shouted from the beach and I saw people gathered." He jerked his chin toward Silas and went on. "He lay in the surf like he was drowned. We carried him to Old Tom's house, where we thought he'd finally died, and bundled the drowned one in blankets to bury later. I went back to my prayers and when I came back again, there sat Old Tom beside the boy, caring for him. I prayed it so, you see? So I was doubly blessed." He looked to the sky where the night and the rain and the stars were. "Great power has prayer, but none so great as our Lord in heaven and His mighty hosts," he whispered.

"I fell off a fishing boat," said Silas abruptly. "Four days out of Frisco and bound for Alaska. Cook's boy. I went over in the middle of the night while I was doing my business over the side. No one heard." He scowled and stared at Charley until the man blinked and looked away.

"Whether he knows it or not or believes it or not," said Charley finally, "he was sent by the Lord, like all children are, and was upon the Lord's own business." He stood and stepped away from the light to sit down on a stone in the outer shadows and stare at the ocean.

Abel nodded absently. His chest and back where they'd beaten him throbbed, and there was a hard, constant ache all along his crooked left arm. Wiping his mouth with the back of his hand, he gave a soft yelp, then shook his head ruefully. "I don't guess I've gotten used to myself without a few chin hairs," he said.

"Your face is cut. Badly," said Edward, his eyes bottomless and dark by the firelight. "They had to shave you to stitch you."

Abel looked at the boy. "Well, I appreciate it, son. I surely do. Reckon I would've died had you-all not come along."

Edward raised his chin. "You have a lot of scars."

Abel wet his upper lip with his lower, then nodded. "I guess I am pretty banged up, at that."

"You were in the war?"

"That's right."

Edward licked his lips and swallowed. "At Gettysburg?" he asked, his voice soft yet tremulous with something like expectation.

Abel pressed his lips together. He nodded.

Edward scooted forward so the flames lit bright the shadowed planes of his angular face. His dark eyes softened. "Were you a part of Pickett's Great Charge?"

Abel's eyebrows jumped. "Great Charge?" he asked. He filled his cheeks and blew, then winced. "No sir," he finally said. "No. I was Second Corps. Under old Clubby. Old Johnson."

"Off on the left, then."

Abel cocked his head and looked at the boy. "That's right," he said. "I did see a little of that Pickett fight, though. Our work was mostly done that day by the time theirs got started."

Edward wrapped his arms around his knees and looked into the fire. Then he looked at Abel's face, scrutinizing, judging. "Johnson's Division," he said. "You don't talk like how I imagine Virginians talk."

Abel grinned and shook his head. "Mine was a regiment of Tar Heels," he said. "But I ain't one of them, neither. My God, no. I got where I got by way of the state of New York and points between."

"There were Tar Heels in the Charge," said Edward. "They went in under Trimble, I think."

Abel shook his head again. "Jesus-by-God, boy. You do know yourself a little history, don't you?"

Edward Poole sat up straight and touched his chest with the points of his four brown fingers. "American," he said simply, looking Abel in the eye.

Abel sighed and looked down at the fire where the flames fed steadily upon the driftwood, crumbling it into glowing coals and long fingers of ash. He shook his head slowly. "Ah, son," he said softly. "You . . ." He looked hard at him. "You're only an Indian," he said sadly.

The expression that passed over Edward's face was hard to watch, and Abel turned from it. Rain dripped slowly, persistently, from the underside of the canopy. A few drops sizzled into the fire. It pattered softly on the understory beyond. Abel turned back and looked at Edward for a long moment that passed slowly, then stared into the flames and sat that way, silently. The waves battered the beach and the fire crackled. The wind came through the forest. Charley Poole moved off to gather more firewood; if he'd heard what Abel said, he didn't show it. Silas had fallen into an uneasy sleep, his soft, little-boy moans of hurt coming at intervals between the surging wind and the snapping fire. After a long while, Abel heard Edward swallow and then, after another pause, ask, "What was it like? That day?"

Abel looked off into the middle distance. "I don't know that I can tell it," he said. "Not really and make it like it was. I don't think any man can, and those that try . . . Well, they either weren't there—in the moment, if you understand me—or it's maybe just their own small version of it. A small part of a big thing." Abel smiled and went on. "I don't know that any one of us, if you was to plunk us back down smack in the middle of any of that mess, could tell one battle from the next, let alone our feet from our heads."

Abel shook his head and shrugged, then shifted about to find comfort. He sat before the fire with his right hand cradling his left, which lay curled tightly to his side. He gave Edward a look. "There was a whole hell of a lot of marching. I can tell you that. If you asked me what it was I did in the war, I'd say: I marched four pair of good boots to their nubbins, and I was just dumb lucky to get that many. Dumb lucky. We had us days of marching. Long days spillin' into weeks. In every kind of weather. But that day—hell, any day we had us a fight, and there was a lot of them, too—that day there was noise and smoke and passels of men all over the damn place and you really couldn't see much of anything. And what you could see—"

"It lasted two hours," said Edward. Abel blinked and came back from wherever he was and looked at him. "The cannonade," the boy explained. "It went on for two hours."

Abel shrugged. "Maybe it did," he said. "I don't know, but I could feel it. I do remember that. Every mother's son of us could feel it. The charge, too, as I recall. So there was that. I was . . . I don't know." Abel paused to catch his breath. He was very tired. His face hurt and his chest and his throat from saying more aloud in the last few hours than he had for six months or more, yet he surprised himself by going on.

"I don't really know how to describe it," he said. "Not at

Gettysburg or Manassas or Malvern Hill. Not in the Wilderness or any other damn place I was at. I seen things I can't forget. They won't turn me loose, and if they did, I can't imagine what I'd do with myself. Who I'd be. No. I can't really tell any of it because they ain't invented the words a man could use to do it justice."

Abel Truman panted, hurting. He sat with Edward's dark eyes upon him, and when he spoke again, he spoke slowly and with as much precision as he could to frame the events of his experience with the poor, rude language at his command. How it had been that afternoon at Gettysburg when the world changed and you could feel that change as though the earth itself was shook to its very core, and maybe it was. That day. Pickett's Great Charge. Up and through the dirt came the sound of them setting out. Through the earth and through the soles of the boots and bare feet of those watching and those who helped to make it happen. All those going across the fields who could never turn back from it forever and still call themselves men in that age. Up their legs came the sound. Up their legs where their muscles were burning and their bladders were voided down their thighs and on past their mean, hard, shrunken bellies to rattle around their hearts that beat so quick with fear and dread and wonder it seemed they'd burst. And finally up over the backs of their heads and down their arms like the feeling that comes upon a body when some momentous thing has happened and the truth of it actually happening is only just beginning to dawn; something willfully done that can never be taken back and that changes the world with its doing. Something, some great deed, seemingly foreordained, that in a stroke is writ in the clouds and in the shadows and in the blood of the living who witness it and in the souls of those who have the eyes to read such a language. But something, finally, that rests solely on the shoulders and in the hearts of men who are by nature born to kill other men. Abel fumbled with the telling of it, trying to make the boy understand. Of flags and men and horses and cannon and hot gore slick upon the green grass of high summer. The heat and the smell of the heat. The sound.

Finally, Abel said, "We had us a fellow in our company. Went all through the war up to the Wilderness where he got himself killed. Simple fella." Abel tapped his temple with a fingertip. "But that boy could shoot a gun like a dream. Like nothing you ever seen. Like he was born to it, that boy was a shooter. Ned. And I got to where I was pretty fond of him. Spent a lot of my time watching out for him and suchlike." Abel swallowed and twisted his head about until his neck cracked like a set of back-folded knuckles. "Anyway, we ended up in reserve that afternoon and was watching from a little ridge south of town as those Pickett boys started off. I recollect somebody saying, 'Mercy God, would you look at that.' Well. Ned, he up and says, 'Yessir, I ain't never seen so much smoke in one place before.' He had him a hunk of real honest-to-God apple pie that he got somewhere or other, some windowsill in town the day before maybe, and he ate that, then lay down to sleep while I went around trying to hunt up a cup of coffee or milk or some such thing and next we knew the army's pulling out. And that's how it was. The world didn't stop that day. It didn't even pause or look up from whatever it is the world does while it's turning. It was only afterwards that it all turned into something more than what it was and that was only because by then we needed it to be. All of us, on both sides of that field. We ended up needing it to be something more than what it was. Which was nothing but slaughter."

Edward frowned deeply. "I don't understand. Are you saying it was . . . That it was all a lot of smoke?"

Abel shook his head. He was suddenly very tired, very sad. He felt old, and the back of his throat was hot and sick. It seemed every other part of him hurt in some way. "No," he finally said. "I ain't told it right, I suppose. All that"—he waved a hand through the smoky, flame-clutched dark—"all that was the bravest goddamned thing I ever heard of. The Charge. Other things too. But I'm like you. I had to read about it later to know how brave it all was."

Edward pursed his lips and sat back, obviously disappointed. "Is that where you got all those scars?" he asked. "At Gettysburg?"

"No," said Abel, shaking his head. "Most of them come later. In the Wilderness, mainly."

Edward cocked his head and shrugged. "I don't guess I know much about that."

Abel wet his lips and moved his shoulders about to try and loosen his cramped muscles. "It don't matter much," he said softly, not to Edward, not to anyone. "Don't matter much at all." Abel blinked and shook his head. "Why Pickett?" he asked.

"What?"

"Seems like Pickett's your man. I was wondering why that was."

"It's not just him," said Edward. He took a breath and looked hard at Abel. When he spoke next, it was with a force and resolution Abel had not yet heard from him, as though he'd spent a long time thinking things through, a long time defending certain things to himself. "I'm American. Like I told you. And I'm American and not something else because they failed that day. They couldn't do it and most of them probably knew they couldn't do it before they even started, but they went anyhow. There's honor in that. I don't reckon there's much of honor left in the world now, but they had it that day and I honor them on both sides by knowing what I can about it. Much as I can."

"Honor?" Abel snorted. "Honor, shit." He ran his hand through his long, smoky gray hair, then leaned close to the flames to peer at the boy. Staring hard, he touched the inside of his cheek with his tongue and said, "There's just two things you need to know about honor. You know what they are?"

Edward shook his head.

"Once you get on her, stay on her," said Abel, grinning and laughing and slapping at his knee. He doubled over with a wheezing, wet cough that brought tears to his eyes. He pressed his palm to the side of his chest until he'd caught his breath, then looked at the boy, who watched him without expression. Abel frowned and licked his lips. "You see? Honor?"

Edward shrugged, his gaze drifted to the flames.

"Well, shit," said Abel, shaking his head. "I guess I'd better try for a little sleep."

Edward nodded and curled down beside the fire and closed his eyes. The old soldier watched until he was asleep and dreaming, then he, himself, lay down beside the fire and closed his eyes.

And dreamed.

He came awake panting. Feverish and wet with rain, Abel rocked back and forth with his hand pressed to his chest. He drug a palm down his face and smeared his eyes dry with a curled forefinger. The night was fully dark and the fire had settled to a bed of red coals pulsing with heat, sizzling with tiny points as raindrops spattered them. Oyster Tom sat in the long red shadows beneath the trees, smoking his pipe. He glanced at Abel and softly apologized for waking him, but Abel waved it off.

The Indian sat with his back to a moss-feathered spruce. The bark crackled against his shoulders, and he said he'd found sign of the thieves. Oyster Tom said that they followed one of the old trails that led through the forest to the foothills and the mountains beyond them, and he said they had Abel's dog with them. Oyster Tom said he reckoned they fought and bet upon and sold dogs as some men did, and he said that the trail more or less followed the Little Sugar Creek. Abel sniffed and wiped beneath his nose with his wristback. Nodding, he said he knew the area well.

"I want to thank you for stopping to patch me up," Abel said.

Oyster Tom nodded. He said that it was nothing more than what

Abel would have done, and then, without preliminary, he leaned forward with his ghostwhite hair haloing the dark about his head and told Abel he was sick. He told the old soldier he was sorry for it, then sat back into the shadows again to watch Abel silently, his dark eyes aglitter.

Abel pressed his right thumb into the fleshy little valleys of bone and sinew between the knuckles of his wrecked left hand. He took a breath, nodded, then spat into the fire. "Well, I trust you know what it is you're talking about," he said, smacking his lips thoughtfully and shrugging. "I reckon I figured as much anyway." He looked up at Oyster Tom. "Old Charley there, he told me how it went with you." Abel jerked his chin up. "How'd you get around it?"

The Indian shrugged and said that he hadn't. That he had only put it off for a while and that only because of the boy, Silas, and because of Charley.

Oyster Tom then grinned. His white, white hair waved and trembled. He said that Silas was only a boy in need of care and that Charley, having lost his father at sea, had become the sort of man who needed angels and devils to keep him upright. He said that many men were like this to greater or lesser degrees and that there was no shame or foolishness in it, and anyway, who was there who would tell them they were wrong in their beliefs? "No," he said softly. "I never got around anything. But the boy, he needed someone at that moment, and Charley needed something also. At that moment. So I got up. This is what men must do. Their true job."

"What's that?"

"Take responsibility for what's theirs and let go the rest."

"Seems the trick, then, is figuring out what you can safely let go."

Oyster Tom shrugged.

Abel shook his head. "I don't know about any of that," he said. "I don't think most people care for anything but themselves anymore."

Oyster Tom said that they were not talking about people but about men. He agreed that most men remain accountable to themselves only, and that but poorly. He said that the proper chore of a man is to be chargeable for those and that dear to him and that this was something women understood and knew how to do without having to be told. It was a thing women looked for in their men, and this was why most women lived lives of bottomless sorrow. "So I got up," said Oyster Tom. "I saw I needed to care for that which I could and left the rest to itself."

"Well," said Abel. "If that's the case, then I believe we're all of us in a mess of trouble. I don't know that it's anywhere in a man to do any goddamned thing that's decent or good." He shook his head. "I don't know what-all you've seen of him, as a species I mean, but I know for a fact he's a mean, self-centered sumbitch when given half a chance."

Oyster Tom shrugged and said that violence was inseparable from living, and who could say that it never brought forth a greater good? He pointed out the example of Abel's war and the black man's freedom, and Abel looked at him and did not reply.

The fire ticked heat into the upper dark. Beside it, Edward turned in his sleep, then settled again, facing away from the heat. "Let me ask you something," said Abel. "What makes that boy go on the way he does? Pickett and Gettysburg and all?"

Oyster Tom took the pipe from his mouth and studied the bowl. He told Abel that he was Edward's age when he met George Edward Pickett at the soldier's fort in Bellingham during the Pig War. He said it was well before the war in the east started, and that he went to the fort to find work because sickness was going up and down the coast. He said his mother died, and then his father. His sister and all his aunts and uncles died, then he touched his scarred cheeks lightly and shrugged and said that he was spared. So he went north to the fort where there was much to do because everyone thought there would be a fight with the British because an American farmer shot an Irish pig. Oyster Tom said nothing came of it in the end, but he still fished and hunted for the soldiers, chopped wood, drew water, things like that. He said the fort commander, Pickett, was very kind to all the Indians and took a Haida for a bride who bore him a child that died not long after. Oyster Tom said that Pickett finally went away to the east when he saw the British would not fight.

The old Indian sucked thoughtfully at his pipe. He nodded to where Edward lay sleeping. "I taught the boy to read English, and he reads very well. Pickett at the fort taught me. So you see, the boy feels a connection to that past." He shrugged. "What can it hurt?"

They were silent then—two old men staring at the glowing remains of a burned-down fire in the dark of a long, wet night. When Oyster Tom spoke again, it was to ask if Abel would go after his dog.

Abel nodded.

Oyster Tom tapped his pipe against a stone to knock the ash from it before taking out a little nail with which to scrape the sides. "You better have a sleep while you can, then," he told Abel.

In the morning, the camp was vacant, though the fire had been built back and there were two cooked salmon steaks lying hot upon a smooth stone beside him. Wincing, Abel stood and looked out at the beach where they stood beside their canoe. They watched Edward as he clambered up the little bluff toward him.

"A few days' supplies to see you through," he said, handing Abel a little sack. "An old knife and a little pistol, but I wouldn't trust either one too much."

The rain had ceased and mist leaked from the trees to hang shroud-like in the forest. The sack was heavy, and Abel stood there with it in his hand. He stood with his head hung and then he thanked the boy, set the sack between his feet, and set his palm on the boy's shoulder.

Looking into Edward's dark, wary eyes, Abel said, "What I told you yesterday . . . What I said . . ." Abel's lips moved about, and he wet them with the tip of his tongue. "Don't you fret it. Any of it. Americans are . . ." He shrugged. "Truth is, I don't know what all we are anymore. We were one thing—now we're something else. The war mixed it all up. That's one thing it did." He let go of Edward's shoulder and stuffed his hand into his pocket. Squinting at the ocean, he said, "Don't ever let anyone else try and tell you what I did yesterday. They'd be wrong, like I was." He looked at the boy and grinned. "And if you do . . . You go on knock 'em down."

Edward looked at the old man. The gray wind blew in his gray hair, and a white crust of spittle had dried at the corners of his mouth and he had to lean against the wind to keep his balance. "What happened to you?" Edward finally asked.

Abel blew and shrugged. "You tell your papa . . . Well, thank the man for me and let him know that about five miles up the beach he'll see him a blood slick on the sand beside the seep that's there. Where that rock that looks like a horse's pizzle stands. Shot me a deer there a few days back and there ought to still be some good meat left to it if them thieves didn't get it all. I buried it a little so it'd keep longer. I couldn't take but a little of it and I'd be obliged if you-all could fetch out the rest. I wouldn't want to think of it going to waste."

Edward stared at him and nodded. He did not thank him. His eyes were wet, and he knew they would not meet again. Finally Edward turned and started back down to the beach where they stood waiting.

Abel called after him, and Edward turned. The old man raised his chin. "You watch out for old Helen, now," he said.

Edward frowned and shook his head, a little grin beginning to play about his lips.

"Helen Damnation," said Abel with a broad smile. "That's something we old soldiers used to say to each other."

Silas was in the canoe and Charley stood calf deep in the surf, fussing over him. Oyster Tom stood in the water near the prow. He looked at Edward, and together they pushed the canoe into the surf, hauled themselves in, and plucked up their paddles. Oyster Tom sang cadence. Edward sat in the stern and steered until they passed the rocky shoals and were beyond the sea stacks that stood like dark sentinels against the gray morning that spread slowly down from the blue foothills. When he looked back, Abel was vanished, and no smoke rose from the cooking fire they'd kindled for him.

# SIX

## *Saunders' Field*

### *May 1864*

SEE THEM ON the road. A white road under a blue sky between fallow fields spreading toward hills and forests green and lush in the springtime sun. What little dust their bare feet raises curls and licks at the roadside grasses, then finally settles after they pass. Two of them, a man and woman, hopeful contraband, walking north along the road. The man's face creased with worry and with pain, hands furrowed with fieldwork, stiffened and rough. He emancipated himself a fortnight ago, and the root-sour stink of fear still rises from the sad folds of his thin shirt. He does not know what to do, where to go. His name was once Dexter but it is not any longer, and he has been walking north with this quiet, careful woman for the past week. The pain in him, carried silently for years now, is all the worse for a taste of freedom and her company.

They have crossed this day the Newfound Creek and the Little Creek. Other, nameless branches meandering the countryside as though they'd nothing better to do. They have heard trains in the distance, seen cavalry flinging themselves up and down parallel roads. But for the hard, fleshy rasping of their bare feet in the dust, the air is filled with birdsong, the sound of wind. Dexter can smell the perfume of new blossoms, of leafed-out trees and new spring grass, but all of it is tainted by his own stink rising against his nostrils. He looks down and sees he's wet himself again. A dark stain spreads along one trouser leg, and he wonders will he weep aloud. Even after so long he is still numb in the places they cut him, still unused to the lack of sensation. When he does not sob, when he merely takes a breath, Dexter looks over at her as they walk, wondering if she has noticed. If she has, she does not show or speak it; merely walks along silently, fingers laced across her belly, steps steady, slow, and assured. He can see stains seeping through her dress front and stiffened cloth where her milk has spoiled. Dexter looks away, walks on.

Her name is Hypatia—a joke of her master, lately dead, for she had no notions of mathematics. For a brief moment she was a mother but is not any longer, and she has been walking northbound roads for over a month.

Together they top a little rise and see the road spool lazily northward. A dark stain of forest on the horizon where the road disappears. And closer, between them and the forest, a plume of dust and the watery impression of a shape within rattling steadily along. Hypatia settles down on a rock just off the road. A soft, satisfied sigh. With slender, strong fingers she prods her ankles and heels for the pleasure of it. Dexter stands in the road with his hands on his hips, watching the dust. Squinting, trying to decide if it be pilgrims like themselves or soldiers or home guard or any one of a dozen other dangers. Trying to decide should they leave the road for the fields and woodlots, for the beds of streams and runs and creeks. His skin is the soft ruddy color of a chestnut in the fall when the weather turns cold. He shakes his head and says, "I don't know. A wagon, I guess."

"But you don't know."

He shrugs. "Nah."

"Then you best get out the road. Up on this hill, they can see you plain as you see them." With another soft sigh, she tilts her face skyward to let the sun fall upon it, then opens her eyes to look for shapes in the clouds.

Dexter looks about himself. The white road, the hill, a dark stand of pine within running distance. Shaking his head and muttering softly to himself, he ducks and scurries out of the dust, coming to a crouch near Hypatia's rock.

"Figure you can make them trees if we got to run?"

Blinking, she looks for a long moment at his face, so tired and careworn and pinched with need and hurt. With the very tips of her fingers she touches an old, puckered scar tatting his cheek. Even with so light and inconsequential a caress, she feels him tremble, so draws back her hand. Shaking her head, she tells him, "You go on. There ain't nothing more they can do to me." A pause. "They can't touch me no more."

His throat bobs and he hangs his head a moment before answering. "I reckon I can wait with you."

The wagon solidifies from the dust. An old white man on the bench seat with a rifle propped up on his thigh. Dexter raises himself to the balls of his feet, tensed, his arms away from his sides. Ready to throw himself before her and shield her. With her long fingers, Hypatia tucks an errant kink of hair back up under the black rag wrapped thrice around her head. She settles her calm gaze upon the wagon as it approaches and slows.

For his part, the old man brakes slow and easy after cresting the hill and looks down at them on the grass. He studies them there for a long time, then rubs his jaw and shakes his head. Setting the rifle down, he raises his chin to Dexter. "You there, nigger. What the hell are you doing out thisaway?"

Dexter cannot meet the old man's eye. He looks down, looks away. His shoulders sag and his expression slackens so as to give up as little of himself as possible. The old posture of submission. He cannot speak.

"We goin' to see Lincum," says Hypatia, rising from her stone.

"Jesus Christ." The old man leans and spits and wipes his mouth with the back of one hand. He ducks his head to try and catch Dexter's eye. "That true, you crazy buck? You look at me here now, boy."

Dexter's eyes roll up to the old man's face. A hard face, cruel about the mouth, and the flesh around the eyes chased with age. He takes a deep breath, stands straight as he's able. "Yes, sir," his voice not more than a whisper.

The old man's face sours and he curses and looks away. Looks back at Hypatia and studies her for a time. "Where's your baby?" he asks.

"Dead, sir."

"Dead where?"

She looks back down the road the way she's come and blinks slowly. "Back behind me now," she says.

"God damn," says the old man. "Just God damn it." Taking a deep breath, he stands and steps into the bed of the wagon, where he roots around through various boxes and sacks, telling them, "You got a fair piece of travel ahead of you. God damn God damn. You have any idea what's happening up the road? What's coming thisaway? Do you?" He does not wait for them to answer. "Them armies is coming together, is what's happening." Pausing, he makes two fists and bangs them together in the air. "There's goin' to be fightin' like you can't imagine, and they're coming right through here. Right down this road. You watch and see if they don't. Now, you listen. If you can, find you a Union soldier, a soldier in blue. Pick you a young one if you get the choice and just go on up and tell him you-all is contraband. Do you know that word?"

"Yes, sir," says Dexter, bobbing his head, looking down at the dust.

"God damn it." The old man spits and transfers items from various boxes into a little canvas sack. "Now, I ain't givin' you any God damn weapons. Not even a blade, and I hope I am well in my grave 'fore niggers start walking around my homeland armed. But here." He hands the sack down to Dexter. Hypatia walks across the grass and stands looking up at the old man. "There's food," he tells them. "A little cornmeal, some salt beef. I put a hunk of cheese, some soft bread, and a jar of milk in there too, but that's for you," he tells Hypatia. "You understand me?"

"Yes," she says. "We thank you."

The old man steps back onto the bench and takes up the reins. "Stay on this road," he says. "But God damn it, be careful. You end up with the wrong army, and that's it. I don't have to tell you what they'll do to you. You got that, boy?"

Dexter's hands fist and unfist, then fist again. He nods.

"All right then. Now. You see that dark patch up yonder? That mess of woods? Called the Wilderness. You'll be there in a day. Maybe two, the way she is." He looked at Hypatia and shook his head, then indicated the long view toward the Wilderness from the top of the hill. "Anyway, odds are the armies'll come out on this side and get down to business. Ain't no white man goin' to start a fight in them woods but they'd be good for hiding. You two head on north, make for the trees, and watch yourselves. A little luck, and you'll be all right."

They thank him together—Dexter still off-looking to some point in the air just beside the old man's shoulder and Hypatia meeting his tired, careworn gaze without blinking. "What are you two?" he asks them. "Husband and wife? Kin?"

"Nah, sir," says Dexter, shuffling his feet in the dust. "We just meet up on the way."

"What's your name, boy?"

Dexter squeezes shut his eyes, opens them again. His name is not Dexter any longer. They took that self six months ago when they cut him for not turning down his gaze quick enough when the missus came out into the yard. The master had been especially worrisome, especially watchful, with the way the war was going and so had Dexter taken to the shed. They held him down. A fast memory of the blade. A curve of metal as silvery and cruel as the crescent moon, quick and ice-cold against his thighs until the warmth of his blood spilt over them. He takes a deep breath, raises his chin, and opens his eyes. "My name?"

The old man frowns. "Yes, God damn it."

"Grant," he says without pause, without lowering his eyes. "Sherman Grant." He squares his shoulders and shows the old man his teeth.

The old man looks stricken, shaken, then sniffs and nods. "Well by God, by God. Don't tell nobody else that." Grins. Says, "Well, Sherman Grant, there'll be time enough for the two of you, I reckon." The old man pauses, leans and spits, then looks over the countryside round about. "Used to be a hell of a country," he says quietly. "A hell of a place to be. This land here, this good farming soil . . . it won't be worth a good God damn in a couple days." And without another word, he shakes the reins over the old swayback's flanks and the dust comes up and he and horse and the wagon are vanished in it.

That was in the morning when the red sun radiated across the rolling hills. Making the pale undersides of the leaves to shine and spinning rubies into the little creeks where they crossed the road. By afternoon of that day, the second of May, 1864, the sky was wholly darkened. The air alive with electricity. They sat out the storm beneath a live oak and Grant drew his blanket up around them. They sat huddled, sharing warmth against the wind and wet, and he could feel her heartbeat against his chest. A shift of a hand stole his breath and unmanned him and he began to weep without control or sound. With soft whispers, Hypatia calmed him, stroked his brow and cheek, and held him tightly in his sorrow. He told her what they'd done to him, what they'd taken from him, and what he'd never known and, now, would never know, and she said nothing. She held him, and he slept. By morning, the storm had blown itself out and they rose without speaking and walked on up the road.

Later that day, as the heat began to gather, they passed the body of a man hung from the neck until dead. He swung from a stout branch and his hands and feet had begun to swell and his hair was damp. He wore a wedding ring but no shoes and the eyes were gone from his head and three crows watched from the branches above. Grant and Hypatia walked on.

A stillness now, as if the world were waiting, breathless. The wind did not blow and the day grew warm. They slept that night on the banks of some nameless stream for the cool of the water in the close, hot dark, and when they rose they could hear a distant, tearing sound as of a sturdy piece of canvas ripped lengthwise. It came banging intermittently through the springtime air all morning and in the afternoon the tearing become a roar and the roar was constant. They could hear shouting. They stopped on a rise on the outskirts of a four-building village that lay abandoned. The Wilderness was before them, studded with powdersmoke that rose, slow, malignant, until the sun was darkened and the shadows grew long.

## May 5, 1864

It was early afternoon when they came out of the woods across the field. They came as they always did: shouting and huzzahing like an organized mechanism geared for war and nothing but. Their lines were as dressed as the Wilderness allowed, running north to south, and they were ranked by regiment in that close space. Small figures uncountable with distance, haze, and dust. The sun on their bayonets like star points against the nightblue backdrop of their uniforms and the greater dark of the woods behind them. They came marching out of the trees. You could feel them coming in the earth.

David's knuckles were white upon his rifle, barrel and stock. His eyes stung with sweat and his own stink rose from his collar. He was distantly aware that his head had stopped its throb and his spectacles had slid down the long, thin line of his nose until he eyed the coming battle over their moon-round tops. He took as deep a breath as he could and looked at Abel. "Don't look like they're fooling around no more," he said.

"About goddamned time," said Abel. The older man took off his hat, gathered his long, dusty hair into a ponytail, tied it off with a thin strip of leather he kept for that purpose, then tucked the works back under his shirt collar and jammed the hat back on. Behind them, officers strode back and forth, their swords unsheathed, steeling the men with words and shouts and curses; getting them ready for what was coming and telling them to charge their weapons and, when they fired, to fire low. A young aide went about cutting blazes into the trees and telling them to fire beneath those marks, and they could see how his revolver shook in his hand.

David checked over his piece, steadying the barrel on a slim branch that lay atop the earthworks to his front. Next to him, Abel hawked up a great gob of phlegm and sent it in a long, dirty yellow arc into the field.

David shook his head, then ducked quickly as a spattering of bullets sent sprays of dirt over him and down through the holes in his wrecked hat. "How d'you do it?" he shouted as he shook out the hat and clawed his fingers through his hair. "My mouth's dry as a stone."

Abel didn't answer. His face was unreadable. He reached out one grimy finger and gently pushed David's spectacles back up his nose, then patted his shoulder with an air of the paternal. As he turned away, David touched his arm and leaned in close to shout, "You been hit."

Frowning, Abel touched his neck. The sunbrowned flesh beneath his ear lay raked open. His fingers came back red and Abel crouched there staring at it amidst all the gathering roar of rifle-fire and shouting. He stared at his fingers with dumb amazement, then looked at David. "That's my blood," he said.

David winced and ducked as a bullet went clipping through the branches above them, sounding for all the world like an angry hornet. He glanced over at Abel's outstretched hand and looked at his face. "Maybe you ought to go on back and find the surgeon. Make sure you didn't take another one you don't know about yet."

Abel shook his head. "This is just the first I was ever shot," he said. He looked at David a moment, then licked his lips and risked a quick peek over the earthworks. At the far left of their line, at the north end of the field, their men had begun firing and the smoke from the discharges moved down the line toward their own position like clockwork. The blue soldiers had not yet reached the gully in the center of the field and yet they had already begun dying. They lay scattered amidst the grass. Abel ducked back down. "Listen a minute," he said. "I want to tell you something."

The Union line reached the gully, went down its far side, nearly disappeared—became but heads planted strangely with the failed crops—then came back up the near side. Some dropped to their knees in the grass to fire and some fell forward into the grass and did not rise again. David breathed. He squeezed shut his eyes and opened them again, but nothing had changed. He was not home, abed, and being woken to breakfast by his mother's call. He panted and made ready to fire, then looked at Abel. "What is it?" he shouted.

"I was married 'fore the war," said Abel. "I was a married man." He paid the gathering violence no mind and held one hand fast to the side of his neck. "Had us a baby girl that died 'fore we even had the chance to name her."

David looked at him. Bullets sent sprays of dirt over them and went clipping through the branches overhead to send down bright, spiraling showers of leaves that flashed in the sun as they fell. A man four feet from them threw his arms skyward and fell back dead without a sound. Someone gave the command to fire, and he and Abel and all the men around them rose to their knees and fired over the works, then rolled over onto their backs to reload. From somewhere in the field, beyond the curtain of smoke that had dropped between them and the Yankees, came the chilling, familiar rumble of cannon being brought up the Old Stone Road.

"I dropt her," said Abel, not looking at David, his hands moving expertly upon his weapon. He tore open a cartridge with his teeth, spat the paper, then pinched the shot and powder into the barrel and drew the rammer, twirled it between his fingers, and rattled it down the barrel to push home the charge.

"I never told anybody," Abel went on, shouting to be heard. "Not even my wife. They all said she died in her sleep, but I know better." He pursed his lips and frowned as he drew out the ramrod, twirled it through his hands again, then shoved it into the loose soil beside him. The long chain of firing had begun again at the far end of the field, and they crouched silent and waiting. "I'd've named her Jane," said Abel, looking absently back into the dark of the Wilderness behind them. He opened and closed his mouth then said, "Would've called her Janey, maybe." He swallowed, swore, and turned away to fit the firing pin onto his piece.

The blue line came on. Steady now, without shouting. Leaning forward and clutching at their caps as though they struggled into a wind. No cheering. Abel rolled his head around on his shoulders.

Beside him, David's hands were busy on his rifle. Abel sniffed and tapped his shoulder. "You reload already?"

"Yes, goddamnit." David was pale, watching them come. He drew out the rammer again.

"Then leave it alone," said Abel.

David took a deep breath. Exhaled. He set the ramrod aside.

"One other thing," said Abel.

"What, goddamnit?"

"When you do fire, point it thataway," said Abel, good-naturedly nodding toward the field.

David looked at him. He shoved the barrel of his rifle up over the works, fired blindly, then began reloading. He looked back at Abel. "You just go straight to hell," he said, grinning.

"Save you a seat," nodded Abel. He rolled onto his stomach, came up on his knees, and fired.

There was no use aiming now, for smoke lay thick upon the field and rose slowly over the trees, as though it was night falling. The rushing enemy had become so many dim ghosts solidifying from the vapor momentarily before dissolving again.

And then they began to fire without order or pause and time compressed upon them all. Firing as fast as hands could load, as fast as tired and tiring arms could lift rifles to bruised and bruising shoulders. Old, familiar aches rose from deep within them as their rifles kicked against their bodies. The sour, charry taste of powder and paper dried their mouths and their jaws hurt and their teeth rattled loosely in their gums as they bit cartridges open.

Out in the field, the Union lines bowed and bent, sections splintered off and went rushing into the deep green woods that grew ever darker for the smoke in them. The Wilderness rang with cries and shouts and tremendous crashes of musketry. Out in the field, the yellow grass was shorn by the hot iron flung across it. Little mobs of men reached the Rebel earthworks and fought there with fists and rifle butts. A few Zouaves, all bedecked in gaudy splashes of red and blue trimmed in yellow and with mud-stained spats, veered toward them and were cut down as though by razorous wind. Their bodies bright in the grass. More came on. Someone gave the command and their section stood from the earthworks, screamed and charged out into the open field. Behind them, back in the Wilderness, smoke hung in tatters from the branches like strange moss . . .

. . . *and had you been there to see it, to hear and taste and feel it, to smell it, it would have been something. It would have been a thing indeed to have been there, that day. At that hour. It was the end of something—all felt that. And the beginning of something else. They'd not line up quite like that again. The flags and banners would not be uncased for this kind of work more than a dozen more times, and though bands would play, they'd not be heard. The cauldron of Saunders' Field was all aboil and the dark trees that ringed it shook and clashed as though under a great wind, as though something truly monstrous prowled between the trunks as countless bullets tore branches, as cannon fire broke them apart. Their roots groaned slowly loose of the boggy soil. Smoke rose in dark, billowy columns and the sun went dark. Men fell dead in the field and they fell across the Rebel earthworks and men fell dead in the Old Stone Road where a section of Union artillery stood firing into the trees and the backs of their own men. The very air was scorched and there was a constant roaring as of a furnace stoked high, running hot. Red smears on the grass, red stains in the road.*

*There: A clean-shaven Union boy with arms too short for the man-sized sleeves of his frock coat is struck on the shoulder by a spent ball, is spun around and skewered on the readied bayonet of the old veteran behind. The boy dies with blood falling from his open, shocked, and terrified mouth. For his part, the veteran shucks the body from the blade, goes on into the wall of smoke, and is gone.*

*And over there: A thin and ragged Confederate, hirsute and wild-looking, falls to hands and knees behind the works as though he means to pray there, then leans with slow, calm, resigned weariness against a bullet-chewed old pine. A neat red hole decorates the center of his forehead and it is not long before the hat, his name stitched with great care into the band by his sister back in Galveston, is stolen from his head.*

*The Union line went down into the gully, came back up out of it shouting into a long gray line of smoke stabbed bright by flame. The Rebel works were ablaze where they were loading and firing and loading again as those Union men, those Billys those bluebellies those northerners those Yankees, fell clawing at their faces and at their arms and legs and stomachs and hips and shoulders, clutching at their soft throats and at their privates and screaming all the while. Covering their eyes with sooty palms, these deadmen stumbled forward, fell, and rose no more forever.*

*The sound that came up out of the field that day, rose through the swirling smoke then echoed down the shocked countryside round about. The smell that day was of heat and smoke and fear and rage and shit and blood—a red-hot stink rising salty and bitter from the shivering grass, the clashing trees, the sweating flesh.*

*And then the Rebels rose from behind their works and stepped off into the grass to meet them.*

*This: A man with his underjaw shot away crawls blindly through the smoke, his red, spastic tongue, suddenly unanchored, become impossibly long, improbably pointed, with bloody slobber running all down the front of him and the tongue still twisting in its socket as he tries to call for his mother.*

*And this: A Union man loses both eyes to a spray of hot shrapnel and staggers forward. Rebel soldiers part before him, do not touch him or allow him to be touched, as though he has become beloved of God. He fumbles past, over the earthworks, and is gone.*

*This: A lean, tall rebel in a shabby suitcoat comes staggering out of the smoke with a bowler hat held beggarwise before his belly and filled with his own entrails spilling from a long, gaping wound that cuts him near in two.*

*And: Great, wide swaths of crisp yellow grass catch fire, the flames jumping and crackling, fanned by soft, spring winds. Black smoke billows from the field as things begin to burn. The sun reddens at its circumference like a bloodshot eye. Flames spread and wash over the dead where they lie, igniting ammo pouches with red, moist reports.*

*And there comes the sweet, sick stench of burning men and burning horses and standing watch over these and other, worse, things, you must wonder, Was there ever war like this before? Ever in all the world's long turning? And would there ever be again? And you must know the answer and take no solace from it.*

*Weeping soldiers take aim at wounded comrades, their friends and mentors and adopted sons. They shoot them dead before the flames can reach them while those hurt beyond the range and sight of their fellows ready what weapons they can and pray for one thing or another while they watch the fires come. One man twists a little jackknife into his own throat, and another wraps weeping lips around a pistol barrel. Men burst apart, their blood flung down upon the living and the other dead like a gentle spring rain . . .*

David Abernathy crouched in the Wilderness and watched the field where the flames gamboled brightly in the grass. Ahead of him, still hunkered behind the earthworks, Virgil Adams fired blindly, tears leaving pale tracks through the dark powder smeared across his cheeks. Deadmen from both armies lay in heaps in the grass, on the works, in the road, and the Union soldiers were falling back stubbornly, stumbling from the dark woods and back across the burning field toward where they'd started their charge.

A hundred men had stepped off into the grass to meet the enemy and had been, in their turn, driven back into the woods where all was green chaos. David soon lost track of his friends. His bottom lip was split from a Yankee rifle butt and he'd not seen Ned since the fighting started. Blood ran down his chin, striping him like a Red Indian. Somewhere out in the field, amidst the roaring, smoke, and flash, they were trying to form up again, and somewhere out there, still in it where it was the worst, was Abel, but David knew not where.

Balls sang past. They drove into the earth and underbrush around him and his hat gained three more holes. Throwing himself forward through the new spring grass, David gained the works and rolled onto his back to load. He slid the rifle down between thighs, grabbed the hot muzzle with his toughened left hand while his right fished around his haversack for a cartridge. He could feel the impact of bullets against the mounded dirt at his back, could hear their sizzling whine as they flew past, leaving momentary trails of clear, blue air through the smoke. As he tore the cartridge open with his teeth, it left a smear of black powder down and away from his lips like a half-painted frown. David dumped powder and ball down the barrel, then tilted the rifle up and banged the butt upon the ground to settle the charge. He'd lost or shot his ramrod during the charge. The right side of his face ached terribly and he wondered how bad tomorrow's bruises would be and would his teeth remain locked in his gums or would he, at some point, end up dumping molars and eyeteeth down the barrel along with powder and ball.

From out in the field, David heard the Union cannon fire again. He ducked and squeezed shut his eyes as thunder, shock, and smoke rolled over the grass. Somewhere up the line came the crackling shriek of another tree falling. To his left and right, as far as the smoke allowed him to see, men were busy at their weapons—those still with rammers drawing them out and twirling them batonlike through the air, then fitting firing pins and raising to their knees to fire in great long sheets of flame. The dark of the field was pricked brightly as the Yankees returned fire.

David discharged his weapon without thought, like a machine or a laboring man working late in the day, and threw himself onto his back again to reload. He glanced over at Virgil. The man had accidentally fired his ramrod and was staring mournfully at it where it was stuck quivering in the grass some ten yards out. Virgil looked at him, his face square and sad and resigned, and before David could raise his voice to stop him, he'd vaulted the works and was running through the burning grass. David rolled over onto his stomach to watch as Virgil's running legs stirred airy coils into the smoke. The cannon near the swale fired. There came the sudden bang, the malignant hissing like a hot rain on a cool day. Shrapnel from their canister sent Virgil's head, the upper portion of his chest, and his entire left arm spinning away while the rest of his body kept to its course—stumbling through the smoke, propelled by momentum with the pale segments of his liberated spine flopping along behind like a bizarre tail.

Swearing and trembling, David ducked back down and was sick. The field was afire on both sides of the road. Black smoke billowed and darkened the sky nightwise and the sun went wholly red. As though the armies fought under some fantastic new star or the old one gone all wrong. There was screaming. Rifles fired and flames crackled in the grass and David could hear ammunition pouches exploding. The moist slap of bullets striking flesh. And again. And again. He finished loading his piece and rolled over to go back to work.

The Union artillerymen were firing obliquely across the smoldering field into the faces of a regiment charging them from the northwest corner of their line, and the shot tore into the backs of their own men still running for the works on that portion of the field. Men threw up their hands in shocked amazement at bright death. Men fell and rose no more. In the deep woods along the road behind him, David could hear a brigade forming for a countercharge. He heard old Spivey bellowing his war cry and laid his rifle barrel atop the works to aim into the smoke blowing about in designs strange and fantastic. Manshaped ghosts flitted through the gloom. Smoke roiled from the grass, from little glowing beds of fire, as though there were oil patches there that had been set ablaze. David fired in the general direction of the cannon, blinked sweat from his eyes, shook his head, and bent once more over his rifle. The roaring sound of the battle was everywhere and unceasing. The very ground was atremble.

A man came toward him through the smoke, running with his rifle raised like a club and a desperate, terrified expression twisting his features monstrously. Gilded eagle buttons twinkled redly on his coat. With nothing like thought, David squeezed his fist around the trigger. He felt the stock kick against his shoulder; a deep bruise there tomorrow like a blue half-moon etched into his shoulder. He did not even hear the sound it made for the sound of musketry was general and unceasing as rain nor did he need to hear it. The man fell, the gilded eagles winked out, and David ducked back down.

As he settled the charge home for the thirty-eighth time that day, the man he'd shot began to scream. He pleaded and sobbed and called for his mother, his father, and his brother and wondered, groaning, why they had forsaken him.

David closed his eyes and counted slowly, and when he opened them again his hands had calmed and he could breathe once more. Lifting the cavalryman's cross from around his neck, he wrapped the cord around his fingers so the cross itself fit neatly into the hollow of his cramped palm. He fit a firing pin onto the cone and rose up on his knees.

It was not a man at all lying there gutshot and dying in the dirt before the works but a boy of fourteen years or so. He wore a Yankee coat and lay with his legs kicking feebly in his urine-soaked trousers. The ground beneath him was red, and the hands he held over the wound in his stomach were the hands of a child.

David's breath left him. He doubled over behind the works with his thumb and forefinger pressed hard to his temples, as though to constrict the veins jangling fresh green pain through his skull. Beyond the works, the boy called again for his father, his brother. He called for his dog and he called for his mother. David pursed his lips and spat. With shaking hands he lay down his musket. He stood. The boy saw him, stared at him through the smoke. His lips moved and he lifted up his gorestained little-boy hands.

David Abernathy was aware of his legs and of his lungs. He was aware of a dull, numb tingling in his hands and he was aware of the bloodred slantings of the late-afternoon sun come cutting through the smoke to stand in strange, ruby-colored columns tilted on the trembling earth. He heard flames crackling orange and red in the dry yellow grass, and he even heard the sound that smoke makes upon the air as it travels—like a soft whisper of lace drug through still, cool water by the hand of a mother who loves her boy.

The boy's mouth moved without sound, and he vomited bloody sputum down the front of his overlarge uniform.

David churned with a thick, weary nausea, and he wondered if his eyes leaked blood or tears from the pain in his head. Smoke fouled his lungs and dried his mouth and he could feel the fast pulse of blood all through him—temples and arms and legs and the small veins behind his eyes and he could feel blood pulsing in the lobes of his ears.

He took a breath.

The cool, stinging wind of a single bullet passed close to his cheek like the first quick kiss of a shy girl.

David took a breath.

Clambering over the shot-torn works, he ran into the field and down the road toward the boy. He ran with the little cross pressed to his palm, pinching his flesh with a peculiar, satisfying pain. From somewhere came the sound of Abel's voice, shouting to him, but David paid it no mind. He ran on, suddenly aware of the good, clean feel of his new shirt upon his hot skin—his chest and arms and back where it had soaked up his sweat and now lay cool on him like the damp towels his mother would press upon his forehead in the beforetimes when he lay abed with headaches—and David suddenly knew beyond knowing, beyond memory, how it had been to be a child with a mother who loved him and how it had felt to run through the tall grass, no trace of pain now, toward her where she stood smiling with her arms open. A dark, welcoming shape against the sun. David was filled with a joy that burned the jolting green pain away. He ran joyously forward, legs fast and blurstruck through the charry smoke.

And, finally, these things: A man runs forward through the smoke, into the field and down the road, to the side of a young boy grievously wounded beside a high wall of flame. This man throws his own tattered coat around the boy and lifts him, mindful not to spill the insides out through the hole in the boy's stomach. Another man shouts to him, and he turns, still holding the boy as protectively as if he were the man's own child or the phantom-boy of himself, come to remind him of something he'd forgotten. He turns to face the cannon, to see them jerk the lanyard, and he has only time to raise one hand before he and boy all but disappear in a gust of hot metal. On the smoldering grass where they'd stood is little but a wet smear.

And this: A lean rebel with a tired face and a seeping wound upon his neck stumbles forward. He finds the place where his friend had stood and falls to his knees, searches about in the grass a moment, then lifts up a little carved cross as though it were a rare flower. He puts it in his pocket, then covers his face with his hands and weeps as the balls go whizzing past, leaving thin, diaphanous trails, like strange webbing, hanging in the smoke.

And look—you cannot help yourself. Look to see dead men and wounded, shattered men and burnt. Men standing to battle with fixed expressions of grim resolve, as though they'd discovered things within themselves that will be hard to live with later, and men frightened beyond all sense, lying facedown and weeping in the grass. Union soldiers in retreat across the howling field and masses of men from both sides lying huddled in the damp of the gully between the lines, passing bottles back and forth. Pennants and standards and flags all brightly waving and shot-torn, proud amidst the smoke and flames. In the woods beyond the field either side, wind-rippled green and yellow hospital flags sprout, drawing the wounded to them like awful heliotropic blossoms. Surgeons stand to their work with bare forearms, fists white upon the handles of their bone saws.

Smoke billowed up in great black sheets that could be seen for miles about. A horse, cut loose from the artillery limber, came screaming down the road past Abel with its mane all afire and its nostrils huge. As he stood to watch it pass, Abel fell again. The sun darkened as though night had come upon Saunders' Field, and when it did come, hours later, it came slowly but with infinite mercy.

He woke well after dark. His eyes slowly opened, and he lay a long time staring into the branch-crossed dark, wondering if he had died. Abel breathed and he blinked and pondered the nature of light and dark, and after a time of this he sat up. Setting his back against a flowering dogwood, he placed his sticky hands in his lap and let his head fall back against the trunk. Tree branch, shrub, and vine traced ink-black lines across the surface of the night, and Abel's chest and legs were sprinkled with pale fallen blossoms.

He was far behind his own army's lines, and how he got there he did not know. Wan circles of sad yellow light cast from cloth-covered lanterns shone here and there through the shadows. Occasionally rifle fire erupted with loud clatterings like someone off-loading planks somewhere, and faintly came the moist grindings of working bone saws. High, falsetto screams of those beneath the blades. The constant tramping through the darkened Wilderness as lost men stumbled about.

Abel pulled himself unsteadily to his feet and leaned against the dogwood. Pain flared blue as ice through his chest. Setting palms to knees to better get his breath, Abel worked his shirt open and sent his fingers exploring his midsection to see if he'd been killed. When he found the wound, he gathered his lips between his teeth and pushed the tip of his little finger into the wet declivity beside his heart. His nail scraped against his fourth rib before he finally drew his finger out and went carefully feeling along the wound's length. The ball had gone through his jacket and his shirt and licked along the side of his chest, laying him open without piercing him. His shirt, along with mud and yellow grass from Saunders' Field, had dried over the wound, making a fist-sized poultice that had stopped the bleeding.

Abel panted, leaning against the tree. He'd begun to sweat, and bile had risen up his throat before subsiding again. His smoke-scorched eyes went grinding dryly in their sockets as he knuckled them with curled forefingers gullied with cuts. He lacked two nails on his left hand and wondered if the thumb on that hand was broken. It surely felt it. When he tried to remember the face of the man he'd clubbed, it would not come to him, though he could still see the look in the man's eyes as he died.

When Abel finally took a step away from the tree, he fell for the pain of it. Sitting up again, he felt along his right leg and found two bullet holes, hip and thigh, and marveled that neither had struck bone. The hip was another grazing wound, but when he pressed against the back of his thigh just above the knee, Abel could feel the hard alien shape of the ball itself embedded deep in the meat of his leg.

Where he sat, back from the lines, the air was somewhat cool and fresh. Abel gulped at it, then hissed and fought hard to keep from vomiting. When the spell had passed, he opened his eyes and slowly began to grope about the dark for his rifle.

His left hand touched a pants leg, his right settled upon a man's chest—cold, sticky, and unmoving. Abel sat very still, letting his eyes adjust to the dark. As shapes faded in from the shadows, he realized he'd risen from a row of deadmen laid out like railroad ties along the road. As he sat there, a wagon slowly congealed from the darkness, its sound describing its shape before he saw the dark silhouette or smelled the horses. The wagon came to a stop down the line from Abel, and he watched two Negroes climb slowly from the bed. A white teamster tied the reins off on the brake, looked about, then pulled his hat brim over his eyes, crossed his arms over his belly, and began a fitful dozing on the jockeybox. One of the blacks lit a tiny lantern and hung it from a nail on the side of the wagon before the two of them walked to the first corpse in line and lifted it between them by the knees and arms. As they rolled the first of their stock into the wagon, a whippoorwill called from the dark, and both blacks paused to look fearfully about. As though the bird call heralded the stirring of the dead; their bright ascension or their long, dark fall. The Negroes watched along the line a moment, and if they saw Abel sitting up amidst the corpses they did not show it; they'd seen deadmen by the score twisted by their endings into every conceivable position of pain and outrage and fear, and so continued with their work.

Abel slowly stood and waited for them. He watched them at their work and reckoned them field slaves long used to heavy loads and wearying labor. Neither spoke as they lifted their charges and carried them to the waiting cart, but neither was there reverence in their actions. They simply worked. The whippoorwill called again, and from somewhere a man cried out once, then fell silent again. The blacks came down the line steadily—lifting, carrying, rolling. Neither looked the other in the eye. Abel could smell them now—the sweat that gilded their foreheads and arms, their rank fear and quiet revulsion, and another, softer scent that Abel had always associated with the race and which seemed to him to have the essence of wet leaves in October.

In that strange, mad dark there were too many dead to count, and as Abel stood waiting in their midst, he wondered if he was, himself, dead or living. He was afraid to look down for fear he'd see his own bullet-gnawed corpse lying at his feet. Abel sniffed deeply, feeling his sinuses rattle soft and wet, and tasted the bitter creosote residue of powder and smoke on his teeth and tongue. His tongue felt dry and huge. He spat into his palm and touched the spittle with two fingers, realized the breath in his lungs, and pressed a palm against his chest to feel the quick, strong beating of his own heart.

The whippoorwill called again. Abel licked his lips and tried a whistle. A soft, mournful note escaped his lips and hung in the darkness, static and sad before fading. The blacks, wrestling a half-headless body that had shat itself, paused in their work to look fearfully down the line. Abel licked his lips again and stepped back from the dead, back into the shadows of the Wilderness. He looked down at the place where he'd been. His body was not there. And he was in pain and discomfort, so knew himself alive. Releasing his held breath, Abel turned and went off slowly through the trees.

He walked a long time. He passed other men, dazed and lost and, like him, out a-wandering. Abel watched them as they stumbled past—dull eyes and slack faces, the shells of their ears crusted with blood. They seemed to vibrate palely in the dark, some of them, as though they'd been afflicted with a palsy that would never quit them. Others merely lurched along or lay curled in tight fetal balls amidst singed leaves and charred undergrowth.

Deadmen from both armies lay scattered about that night. Walking, his way lit by smoldering little fires and distant pale lanterns, Abel passed men fallen with their arms frozen in the rigid postures of rifle-carrying, men whose pockets had already been turned out by thieves that slipped unseen from shadow to body to shadow again. Men whose powder-blacked flesh swelled monstrously in the heat.

There were many fires burning in the Wilderness that night, and as Abel stumbled along he began to see what shapes their light revealed. Dead horses and chunks of dead horses and now a thicker waste of deadmen lying in heaps and rows throughout the thickets. There were fires that flared in the canopy overhead, lighting yellow the dark, moonless welkin where tree branches laced black as snakes. Little weaverbirds, their nests destroyed by fire, flitted worriedly and quiet through the dark and gone again. And here and there, like signal beacons, whole trees stood blazing, pulsing smoke down the floor of the night. Sound bled slowly back into the world, and Abel could now hear the wounded groaning and the soft rumbling of distant wagons and of marching men and the cries of the lost and hurt and the calls of those that sought them. He heard men praying Jesus, and somewhere someone sang a snippet of song Abel did not recognize but that was furious and sad and that he would remember ever after. And beneath all this other sound, staccato and enthusiastic bursts of rifle fire from jumpy men out on picket kept the night lively.

After a time of walking, Abel settled painfully upon an old blown-down log to rest. His head was light, and even for all the hot, smoky darkness, he was very cold. Flames shivered and Abel rubbed his face, dragging his palm down from temple to jaw, and then he blinked and looked about again. "Well, I'll be goddamned," he said softly when he recognized the flags of his division's hospital strung limp and backlit between the trees, and beyond them the ghost-pale shapes of surgeon's tents. He swore again when he then saw yet more lines of deadmen and wounded men and men soon to be dead lying in lines like the spokes of a wheel radiating from the tenting. Among the dead of that place, and not far from where Abel sat, lay O. W. with the lower half of his face shot away and his red, red tongue lying like the bow of some ill-shaped tie upon his throat.

On the stained blanket beside him lay his tricorn, and on his big toe a tag that told his name, his county, and his town.

Abel sat quietly. More sound slowly reached him, and he idly wondered if his eardrums were ruptured. He identified the high-pitched grating he'd been hearing for the last half hour as the singing of bone saws brandished by the operators in their tents. Those beneath the cold teeth screamed like children, begging for it to stop even if it meant certain death. Abel broke a filthy-feeling sweat to hear it and felt his stomach churn.

After a while, he crossed to O. W. and stood looking down at the man. Abel bent and picked up the tricorn. Brushing it off as best he could, he settled the old war bonnet over what was left of O. W.'s face and took a moment to straighten out his clothes and touch his hair. It was as he stood again to leave that Abel heard Ned calling to him from two rows over, where a line of dead lay beneath the branches of an old black oak.

Abel picked his way carefully over men dying and men dead. Every one a broken thing that could never be set right. When he reached Ned's side and knelt, Abel did not recognize the boy. His moon-round face was powder-burnt and bruised from temple to jaw on the right side. He was shirtless and mud-spattered, and his arms were gone.

Ned was hatless, his thin hair mussed with his cowlick rooster-tailing the way it did, and when he saw the way Abel looked at him, he began to weep. "Look what they done to me," he sobbed. He tried to lift himself from the foul blanket where he lay and failed.

His right arm had been taken cleanly at the elbow and his left mangled at the armpit. The surgeons had been fast and sloppy in their work—isinglass was slathered in patches onto the red, puckered flesh at the tips of his stumps, but much of it had flaked off into the dirt. Black thread bristled like wiry antennae, and a little splinter

145

of unsmoothed bone protruded jaggedly from the drain hole of his left stub. Ned gasped with pain or fear and tried to reach for Abel with arms that were not there, then cried out again.

"God damn it, Ned," breathed Abel. He reached and cupped the boy's face with his hands. He touched Ned's mouth with the pad of his thumb and asked him if he was thirsty. "Oh my Lord," whispered Ned, rolling his eyes and smacking his lips. "Oh God, yes."

They'd left him his canteen when they put him in line for the deadcart and Abel unstoppered it. He lifted Ned's head carefully with the palm of his hand and tilted the water against the boy's lips. Water ran from the sides of his mouth but he managed to get a little down. Abel lowered the boy and fussed with his hair a little, for he knew not what else to do. "What all did they do for you, Ned?" he finally asked, trying hard to keep his voice steady. "Them sawbones . . . they give you something? For the pain?"

Ned swallowed and blinked. He opened his mouth and closed it again. "They put a rag on my face," he whispered. "White rag what smelled a hunk . . . like a hunk of sugar cane. Smelled like candy." Ned moaned. Swallowed. Went on. "When I woked up—when I woked up there was a big ol' fly that was on my face." His eyes rolled. "I reached up to brush it off but I couldn't do it. I couldn't." His mouth opened wide and closed again, and he began to weep. "Abel, I couldn't. I couldn't reach it. I couldn't."

Abel looked away, for he did not want Ned to see his face. He tried not to listen anymore, tried not to see all the other mangled bodies lying round about, but could not. He tried to concentrate on the lights of countless little fires burning in the night, but the wounded and the dead would not be discounted in either sound or sight, and Ned went on.

"Fly . . . that goddamned fly. It lit on my arm. On the end of it. I felt it on me. Then it come back and landed on my face. You see it?

Abel? You see it on me? Oh God, get it off me, Abel! Get it off me!" And Ned began screaming. He screamed with fear and pain and outrage and drew the attention of the dying men around him. They looked up from their places, watched the boy thrashing, then settled down again without comment.

Abel made soft, soothing sounds and brushed at Ned's face, and after a while Ned hushed. He closed his eyes. His breath was quick and shallow. Abel tore a section from the tail of his shirt, tilted the canteen against the cloth, and commenced cleaning the boy's face with cool water, all the while speaking to him in the same low, comforting tones of a man calming a good dog that needed to be put down. And as he cooled Ned's temples with the wet rag, Abel peeled back the blanket that covered his lower half and understood why the surgeons had done such poor work upon his arms.

Ned was lying in a pool of his own blood that spread like a dark wing from his side, and when Abel held a palm over his belly he could feel the fierce, sick heat of a lethal wound. It bled but slowly, yet the blanket and ground beneath were soaked. Abel wondered if it was his kidney or his bowels or both all torn up within him, then decided it didn't matter. He figured the surgeons, forearms huge with straining and punchily tired from who-knew-how-many hours plying their trade, had only discovered this mortal wound after they taken his arms and begun to sew the stumps. Swearing softly, Abel turned away and set his temples into the cradle of his palm. When he turned back, Ned's eyes were open, clear, and focused.

He took a breath. "Pretty bad?"

"Jesus, Ned." Abel's voice finally broke. He looked at Ned, then looked to find the stars above. He could not see them. "Someday," he told Ned. "Someday, I'm goin' to be somewhere where I can find the stars at night whenever I want them." He licked his lips and looked down at Ned again. "All right, Neddy. You tell me what you want. You tell me what you want me to do, and I'll do it."

Ned licked his lips and blinked and looked at Abel. He shook his head. "You just go on do what you think's best, Abel. It'll be all right." He closed his eyes. "It'll be just fine."

Abel pressed his lips together and squeezed shut his eyes. He took a breath, then stood. He could only put a little weight on his leg. Slowly crossing the ghastly clearing, he drew to a stop outside one of the tents where the surgeons were still busy at their work. Monstrous shadows gamboled outsized upon the dingy canvas. Unspeakable sounds issued forth and would continue, forever, in his dreams. Screams and rhythmic grindings. The soft ticking of bone dust falling in a cone beneath the bench where three strong men held another down as the operator, like some pagan god all gore-bespattered, took pieces of him away to add to a great, slippery mound of legs and arms, hands and feet, that would be buried later in a long, shallow trench and thence forgotten by all save those who lost them.

Aides came and went and paid Abel no mind. After a while, he blinked and looked around. There was a table nearby, and upon it stood basins of foul, pinkish water, squares of lint, spools of thread, and surgeons' tools. Gleaming scalpels and long, exquisite needles, pliers and little chain saws and fleams and scissors and, crossed at one end of the table, redly wet, were two huge bone saws like great serrated dragoons' knives.

Abel took a deep breath, fought down his rising gorge, and went to the opposite end of the table where there stood some half-dozen glass vials and a few squares of somewhat clean linen. Uncapping the bottles each in its turn, Abel sniffed cautiously until he found what he was looking for, then slipped it into his pocket, took a thick square of linen, and returned to where Ned lay dying.

Abel asked him how he was, but Ned did not reply, merely blinked and watched Abel with his eyes wide. Abel gave him more water, and Ned closed his eyes. Abel breathed. He breathed and opened his mouth as though to speak but only made a choking sound, so turned away a moment to collect himself. He took the vial from his pocket and set it to the side. He doused his hands with cool water and ran his fingers through Ned's hair. Ned sighed and a long shudder passed through him. Abel looked at Ned's face, then began to sing to him the Hush-a-Bye song. His voice was soft and it was good, and Abel smiled as he sang. Those men who still remained alive round about quieted their moaning as best they could to hear Abel singing and Abel sang to them and he sang to Ned and he held Ned's eyes with his own to show him that he shouldn't fear and as he did his hands were busy opening the vial and soaking the linen with its contents.

Finally, Ned closed his eyes again. His face relaxed. He spoke but softly, as though already far away, and Abel never knew what he said. Abel sang and covered the boy's mouth and nose. Ned's eyes came open and he tried to rise, but then they closed again and opened no more forever.

Abel covered the boy's face with a blanket, then pushed himself to his feet and turned away. His hands, fingers splayed, were in the air before him as though to push something back, and his shoulders shook. He took a great, deep breath that hurt him terribly, then walked away from that place into the dark, flamestruck Wilderness and did not look back.

Abel staggered on through the Wilderness. He saw things that night that would never leave him. He saw a Yankee soldier bound to a thick oak with his throat cut, and he saw a Yankee drummer boy lying dead beside his drum with not a mark upon him. Abel saw three suicides and a naked man hanged by the neck from the branch of a scrub pine, his blue uniform neatly folded and set upon a nearby log. And he came upon a dented tuba lying lost in the middle of a swampy little creek and loose horses too numerous for counting. He walked and walked and by and by came upon a little clearing floored with soft moss. Abel sat down at the clearing's edge and closed his eyes.

There came a soft jangle and creak from the opposite side of the glade, a soft, choking cough, and, muttering to himself, Abel stood and looked. A man lay crumpled against the base of an old, furrow-barked box elder. His haversack had spilt and his papers and possibles lay in a jumble on his lap and off. He was a Union man, tow-haired and all but dead. He'd taken balls in both knees and there was no way to tell what other wounds he had. His face was cut and burnt, and somehow he'd lost both his eyes. Yet still the man lived, and still he held a pistol pointed blindly, yet accurately, at Abel.

Abel licked his lips and spat, and even though the Yankee could not see it, he made steadying motions with his hands. "Hold on," he said softly. "Just ease on up and hold on, now."

"Who's that?" the man cried out. "Who is that?" His mouth was open and his upper lip damp. From somewhere, not far away, a man screamed once and loudly, then fell silent.

"It's just nobody," said Abel. "Just another fella hurt like yourself."

At the sound of Abel's voice, the Yankee fired the gun. Abel sat down hard. He'd felt a sharp tug at his left shirtsleeve and looked that way to see who was wanting him. There was no one there, and after a moment Abel toppled over. He lay very still, looking starward, but there were still no stars, only long shivering streaks of red laid out across the floor of the sky. Behind him, Abel heard the Yankee die—a soft rustling in his clothes and a softer thud as the pistol fell to the moss.

After a while, Abel pushed himself up and looked over at the man where he lay dead. Taking his upper lip between his teeth, he looked down at his arm. From hand to forearm, he was gloved in blood. He could not move his fingers or bend his arm, and it looked all wrong where it hung from his body. Somehow he got to his feet and staggered over to the dead Yankee. He was but a boy of twenty or so, and there was room beside him at the base of the box elder for another, so Abel settled down. He stretched out his legs. He took a breath. Let it out. "Right comfortable," he said.

The boy's haversack lay near Abel's thigh, and he reached inside. His good right hand closed around a paper-wrapped square of metal, and when he took it from the sack he saw it was a lidded tintype wrapped in the boy's last letter to his wife. The metal was emblazoned with the Union Fifth Corps cross and the letter was blood-stained. Clumsily, Abel prised open the frame and looked upon the little image of wife and daughter within. He swallowed deeply. His shattered arm crawled with the beginnings of pain and he thought for a moment of the surgeons' tents and of Ned. Abel blinked and shook his head. He looked at the letter and began to read.

*May 5,*
*Catherine Schwartzenbach*
*Grape Glen, Pensyl.*

*My Darling Catherine,*
*Yest'day we left camp—our Home for the last three months as You know. We started South right away. Richmond bound again or so they say. This morning saw Genl Grant. He is not much too look at but they say he is a good Genl and we need a good Genl if ever we want to lay down our arms and be One Nation again so I hope that they are rite and He is a Good Genl. I guess today we are going to have a Big Battle. When I look I can see Rebs just across the way. There is a little field here and the sun is pretty on the yellow grass. The Rebs are*

*on the other side and we can all hear them plain as day. I think they are all fine Fellows and am not ashamed to say so. Many others think as I do and do not hate the Rebs but rather hate the War because it is a Bad and Hateful thing. Darling Catherine there are no words to describe the things I seen and if there were I wouldn't use them because I dont want you to know the things I seen. They are all so bad. But the Rebs. They are all Americans same as us and only gone astray and tho War is very hard and terrible in its aspeck it is nessary to save and Preserve the Union. Youve heard me talk this way before and I still think it. It is hard to Kill a man and sad too because they are everyone of them our true Brothers and whenever we see Them coming we are very Proud to see them coming. Even when we are told to Fire! Fire! and watch as They fall we are Proud still because they are the same as us only gone astray somehow. It is hard to talk about but True.*

*My friend Harding who I wrote you of comes from the Oregon Territory and has been telling me about the Blue Pacific and the trees Out There. He says that everything is Green and Lovely and a man has only to rise up in the morning to feed from the Fat of the Land. And there are Mountains and Noble Indians and so few People that you could walk a full day and not meet your Naybor. I am thinking now that if the Lord in His Wisdom sees fit to spare me that we should Move There when I muster out. I don't want to see these places I've been no more and these places are Everywhere in this country. Harding says the forests Out There are greener and bigger than here and the trees are Three Times as big as here and I surely would like to see Them. Harding says at night you can see stars forever. I surely would like to leave these places where wev been fighting so promise me youll think about it and write me soon with your anser. I so love your letters and never told you that I*

*Darling the officers are calling for us now so now your Husband has to go to work. Did you get the money I sent? With Gods Own Blessing I will be Home Soon and I Pray to Him everyday to watch over*

*you and the Baby. I think about you Every minute of Every day. I love
you More and More Every Day. Kiss the Baby for me.*

*Your Loving Husband
Henry*

And beside Henry Schwartzenbach, Abel Truman fisted up his
good right hand and held it before his mouth and began to weep,
and after a while he stood and left that place.

# SEVEN

## *Time before Sleep*

### *1899*

THE STINK WOKE him before the sun did. In truth, the stench never really let him sleep much, and the sun that morning was nothing but dim gray light that shed no heat, yet Glenn Makers was surprised nonetheless to open his eyes blinking against pale slats of day seeping through the cracks in the outhouse roof.

Standing, he leaned against the door opposite the shithole and rubbed his eyes. The chain between the irons round his wrists clanked softly in the morning quiet. Makers muttered to himself and flapped his right hand about as though to shake the pain from it. A jangling, metal sound in the close, dim dark. Holding his right wrist with his left hand, he put his dark flesh into what light he could to study his fingers after the fashion of elegant women of society. The nail of his ring finger was torn out, snagged on a buttonhole or loose thread on Farley's shirt when Makers wrestled the man before beating him senseless yesterday afternoon. His examination of the soft, red pulp prompted further inspection of his various hurts, and Makers winced to touch pump knots at cheekbone and temple. He thought of Farley's fat turquoise ring sparkling through the light and winced again.

But nothing felt broken, and Makers grunted and stepped to the hole to piss into the stinking dark. He heard it spattering not quite far enough down for his comfort and turned his face from the warm reek rising upward with the day. Other peoples' smells, telling of strange foods and strange ways. Presently, his eyes began to burn, and he halfheartedly tried the door, but it was still locked. He briefly poked about for a sack of quicklime amongst the greasy rags and old paint cans, but there was nothing and so he settled down in one corner with both palms covering the lower half of his face.

He'd been awake for the better part of an hour when he heard the stamp, jangle, and creak of horse and wagon in the yard outside. He could tell by the gait that it was his own wagon, and the creak reminded him that once he was home he'd need to grease the axles before the cold came down from the mountains. When a key rattled the padlock and the door opened, Makers was standing athwart the jamb. He took a great, deep breath of fresh air and let it out again. Below him, Sheriff Henry Lee Jensen squinted up at him, then leaned to the side to spit a long brown chain of juice out from under his yellowy mustache. The sheriff put his bootheel up on the step to block Makers's way and hitched his thumbs to his back pockets. Tilting his head farther back, he looked Makers up and down appraisingly. "You can be damn sure the only reason I'm letting you out already is I got to use the shitter," he said good-naturedly.

"And you can bet that after a night locked in with your stink I'm a deeply remorseful man," answered Makers. He raised his chained hands.

Jensen looked at the hands hanging fisted and huge in the air between them. The sheriff squinted again, unlocked the irons, and

155

stepped out of Makers's way. "I guess I ought to tell you to shut your goddamned African mouth," he told him. "But I ain't got it in me to lock you up again if you react poorly."

He'd brought Makers's wagon with him, and Emerson stood quietly in the traces, his breath pluming against the morning chill. Makers walked over and let his hand trail along the horse's neck and shoulder and stood beside its head so he could breathe in the animal's exhalations. A good smell from another, cleaner world. He took in the earthy scent as though it alone could refresh him, then leaned to look into the wagon bed, scanning the boxes and sacks there. After a moment, he lifted out his coat.

"Your gear's all there, don't worry," said the sheriff. "I know you're laying in for winter and I don't particularly want you back to town any faster'n need be, so, just like you, I kept it all locked up last night."

Makers nodded and pulled on the coat. "You could have at least given me this," he said, fixing his shirt beneath and tugging down the sleeves. "It's almost November. It's not warm."

Jensen shrugged. "I could've done a lot of things," he said. "I could've been the sort of fella, the sort of lawman, that'd string a nigger up for beating on a white man." He leaned and spat again, then plucked a pebble from the mud at his feet and absently rolled it between his palms. "Hell," he went on. "I could've been the sort of man who'd cut the balls off a nigger just for looking at a white woman, let alone marryin' one." He shrugged again. "There's any number of men like that around here."

"Watch it now," warned Makers. "How you speak to me."

Jensen pursed his lips, then nodded. "All right," he said. "All right. You're right, I am sorry. But even though this ain't Georgia or wherever the hell you come from, you don't watch your ass and your mouth, Glenn, you'll find out quick there ain't a whole lot of . . .

What's the word? . . . philosophical differences between here and there."

Makers considered the sheriff a long moment before swinging himself up into the wagon. Wrapping a fist around the brake post, he asked, "Are you threatening me? Or asking me to thank you for locking me in the shithouse all night?"

Jensen spat and wiped his damp, brown-speckled lip with the back of his hand. "Neither," he said, shaking his head. He hitched his thumbs to his back pockets once more and stood with his lean face tilted skyward as though to judge from the fog the character of the day to come. He looked back at Makers from under the round brim of his hat. "No, sir," he said. "But I am saying you have congress with, you give ear to, ignorant folk, and you got to expect them to act ignorantly. To say ignorant things. And, mister, there ain't a shortage of ignorance no matter where you go. Smart, well-read fella like you ought to know that."

Makers put his feet up on the jockeybox and gathered the reins. Emerson stamped impatiently and put his ears up. Makers sat regarding his boots. "Those Chinese make it out all right?" he finally asked.

Jensen frowned and pulled a face. "Left town two days ago. Same day your sorry ass came in."

Makers nodded. "Farley was saying something. I thought maybe he'd cause trouble for them."

The sheriff grinned lopsidedly and shook his head. "After what you done to him? I ain't heard yet that he's even woke up. And without him, them other boys is just trifling." Jensen's grin faded, and he looked seriously at Makers. "I didn't know you run into them Chinese."

Makers shrugged. He picked a splinter off the brake post with his free hand. "I told them stop by the house before they tried the Pass.

157

Hoping maybe Ellen can talk some sense into them. If she can, you'll see them back here in a day or two. Then you'd better watch Farley."

Jensen nodded. "Snowing up there already?"

"Not at our place, but judging from the view from the porch, I'd say it's come down into the tree line. And we've already had one hard frost."

The sheriff bobbed his head. "They'd best not try it till spring, then." He sighed. "That'll make my winter busy."

Makers pushed his tongue into the side of his cheek thoughtfully. After a moment of contemplation, he shifted about and said, "Well, maybe we can put them up. Depending on how well geared up they are, it might mean another trip back down here for me, though."

"Well, whatever you think best," Jensen said, then grinned wistfully. "My God, was that not a beautiful child?"

"Sure," said Makers. "She was a pretty little thing." He smiled broadly at the sheriff and said, "Listen to you. Who'd have thought it?"

"Fuck you," said Jensen good-naturedly.

"How is Farley?" Makers finally asked. "I guess I didn't kill him."

The sheriff grinned and waved a hand through the air. "Shit," he snorted. "You must have some deep goddamned faith in my peace-keeping abilities if you think I could stop you getting strung up and worse if you'd killed that fool." He snorted again, hawked up a great gob of phlegm, and sent it spinning off into the brush. "Naw," he went on. "Farley ain't killed. Like I say, I ain't sure he's come awake yet, but he's only a little torn up. Maybe a mite worse'n you. Still and all, I'm glad you're not wintering over down here. Give him a chance to cool off and forget about it."

"A man like that doesn't forget anything," said Makers. He shifted on the seat and released the brake. Thumbing the bill of his hat,

Makers clucked his tongue and Emerson started forward, but the sheriff stepped up and took hold of the halter.

"I need to know, Glenn," he said. "What started it? For my records."

Makers raised an eyebrow. "You keep records? I didn't even know they'd taught you to read."

"All right, I'll go on and say it then: Fuck you, you African bastard. There. You want to try and knock me down now?"

Makers shook his head and grinned. "Naw," he said. "I'll leave it go this time."

"Then maybe I ought to say it again. Make myself feel better about letting you out so soon."

"Fair enough."

"Glenn." The sheriff looked at him. "What'd that fool say to set you off like that? Something about them Chinese?"

Makers shook his head and looked down at him. He filled his cheeks with air and blew, then looked up the road where it ran dark and muddy between green trees toward the blue Olympics brushed with early snow. She was waiting for him, and he was late. He was always late, and she always suffered for it. Behind him, beyond the screen of forest, Makers heard the town coming to life—heard the soft sounds of mothers calling children from their sleep, of chickens clucking over morning feed, of hooves stamping muddy paths amidst the tangled green, and then, distantly, the shrill blare of the mill whistle out on the harbor. "He called her a mud shark, Hank," he finally said.

The sheriff pursed his lips. "That it?"

Makers looked at him again, hard this time, with no trace of a smile. "It's the same as those others called her."

"Aw shit, Glenn," said Jensen. "You know Farley had nothing to do with any of that. He's a bully, sure, but he ain't goin' to do that to a woman."

159

Makers pulled down on the brim of his hat so his eyes were shaded against a day that was still without sun. Said: "It doesn't matter. I won't hear it, Hank. I can't."

The sheriff stroked his mustache. He looked up at Makers. "How is Ellen these days, Glenn?"

Glenn Makers thought of her waiting for him. The bright shine of fear deep in her eyes. He finally shrugged and shook his head. "She won't ever be the same," he said. "She's hurt too deep." He took a deep breath and looked at the foggy sky. "Now let go my horse," he said and clucked his tongue and the horse and wagon and driver started up the muddy road between the green trees.

"Hey, Sheriff," Makers called just before he rounded the bend.

"What?"

"Start eating better, would you? Your shithouse is monstrous."

Jensen favored him with a casually crude gesture, and Makers laughed and waved and presently was gone down the narrow, treebound road leading home. Where she was waiting. Where she'd been waiting two days longer than he'd intended.

Two nights after leaving the coast, Abel Truman crouched sore and cold in the dark forest amidst the dead branches of a fallen spruce some fifty yards from their fire. The raw, splintered stumps and snapped trunks of a wide tract of blowdown left in the wake of last year's big storm lay without design through the dark wood. The downed trees were already jacketed with moss and studded with little seedlings as the wilderness worked to claim them back. Willis and the Haida squatted like apes on either side of their fire, forearms resting on the points of their knees, their fingers splayed toward the flames as though they'd grasp and hold what meager heat they shed. Their breath steamed, and for all his age, Abel's eyes were good and he could see the play of light and shadow on the Haida's long face. Occasionally they passed a word or two along with a bottle, but

Abel could not make out their conversation for the distance. And every so often he'd hear the dog's low growl, though he could not see it for the shadows beyond the fire. Abel fixed its place back in the trees, in the dark of the nightblown forest. He wondered if it had smelled him yet, then decided it had not.

There was but half a moon now, and the night was clear, starry and blue. A bright silver cold lay upon the land. The flames leapt in their fire like the ghosts of flames and the pair were nothing but sil-houettes in the dark. Bands of shadow cut slantwise down their faces, and witch hair moss hung in great hanks from the lower branches so they resembled trolls squatting in a grotto. Abel had been watching them since dusk, and it was getting on late now for an old man to be up and about in the woods in winter. He fisted his hand before his lips and blew warmth into his cold fingers. Every now and again a great nausea would surge through him, hot, salty waves breaking against the back of his throat, and he had to fight to keep from coughing. When he hung his pale hand in the dark before him, it trembled and he could not stop it. Abel sniffed softly and rubbed his prickly, hairless chin. Taking a breath, he softly blew and figured it was November.

After the Indians had left him on the beach, Abel kicked over the remains of the fire, ate the salmon steaks, buried the bones, and set out into the forest. He walked on soil, and he walked on a red carpet of fallen needles. But for the play of wind in the creaking trees, all was silent. At one point, Abel heard a furious barking, very faint and far away, but when he stopped to listen, all he heard was squirrel chatter from the branches. Here and there along the trail, every mile or so, stood little stone cairns erected to keep travelers on the path and help them mark their distance. By late afternoon, Abel had counted seven such markers and come upon their previous night's camping place.

The little clearing was just off the trail, and Abel paced it carefully, then crouched beside the dregs of their fire. Little hunks of wood lay crosswise and smoking in a ring of soot-blacked stones. The ashes beneath were warm. Gray and papery, they took flight and spiraled about like merry dust motes when Abel put his hand into them to search out a kernel of living coal. All within was dead, and when he put his fingers to his face he could smell burnt blood and melted fat and presently found the wet bones of a hare in the underbrush.

He found where they'd made their toilet and he found where they'd roped the dog to a spruce. Its tracks circled the tree, the moss torn and the bark raw and the underbrush 'round about savaged. The old man took a deep breath and went on up the trail.

At some point during the long day, he realized he could no longer smell the ocean. The scent of salt, of wet sand and rotting bull kelp, was gone, replaced by freshening breezes through branches and the faint odor of earthy rot as things dead and things recently dead decomposed upon the soft, mossy floor. A flash of unbidden memory brought the loose dirt and dry leaves of Saunders' Field to mind, and on his tongue came the charry residue of old battles past. He wanted none of it. The way David died, and armless Ned. Abel sniffed and spat, then leaned over with his good hand on his knee to catch his breath. After a while, he straightened and went on.

Abel camped that night just off the trail near a rushing stream of water pale with glacial milk. He slept sitting up, his back against a smooth boulder, and he lit no fire. For a time before sleep, he watched the sky where it lay dark and star-crusted, with but a few airy wisps of cloud to the east where the mountains blackly stood. He tried to sleep but could not, for he missed the dog's company and so lay there awake, remembering the night it appeared.

The dog had come out of the forest on a cold night four years ago. The month of the new year, with the weather raw and wild. Freezing rain and a darkly frigid wind, yet there were breaks in the clouds that showed the icy stars above as Abel crouched in the wet sand beside his cooking fire. A rime of frost scaled the stones, and his hands ached with cold as he gutted a middling-sized sockeye for his supper. He did not hear it approach but was suddenly aware of its presence. One moment there was the empty brown trail that ran between the rocks past the driftwood to the shadowy trees, and the next the dog was there upon that trail. Panting, its eyes red in the firelight. The flickering light shimmered yellow on its redblonde fur.

Abel set the fish down. He stood slowly, wide-eyed and suddenly atremble. His mouth hung open. His hands, slick and red, hung limply at his sides, themselves like two skinned fish. He didn't know the last time he'd seen a dog. He didn't move. He barely breathed.

For its part, the dog stood just without the forest, at the very edge of the apron of firelight. Its breath smoked around its muzzle, and it lifted a quivering nose to gather Abel's scent. The dog then sniffed the ground as though to be sure of the rocks and the sand and the fallen pine needles sugared with tiny points of ice. When it finally moved, Abel saw it limped, and there was a large, round wound on one thigh, all red and scabbed over.

The dog approached by fits and starts, pausing now and again to sniff a rock, some piece of ground, and studiously ignoring Abel as though he was beneath its rightful attention. And Abel stood, his breath so shallow you could hardly call it breath at all. The dog came to him through the honey-colored firelight like a dream of a dog, like an answered prayer he could not remember praying, and finally it settled painfully beside the fire.

Abel wiped his palm down the thigh of his trousers, then walked around the flames. Slowly, slowly, he crouched and put his right hand out, and the dog lifted its head as though beyond fatigue and sniffed cautiously at his fingers, its lip curling a little over the fish smell. Abel reached and touched the dog on its wide brow, where the fur was damp but still very soft. "Dog," he whispered, trying the word out. The dog looked at him, and Abel closed his own eyes, then opened them again.

As it warmed itself beside the fire, the dog began to steam. Abel stroked its cheek with the backs of his fingers and ran his palm along the underside of its jaw to softly scratch the point of its chin. He pressed his palm against its chest to feel the steady beating of the heart behind the bone. "My Lord," Abel said softly.

The dog watched him and was silent. It closed its eyes and sighed. Abel settled beside it in the sand. The fire crackled suddenly on a wet log and shot loud sparks against the dark. Frightened, the dog tried to rear up but fell back for its bad leg, with its eyes wild and its nose running. Fur stood in a bristling ridge between its shoulders and down its back. Abel spoke to hush it and surprised himself with his own voice. He coaxed the dog calm, telling it what a good dog it was, and when it had settled again, he bent to examine its hurts.

Four ill-healed claw marks that could have come from anything in that country—bear or cougar, raccoon, skunk, or barbed wire— raked its left thigh. The long fur behind one leg was dizzied into a mat the size of Abel's heart that did not allow the dog to unbend it. Abel sighed and rocked back on his heels, speaking quietly to the dog, looking the rest of it over.

The dog watched him and did not growl when Abel wiped his knife off on his pants leg, then cut free the mat. He set the knife down and tossed the fur into the fire, where it crackled softly, and presently the dog climbed stiffly to its feet. It gentled its leg to the ground as though unsure yet whether to trust it. Abel nodded and praised it and the dog stood looking at him for a long time. Then it limped over to the half-open shack door, looked over its shoulder at Abel, and went into the dark to lie down beside his cot. Abel followed and eased shut the door against the cold. Lying down, he let his hand dangle until he could twist his fingers into the soft fur behind the dog's ears. He spoke to it a long time that night. And finally, just before sleep, Abel breathed deeply and said, "I'll be goddamned if it don't smell like wet dog in here now."

Abel smiled broadly to remember the moment and felt himself slip slowly to sleep.

The afternoon of the next day found him in an old field that stretched a half mile in every direction. A Swede's homestead from years ago, but the ground had been too boggy to support his claim— not farm or outbuilding, let alone any sort of crop. Old timbers dressed greenly in scissor-leaf lay abandoned in dry, waist-high grass that shivered and clashed softly in the wind. The sky was gray with clouds but rainless yet. Upon the air was the brass taste of winter, the sharpness of a coming cold snap. The forest began again on the far side of the field—a green wall cut with brown trunks and shadows. Abel thought for a moment he could hear them somewhere in the field ahead or in the darkness beyond, but a great weariness settled over him, and he covered his face with his hands as though in despair. After a time, he went to an outcropping of stone where the old Swede had thought to build a wall near the center of the field where there grew a bent apple tree. Abel picked a few pieces of spoiling fruit that still, improbably, clung to the branches, and settled upon the stones to rest.

He broke the apples open in his hands. The meat was soft and orange and smelled winesweet. Abel pushed the pulp off the cores with the pad of his thumb and ate the cores, then spat the seeds to the side. The Indians had given him a water skin, and he rinsed his mouth and cleaned the fronts of his teeth with his tongue, then spat and took a long drink. The water was cold and sweet, tasting of rain. After a while, Abel closed his eyes.

He dreamed a dream of empty houses. He dreamed of ancient

stones, cold and moss-covered. He dreamed of a yellow woman whom he knew well, and when he opened his eyes again, he rose and went on.

When they finally bedded down, neither stood guard. After a while, Abel rose from the blowdown and by starlight checked the pistol the Indians had given him. It was an old Adams .32 pocket revolver with but half a grip and a dangerous-looking dent in the barrel. Abel swallowed quickly to ease the itchy burn at the back of his throat. He turned the single bullet out onto his palm, squinted through the chamber, blew it clear, then replaced the bullet and snapped the cylinder back. "All right," he said softly. "You checked it. You did that, so there ain't no cause to go checking it again." Abel took a deep breath and crept through the blowdown toward the red glow of their coals.

When he was close, Abel stopped just without a little box-shaped patch of moonlight, filtering silvery and fine through the canopy. He crouched and listened to them at their slumber—snoring and sighing and soft whimpering. Abel put his hands into the moonlight and broke open the gun to check it once more. Satisfied, he put it back, and the parts clacked softly as he fumbled in the dark. The old man stilled, and he waited a moment to see if they would stir before he continued.

It was very cold now; his breath steamed and rose through the trees like moss vapor in the morning sun. Abel clutched the broken grip where the metal was jagged and tried to control his breath, to ignore the thin, high, icy itch at the back of his throat. He could smell himself, root-sour and fusty, speaking of fear and sickness and age and anger and hurt. He went slowly forward once more, and only stopped when he saw the dog's eyes glowing redly from across the burned-down fire.

It growled, low and deep, ancient in intent, and Abel made a quick, soft shushing sound and the dog fell silent. The old man crouched and let his eyes adjust to the glow of the fire shivering up the tree trunks and paling red the darkness beyond. The dog's legs were tied fast, and a heavy rope was looped tightly around its neck and secured to a tree. It was muzzled with strips of knotted cloth, and a white scrim of drool decorated its underjaw. The dog raised its head to peer at Abel. He made a sign and it settled once more, ears raised.

Abel stepped into the clearing. There was a high burning in his chest and he could feel the action of his heart at work. Above, the stars glittered like fool's gold, and beside the coals the two men slept. Abel eased out the knife the Indians had given him, trod softly around the perimeter of their camp, and crouched beside the dog to cut away its bonds. He cut the rope from its neck but left its muzzle bound for the quiet it gave. Because it could not help it, the dog's tail began to work, sweeping through the ferns once and twice before Abel clutched hard at the loose flesh at the back of its neck and stilled it with a glare. The dog calmed, and Abel nodded, then ran the backs of his fingers over its cheek. He nodded again and jerked his chin toward the dark, and the dog turned and disappeared into the shadows.

The old man pressed his lips together and breathed. He looked at the two men where they lay reddened by coal light. The Haida slept with his face starward, and even in sleep his lips framed a soft, cruel smirk as though his dreams well satisfied him. The big Indian's hands lay composed just so upon his chest in the unnatural manner of the dead in their caskets, and his rifle lay beside him. For his part, Willis slept curled on his side. His thin white hands covered the ruins of his mouth as though he were mocking some proverb-monkey, and his eyes and shoulders twitched as though his dreams showed him things he'd not otherwise see. He whimpered softly, and the toes of his wretched boots dug shallow troughs through the dirt.

Abel moved quietly to the edge of the clearing, then around to where they'd piled their gear, and quickly found his haversack, rifle, and walking stick amongst their reeking equipment. Distantly, he heard the dog barking and frowned and stood stock-still until he was sure the sleepers had not woken. After a moment, he gathered his things and made to turn, but chanced to look starward, where he saw them falling out of the night.

It was no repetition of the Leonids of '33 or even the lesser shower after the war, but perhaps some celestial precursor of other, greater star showers yet to come. Long white trails etched flashing across the glassy night soundlessly in cold parabola. They glittered in the old man's eyes, and for an instant he was a child again, clutching tightly his father's strong hand in the starlit dark, and then he was a man and young and without anyone at all on the long, lonely trail to the blue Pacific and the forests Out There. And then, just before the long white arcs of light faded and were gone, Abel's breath caught in his throat and he began to sputter and to gag. He sputtered and gagged, then drew a great, shuddering breath that forced the caution from him along with a cough that rattled from him harsh and loud.

He doubled over, blood on his lips, and felt strange, damp chunks of matter spray against the backs of his teeth and a tearing within him. Abel spat. He fell to his knees with the pistol falling from his pocket and gone amidst the red-clothed shadows. On either side the sleepers woke and rose.

The dog came silently out of the forest to the left of the road, and had Emerson not spooked, Glenn Makers might not have seen it at all until it was in the bed of the wagon behind him. As it was, all he did see was a dark shape, low to the ground and swift as he took up his rifle. The wagon creaked to a stop in the middle of the road as Emerson stamped and blew and rolled his eyes. Makers told him hush and pointed the barrel out at the dark, cursing himself for a fool for traveling after nightfall with Farley's friends about.

He stood ready that way and, when he saw and heard nothing, lit a little lantern on the seat beside him and held it over his head. The dog's eyes flared in the lamplight as it scrambled into the wagon, and Makers saw it for what it was and saw how its mouth was bound, its neck rope-burnt and raw.

He set the rifle by and stepped into the bed. "That you, Buster?" he asked the dog, and it came to him, whining softly and pawing at its muzzle as Makers took out his knife and cut away the bindings.

Immediately, the dog began a furious barking. It leapt from the wagon and ran into the forest, then turned and barked and ran back out into the road.

Makers looked at the dog. He looked up the road and out at the dark forest, and the dog began barking again. Cursing softly, Makers stepped down into the road to follow the dog where it would lead him, then looked to the sky, where the stars were falling by the hundreds.

They arced in reflection across the dark panes of his eyes, and his mouth dropped open to see them falling so. He thought there should be sound but could not imagine the uproar that might accompany such a spectacle.

Then, quickly as they began, the stars quit falling, and the myriad that remained sparkled from all their right places in the western night. Makers tied the reins around a thin alder nearby, then turned to follow the dog just as the sound of gunfire and outraged screaming crackled from the woods not more than a hundred yards away.

The Haida pushed the barrel of his shotgun against Abel's temple as tenderly as a kiss. Abel was on his knees, and slow, sick blood dripped from his lip to spatter softly in the springy moss. "Old man, old man, old man." The Haida sighed. "You should have just died."

Willis fisted a hand into Abel's long hair and lifted the old man's head. Abel blinked away tears and saw the little man had scooped up the pistol the Indians had gifted him. His eyes widened, and he tongued the red edges of his ruined cheek. In the red light, the little man had a fearsome, scarecrow aspect, and he let go Abel's hair and stepped back. "Shit, Buddy," he gurgled. "This man's sicker'n a dog."

The Haida nodded and withdrew the shotgun. "It would be interesting, I think, to watch it take him. To watch him at the end. An interesting thing." He shrugged and looked up at Willis. "Fuck it. You know what to do with a sick dog."

Willis leaned and spat blood onto the coals, where a yellow flame flared and sizzled and died. He thumbed back the hammer of the Indians' pistol and pointed it at Abel. "Same thing you do to a hurt one," he said.

Abel pushed himself up so he was kneeling between them with the coals of their fire warming his right side. He put his palm on his thigh and breathed as best he could for the pain in his chest and held his ruined left arm in such a way as to ease that pain. From somewhere he heard the dog barking. After a moment, he raised his face to stare into the cold, round dark of Willis's eyes.

There was an explosion, and Abel felt heat scorch his eyelids and his forehead. There was a scream, and he opened his eyes to see Willis fallen to the side with the Haida bent over him. Their shadows on the pines were monstrous in the lurid light. The pistol lay here and there in so many pieces, and Abel blinked and shook his head to try and rid his ears of ringing. As he pushed himself to standing, he reached into the coals and scooped up a bright handful that sizzled mournfully in his bare palm.

The Haida stood and swung the shotgun around as Abel flung his hand forward and released the coals. They went hissing starwise through the dark space between them, and the Indian ducked. The shot went wide but not by much, the pellets slicing through the underbrush and thocking loudly into the trees.

Abel turned and grabbed his haversack and rifle as the Haida broke his own gun to reload. Willis pushed himself to his knees, holding with his left hand the remains of his right, where the exploding pistol had blown it apart.

Abel had no way to know how far he'd run before he finally fell gasping and sick to the moss, but he reckoned it could not have been far. He could still plainly hear Willis screaming with thick choking sounds as his broken mouth tried to find the proper shape for his pain. Abel lay on his back in the moss with one hand clutching the straps of the haversack and the rifle fallen beside him. He lay with his chin wet and he lay with his heart racing all out of time to the pulse of blood he could plainly feel pounding at his temples.

And then the dog was there—worrying his neck and ears with its soft, warm tongue—and then another figure, a man who looked him over, swore, and helped him to his feet. He fetched Abel's rifle, and together they stumbled through the brush. Moonlight came through the forest like the ghosts of trees, and they heard crashing in the brush behind them. A hoarse and maddened shouting.

They came out of the woods onto the road, and Abel pulled himself up into the wagon bed as it lurched forward. He whistled for the dog to join him and when it did, Abel told it what a good dog it was. Then with his hurt but still expert hand, Abel checked the rifle over, cocked it, and lay the barrel against the backboard to aim out into the dark forest as it passed by along either side. They were moving fast now, up the road, but the road was not good, and as he was jostled about Abel felt what little strength he still had begin to fail him. When he saw there was nothing, and would be nothing, behind them, he lay back.

"Glenn Makers," he called out after a few moments.

"Abel Truman," said Makers over his shoulder. "You all right?"

"Passable," said Abel. "You can probably slow up a little now."

"If it's all the same to you, we'll keep along like this for a bit."

"All right then," said Abel. His burnt face felt light and numb and his right hand itched, the skin tightening. He looked at the little sacks and packages laying heaped in the wagon bed with him. "You-all layin' in for winter?" he asked.

"That's right," said Glenn. His shoulders rose to his earlobes as though he felt a sudden shudder, then fell again.

Abel lay back and quietly panted for a short time. "Well," he finally said. "Looks like you'll have plenty. You two must be doing all right up there."

"We're doing fine."

Abel nodded and cleared his throat. He sat up and spat over the side. "Ellen ever get better?"

"She's just the same."

"Well, that's too damned bad." Abel began a weary, wet coughing that he soon lost control of. Makers slowed the wagon and finally stopped when Abel vomited over the side. It went on for a time before the old man finally fell back gasping, and Makers started the wagon forward again.

"You see them stars, Glenn?"

"Yes, I did."

"Pretty things, them. Pretty things."

They went along quietly for a while. Makers wondered if the old man had died until a voice came from the wagon bed. "I brung back your book."

Makers spoke to Emerson, and the horse picked up the pace again. "Did you?" he answered after thinking about it a moment. "I'd forgotten you had had it."

Abel stirred about in the dark. "I didn't," he said softly.

Again, there was a long period of quiet, and Makers finally stopped the wagon and climbed into the bed to kneel beside the old man. Looking at him, Makers thought again that he was dead until Abel made a soft sound and grimaced in his sleep. Makers got a blanket from his supplies and settled it over him, and the old soldier slept and Makers nodded and got the wagon moving again.

# EIGHT

## Like a Distant Storm

### The Wilderness of Spotsylvania, May 7, 1864

A SINGLE RAINDROP struck his face. A fat drop, filled with spring-time promise and tainted now, too, with the smoky pollutants of war, for it had fallen through layers of stale powdersmoke. Risen days past from the solid world below, it plunged. The herald of a hard shower coming, as it fell to the dark green world it gathered to itself dust and chaff and particles of violence that threaded invisibly through the dirty air like shuddering ectoplasm.

The drop smacked against him, pooling neatly at the center of his brow then sliding along his temple, running atop a month's accumulation of dried sweat and grime and tracing the delicately curved intricacies of his ear before dropping, finally and forever, into the grass, where it seeped into the ruined soil of the Wilderness of Spotsylvania.

Sherman Grant opened his eyes. He blinked and breathed with his flesh all damp and aching in his joints. Filthy and hungry, badly frightened by the memory of what they'd seen of the fighting the day before, he shook his head to try and dislodge the terrible dreams from his mind's eye. He tried to forget other, worse things that were not dreams at all but that he would remember always in nightmares.

He lay on his back in the grass, watching the undersides of dark clouds flowing southward. Carried by high winds, they lay seamed each to each and complex as a Chinese puzzle box whose secrets held blue sky and sunlight. Grant smelled the smells of rain and things burnt, and when a blocky rattling came to him upon the wind, he stood.

He looked southward toward a dense screen of trees. Dark smoke stood like tilted columns holding up the gray sky. The artillery rumbled again, and he marked its place by sound and distant flashes of light against the low belly of cloud. Like thunder it rolled, like a distant storm a farmer will watch with worry. He wondered where the armies were meeting again and stared south, trying to see beyond the green rim of the forest. He wondered how far they'd gotten before turning on each other again.

They'd hidden in the woods for three days now, afraid to move for fear of capture or worse. For the first two days and nights they'd heard the sounds of battle issuing out of the dark all around them like nothing either had ever known. Like two animals at each other ceaselessly, they did not stop their fighting for dark of night, merely slackened the pace a little. On the third day the armies moved south. He and Hypatia stayed still as the marching soldiers flowed past. Lights stabbed through the shadows all night long, and the trees filled with the sounds of shouting and the stamping of hooves, the creaking of tack and the clatter of wagon wheels.

At some point they pulled each other to their feet and started stumbling forward through the dark in a direction they hoped was north. They heard caissons rumbling down newly cut roads and the irate shouts of teamsters. Smoke seethed through the trees. Grant and Hypatia walked the night long and at dawn lay themselves down to sleep.

Hypatia still slept. With knees drawn up and one hand fisted against her neck, her brow was pinched, even in rest, and her head-wrap was discarded, her cropped hair as dusty as her bare feet. Her dressfront was damp, and she pleaded quietly with her dreams. Grant watched her at her dreaming and held a palm before her mouth to feel her breath upon his skin. Closing his eyes, he grimaced and stood, then went a short way through the wood to make his toilet. He lowered his trousers and squatted to let his water spill. He tried hard not to give in to the temptation to examine his mangled sex, and as he fastened up, Grant spied a thin trail winding through the trees. He looked back at Hypatia. She had not moved. After a moment, he turned and went up the trail.

Gaining the top of a small hill, he marked her place in his mind and turned to look out over the Wilderness. Here and there individual trees swayed and clashed with wind or, in the far south, with men fighting and dying at their trunks. The booming artillery swelled and echoed, joined now with tremendous crashes of musketry. Grant stood watching a while longer and a lean wind disturbed the leaves and drew his attention to a burnt yellow field in the dark of the Wilderness. Figures moved slowly through the clipped grass that lay smoking in the afternoon light.

Turning, he started down another trail that followed the back of the hill down into the trees. A donkey lay dead on its side, its belly swollen and its three remaining legs cocked grotesquely skyward. A hickory tree stood split asunder with its shredded meat white and shocking in the gloom. Branches and fallen logs, all nicked and torn by various pieces of flung metal, lay all about the mouth of the trail as though the path had been hard fought for and taken and lost too many times to count. Grant took a breath and walked down into the dark.

He passed trees swollen with bullets, broken by cannon fire, and singed black by flame. He saw fine-bred horses dead amidst the fallen leaves and dead soldiers lying beside them, weaponless and with their backs shredded. As he picked his way carefully along, Grant could hear the crackling of fire but saw no living flame. Smoke ghosted where the trees kept the wind from blowing, and about the trunks the moss was singed.

When he reached the edge of the field, Grant tilted his face into the breeze, for here it blew softly and fresh upon the outraged grass. He sniffed deeply, his eyes closed. Off in the distance, the sound of battle was dim but constant. Grant rubbed his nose with the back of his hand and stepped out into Saunders' Field.

The armies had moved on, but had left a goodly portion of themselves behind. Deadmen lay scattered in numbers beyond those he'd learned, yet Grant thought that someone besides God should be counting them. Entering names and dates and sorrowful histories into some great ledger for generations hence to study. He gasped and retched, for the breeze suddenly fell away and the charry stink of death in bedlam rose again. He could see the rounded humps of corpse backs, gray and smooth and common as stones about him in the yellow grass. Men and pieces of men lay smoking like grease fires. A horse knelt dead with its hindlegs standing to and its forelegs drawn under its great chest as though presented for some terrible dressage. Little flames, brightly orange under the dark gloom of the sky, still whispered about so that those few stragglers moving on the field's perimeter, stranded in the red wake of clashing armies, were obliged to step carefully.

Grant stood looking out onto the field with his arms wrapped about himself. His face was streaked with dirt and sweat and old hurts. His eyes as burnt and wasted as the chewed grass. Another cool afternoon breeze blew mockingly past, billowing his thin shirt and turning leaves about on their stems so their lighter backs flashed dazzlingly in the shadows.

Out in the center of the field, through the smoking grass, other Negroes moved amidst the dead. They walked slowly, stooped and bent-backed, their hard, worksore hands dipping now and again past the shivery grass tops to touch a body where it lay. Or, if not bending to feel for pulse or breath, then idly nudging the deadmen with the balls of their feet or the toes of their shoes. Some moved about carefully and with an exhausted attentiveness, while others did such work with a passivity that bordered on the sullen, but all took the time to arrange the bodies flat so they would not mortify in positions that would make it hard to later move them. The Negroes moved about amidst the fallen all along the length and breadth of the field, sidestepping the flames and working with an unhurried lassitude that seemed like careful respect and weary shame in equal part.

Standing there, Grant felt the bottomless sorrow that hung in the air and knew, suddenly, that the grief still to come would be infinitely harder than the work at hand. He also knew that brighter still would be the Jubilee, if and when it came. He took a breath and walked from that place with his head hung as though he'd seen, and by witnessing taken part in, some thing he'd no right to.

He walked back slowly through the Wilderness and passed by death in every posture. Beside a white road slanting through the dark green he came upon an old black man weeping without control beside the body of a young boy in a blue uniform. The old man pressed the boy's small hand against his cheek, and the other hand was spidered darkly over the child's face. His grief was violent and soundless, and if he saw Grant he paid him no mind. Grant moved on without a word, and by and by he found a Union sack coat folded neatly upon a log with a forage cap perched atop. He stopped, breathless.

Sherman Grant lifted up the cap. It bore a badly sewn Maltese Cross, and the leather brim was cracked and creased and torn. The brass eagles on the coat glittered dully, and there was a neatly folded pair of trousers beneath. He wondered what had become of the soldier and looked about himself for a naked body lying dead nearby, but there was only a clothed, sandy-haired fellow lying in a fetal ball.

Grant sniffed. He blinked and looked once more about himself, then lifted up the uniform and carried it away.

He went on up the road past the Union fieldworks until the Wilderness darkened around him. A thin, sallow white man driving a dilapidated carriage rattled up in a swirling cloud of white dust. The rear of the wagon was filled with spades and shovels, and in one corner, half under a small pile of onion sacks, lay a dead Negro boy. A frightened, shocked face and an ugly wound in his throat. The man stopped the carriage opposite Grant and looked him up and down appraisingly. Grant was well familiar with the stare of valuation and bent his gaze away, hoping the man would not demand to see his teeth.

The man let go the reins, took a deep breath, then blocked one nostril with the tip of his forefinger and blew his nose into the opposite palm. He spent a moment studying the mess as though he'd read his fortune there, then scowled and wiped it off along his thigh. "What're ye doin' out here, boy? Ye run off?"

Grant opened his mouth. He shut it again.

The man shook his head and shifted about on the seat, and when Grant looked up he saw the man held a revolver. "I'll ask ye agin," said the man. "And this time I'll warrant ye'll answer. Ye run off?"

Grant rolled his eyes about as though he'd seek escape. He opened his mouth. He shut it again.

"Damn it all to hell," snarled the man. He stood and turned to step down, and the carriage trembled with his weight. The dead boy's head rolled as though he'd look away. "Damn it all to hell if the woods ain't bleeding niggers today," the man said. "Getting dark early these days." He chuckled to himself and leaned to spit. As he wiped his mouth, his eyes fell on the uniform under Grant's arm and his face split into a wide, malicious grin.

"Where is ye goin' with that shoddy?" he asked, walking around Grant, looking him up and down as though to evaluate his worth against fair market value. "Why, I'd bet ye're nothing but a field buck found hisself a fuckin' blue monkey suit. That right, ye black devil?" He shoved Grant, and Grant stumbled against the carriage. The uniform fell into the dust, and Grant found himself staring into the dead boy's ever-open eyes. He had a tiny mole at one corner of his mouth, and Grant could see his small white teeth past his lips and the dried salt traces at the corners of his eyes. Grant gripped the rail and closed his eyes as though to prepare himself for a beating.

"What're ye goin' to do?" The man laughed. "Ye goin' to volunteer in old Uncle Abe's army? Shit. Y'know, I heard tell there's a whole brigade of you fuckin' chimps marching around out here somewhere. Like they thought it was fuckin' Africa or Cuba or some fuckin' place. Marchin' round like they thought they was men, if ye can believe it."

Grant heard him cock the revolver. His eyes were hot and dry. He knelt, staring at the boy in the back of the carriage, and felt a sharp, pleasant quickness at the back of his throat, and he felt no fear. All his varied pains, all his deep, dark, weary aches, were lifted from him as though caught by a risen wind to which his breath was joined and made part of and would now never be separate from. Grant breathed. Quicker than he thought himself capable, he reached into the wagon, grasped a shovel, and swung it.

The man put an arm before his face, and the pistol went off, but the shot was in the air. Grant wrenched back the blade of the shovel from where it had bit into the man's arm. He was on the ground, and Grant was screaming. A sound raw and bestial. And for the first time, Grant did not stand apart from his anger but gave himself over completely, and his anger was red.

Grant blinked. At some point, the shovel had broken into two pieces, and the blade was sunk to the scruff in the man's face. He gripped the broken handle in both hands, and the end of it was dripping and covered with matter. Grant straddled the man's chest, and the man was wholly destroyed.

Grant stood. His knees were weak, and he walked to the wagon and wiped his face with an onion sack, then walked back and pried the pistol from the man's fingers and put it in his pocket. He put the man's ammo pouch around his neck, then retrieved the uniform, dusted it off, and put it into a clean onion sack. Grant stood a moment or two watching up and down the road. He took another shovel from the wagon and lifted the dead boy and carried him into the trees.

By the time he returned it was evening and dark. She'd risked a little fire and had somehow caught a squirrel to roast upon a stick. When Grant came out of the Wilderness, Hypatia saw how he was and pulled the stringy, brown meat from the bones and laid it on a smooth stone for him to eat. He licked his lips and asked her had she eaten and she said she had and he crouched beside the flames and ate. He licked his slick fingers each by each, and juice ran from the corners of his mouth to sparkle in his growth of beard like tiny red-hued jewels.

She did not ask him his business that day, nor did she question the uniform in the onion sack or the dried blood on his fists and face. She watched him eat, and when he finished, she watched him stare into the flames with things happening in his eyes that she'd not seen since he fell in with her. Several times he opened his mouth to speak and each time shut it again. After a while he wept. He covered his eyes with the shells of his palms and wept against his hands and

Hypatia watched without movement or comment. Courteous and respectful of his grief.

The fire had burnt to embers when he finally stood and walked to the edge of the little clearing. Hypatia heard him making water there, heard it spray forcefully into the brush and heard him sigh with simple, cool pleasure. He came to her after, and they lay holding each other the night long with the shimmering coals painting them red and ushering them to a sleep dreamless and fine.

In the morning they rose hungry and cold. Having no food or possibles about, they picked a direction they hoped was north and started walking through the green gloom. The venomous crackling of innumerable unseen fires made the morning air shudder and the smoke was such it blocked what little sky came through the canopy. But they kept moving. Through the morning and into early afternoon, with the brambles making further mockery of their clothing. Grant kept the uniform safe and gave his arm to Hypatia when she needed it, which was not often. Several times they stopped to try and reckon their course but could not find the sun, and neither was skilled in woodcraft enough to read the moss or stones or any of the other common markers set by nature to help lost travelers. Now and again they rested beside dark little streams, then rose again and went on. By and by they struck a road running through all that charry dark and they stood watching where it ran yellowy and straight to deeper darknesses beyond.

The debris of last year's Chancellorsville battle lay scattered about. A broken wagon wheel scaled with moss. The rusted hoop of a long-decayed barrel. Bits of colored cloth and bits of boots. Grant stooped and plucked a little chess piece from the dust, looked at it briefly, then tossed it away. Hypatia breathed deeply, for the smoke was less in that place and the sun fell suddenly and bright upon the face of the road. As Grant toed the wreckage about, Hypatia walked

to a smooth stone lying in the sun beside an old blackjack. Beside
the stone, a short lane ran to a tiny cabin with a door painted sun-
shine blue. She saw there a covered porch, wild roses blooming in
the dooryard. Red bricks framed an earthen path. Hypatia sighed
and smiled and walked to the porch.

There was a stool there, and an old crate. A soft breeze came up,
and she smelled the roses where they quivered amidst their thorns.
The porch boards were littered with rusty, shriveled petals. The air
was cool and fragrant. Inside the cabin was a packed-earth floor, a
stone hearth. A thin rectangle of ticking in one corner suggested a
mattress, and a sagging desk with the drawers turned out stood abandoned along one wall. A Dutch door swung out onto the Wilderness
where it reared up behind the cabin. She stood looking at the door,
wondering what its business was, being in halves, but could not
fathom it. When she came back onto the porch Grant was there, with
his big, scarred hands on the rail, looking out at the road. She smiled,
and to her surprise, he returned the grin, and they stood shoulder-to-
shoulder, watching the road without speech.

In the late afternoon they kindled a fire in the hearth to draw the
damp chill from the air, and to their relief, the chimney was sound
and drew well. The smoke added itself to what still drifted through
the Wilderness, and all moved southward. They heard rifle fire all
day, and as the light began to fade, a rain began falling and the firing
slowly tapered off. It cooled, but the cabin warmed nicely as the fire
crackled on the sagging andiron. And there, in the lengthening shadows that laced the porch and the lane leading to it, they sat as though
waiting for something yet to come.

After a time a soldier came limping along the road, careering from
side to side like an unmoored ship and spattered with blood from
head to toe. He came stirring coils of dust into the darkening air. At
the lane, he paused and looked their way and stood looking for a
long moment. Neither Hypatia or Grant moved or breathed, for

they recognized his affiliation by the ruins of his uniform and his lean haggardness. The rebel was hatless and his hair was wild and he stood there swaying at the mouth of the lane, staring at them until finally he fell face-first into the dust and did not rise.

Hypatia leaned forward on the crate and the crate creaked and the soldier reared up out of the dust as though from a dream of terror. He gave them another long look, then turned and staggered on down the road and was gone.

With the same silence that had characterized their relationship to that point, Grant and Hypatia stood together and walked up the lane to the road. Squinting through the smoke and gloom and slanting evening shadows, they made him out where he stumbled along. One arm was cocked protectively to his chest like a hurt bird's wing, and he waved the other before him in the manner of a blindman.

Their faces as they watched him. She: motherhearted and quiet with a grief that drew hard lines about her mouth yet softened her round, almond eyes; he: silent and atremble with a newfound courage that allowed his hate to fist up his hands and bring out the weary veins in his forearms. Together they stood, not touching, and watched as Abel fell into the road again and did not rise.

They watched down the road. The white dust settled in the gloom. The whippoorwills began to call soft and low from the dark of the wood. Grant swore and walked down the road into the dark. Then he came back.

"He ain't dead," he said.

"Well," said Hypatia. With two fingers she delicately shifted about her damp dressfront. "Well," she said again.

Grant sighed. "Goddamnit. Just God damn it."

She nodded. "You may as well," she said. "He ain't goin' to do us no harm all busted up like that."

He did as she told him and brought the soldier into the cabin. He was very light and Grant handled him easily and together they tended him by firelight, their shadows antic on the wall behind. They cleaned the blood from his flesh to separate wound from waste and found the bullet where it had shorn up in his thigh, the snub, dark shape of it just below the skin of the off-side. The flesh there tight and hot and red. Hypatia cut the bullet from him with the blade of his own little pocketknife and bandaged the leg with strips torn from her dress. Then Grant rolled the soldier up so she could judge his hurt chest. As she cleaned carefully around the red mouth of the wound, she accidentally scraped his exposed rib with a fingernail and he whimpered in his sleep, shuddered, then settled again. It was not as bad as it looked, and when it was cleaned Hypatia tore more fabric from her woeful dress and wound it tightly around him. When they laid him back down before the fire he called out blindly for water and they gave him a sip from what they had. He called again for food but there was nothing to give and so they looked, instead, to his mangled, red-gloved arm.

She cleaned it as carefully as she had his other wounds, and when she saw the wreckage of the soldier's elbow she sighed and settled back on her hard, naked heels. She bid Grant to hold the soldier down and cocked her head, then worked the tip of her finger into the wound to feel the condition of the bone within. The soldier kicked soundlessly about as Hypatia felt along the path of the bullet, working her little finger into his arm nearly to the second joint. Then, with a sharp hiss, she drew it quickly out and flapped her hand through the air.

"What is it?" asked Grant. "What happened?"

Hypatia fisted her off-hand around her finger and made a face. After a few moments she looked at it and shook her head. "He's all broke up inside," she said. "Around the elbow, like I thought. Sliced myself on a hunk of bone somewhere in there." She hissed again, looked at her finger mournfully as she wiped it off, then picked up the soldier's pocketknife again.

She took a corner of an old rag they'd found in the cabin and began to carefully clean the blade, pushing long, curling strips of gummed blood from the helve with her thumbnail and polishing the blade itself until it sparkled in the firelight. After a time, she looked up at Grant and said, "Hold him tight now, he'll be kicking up a fuss."

Grant looked from Hypatia to the rebel and back again. And back and again once more, as though deciding how much of their care this man deserved. Finally, he sighed and grasped the soldier. Grant looked at her where she knelt, looking hard at the soldier's ruined arm in her lap. "Where'd you learn all this?" he asked.

She did not answer right away, and when she did her voice was soft. "I don't really know nothin' about anything," she said. "But I been told I got the knack by folk that was suffering. I'd help the surgeon when he come 'round where I run off from." She shrugged. "You hold him now," she instructed.

In the end, she saved the arm but not its use. The bullet had splayed and flattened against the bone, shattering and twisting into the tendons coiling like slick cables through the joint. Hypatia struggled for a long while to work the bullet out with the pocketknife as the soldier kicked and cried and shouted and wept but did not wake. She braced the shaft of the blade against her knuckle back and grasped the knob of his ulna where it split his skin while prying under the bullet with the point. When it finally dropped onto the floor, Hypatia put the bullet into one of the soldier's pockets, then stood to tear strips from her undergarments to bandage him with. Grant watched her, his face hot, but when she caught him looking he turned away to tend the fire.

Crouching like a hunter before the flames, he scraped old blood from his knuckles with a thumbnail and tried not to think of the boy he'd buried. After a while, the soldier woke and called for food and he heard Hypatia give a heavy sigh and then came the old,

familiar, heartbreaking rustle of clothing followed by a sound of feeding that he remembered coming from the candlelit corners of cabins where his master put new mothers.

Grant turned. He watched for only a moment as Hypatia held the wounded man's face to her bared breast. The soldier's eyes were closed, and so now, too, were her own. Her fingers were caught up in his hair as she smoothed his brow, and his good hand was fisted in the folds of her dress. His cheeks caved and his Adam's apple bobbed in his lean, grimy throat. Grant took a breath and walked out the door into the dark.

There was sound and light from the road where a column of men marched, their way lit by lanterns and torches. They did not sing as they marched, these men, and their officers urged them on in tones as hushed as they were urgent. Grant recognized them by their dark uniforms as Union men, and he stood on the porch watching them pass. Their steps in perfect union, their arms to shoulder, and even with the dust boiling up around their waists, he could see the piping on their trousers, the dull gleaming of brass eagles on their coats.

His mouth open with wonder and delight, Grant stepped off the porch into the lane. He did not call out, for his throat tightened and he choked off tears. The soldiers marched past, their shadows slanting through the Wilderness. They were black men, marching, and they held their weapons easily, as though without thought, as though they knew they'd earned the right, and they all stepped together through the night southward.

Grant stumbled down the lane as the last of them passed on the road. A man at the rear of the column spied him where he stood with his hands cupped before his belly in the manner of those witness to a precious thing that know not what to do with idle palms. This man, this black soldiering man, smiled easily and doffed his forage cap and gave it a little twirl like he was McClellan himself before settling it back onto his head. And then he was gone with the rest of them.

Grant stood alone in the road watching the torch lights flicker and fade in the black of the Wilderness. He listened to the steady, comforting, monotonous tramping of their feet fade into cricket song, the cries of the whippoorwills somewhere out in the dark. His face was wet and smoothed of care, his mouth open, his eyes wide and hands atremble.

He walked back to the cabin. He did not look at her but could tell by the air in the room that she'd fastened back up. The thin rebel lay asleep by the fire, the shadows making him look infinitely sad. Grant paused a moment to watch, then turned away and went to the desk and lifted the onion sack with the uniform and held it to his chest. He stood breathing with his face to the dark wall.

"You're goin' with them, ain't you?" she said.

"Yes," he said.

"It's all right," she said softly. "You go on do that."

Grant turned to look at her. Her face had thinned since the day he met her, and little streaks of fresh sweat cut through the pale dust on her forehead and upper lip. She managed a smile and he took a deep breath and looked hard at her. "Ain't I a man?" he asked. "Still?"

Hypatia nodded. "Yes," she said. "Yes, you is."

He looked over at the soldier, then back at her. "Then goddamnit, Hypatia, I—" He gaped fishwise, then looked away again. "Just goddamnit. God damn it."

"Another time, maybe," she said. "Some other time it would've all been different. We could have been something another time, maybe."

He looked her in the eye and finally said, "Nah. There never was any way, and there ain't never goin' to be another time. I know it and you do too." And when she looked away, he smiled tightly and nodded while she took a single, shuddery breath, then smiled back at him. "Well," he said, drawing breath. "All right then. You goin' to be all right here, girl?"

"Go on," she said softly. "I seen 'em through the window, and the way they was marchin', you goin' to fall behind lessen you scoot."

He bent and took her hand, pausing a moment to look at their two hands joined there in the flickering light. Her cinnamon wrist-back wrapped in his dark fingers. They looked into each other's eyes, and he leaned and kissed her lips, pressed the dead man's revolver into her hand, straightened, and walked out the door.

He stepped into the cool dark. He heard horses on the road, and he stripped and put on the uniform. It fit him well, and for a moment he longed for a looking glass. As he strode out into the road, Grant wondered where he'd find a musket, and then the horses were upon him. A Union officer asked was he of Ferrero's Division, and Grant answered yes and the officer cursed him roundly for laziness and for the color of his skin and for his African heritage and for a general lack of intellect. Then the horseman helped Grant climb painfully up behind him, and they galloped together on up the road until they vanished into the Wilderness.

# NINE

## *Makers' Acres*

### *1899*

HE WAS ALREADY two days late getting back, and she had, thusly, already two days' more worry than she should have had. Fretting deepened the lines about her eyes and at the corners of her mouth. And when she heard the sound of gunfire crackling up out of the nightdark valley like the sound of fire on wet wood, Ellen Makers stood quickly from the rough table in their cabin to stare through the paned window. Her breath shallowed as she set the paring knife down near the wooden bowl of apples, touching the blade with two fingers to turn it from the table edge. Earlier, she'd dusted half the table with flour to keep the dough from sticking, and now Ellen stood staring at the strange designs of finger pad, thumb, and palm heel drawn there. A strange language, unpronounceable and sad.

She stood listening. The little pygmy owl that had been calling from the dark of the slope behind the cabin had flown or, perhaps, merely quieted at the dull, metallic echo of violence. Ellen took her lower lip between her teeth, took air to fill her lungs, and stepped out the front door onto the covered porch, where the cold night had gathered shadows from the forest and laid them in a star-strewn sheet across the sky.

From somewhere down in the valley, a dog barked savagely and wild, then fell quiet again. And another, distant shot with its attendant echo. Ellen stood listening until the fading sound was joined by a wolf's howl from the pitchblack far away. She turned quickly, eyes wide, one hand white upon the porch rail, and tilted her face toward the mountains like a blind woman. But there was no other sound to hear—only the soft, silvery splashing of the Little Sugar Creek where it flipped and danced through the trees on the lee side of the ridgeline.

Thoughtfully, Ellen set her fingers to her lips and waited for what more might come. She'd been paring the last of the apples and smelled cinnamon and juice on her fingers, so touched them to her tongue one by one to taste the aftersweetness of a vanished summer. Just before the gunfire there had been a star shower, and she had seen them falling by the dozens. Bright streaks across the night, and she had rested her chin on clasped hands to watch them prayerwise as they flared and fell and faded and were gone. And as the last star vanished beyond the far rim of the world, the gunfire began.

And now the night was still and cold and quiet. A few thin clouds drifted sluggishly amidst the twinkling stars. A fat portion of moon hung left of center in the night, but Ellen could not recall its proper name, only that it was neither full nor crescentic. Ellen sighed. Her breath appeared and vanished and appeared again. She reckoned the moon might soon pull another frost from the ground, might limn the dead, stiff grass in a hard, white shell and mark precisely the Byzantine curls of moss and fern, the curling leaves of weeds wilting along the lane. In two weeks, maybe, the frost would freeze hard, inches down into the soil, and turn their landscape wintery—hard, silver, joyously beautiful.

Taking another deep breath, Ellen stepped down into the yard to walk the path to the lane and thence to the edge of the long, easy hill that looked down into the dark valley. The lane ran pale and untroubled to the first curve and was lost in the tall firs and shadows they hoarded to their trunks. She leaned against the fence post and the sign upon it that Glenn had carved and painted and that read: "Makers' Acres." Smiling softly, she remembered the day and his fierce joy over the sign, their land, and their first payment upon it. To her right, something went skittering across the roof of the tool-shed and into the trees. Squirrel or night bird or some other thing. Ellen watched in that direction for a time, eyes straining in the dark, and when nothing showed itself she turned and made her way back to the porch.

Rubbing her forearms to hoard her warmth, she stood with her arms crossed against the cold for a half hour, but there was nothing else to hear now save the owl when it started in again, calling softly, softly from its shadowed woods.

Ellen finally went back inside to blow out the lamps until all within the cabin was dark save the smoldering hearth fire, where it glowed to cast a flickering red light upon the walls and furniture. She stood in the center of the room, regarding the speckled little coals, then drew a breath and put on more wood.

She went about the cabin in the firelit dark: the three rooms, touching things absently, righting books on their shelves, blowing motes of dust from atop counters, fussing with the way Glenn's second pair of trousers hung from their peg on the bedroom wall. After a time of this, she stopped before the cabinet near the door, where they kept the second rifle.

Flames crackled from the hearth and softly lit the room. Ellen opened the cabinet and took out the gun and broke it to be sure of the shell, then set it down again beside the door and turned away. Dragging the chair from the table, she set it on the porch, then drew a dipper of water from the rain barrel, filled the teapot, and waited while it boiled. She did not look at the rifle again. Ellen brewed herself a mug of strong coffee and stepped back out onto the porch.

Setting the coffee on the porch boards beside the chair, she retrieved the rifle, and shut the front door so no light would reveal her to anyone on the lane. She sat straight with the rifle crosswise on her knees and touched it no more. She sat waiting, leaning now and again to lift the coffee to her lips and feel its bitter warmth trickle down the center of her. Seep slowly down her limbs and put heat in her belly.

And with the rifle came the sudden, unwanted remembrance of bright, tearing pain as they held her down and worked the cold barrel into her. Their greasy stink and their damp, rough hands and their outsize shadows rearing wildly on the tent wall.

Ellen put a palm to her stomach and tried to imagine how she'd once been. "Damn it, Glenn," she said, her breath a hushed, feathery plume on the cold, starlit air. "You come home to me."

Ellen Makers sat in the cold with the rifle ready on her lap. Listening. The little owl called quietly. A soft wind came up the long slope from the valley floor. Trees creaked and shed needles; she could hear them falling like strange rain tap-tapping into the moss. The understory was rife with movement. She sipped her coffee and took an apple wedge from her dress pocket. By starlight, she looked at the backs of her hands where the bones ran wrist-to-knuckle like rake tines, like the hard implements of labor they were. By starlight, her tough hands seemed luminous, aglow, as though built of light. She wondered if she was old as all that. Maybe not. Perhaps she'd not yet begun the slow, hard decline she knew would quicken as the years passed. She pressed her palm forcefully against her belly as had become her custom since they'd ruined her, as though to divine the broken, torn places inside and set them right again. But then a sound rose from the bottom of the hill where the lane ran into the road.

It was a wagon coming along—she could tell that much from the soft rattle of loose boards and the softer knocking of hooves upon the packed earth. Ellen put by her fear and set her hands upon the rifle. Standing from the chair, she strained with listening, but there was no voice to hear or recognize, so she put the chair out of her way and held on to the rifle.

She stood waiting, trembling a little now. The wagon came through the dark, coming steadily between the trees that flanked the pale road, and she began to tell its shape where those trees thinned before finally opening into the yard. A dark, boxy thing moving slowly along. She pursed her lips and gulped air.

A dog ran out of the brush beside the cabin and stopped before the porch with its head cocked and its breath smoking the air around its muzzle. Ellen raised the rifle, quickly and without thought, and sighted down the barrel, then looked around it, frowning. The dog barked once and without menace, and she knew it then for a dog she somehow recognized, so lowered the gun once more.

And then the wagon was pulling in beside the shed and she heard Glenn's voice—quiet, deep, with that soft, melodious quality of calm assurance she so loved. He spoke to Emerson, telling him what a good horse he was, his voice all the while so quiet as to be more whispery emotion than true speech.

Ellen went quickly down the steps into the yard. She could sense that something was not yet right, even though he was home, and so took the rifle with her. But then he was down from the wagon and she could see his teeth in the dark and his open arms. His white shirt flashing beneath his dark fall coat. She went to him who was her husband and he put his arms around her and she tilted her forehead into the hollow of his neck. His scent enclosed her and she released her breath. They stood so, together, for a long moment with only the moon and wild stars to light them and were quiet.

And then she stepped back with one palm flat to his chest. "What is it?" she asked. She blinked and her pale hand darted to his dark, swollen face. "Glenn," she breathed. "What did they do to you?"

Glenn Makers took her slim white hand in his own two dark and put his lips against her palm where he could smell cinnamon and apples. "I'm sorry," he whispered.

She looked at him and sighed and kissed his hurts and they were silent together again.

There came a soft groan from the back of the wagon, and the dog, forgotten, began barking furiously.

"What is it?" she asked, peering past Glenn's shoulder toward the bed of the wagon. "I heard gunshots."

Glenn opened his mouth and shut it again. The dog barked and paced. Glenn turned toward it then looked back at her. "It's that old man," he said. "It's Abel Truman." And he went around to the back of the wagon and lifted Abel in his arms as easily as if he were a child.

Glenn carried him to the back room while Ellen relit the lamps and bore one after them down the dark hall. They had no second bed or cot, so she spread thick blankets on the floor for Glenn to gentle the old man down upon. There was nothing else in the little room save a small table where Ellen set the lamp. As they stood looking at him, their hands sought each other's through the shadows and their fingers hooked thoughtlessly after the fashion of those long together in love. The old man's eyes were closed, and his chest rose and fell steadily, a faint, wet gurgle high in his throat and soft whistle with each out-breath.

"What happened to him?" Ellen finally asked.

"Hell if I know." Glenn shrugged. "I think he's sick. Hurt, but sick too. Leastways, he sounded it earlier." He looked at her. "You heard the gunfire?" he asked, glancing in the direction of the gun cabinet. When she told him yes, he nodded and told her how he'd found the old man and shrugged again as though there were other things that needed saying that would keep until later.

Ellen let go his hand and squeezed his arm. "But you're all right?"

"Ah, they weren't shooting at me." She looked at him sharply, and he grinned and nodded. "Well, I might've gotten a little banged up in town, but they tell me Farley got worse than what he tried to give."

"Glenn . . . He's going to be the death of you."

He touched the pads of his fingers to her lips, then leaned to gently kiss her forehead. "It's over and it's done and it's nothing for you to worry yourself over," he said. "It's nothing now and wasn't much of anything to start with."

Abel groaned wearily in his sleep and smacked his lips. Ellen squatted near the old man's feet, pushed her hair back from her face, and began to unlace his boots where they were stiff with mud and tight with old rains soaked and dried into the leather. Wrinkling her nose, she put a hand over her mouth. "Good Lord above," she breathed. "When do you reckon this man bathed last?" she asked the air, then stood and rolled up her sleeves. Looking at Glenn, she said, "Why don't you go on put up Emerson and bring the things in while I settle him." He nodded and she watched him leave the room. After a few moments she heard his footsteps crunching through the icy grass, could hear him speaking alternately to horse and dog.

Ellen finally levered Abel's boots from his feet and paired them by the wall. The old man had been traveling sockless, and his ankles were ringed with raw sores where the old leather rubbed bare flesh. Remembering the teapot, she fetched it and added to it and brought back with her a bowl and some clean cloth. Kneeling beside him again, she washed his feet. She washed Abel's hands and cleaned his fingers and slipped his thin coat from his hunched shoulders. Curls of steam stood from the bowl. Ellen's strong fingers worked loose the buttons of his shirt, and she gasped to see the varicolored bruises chaining the old man's chest, the little maps of blood that had dried to hard ridges along the lines of old white scars—a lifetime of hurting plotted there for any to follow who could read such charts. Ellen peered at the bruises and the long, stitched cut arcing redly down his face, then pursed her lips thoughtfully. "Someone's been caring for you," she told his sleeping face. "I'm glad." Then, clucking her tongue, she continued washing him. Abel's lips moved and his eyes jerked beneath their lids. He whimpered in his sleep as she washed his back, and when she settled him down again he yawned widely and silent before falling back into a deeper sleep.

Ellen released her breath and mastered her nausea. She cleaned the road dust from his crow's feet and from the deep lines at the corners of his mouth, his sad face pale and shrunken-looking where his beard had been shaved. By the time she'd finished, Glenn had brought the supplies in—stacking boxes and small crates, bags and canvas sacks filled with oil and saw blades, potatoes, onions, and flour, extra linen, and all the other makings for the long winter—and was done with what outside chores he could do by moonlight. He'd stoked the fire for the night, banking the coals to keep back the cold, and it was after two o'clock in the morning and even the little owl had gone quiet.

Ellen shut the back room door and she and Glenn walked word-lessly together to the bedroom to undress by what little star- and moonlight filtered through the windowdrapes. She: pale and wan by darkness. He: a splinter of shadow and warm. They embraced silently before putting on bedclothes—flesh to flesh and pressed tightly along the lengths of their bodies and their mouths fast upon one another. Silent but for the moistness of lips and tongues and the dry, cool drag of fingertips on flesh. And after, still silent and now clothed for sleeping, they slipped beneath the covers and lay quietly together. The soft hush of the wind blew over the eaves and they could hear it in the forest as it passed through the trees. After a while, he asked into the dark, "Did you . . ." He stopped and sighed and went on haltingly, "What I mean is, are you . . ."

She put her hand to her stomach and pressed. "No," she told him. "I'm not expecting. I was only . . . late. It's mostly done now, I think."

She felt him nod, and he told her how sorry he was, as though that would help. He took her hand and held it in his own and said nothing more at all and she stayed silent in the soft, cool dark beside him until he was asleep. She felt his warmth all along her side and in the quiet moments before sleep she fancied she could hear, too, the sound of his blood within his body—ancient, African, noble, fast, and hot—as it rushed through the fine, thin veins of his arms and his neck and legs and in his belly through to the very center of him. The largeness of him seemed to cast a warm, soft glow over her in the dark, and she wondered, could he ever hear her blood? The fast, nervous thrum as it raced through her? Slowly, half shy, Ellen cupped his sex in her palm, holding it there a long time before drawing back her hand and making a tight fist against her belly as though to push his fierce, slow heat into her for keeping as she would. She desperately needed to warm the hollow cold they'd put inside her along with the gun barrel that summer's night beside the tide-swollen river. And when she finally slept, it was only a light sleep peppered by dreams that twisted the sheets about her legs.

Ellen woke. Beside her, Glenn breathed softly, dreaming his own dreams and of what she had no inkling. She stepped from the bed into the dull, dark cold and went to the front door. The dog came inside and turned three tight circles before the hearth, where the backlog had burned down to red coals, sighing softly as it settled before the heat. Ellen stood watching it for a time before finally returning to bed and sleeping a sleep dreamless and deep.

Abel did not wake all the next day, and the hard frost that Ellen had expected did not come. Instead, the day dawned to a sky darkly clouded and the rain came lightly back. The sky was a puzzle of clouds of gray and darker gray. And through the woods came the sound of water falling, running, dripping upon the trees and through the trees and beneath the trees where it ran in little rivulets that lifted burnt-colored pine needles and sent them flowing into Little Sugar Creek and thence down into the green, fog-bound valley.

Glenn spent that day resting and chopping wood for winter—an activity that was, for him, a sort of rest itself where he could lose himself in the easy motion of his arms. Lifting the axe, letting it fall precisely where he wanted into the wood with great thunking sounds, then wrenching it free, lifting and letting fall again and again. The sound of the axe on the wood like the sound of the season's own heart. For her part, Ellen swept out the cabin while she listened to Glenn. She shooed Abel's dog outside and beat the dander from the rug on which it slept. She mended the holes in the knees of Abel's trousers and used cold water, salt, and extract of lemon to scrub the blood from his shirt where it had spotted in designs strange and repugnant. A story of violence there that she had no desire to read.

After a time, she went to the back room where the old man lay sleeping and stood looking down at him. A rank smell had settled into the room, fouling the air and tainting the curtains. Ellen thought, suddenly, of her father and the way he'd died—from the inside out and so slowly you could smell death in him like turned meat, as though his very pores exhaled it. The flesh itself, her father's flesh that had rocked her to sleep and brushed her hair and held her close during storms when it seemed the very world would end, had turned suddenly contrary. Had tightened and loosened, moistened and dried, and, in the end, shuddered all on its own like horsehide touched by flies. His flesh imposed its will upon his mind and he'd gone to sleep and never woke, her father when he died, and Ellen had come to reckon that as about the only part of his sickness that was kindly in the least.

And even though she'd washed him the night before, Abel still looked roadsore and dirty. He'd woken enough at some point to use the night jar she'd set out for him, and Ellen carried it to the outhouse. The stink of age and strange food. When she returned she brought with her a small sack and the scissors and she knelt on the floor beside the old man's head. Lifting a hank of his long, metal-colored hair, she rubbed it between her fingers. It was not soft and smelled like the smokes of countless cooking fires. It hung limp and bedraggled to his shoulders and was, on the whole, impossibly dirty and ill-kept, matted and shot through with all manner of dirt and moss and pine needles, bits of mud and tiny stones and other matter that she hoped was merely mud and tiny stones. Clumps of things snarled the ends like decorative beads or small, strange berries. "Looks to me like you're about half tree," she told him, shaking her head.

Ellen clucked her tongue and began to cut back Abel's hair. It was slow work and she cut it back to finger-width so it stood straight and bristly from his scalp. When she finished, Ellen fetched and warmed a bowl of water and washed what hair remained, feeling the hard ridges of scar tissue that, even here, laced his skull like the stitching of a well-used ball. "It's a good thing your dog's away and you're sleeping," she told him. "Elsewise neither of you would let me near."

That night, Ellen let the dog indoors again. It followed her down the hall to the back room and when she opened the door it went inside where the old man still lay sleeping. Sniffing the floor cautiously all around him, it licked his ears and face and, as Ellen watched, turned three circles and settled down on the corner of the blanket just beside him. Shaking her head, she shut the door and went to the bedroom where Glenn lay waiting for her.

They held hands beneath the covers in the dark. Glenn lay on his back, staring at the shadowed ceiling, and Ellen knew what needed discussing and knew, also, that she would have to be the one to broach the subject, speak aloud the decision each had already separately made but neither had yet found the voice for. She took a breath and squeezed his hand. "We can't turn him out," she said softly, addressing the dark. "We both know it. Even if we don't want him here."

Glenn sighed deeply and long as though a great weight had been lifted from him. "I know," he said, his voice deep and soft and close as shadows. "I know it."

And then silence came between them, broken only later when Ellen said, "I think he's sick." She shook her head in the dark. "No," she said. "I don't think it. I know it. I can smell it. I think he's dying."

She felt Glenn nod. "I know that too."

She wet her lips. "But?"

"But what?"

"You tell me. You say it."

He let go her hand and cradled his head with laced fingers, still staring upward through the dark. "You're right, we can't turn him out. Not with winter coming."

Ellen sighed. "Do you really think he'd stay? That he'd even want to? To settle for that little room?"

"Do you think he can do much more?" asked Glenn. And then, softly, "No. No, I don't. But what can we do? . . . What I'll do," he said, thinking aloud. "What I'll do is tell him I need help clearing the upper field. Which I do. He could drive the wagon back and forth, if nothing else."

"He won't," said Ellen. "Granted, I don't know him well, nor do I really want to, but a man like that driving for you? He couldn't conceive of it, I'm sure." She sighed. "When he wakes," she said with a certain, heavy resignation, "I'll offer him the room for the winter. That's all we can do and that's what we *have* to do. We'll offer the room, and he can decide on his own."

"You don't think we should force him? For his own good?"

"I don't, and we couldn't," she said. "There's his good and the world's and then there's ours. Our good, Glenn. It might not be Christian, but I don't care. If it comes to it, ours has got to win out over his, over the world's. After everything we've . . ." Ellen took a fast, hot breath and Glenn took up her hand and pressed his lips to each of her knuckles in its turn. She watched his shadow in the dark beside her—how he moved, the soft rustling of fabric as he shed his union suit. The sudden warmth of him pressed flush against her. His fingers at her knees, bunching the nightdress around her hips, and the cool kiss of wintery air upon her flesh.

And she was conscious of her own breath and his, suddenly synchronous. Their frantic pulses of blood beating in time as their tired, hurt hearts thrashed against each other with only thin walls of flesh and bone to keep them separate. She opened her eyes, trembling in the soft, cool dark, and saw his sad, lonely face hovering close. His eyes closed and his face held as though he'd weep. She said his name and he told her he loved her. "Can you see me?" she whispered against his ear. "Can you feel my skin?" He told her yes and yes and their hands fisted together atop the sheets as though struggling quietly, desperately. But before it was beautifully finished things went all wrong within her as they often did and she cried out, pushed him back. Away. Kicking the sheets from her legs and her legs pale and thin in the dark where they were tucked under her. She clawed at the wall beside the bed and scuttled into the corner, covering her face and trying to will away their smell, the old, cold feel of the gun barrel going into her.

Glenn covered his eyes with his forearm and breathed deeply until his heart had slowed. He knew better than to talk or try and touch her, so lay instead damning them for what they'd done and damning himself because he'd not been there to stop them doing it. Ellen wept. She told him she was sorry, and after a time he sat up

and held out his hand and after a time she took it and without another word they lay back down together.

She lay, telling him how she loved him, and he answered. Their
hearts slowed, the sweat and tears evaporated from their flesh into the
dark cold—rising through the shadows and through the roof and on
into the clouds where they would, days hence, fall again as rain upon
the town below and the townsfolk would look up from their lives,
suddenly melancholy and for what reason they would never know.
And finally, in the cold, moonshot dark, Glenn and Ellen fell asleep
and dreamed dreams quiet and weary and sad.

Down the hall, Abel woke in the dark. He could hear their urgent, soft, grief-struck lovemaking and could hear them when they
fell apart. At the change of his breath, the dog rose and licked the
side of his face. Abel grinned and swore softly and when he finally
did fall back to sleep it was with his good arm outflung over the dog,
fingers curling into the soft fur behind its ear.

The next morning, Glenn rose early. The rain had ceased and the
sky was gray, charged with a high wind that you sensed more than
felt. He hiked to the upper field to judge the work that needed doing, calculating two men's labor against the scant days remaining
before the first snowfall. Ellen stayed behind to warm water on the
stove for bathing. It was cool and she spent some little time coaxing
flames from the ash-hidden coals. By the time the fire was crackling
the water was warm, and she cupped her pale hands into the pot to
raise the awkward bowl of her palms to her face. Running wet fingers through her brown hair until her face and neck and scalp were
damp, she was lost for the briefest of moments in the pleasant steam,
the water's soft warmth. When next she looked up, Abel stood with
his dog just without the room in the dark of the hall, looking studiously at the floor with his old boots in his hands.

When he sensed her eyes on him, the old soldier looked up and grinned lopsidedly. Wincing a little, he ran a hand over his shorn head. "I'll be damned if every time I wake up anymore someone hasn't barbered me," he said softly.

Ellen smiled and Abel nodded and ducked his head and pressed his tongue to the inside of his cheek. The deeply callused soles of his bare feet rasped on the swept floorboards like shy whispers. After a few silent moments, they both raised their voices to speak, then both fell quiet again. Abel raised a palm. "You go on," he said.

Ellen nodded. "I was just going to ask how you were feeling. You've had us worried."

"Yes ma'am, I reckon I was pretty worn out. Still a mite woozy, but I do feel one whole lot better'n I did." Sniffing, he looked at her. "Must've been you who doctored me?"

Ellen nodded, plucking up a towel and pressing her damp hair into it. "I didn't do all that much, really. Just cleaned you up a bit and gave you a little trim." She patted her forehead with the towel and dried her cheeks, then raised her chin. "That cut on your face looks like it's healing pretty well. Whoever stitched it did a good job."

Abel touched the long cut that ran the length of his face. "That was old Charley Poole and his kin," he said, nodding. "Like Glenn, they come crost me when I was in a bad way."

Ellen set the towel aside and looked at the old man. "Glenn said he found you in the woods north of town."

"That could be," said Abel. "And I'm obliged to both of you." He looked down at the dog where it sat next to him, leaning against his leg and dampening a spot on his trousers with its wet panting. "And for takin' in this fool, too."

Ellen shook her head. "It's nothing," she said. "But it looks to me like someone beat you."

"Yes, ma'am," said Abel, looking away. "I reckon it would. I reckon they have been."

Ellen sighed heavily and crossed her arms. "Abel Truman," she said. "What happened to you?"

The old man stared off into the corner of the room. He whistled flatly through his teeth. After a moment, he reached down and scratched behind the dog's ears, then looked back up at Ellen. "Ah," he said. "That'd be a long tale."

She pursed her lips and stared at him until he shuffled his feet and shrugged. "We run afoul of brigands," he finally said, nodding to include the dog.

She looked from the old man's face to the dog's and back again. "Brigands?" she asked, raising her fingers to her lips to cover the smile forming there.

"Well," said Abel, shrugging again. "They was bad men, sure enough."

Ellen's smile faded and she nodded. "There are a few of those about," she said.

Abel squinted at her and raised his chin. "I reckon I'll step outside, if you don't mind," he said. "Pull on my boots and take the air."

Ellen nodded again. "I tucked some socks down into them for you," she told him. "You'd better go on and put those on too."

Abel blinked rapidly with surprise, then felt inside the boots and smiled. As he went to the door, Ellen stepped aside, and as he passed her, she caught again the faint, metallic whiff of something gone or going wrong within him and for just a moment she was unbearably sad. Taking a quick, deep breath through her mouth to master herself, she squared her shoulders, and as Abel opened the door the ferrous odor disappeared with the cool air that rushed in.

The old man turned in the open door and looked back at the dog where it still sat in the hall with its mouth open, looking at Ellen. "What're you grinnin' at, dumbass?" he asked it. "This nice lady don't want you. Now you come on here now." Abel slapped his thigh twice and the dog stretched its front legs out, raising its hindquarters and squinting with a pleasurable stretch. "Look at you," said Abel with mock disgust, shaking his head as the dog trotted leisurely out the door. "You are pitiful, is what you are."

Before following, Abel turned to Ellen and raised his hand as though to tug down on the brim of his hat, but he was bareheaded so only frowned briefly, then nodded to her and closed the door.

Abel Truman stepped across the Makers' porch and sat upon the top step. The day was overcast but not too cold, and Abel reckoned that on clear days the Makerses had a view that stretched over the trees and gentle foothills to the distant ocean. Trees rose through the fog like strange steeples, their trunks looming as though some great, quiet city existed there in the fog without motion or sound. Abel closed his eyes while the dog scampered off, and when he opened them again, Ellen was crouched beside him on the step with her wet hair pushed back behind her ears so it hung in dark ringlets below the sharp hinges of her jaw. She smelled of soap, and Abel blinked rapidly.

"Are you all right?" she asked, settling a hand upon his shoulder.

Abel cleared his throat loudly. It became a harsh, hot cough that doubled him over and chased tears into his eyes. He wheezed, though he tried hard not to, and when it was done with him he spat to the side and apologized. Ellen shook her head and handed him his old slouch hat. "You left that in . . . in your room," she told him.

"Goddamn," murmured Abel, taking the hat from her. Grinning his pleasure, he blocked out the crown with his fist and turned it about by the brim, marveling. "Well, I just knew I'd lost it some-wheres," he said, snugging it down on his head, settling and situating it slightly front and back to account for his haircut.

Ellen set a mug of coffee on the step beside him along with a little wooden box painted with Chinese dragons in red and gold. "I thought it might have been awhile since you had a decent cup of coffee," she said, then nodded to the box. "Let alone tobacco."

Abel looked at the coffee. He smelled it on the damp air and wiped his eyes, for a fierce heat suddenly troubled them. As Ellen turned to go back inside, Abel shifted on the step and found his voice. "But I couldn't take none of Glenn's 'bacca, could I?"

She paused at the door and looked back at the old man. Very small and worn he perched, half in tears over the prospect of coffee and tobacco. "Glenn doesn't use it much," she told him, waving her palm. "You go on, help yourself." She nodded and winked. "Glenn'll be down from the field in a little while and we'll all have some breakfast then and talk things over a little. Is that all right with you?"

Abel ducked his head and nodded. Ellen returned the nod with one of her own and went back into the cabin.

Left alone again, Abel took a deep breath and drug his palm down his face. He scowled to remember his beard was gone, then picked up the little box of makings and stared off into the forest. Distantly, he heard the dog barking and Glenn calling to it. Abel smiled and set the box to the side. He lifted the coffee and held the mug by its base in his damaged hand, cupped it with his good one and put his face over the white china rim, closing his eyes to the rich scent and letting it conjure what memories it would. All those unbidden recollections suddenly fine and easy and bright there in the cool morning air. He sipped the coffee and, for the first time in a long while, enjoyed his thoughts. And after a while, Glenn came along the uphill trail beyond the tool shed.

Abel watched him cross the yard and bid him good morning when he drew near. Glenn nodded in return and settled down on the step beside him, setting the veiny slabs of his forearms on the peaks of his knees and clasping his work-raw hands together in the air before him. They sat together silently and Abel sipped the coffee. In the cabin behind, they could hear Ellen moving about, and presently there came the sound and smells of breakfast cooking—the clatter of crockery upon the wooden table, a sizzling in the pan, and the soft, unbearably clean, fine scent of broken eggs. After a while longer Abel said, "She seems well."

Glenn nodded, pursed his lips, then nodded again. "She does," he said.

"They ever catch 'em?"

Glenn filled his cheeks and blew. "No," he said. "But I don't figure they're still around. If they were, even old Jensen would've found 'em by now." He unlaced his fingers then laced them again, trying by small movements not to think of any of it, though, in truth, there was seldom a moment that he wasn't turning it all over again in his mind. As though it was the punishment for his tardiness that day, it came constantly back, kinking and tangling in his mind like fencing wire that's slipped the post.

He recalled paying cash for the down payment on the land and how carefully he folded the paper receipt into his breast pocket. He remembered making a proud show of it in Wheelock afterward so everyone could see he'd finished a legal transaction and by God this land was his now, and he remembered felling trees for three months straight. And then came a warm spring, a hot summer. Nights spent in a mud-spattered canvas tent beside the river at the edge of town as they resupplied. They could hear at night the soft crashing of the ocean beyond the forest and knew its constant presence by the rise and fall of the river in its bank. And Glenn remembered that last week in August when he spent the night alone on the property, hurrying the cabin along, getting it ready to receive them while Ellen waited for him in the tent beside the river swollen by the tide.

They came in the night while he was away, their boot prints crazing the mud along the riverbank and not a man in Wheelock willing to follow them the next morning save Jensen, who knew little in the way of tracking. Glenn remembered how he'd found her on the floor of the tent, her thighs smeared with blood, her eyes wide without sleep or thought. She didn't speak for six days after, and on the seventh she wept. Some nights, Glenn's dreaming mind still recalled the blood on the tent wall where they'd written the word "mudshark" and how he'd naively turned to Jensen, who said past his stained mustache, "What some fools call a white woman who lays with a black man." And then the rage; the great, hot, red, dirty rage that unmanned him until they'd struck him a blow on the temple and he fell into the dark.

On their great, grand moving-in day, Jensen was with them and stood beside the wagon, his fingers absently wrapped up in Emerson's mane, telling them how sorry he was, how there was nothing for it but to put it behind them, that they were most likely long gone and not coming back. And finally, Glenn remembered leaning over to wrap his fist into the front of the sheriff's coat and saying very softly, "It shouldn't be hard. You just keep looking until you find the son of a bitch with a bloody rifle barrel and you point him out to me." And Jensen had eyed him and stepped back as they left for their new home, on their own land, mud from the churning wagon wheels flying through the air like dark, cast-off chains.

Glenn stood. He stretched and squeezed shut his eyes. Opened them again. He felt the blood, fast and hot, in his arms, and his face was warm with the old anger he'd grown to know so well. Taking a deep breath, he looked down at Abel. "You not smoking?" he asked the old man.

Abel shrugged and grinned in a small way. "Not that I wouldn't like to," he said. "But I ain't even used to this coffee yet. I want to be careful of all this rich living." He grinned until Glenn gave back a small smile in return, then stood from the step.

Stretching his arms over his head, Glenn groaned softly and said, "Well, I'm going to see a man about a horse," and walked toward the outhouse where it stood screened by filmy curtains of hanging moss at the base of a giant fir.

Abel stood and said his name and Glenn turned. The old man set his lips together and nodded solemnly. "I am obliged, Glenn," he said quietly. He ran his palm over his close-shorn scalp and smirked. "To both of you."

Glenn looked at the old man standing on the step so small and feeble, nodded, said nothing, and turned away.

The breakfast was eggs and potatoes flavored with shavings of wild onion and flecks of pepper, served simply and hot on thick slabs of crockery etched with blue floral designs. The three of them ate in silence until Glenn slapped the table suddenly and touched his forehead. "Lord God," he said with quiet urgency. "I almost forgot."

Ellen's eyes went round with sudden fear, and she looked to the window and the gun cabinet, then back again to Glenn's face. For his part, Abel patted his lips with his napkin, then fisted it in his good hand and waited.

Looking up at his wife, Glenn saw her face and held up a palm. "No," he said quickly. "No. It's nothing really."

"Then what?" asked Ellen.

"Before I left town," he said, chasing bits of food from about his gums with the point of his tongue. "I met up with a family of Chinese that were going to try and make it over the pass before the snows."

Ellen frowned and Abel opened his mouth to comment on the danger of such a course at this time of year, and Glenn raised his palm again. "I tried to talk them out of it," he said. "I did. But I think Farley put some kind of scare into them. At any rate, I thought I'd gotten their promise to stop here before they tried it." He looked at Ellen and raised his eyebrows.

Ellen shook her head and glanced through the little kitchen window toward the Olympics, where they slumped hugely northward in shades of pale blue and white. "I heard a wolf howl the other night, but nobody's passed by that I saw," she said.

"Damn it," sighed Glenn, resting his chin on the dark bridge of his two linked hands. "I'm not sure that I shouldn't go looking for them." Pursing his lips, he stabbed a bit of egg with his fork and looked thoughtfully at it where it quivered on the tines. After a moment, he looked up at her again. "Wolf?" he asked.

Ellen nodded. "The night you got back."

Glenn frowned deeply. "Are you sure it wasn't Abel's dog carrying on?" he asked, lifting his chin in the old man's direction.

She shook her head. And Abel set his napkin down and cleared his throat, then picked it back up and held it before his lips as he coughed. They watched his face go red, but when Glenn made to rise and help, Abel shook his head and set his upper arm over his mouth. Clearing his throat again, he apologized and said, "Them fellers that took Buster was hunting a dog they thought was half wolf that got away from them, they said." He looked at Ellen and grinned weakly. "Them brigands," he said.

Glenn looked at him. "They lost a wolf?"

Abel nodded. "Crossbred, they said. Dog fighters. It tore one of them up pretty good."

Ellen looked to her husband as he set down his napkin and stood from the table. "Glenn," she said. "What are you doing?"

He wiped his mouth and leaned over her to kiss her forehead. "There's a blowdown across the crick down by the road I need to clear," he said, squinting to the toolshed. "I reckon I'll go work on that."

"That's not what I mean."

"I know it." He went to the door. When Abel stood to accompany him, Glenn motioned him down again, saying, "This'll be just a one-man job, I think. Two'd just get in the way of each other. Besides, I need to think on things." He looked at Ellen a long moment and she returned the look and then he was outside, where presently they heard him loading tools into the wagon and harnessing Emerson.

Abel ate slowly. He held his fork as though made uncomfortable by it, and when Ellen questioned his appetite the old man quickly said, "Oh no, it ain't that, ma'am." He sniffed and blinked wearily and smiled. "I'm just still a mite bit tired and I'd forgotten that people do this. Eat this way. Meals and such where they set down together whatnot."

"Well," said Ellen, smiling at him. "It's what we like to do."

Abel's head bobbed as he swallowed. "I like it," he said. "I think it's good. I did notice you-all didn't say no Grace, though."

Ellen pursed her lips and nodded. "You're right. I suppose that's a custom we've more or less let fall by the wayside here on Hard-scrabble Mountain."

Abel looked out the window with his brow furrowed then squinted over at her. "That ain't the name of this hill," he said.

She smiled. "No," she admitted, shaking her head. "But that's what Glenn started calling it right after we moved in. He said now he knew how President Grant must have felt, only more so." She grinned wide with that one delicious memory amidst all the other badness of that time but did not share or linger over it and after a few moments asked, "Are you a religious man, Mr. Truman?"

Abel pushed back his plate with his thumb and rested his elbow on the table. Moving his shoulders about, he winced a little as though the frayed and atrophied places within his arm were troubling him, and seemed to think the question over a long moment before answering. "I have been once, I suppose," he said. "I don't reckon there's a man born who can claim he's never prayed for one thing or another." Abel smiled and shook his head. "'Specially when he's got some other man shooting a gun at him." Sitting back, he cocked his head and stared off into the middle distance. "In the war . . . ," he went on slowly, "it seemed like every other son of a bitch . . . pardon me, ma'am. But it seemed like every other fella you run into could quote you Scripture up, down, and crossways—we even had us a fella was named Scripture—but I never could. It just never did stick with me."

Ellen nodded. "It must have been quite a thing."

"Ma'am?"

Ellen looked at the old man. "The war, I mean. It's all very sad, isn't it? Sad and useless, it seems to me."

An expression inscrutable passed across the old soldier's face and he shook his head and rubbed at his hairless chin. "Oh no, ma'am. If you'd pardon me, but you've only got it about half right."

"How do you mean?"

Abel pushed his tongue into his cheek, looked at her briefly, a little judgmentally, then looked down at the table. As he spoke, he pressed the pad of his finger down on little grains of salt where they'd been spilt and rubbed them a few times with his thumb before tossing them over his shoulder. "Way I figure it," he said. "All that, all that back then, it decided some things about how things was going to be that couldn't be decided no other way. Not the way people are, anyways." Outside they could hear Glenn loading tools—saw and crowbar, rope and pulley—into the back of the wagon. They heard the wagon creak and groan as his weight settled onto the jockeybox, and presently came the soft clopping of Emerson's hooves. Abel pursed his lips, flicked salt over his shoulder. "I suppose things turned out the way they should ought to have," he said.

Ellen looked at him a long, hard moment. "I'm surprised to hear you say that," she finally said. "Considering what it was your side was fighting for."

He raised his eyebrows to meet her stare for a moment, then shrugged and continued with the salt even though there was none to be seen. "I suppose I could say I wasn't fighting for no niggers," he said very softly. "I heard men say that very thing all along, but didn't nobody ever believe it." He finally left off the salt and reached, instead, to absently turn the plate around and around in its place before him. "Truth is," he went on. "Truth is, every one of us on both sides was fighting for the nigs and every one of us on both sides hated that fact. That's why it was so bad. Why it went on so long." Abel sighed, and across the table, Ellen turned her head to the side to escape the faint, foul stink of the old man's breath.

"Shit," muttered Abel, unmindful now of her presence. "Even if I didn't join up for that reason, and I didn't, my reasons was all my own . . . But even if I didn't join up to fight it out over the nigger question, I did come to be convinced that freeing 'em was wrong. For a while there I was a true believer." He fell silent for a long time, and Ellen stayed still, her face as much a puzzle as the clouds.

Abel took a great, deep breath, stared hard at the plate, and did not look up. "Somewhere along the line, though," he said, "and I will admit it was well along toward the end of the things, my mind was changed. I don't want to talk about much of it 'ceptin' to say I was in a bad way, a real bad way, in the Wilderness, and two folks helped me when they had good reason to do the opposite. And they was just folks. Folks trying to get by in a bad place." He nodded, pursed his lips, and shook his head. "So, like I say, things ended up pretty much the way they should have, but it ain't over yet. I figure there's still a long ways to go 'fore the issue's decided well and truly." He looked at Ellen and made a face. "Otherwise, would you and old Glenn really be all the way up here on Hard-scrabble Mountain?" he asked her. "Otherwise," said Abel, shrugging. "You hit the nail right on the head. Like you said, it was a sad, sad thing."

Ellen sat back in her chair and crossed her arms, looking at the old man where he sat small and sick and hurt and sad. "Did you ever run?" she asked him. "You must have wanted to."

Abel shook his head and grinned. "I ain't talked about any of this for twenty years, and here in the last few days I've been answering questions about that damn war till I thought I'd lose my voice."

"If you'd rather not—"

"Oh, it ain't that," said Abel. "It ain't that. Just queer is all. People interested in a thing like that. From that long ago. Says to me that nobody's got it puzzled out yet—just like I always thought." He shrugged and grinned again. "But to answer your question," he said, shaking his head. "Nah, I never did run. Not from them."

Outside, the day was clearing, and a single ray of sunlight slanted through the dusty window onto the table. Abel tilted his face from it but put his good hand into the light, fingers spread to soak up the heat. He squinted at Ellen. "But I'll tell you," he said. "There was plenty of times I walked away from 'em pretty goddamned fast."

Ellen shared his smile and stood from the table. With quick efficiency, she gathered the dishes and moved them to the counter where there sat a white enameled bowl filled with cooling water. Abel offered his help and half stood, but she bid him sit. Turning away, she put her hands in the water and began to wash. Without turning around, she asked, "What are you doing here, Abel?"

"Ma'am?"

"Why are you here?"

There was a long pause while he sought his answer. Ellen watched out the window, but Glenn was gone, and there was nothing to see but sunlight filtering through the trees and making sparkle like treasure the emerald moss and the last of the little jewel-winged deerflies flitting through the air. She uncurled her fingers in the water, trying to relax, trying to force heat up through her arms and into the dark, windy cavity where beat her tired heart.

"I was out front of my shack where I lived," said Abel, choosing words carefully. "I like to sit and watch the ocean of an evening. The way the tide comes in and the different colors the sun puts on the water when it sets. At any rate, I remember standing up one day just as the last light was going out, and when I turned round it was shining back in the trees behind like there was fire in them. I seen fire in trees plenty of times, of course, but this was . . . But this was like how it was in the Wilderness, in the war. The light and the trees and I could suddenly . . . smell things I haven't smelled in more'n thirty years. I had to up and practically pinch myself to be sure of where I really, truly was." Abel sniffed and sighed. "It greatly disturbed me, as they say."

He hushed for a moment. Ellen fisted her hands beneath the water, unfisted them again, and plucked a plate from the counter. She began to scrub it. When Abel spoke again, his voice wheezed softly as though his breath were coming from a place fallen into dis-repair within him—as though his voice were an old, ill-oiled ma-chine seized with neglect.

"I was remembering how it had been when I realized how much I'd forgot. I don't remember exactly what kind of trees there was back there. What kind of flowers there was. My wife, she planted us a little garden back behind our house when we was married, and I can't, for the life of me, I can't remember what it was she planted. Melons or corn or tomatoes or just a mess of flowers. A man ought to be able to remember something like that. And the color of her dress that day . . ." He faltered. "I can't see it," he said. "I can't even see her face clear no more."

Ellen turned from the dishes. She looked at the old man where he sat slump-shouldered, warming his one good hand in a patch of sunlight on the table. "I didn't know you were ever married," she said.

Abel nodded. His lips moved around the lower half of his face and he shook his head as though to chase away thoughts he'd rather not have. "I just figured it was time for me to go on back home while I still can," he said, glancing up at her for a moment before looking away.

Ellen pursed her lips and said slowly, "Glenn and I talked it over, and we'd be proud to have you stay on with us for a while. You'll have your strength back by spring, and your trip will be easier then."

Abel smiled up at her. "Well," he said softly. "Well, that's right kindly and I do thank you, but I can't do it. You folks is good people, but I need to keep moving while I still can, I reckon." Poking his tongue thoughtfully to the inside of his cheek, Abel nodded and went on. "'Sides, if I can catch up with 'em, it sounds like them Chinese might need some help over the pass. And that'd help me, too." He looked at her and blinked. "I reckon you know what it is I'm talkin' about."

Ellen nodded and looked out the window where, within its frame, she saw a doe and its fawn nosing the dying grass and thistle at the edge of the yard. After a moment, the doe stepped with light, articulated precision into the trees and the fawn clumsily followed, until both were vanished in the shadows of the wilderness beyond the clearing.

Abel swallowed as though it pained him and pushed himself up from the table. When Ellen asked if he was all right, he nodded and said, "I'm just not so used to talking to folk, I reckon. I'd forgotten what hard work it can be." He grinned a little and looked at her. "Good work, though. Old numb-nuts there, he's a good dog but he don't answer much when I talk at him." Abel looked down at the floor as though suddenly embarrassed. "If it's no trouble," he said softly, "I might go on into that room back there and rest a spell."

She nodded and watched as he shuffled across the room toward the hall, where he paused. "The dumb old cuss of a dog of mine'll probably be running around out there a while longer. Could you, if you think of it, check up on him 'fore it gets dark? He don't much care for bein' out in the wild in the dark of night." Ellen told him she would and told him not to worry and the old man nodded and walked on down the hall. She heard the door open and close again and then all was silent save for the birdcalls that drifted through the forest like happy, wandering spirits.

Abel woke in the dark and lay quietly staring at the ceiling until he knew they were sleeping in their bedroom. It was a clear night, and bright moonlight washed the walls silvery and pale. A cold wind, near to freezing, breathed along the eaves and made the branches shudder. From somewhere on the hill behind the cabin an owl called softly.

Abel rose from the floor, and beside him, the dog pushed itself up. The old man put a finger to his lips and gave the dog a look and it ceased panting and closed its mouth. Abel nodded his satisfaction and pulled his trousers on. He buttoned his shirt and put on his coat, then pulled on his socks and tied himself into his boots. He gathered his things in the cold dark but could not find his haversack. Standing in the center of the room, he rubbed his chin with his palm, frowned deeply, and swore. After a while, he went to the door and let himself out.

By moonlight, he saw the haversack on the floor beside the front door and he went to it and slung it over his shoulder. He looked around the little room—the tables and cupboards and chairs, the enormous stove and the gun cabinet and the little porcelain figurines and found stones and other knickknacks about the shelves, the knitted quilt draped over the arm of a chair pulled close to the fire, all things around him that proclaimed hearth and home and life and love—then went out the door onto the porch.

"I thought you'd be leaving, so I put some things in that sack of yours for you," said Ellen.

Startled, Abel jumped, swore, and turned. She stood by herself just within the shadows near the rain barrel, smoking with the hand-

rolled cigarette held near her ear. He touched the brim of his hat. "Well, I'm obliged, ma'am," he said softly.

Nodding, she stepped out of the dark and crushed the cigarette into an old jelly-jar lid before crossing the porch boards to him. She wore a heavy robe against the cold, and she stopped before Abel with the moon lighting up her skin and caught up silver in her hair, so that she was ghostlike, all ashimmer. And even in the dark he could tell she'd been weeping, could smell the hot salt rising from her mannish cheeks like warm seawater. "I won't ever have a child," she breathed. "They took that away from me. They took it all away." Her voice bucked and kicked against the grief that rode her and that she'd suddenly loosed from wherever she'd penned it.

Abel stepped back, her naked misery disorienting and overpowering him. The dog had scampered off into the forest, and for a moment he looked about for it as if it could help, give him guidance or good advice, but he could not find it.

She came close, and he could feel the heat of her flesh. He wondered how long it had been since he'd felt such a thing. Her arms hung limply and her head was tilted forward so her moongilded hair fell past her face. She wore heavy, unlaced boots that set the boards to creaking.

Abel put a tentative hand on her shoulder and could feel its round, firm warmth even through the robe. With a breath, he stepped to her and wrapped his arm about her so that the tough flat of his hand touched the center of her back. He closed his eyes and could feel the knuckles of her spine and her jutting scapulae like the knobs of withered wings.

Ellen fisted her hands into the facing of Abel's coat and pressed her face against his shoulder, shaking in his awkward embrace. He stood as best he could against her wild, salty grief, and when it was finally done she stood trembling and panting against him. He felt the workings of

the wide muscles in her back and her small breasts against his chest as she drew breath, shimmering cones into the cold.

Abel closed his eyes. He pressed with the flat of his palm against the small of her back. He breathed in the scent of her hair and her tears and her pale, shimmering flesh. For just a moment he allowed himself a dream and when the world returned he took her by the shoulder and pushed her away.

He was panting a little and ducked his head to better see her face. "Are you all right?" he asked.

Ellen was quiet. She said nothing.

"Well," said Abel slowly. "Maybe . . . maybe it's for the best."

She stared at him, her eyes wet.

"What I mean is . . . if you-all had a child . . . It'd have a hard life, don't you think? Harder, maybe, than it should, way I see it."

Ellen opened her mouth and shut it. The pink wedge of her tongue darted to her lips. "What—what are you saying to me?"

"I'm just saying that any child you and Glenn have'd be mixed, wouldn't it? That . . . that's no—hell, I don't know."

Ellen straightened and stared coldly at the old man. She took a step back and touched her wrist to her lips, then shook her head. "You son of a bitch," she hissed. "You get on out of here." She dug the heels of her palms into the orbits of her eyes and grimaced.

Abel stepped back. He stumbled down the steps into the yard, where he could smell flowers rotting in the garden along the wall— little wilted rhododendron bugles fallen to the soil, sweetening it for the next year. Ellen stood at the edge of the porch, gripping the rail as though her grief and anger had given her a pale sort of strength. She raised her arm and pointed toward the uphill trail and Abel turned. He walked across the yard, then looked back at the cabin, where now their bedroom window was lit yellow. As he passed the shed, he smelled within the metallic scents of tools, fusty rainclothes with sap-treated seams, bottles of kerosene. Abel could see the

outhouse in silhouette behind its hanging screen of moss, and he could see the square back of the Makers' Acres sign on the fence post at the end of the lane. He smelled the good, rich dirt of their yard and the fresh, grassy stink of the horse in its little stable. As he ducked his head to enter the forest, he heard a creaking on the cabin porch and turned again.

Glenn crossed the yard and Abel listened to him breathing in the dark and they stood together silently for some time. Finally, Abel said, "I'm sorry, Glenn. I said a thing I shouldn't ought have. I don't really think it. I don't know why I said it."

"Well, whatever it was, she's mad as a hornet. Hurt some, too, I think."

"She didn't say?"

"No, she didn't. And I don't want to know nothing more about any of it."

"Well," said Abel, nodding and turning. He walked a short distance, then turned back. "I thank you for the hospitality. For the borrowing of the book."

"Abel," said Glenn flatly. "If the snow catches you while you're up there, you head for the flats up near Little Sugar Pass. Just beneath the saddle."

"What for?"

"There's a little trapper's cabin where I sleep over some nights when I'm hunting. It hasn't been used in I don't know how long, but there's firewood and a little stove. Not much by a long shot, but it's shelter."

Abel nodded and turned back to the trail where it sloped up into the dark. The mountains stood black against the night, carving jagged pieces from the starlight and darkening the floor of the forest. When he turned back again, Glenn had become a small figure, diminishing constantly toward the cabin. Abel watched him go. A sudden rectangle of yellow light flashed magical and lovely as the cabin door opened and closed again. Abel turned again and started up the trail into the mountains.

He'd walked a hundred yards or so before stopping and turning with a frown. Swearing softly, he put two fingers to his lips and gave a shrill whistle. And when he heard the dog racing up the trail toward him, Abel Truman turned and walked on through the night while an owl on the slope sang him mournfully on.

# TEN

## Through the Wilderness and After

*May 1864*

AFTER GRANT HAD gone, Hypatia stood for a time watching the road where he'd been. She watched the road until the sound of hoof-beats faded with distance and time and was replaced with the crack-lings of the forest. Rain fell fitfully but did not seem to wet anything. She could smell wild roses in the dooryard, could hear the distant calls of whippoorwills and felt, for a moment, a soft cool breeze dis-turbing tree branch and vine. The wind moved with a quiet rustling, as though searching for something. After a while she went back in-side, set the revolver on the desk, and settled down to sleep on the floor, not far from where the wounded soldier lay all ashudder and whimpering softly.

She had no way to know how long she'd slept, for when she woke the sky was gray and the air wild with rain. To her bottomless sur-prise, she found herself spooned tightly to the rebel's back with one hand caught up in his dusty hair and the other lying on the shoulder of his wounded arm, as though by touch she'd ease his pain. She lay without moving, listening to and feeling him breathe and smelling his scent—tarry powdersmoke and stale sweat and old terrors and the fearsome stink of warring all mixed up in his hair and coating his skin like a fine powder. Pressing her lips in a thin line, Hypatia slowly raised her arm from around him and in one fast motion rolled away and stood. She scooped the pistol from the desk and fumbled with it a moment before getting it pointed at the soldier.

He lay awake, looking at her. His gaze was steadily tired, and he opened his mouth, then closed it again.

Hypatia swallowed and tried to keep her hands from shaking. "You better believe I know how to use this," she told him.

The soldier blinked and nodded. "Good God," he breathed, before closing his eyes and slipping away once more. "You're pretty as a picture . . ."

She held the pistol on him for a long time, waiting to be sure he wasn't trying to fox her. When she could finally control her breath, Hypatia eased her grip and yelped with pain as her hurt finger unkinked from around the trigger.

Holding the gun in her off-hand, she stepped out onto the porch to look at the cut in the cool, gray, rainswept light. The soldier's shattered elbow had cut the pad of her forefinger lengthwise, and when she flexed it the sides of the gash bent stiffly open and she saw a quick flash of pale bone. Gritting her teeth and shaking her hand, she went quickly through the cabin, gathering her few and various possessions. Wrapping everything in her thin blanket, Hypatia slung it over her shoulder, tucked the pistol into her dress pocket, and went out the door again.

As her feet touched the porch boards the sound of riflefire to the south swelled abruptly and kept on in a noisome clatter, made more so by the rain, which had turned from a shower to a driving storm complete with a howling wind to clash through the branches round about. Hypatia glanced back at the rebel huddled against his hurts. Then she turned and walked out into the storm.

Soon enough she was soaked through, with rainwater running down her face in streams. It was fresh and cool on her lips, and she walked the road with her shoulders hunched, and by and by she came to a fork and in the center of the fork lay a horse-sized boulder cleft down its center as though by some long-ago and hopeful farmer with an eye toward clearing the land for fieldwork. Hypatia stopped before the stone. The air quivered electrically and the distant gunfire had neither ceased nor eased and neither had the rain. As though the weather itself had been afflicted by the violence. Hypatia stepped into the forest behind the stone and found there, in the dry, leeward side, a sack filled with flour, salt, a little pork, and a small glass bottle half full of molasses. A soldier's dropped treasure, it lay as though left there for her alone to find.

She thought to give thanks by prayer but did not have the strength for proper devotions so inclined her face rainward to murmur thanks then took the bag, stepped out of the trees, and turned back the way she'd come. The wind and the rain and the distant clamor of war followed her as she made her slow way back. It was evening when she opened the cabin door again. The soldier lay where she had left him and for a moment she thought him dead. But then he stirred and called out a name. Son, brother, father, comrade—she did not know. Standing there dripping in the doorway, looking at him, Hypatia shook her head with tired resignation. "I don't know what it is I think that I'm doin'," she said to him. "But there ain't nothing else I know how to do, even if I thought I could."

She walked into the cabin and closed the door. And later, when he woke, they gave each other their names and Hypatia handed Abel Truman a cooked piece of pork and a biscuit with molasses drizzlings that she'd fixed in the hearth fire.

They slept on opposite sides of the cabin. He lay before the fire to keep the chill away and she near the door, with the cool, dead weight of the pistol in her dress pocket. Numberless times she came awake to sporadic gunfire from the south or merely chased from sleeping by strange, hot dreams. In the morning, when she finally truly woke, Hypatia's right hand ached sore from her cut finger to the pale base of her thumb, where the small veins ran straight as ill-tuned guitar strings through her wrist, each one vibrating with notes of dull pain as though recently plucked.

It was not warm in the cabin, for the fire had burned down to but a few bright coals, yet she sweated terribly. When she crouched beside Abel where he still slumbered, she found that he, too, had sweat through his clothes. His hair lay loose about his head like damp netting, and his face was flushed. Hypatia laid a palm across his forehead to feel the fierce heat of his gathering infection.

Sniffing dryly, she peeled the bandages from around his arm and prodded the swollen wound until a watery trickle ran. His injury was hot to the touch, and when she tried to straighten Abel's arm from the angle he'd cocked it, he cried out with such pain that after but a few halfhearted tries she let it be. As she attended to his other, various hurts, Abel muttered something through his sleep and gnashed his teeth. He called a woman's name and he called a man's and in the end began to shake with a bone-deep cold.

After a while, Hypatia went outside to collect leaves and roots into a small linen bag she kept about her person. She did not stay out long, for she was unaccountably tired, and the constant sound of the southward fighting was as oppressive as the rain. When she returned to the cabin, she mixed the ingredients she'd gathered with water heated over the fire in a little tin cup until a steaming mash filled the bag. Laying the poultice on Abel's shattered elbow, she left it for an hour, then changed out the contents with fresh and laid it on his hurt chest. After another hour, she took the used plaster off him and wrapped it around her finger. She could feel its fading warmth seeping deep into her flesh and felt it settle, it seemed, into her bones, where it hurt like the very devil. Hypatia kept it on as long as she could stand, then carefully rinsed the bag with a portion of their drinking water, turned it inside out, and hung it near the fire to dry. Then she settled herself on the floor near the door with her eyes shut and her forehead cradled in the web of her thumb and forefinger.

She breathed deeply, trying to steady herself. Her eyes were hot and her joints ached, elbow, knee, and hip. After a while she began to cough and could not stop, and by the time she'd finished, Abel had woken and propped himself up to look at her.

"You got yourself sick runnin' 'round in the weather, auntie," he said, panting a little with the effort of lifting himself from the floor.

Hypatia gave him a sour look and said, "Don't you call me that. I done give you my name last night."

Abel nodded an apology and she returned the nod and shifted the stale, milk-sour front of her dress about for the comfort of it and to feel the reassuring weight of the pistol in her pocket. After a few moments, she cocked her head and asked, "How you feeling this morning?"

Abel swallowed and made a face, then said without thinking, "Like I been ate by a bear and shit out over a cliff."

Hypatia looked at him and Abel cleared his throat and pursed his lips and said with strained decorum, "I reckon I'd be feeling more'n a bit worse if you hadn't stayed around to tend me."

She nodded at the implied gratitude while Abel wet his lips and asked, "Where did your man go?"

"He wasn't my man," she said. "I didn't have no claim on him and I didn't think you were awake enough to even know he was here."

"Well," said Abel. "I had moments."

Hypatia frowned. "He went on with some African soldiers what marched right by here two nights ago." She looked hard at him. "You should know there's blue soldiers all over these woods. Wouldn't take long at all for them to show up if I was to yell."

"Goddamn," said Abel, snorting. "Nigger soldiers. This war's lost." He shook his head and settled back down. "I couldn't give you no trouble even if I wanted to," he said. "But I reckon you know that."

"You never did answer my question straight-on," she said after a few moments. "How does your arm feel? I'm askin' for a reason." She met his eyes and went on. "Are you dizzy? Sick at your stomach? Tell me, so I can figure what needs doing."

Abel looked at her, then nodded. "I'm cold," he said. "Awful cold, and I can't get no breath. And my arm hurts all the way down into my hand."

"How bad?"

He snorted again and shook his head. "Pretty goddamned bad."

Hypatia lifted her chin. "You just stay down on the floor, then," she said. "You got to try and relax that arm if you want to hang on to it."

He nodded and said, "A surgeon would've took one look and lopped it off."

"I ain't no surgeon."

"I know that."

"Fine."

"I was fixin' to thank you."

"Well, don't. Yest'day, I was two steps gone from here. Next time I go out that door I might well could be four."

Abel shook his head and grimaced as he shifted about. "I reckon you're free now," he said. "You do what you want."

She gaped at him and opened her mouth, then slowly closed it and shook her head from side to side. "You got that all wrong," she said.

Abel frowned. "Well, sure you are," he said. "You must be." Outside, somewhere to the south in the rain and the wind, gunfire crackled like strange, terrible thunder. "I got to believe we all lost that fight, otherwise we wouldn't be hearing 'em tear into each other down south of here like we are. I figure Marse Robert's scootin' back toward Richmond, and if that's so, it's on account of he can't go forward." He shrugged and looked at her. "Way I see it, this land's liberated. You're in Union territory now, and according to Abe Lincoln, you're a freedman. Woman. At any rate, that's the way I see it."

Hypatia shook her head again. "You don't know nothing," she said, her voice low and cold. "It's almost funny, how you don't know the first thing about anything." She held her right forefinger tightly in the ball of her left fist. "Such a thing gets onto you, gets put onto you, you can't never get shut of it. You're always bound ever after on account of you can't 'magine no other thing. And there can't never be nothing else. Not in your hands and not in your heart, so don't you go on speechifyin' 'bout freedom when you don't know what the other is. You just keep your mouth shut about that."

Abel shuddered with a sudden flare of pain. A soft, mewing sound escaped his lips and he coughed—quick, harsh, and dry—then looked at her with his gaze gone soft and worrisome. "How did you lose your child?" he asked.

She took a great, deep breath, then slowly took the pistol from her pocket, handling it in such a way and with such an expression that she'd have him know her resolve. Moving her lips soundlessly for a moment, she finally said, "Down south of Charles-town while I was still carryin' him inside me—he was a boy—I went up to a Yankee wagon to try and see if'n they had a little food. A little water. Any work, washing or some such, I could do in trade for it." Her face went flat. "They got in a circle. It was going on evening and I remember seein' the sun goin' down all red behind the trees."

Hypatia took another breath, her eyes and face now tilted upward, her voice dispassionate as though her memory of events had removed her from them, made of her a witness to her own tragedies.

229

"Well, you can imagine what happened," she said. "One went twice and one of them gave me a boot in my belly after."

Abel said nothing, and Hypatia lapsed to silence. She stared into the fire, and the light washed over her face in sheets of gold and bronze. "When he finally got born, he only lived a little while and he never did make a sound," she finally said. "Not once. He was such a good baby. Just an eency little thing. Had a little spot on his head that was stove in and I buried him in a shady spot by a little crick. I was so tired, I couldn't think of no name for him so I just let him be, hoping Lord Jesus would do it for me." She blinked, her eyes wet, and licked her lips. "I come aways since . . . and now I don't even know what county it was. I ain't never ever goin' to find that spot again. My head's the onliest place he is now." This last she said in a grief-propelled rush, and by the time she'd finished she'd covered her face with her palms.

Abel was silent for a long time after. Finally, he told her how sorry he was for her troubles, and anger flared up across her face. She asked him what he thought he knew about it, and he answered her honestly. Raising her chin, she looked at him, then nodded, stood, and moved so fast to the door the pistol clattered away and was left behind. Hypatia stepped out onto the porch and into the rain, flexing her hurt finger back and forth.

Rain fell; it plunged through the thick canopy in such a manner that she could spy each drop falling and count it as though she'd keep a record of such a thing. Writ upon her heart perhaps. The leaves quivered joyously in the wet and the sound of it falling melded with the iron clang of battle to the south. She looked at her hands, the cut-swollen finger, the work-cracked knuckles and ragged nails. Sighing, she put her hands out into the rain, holding them there until they were wet and the blood was loosed from them, dripping in pale, red drops to the earth. Then she drew them back and went inside again.

The cabin stank with a sickly sweetness that reminded her of fried onions, and Hypatia wondered if it was all from Abel's wound or just her own fear tainting the breathable air. Closing the door, she turned to Abel and froze.

He stood shakily in the center of the room, bright with fever and holding by its barrel the pistol she'd dropped. He stood hunched with his wounded arm cocked tightly to his chest like a folded bird's wing. Abel looked down at the gun in his hand as though to puzzle a course to take, some right decision. After a while he looked at her and blinked heavily, his weary eyes tatted with red lace and his lips cracked with an inner heat. Nodding, Abel made as if to swallow, grimaced instead, then wiped his mouth with the back of the hand that held the gun.

Hypatia lifted her chin and finally said, "You're all busted up and need to be lyin' flat."

Abel nodded again and squeezed his eyes shut tight, then slowly opened them once more. He took a step and held the pistol out to her. Hypatia took it back, stuffed it in her pocket, and managed to get an arm around him before he fell. Panting, Abel steadied himself against her, his face close to her own. He looked away. "There's something else," he finally managed.

"What is it?" she asked. "You hurt someplace I didn't find?"

"Nah," said Abel. "It's . . . I just need to—" He broke off. His eyes sought the dark upper corners of the room, and he swallowed again. "I got to go make dirt," he finally said.

Hypatia nodded without comment. Helping him across the cabin to the door, she let him find his balance there while she stepped down from the porch and walked around behind the shack.

It was going on evening now, the shadows deepening between the trees. Gunfire and the echo of gunfire haunted the wood. Hypatia looked about the little parcel of land and found no outhouse and the rain kept falling. Going into the Wilderness, she found a sturdy stick and with it dug a shallow hole. Her finger pained her all the while but she paid it little mind. When she went to fetch Abel, he stood slumped in the doorway and together they made their slow, stumbling way into the trees.

In the end, he could not keep his balance alone, and his legs were too weak to hold him aright regardless. Hypatia looked for the moon behind the clouds as he gripped her shoulder. Cords stood from his neck and his forearm trembled. That he had to strain at all told her his infection had not yet overpowered him and neither spoke as she gathered the softest, driest leaves she could find to clean him with.

Hypatia built the fire up in the hearth and they slept that night in their usual places: he before the fire for the warmth of it and she beside the door with the pistol. At some point the firing to the south tapered away to a dreadful silence and the night stilled, but neither noticed.

The next day, Hypatia woke late again, and again to the sound of gunfire from the south. As the light bled slowly into the absolute dark in which she'd slept and nightmared, she began a hot coughing that made her legs kick upon the floorboards. When it had spent it-self, she pushed herself up and cried for the sharpness of the pain that lanced up her arm, into her shoulder, and across her chest. Up her neck and into her jaw. Hypatia carefully got herself sitting up before looking down at her hand where it lay upon her thigh.

She gave a small moan and turned away. Her hand had become something not her own, something unrecognizable. Fingers like so many overstuffed sausages, the dirty cuff of her dress bit tightly into the puffy flesh of her wrist where previously it flapped loosely in the wind. When she dipped her head to sniff at the cut that had now lengthened into the heart of her palm, Hypatia drew back with her stomach heaving. Speaking softly, fearfully, the Lord's Own Name as she knew it, she struggled to her feet and looked toward Abel, but the soldier was not about.

She wrinkled her brow. She filled her lungs, then waited a few long, weary moments for the nausea that had bubbled up within her to recede. Picking up her blanket, Hypatia wrapped it around herself like a shawl, careful to fold it over her hand and hide it so. Through the tiny window near the door, she saw Abel sitting on the porch step with his own blanket around his shoulders and those shoulders hunched.

When she stepped out onto the porch to join him, he glanced her way, nodded the morning, then looked off to the south again. The warring in that direction had risen once more. Hypatia sat beside him, keeping her swollen hand to her off-side, and together they sat watching the rain fall and listening to the unseen battle.

Abel was silent for a long time before finally lifting his chin and saying, "I don't understand it. They ain't in the Wilderness no more, haven't been for days, but listen." He looked hard at her without seeing her at all.

Hypatia shook her head and trembled. She was very cold, yet sweat trickled down her spine. "What am I supposed to hear?" she asked.

"It's what we ain't hearing so much of," said Abel, looking off through the trees into the furious wave of sound that rolled over them like something visible and terrible. "They're not in the Wilderness," he said again. "And they ain't moved no farther south either. That means Lee's holding." Abel grinned for a moment, then shook his head, his face gone serious and resigned. "Still and all," he went on. "He ain't got the men to hold Grant up for very long. And if they keep on like they been—" He paused a moment as the thunderous sound of cannon swelled. "If they keep fightin' this way, Lee ain't goin' to have an army left to fight with. Bloody old son of a bitch." Abel shook his head and fell silent.

They stayed on the porch throughout the day, listening and watching the rain fall, which, like the battle, did not let up. There was still food left, but neither was hungry. Abel complained of his arm but his eyes were clear, he looked stronger, and his face was not as drawn and haggard as it had been. For her part, Hypatia settled with her back to the wall and her legs straight out before her. She was bilious and made a conscious effort to keep her arm still for the bright, sick pain it caused her when she didn't. She borrowed Abel's pocket-knife, outwardly for cutting rags with which to fashion a sling for his arm, but when he was not looking she cut hashmarks crosswise over her finger as though she were snakebit.

And in the evening of that day, as light faded from the raindark clouds, Hypatia rolled her head and looked at Abel where he still sat, trying to follow a battle he could not see—that went on and on and would go on and on. "They ain't never goin' to stop," she said. "Even when they come say it's over."

Abel nodded.

"They'll still be goin' at it a hundred years from now."

"I know it."

"What'll you do?"

Glancing her way, Abel asked, "What do you mean?"

"I mean where will you go?"

"When?" he asked. "After?"

"That's right." She closed her eyes and opened them again. Her lips were cool and numb and her scalp tingled. "After."

Abel shrugged, wincing a little with the pain of it. "It's funny, you askin' that," he said thoughtfully, watching a curl of mist leak from the trees to explore the air over their heads. "I never thought much about it till just a bit ago." He leaned and spat and took a moment to examine the spittle on the ground. "Fella what done this," he went on, nodding to his shattered elbow where he held it tight against his ribcage. "Well, he had him a letter . . . I had the damn thing, but I suppose it's lost now . . ." He looked at Hypatia for a moment but did not really see her for the gathering shadows. "You didn't see nothing like a letter with all my possibles when you come 'crost me, did you?"

Hypatia shook her head and moved her legs about in front of her. Her heels rasped softly on the boards. "Too bad," said Abel. "Too bad. I'd've mailed it for him. Thing like that ought not to get lost." He shrugged again and winced again with a soft swear. "Anyway, in this letter the fella went on about going out west after the show. He wrote about the Oregon Territory and the blue Pacific."

"The blue Pacific," said Hypatia softly, her eyes closed, her voice soft. "That sounds nice."

Abel nodded. "Don't it? Letter said the landscape out there isn't nothing like here, and that that was a good thing." Abel looked about at the dark of the Wilderness. "And I'm inclined to agree," he said. "I seen just about all of this part of the country I care to, I reckon, so I figure when it's finally over, if I survive it, I'll take a walk out that way. See what it is I'll see."

"Would you take me?" Hypatia asked. Her voice was a small thing, and when he heard it, Abel turned.

And then he stood as quickly as he was able and crossed to her. Pressing the palm of his good hand against her forehead, he drew it back quickly. Hypatia watched him as he swore and fussed about her, and when he took up her hand she cried out.

Abel carefully examined the wound and her hand was like a gob of sour dough; the lines, creases, and wrinkles smoothed out to become giving and moist and without character.

Abel wet his lips and swore, then swore again. He touched her shoulder and ducked his head to meet her weary eyes. "Tell me what you need," he said. "You tell me what to do."

Hypatia smacked her lips and smiled a small smile. She shook her head. "Answer my question," she said.

"What?" Abel asked. "What question?"

Hypatia swallowed and panted. She closed her eyes and opened them again. "If you could, would you take me?"

"Sure," he said quickly. "Sure I would."

Hypatia smiled and closed her eyes again. "Liar," she said so softly that Abel had to lean near her mouth to hear.

She was quiet for a long time, and after a while, Abel half carried, half dragged her into the shack. Night drew down around them, and it became dark. The firing to the south had not diminished. He stood for a time regarding the hearth where the fire she'd kindled had burnt down to one or two live coals. Outside it began to rain and the wind came up to set the door rattling in its frame while the remains of the rosebush in the dooryard scratched along the wall and all the trees in the Wilderness round about swayed and clashed.

Hypatia's eyes came open, and she looked at him. "I never knew what to name him," she said softly. "I just never did know."

Abel made soft shushing sounds. He told her he understood and she said it would have been a fine thing to call him home to supper of a fall evening with the sun going down behind the trees and the wind coming in off the blue Pacific. And Abel told her it would have been a fine thing, indeed, and she opened her mouth to say more but did not. Abel knelt beside her, wonderingly. His hand just so upon her shoulder as though he were a clumsy usher.

After a while he reached and carefully closed her eyes, then knelt for a time with his palm upon her cheek like a blind man graving a face to memory before a parting.

In the end, he built the fire up in the hearth and surrounded the place where she lay with brush and what dry timber he could find. He said no words aloud, merely nodded after a few moments' silence, then went about the shack one last time with a burning stick, touching flames here and there before leaving.

Abel stood outside the shack and watched it burn. By the time the roof fell in, he realized that the firing to the south had finally stopped and that, but for the rattling of the fire, the night was quiet. The rain had stopped and the air was fresh. And when he heard the sound of cavalry coming fast up the road, Abel turned and walked down the lane to meet them.

In April, the dead-house wagon came at night and it came every morning. After breakfast yet before the day could turn fine enough to start the corpses stinking, Abel heard it coming up the sandy road from his reeking cot in the long hospital tent. A two-horse wagon driven by a pair of teamsters with faces scarved nose-to-neck like villains. After a bad night in the tents it would take them an hour to load, stacking the bodies up like cut wood, less from respect as for the way neatness would maximize their load, for the way Abel figured it, they surely would not want to make another trip in the afternoon. The drivers worked with flat, repetitious efficiency all out of proportion to their gruesome task, and if Abel propped himself up on his good elbow, he could watch them at their labor. He looked for friends amidst the stiffening limbs and thrown-back chins or salt-stiffened shocks of hair that, perhaps, he'd once helped to wash in the cold Potomac off Lookout Point where the prison camp was. If it was a hard day and he was awash in slow tides of nausea, his shattered left elbow hotly throbbing in time with his weary heart, Abel could still see the teamsters' long shadows, made indistinct and monstrous with distance and slanting sunlight, as they flickered and moved across the stained canvas tenting with metronomic steadiness. Regardless of his angle, there was always the sound of the patient horses nickering and softly stamping in their traces and, softer still, the low grunting of the men at their work, and punctuating all this, the horrid, dry, heavy, solid smacking of falling bodies settling against each other.

This was April then, as it had been March before it, and Abel did not know what to expect of the month save more of the same. His coughs joined a throaty chorus of moist and dry lungsounds rattling his tent, one of thirty arranged like the spokes of a wheel outside the stockade and hard by the lighthouse. The moment one of their number was carried to the dead-house to lie uncasketed upon its earthen floor, another would be laid in his place, the ticking still warm. The nurses, other prisoners furloughed from the stockade, carried the dead to their house with the same tired steadiness as the teamsters, and under the guard of Negro soldiers charged to keep them from escaping. This was April, then, with the wind brisk and freshening the air with the smell of the bay, the faint taste of brine, and that oceanic odor of iodine and decomposition that was so much better than the yellow stink of the tents. As he had been since entering the hospital, Abel was thankful that his cot was at the end of the line near the open flaps.

At April's opening, his fever broke and his breathing eased, though his bowels still pursued some strange, twisting campaign within him that forced his knees chestward and set his teeth to chattering. A week more went by with things expelled from him that he did not recognize, for which he had no definitions or referents, and his sweats were God-awful. But one morning, with the sun slowly rising to turn the tent's crosspieces to black lines drawn upon a surging white canvas, Abel found himself feeling tolerable. He lay back, eyes closed, listening to the sounds of the wagon recede as it went trundling back up the road with its sad cargo. Presently, the space left behind was filled with wind clashing in beach grass and the seething of sand. He could hear the calls of sailors on barges in the bay, the slap of waves against hulls, and soldiers drilling in the field out past the stables. But then the confused, staccato racket of coughing and suffering rose to sweep over all the other sounds of the world outside the camp.

"How you feeling today, Johnny Reb?"

Abel snorted awake. "Just about ready to take me a French leave," he muttered, opening one eye to squint up at the Negro soldier standing over him. "Mornin', Noé," he said.

"*Afternoon*, Abel," said Noé, his stern, dark face warming with a grin. "Let's hear it," he said, grinning wider.

Abel blinked, rolled his eyes theatrically. "What? Again?" he asked. "Fine, fine: How's things today, soldier?"

Noé's head bobbed with delight and he shifted his rifle so his right hand could describe a rising arc through the air as he said, "Bottom rail? Still up top. And listen here: Old Uncle Abe went on down to Richmond. Sat right down at Jeff Davis's desk. This war's about done."

Abel blinked and looked at him, then blinked again. "You're just tellin' tales," he finally said.

Noé shook his head. "They done told us 'bout it this morning.'"

Abel shrugged. "It don't mean nothing. Not a thing. This war? It ain't never goin' to stop. That's what I say. That's what I've always said." Abel shook his head and waved dismissively, wincing with pain as the shift in weight sent a spasm of pain through his wounded arm.

Noé pursed his lips and set his forage cap back on his head. "You know, that arm ain't never goin' to be no use to you no more," he said.

Nodding, Abel shifted about for the comfort of it and looked down at the claw his left hand had become. "I know it," he said. "But I'm still glad some sawbones son of a bitch didn't lop it off. Rather have it useless than not at all."

Noé shrugged and cocked his head. "And the flux?" he asked.

Abel sniffed. "Well, I ain't quick-steppin' like I was, thank the Lord."

Noé reached out, paused for the space of half a heartbeat, then settled a brotherly palm on Abel's shoulder. It took a conscious effort for Abel not to stiffen, wince, or draw back. And though he did none of these things, the truth of that effort reddened him with a alien shame that he was not sure he understood while the dying johnny in the cot across the aisle snarled and spat and called him a mudsill.

Abel and Noé looked over at the soldier, who grimaced at them, showing a mouthful of gray teeth and bleeding gums.

"Old Abe's notions 'bout charity and malice toward nobody is a hard row," sighed Noé, shaking his head and shouldering his rifle. "I'm off," he said. "You need for anything?"

"You want to look away for the space of time it takes me to get on down the road, I'd be obliged."

Noé grinned again, as sudden and startling and fine as the first time Abel had ever seen a Negro smile. "Nope," he said, and walked out of the tent.

In March, he'd spent nights wracked with cramps, watching lamp-flames waver in sooty vases of glass curved like the hips of women. Those nights were long and dark and tiresome as nights spent in sickness always are. He'd hear the Negro soldiers gathered round their campfires, speaking softly, softly singing, softly laughing beneath the star-struck dome of night like real soldiers. Like real men. And it was in March that Noé began his nightly visits to Abel's bedside.

With a soft whisper to draw him from his inner landscape of quivering bowels and bubbling nausea, Noé would set a cool rag across Abel's forehead, and Abel would open his mouth to let him press mashed blackberry root against his tongue. The taste of the river water Noé had used to wash it followed by the tuber's bitter styptic.

"Why?" Abel had croaked that first time.

Crouched beside his cot, Noé had stared at him in his misery, his eyes pale in the lamplit dark, his face a shadowy cypher. The soft rustle of his shrug. "I hate you," said Noé finally. "Ever' goddamned one of you."

"All right."

"My hate's so deep it might well could be bottomless. Leastways . . . leastways, I ain't never found no end to it."

"That's all right."

"No, it ain't. It ain't no way to be. Old Abe, he said we mustn't be enemies. He says now we got to bind up the nation's wounds." Again that soft rustle. "I choose you. And that's the best I reckon I can do."

In April, Noé's voice drew him from dreams of rills of black water fanning over stone and a moon cut by clouds that rippled like black crepe.

"Abel. Grant, he gone done it."

"What?"

"Found him the end. You rebs done give it up today."

And before Abel could frame a question there came the sudden firing of muskets all in disagreement; there gathered beyond the woodsheds near the kitchen an unharmonious and impromptu philharmonic instrumented with pots and pans and wooden spoons for clappers; there rose great whooping shouts of joy from all about the stockade as soldiering men tumbled from their hammocks, pushed back their tent flaps, and capered gleefully in the sweetened dark; and there also came shouts of outrage and misery, despair and heartbreak, from within the dead-line where the prisoners' fondest dreams met their ends. Eventually, someone would organize fireworks to give shape to his explosive delight, but at that moment, in the smoky lamplit April dark of the hospital tent, Abel put up his good right hand and Noé took it while across the aisle the johnny gnashed his rotting teeth and muttered darkly.

Noé came to his cotside one last time. Deep in the lonely watches of the night he softly called to Abel, and Abel grunted, for he was well awake and had been for some time.

"You fit, reb?"

"As a fiddle. And from what I'm told? Ain't no rebs no more. Just folk."

Noé grunted. "Get on up," he whispered. "Get these on and come outside."

Noé handed over clothing: a pair of frayed blue sergeant's trousers with the piping stripped off, leaving behind a paler stripe of frazzled cloth, a thin and well-worn flannel shirt in red and black, a set of black suspenders and an old pair of Federal-issue mudscows with no laces and a hole in the right sole the size of a half-dollar. The clothes had not been laundered and smelled of sweat, soil, sun, and saltwater.

Abel set his feet on the ground. Noé stood at the entrance to the tent, watching the space between the hospital grounds and the barracks beyond the woodlot. "What's this all about?" asked Abel.

Noé glanced over. "Just put on that shoddy."

Abel shrugged. "What?" he asked. "No socks?"

Noé shook his head.

Abel dressed and went outside where the night air was crisp and cool, smelling of woodsmoke and horses. He heard the sound of the Potomac rushing into the Chesapeake as constant as the blood rushing within him. Noé looked him up and down and grinned in the dark. "Well, look at you. How do you feel?"

"I'm standing." Abel shuffled his feet in the dirt and cupped his ruined elbow with his palm. Though the clothes were poor, they were finery compared with the rags he'd been wearing since his capture. He had been on the tip of the peninsula where the stockade was for three seasons before falling ill, and it had taken a toll on his clothing. No trees or brush kept the elements from any of the thousands packed into the forty acres of fenced-in sand, just narrow alleys between miserable little shebangs and one street to speak of. This street, Pennsylvania Avenue as it came to be called, was always clogged with men hoping for a fresh breeze to lift the stink from their faces for a moment. Shamelessly desperate men turned out the pockets of those too weak to stop them and men carved charms and bracelets and rude, mean-faced chessmen from beef bones and still others offered service cobbling or barbering or tailoring for a quarter-ration of muley meat, a twist of firewood, a rare knuckle of soft bread. Abel had seen processions of men blinded by the unceasing glare of sun on sand and water, stumbling about hand-to-shoulder like wretched peasants from some medieval painting.

And now he stood in the dark outside the stinking hospital tent. He released his elbow and pressed his fingertips to his sternum, moving them about slightly to feel the luxury of napless cloth against his skin. Rolling about his right shoulder, he licked his lips and looked at Noé. "Well?"

Noé handed him a black slouch hat and bid him follow. Abel snugged the hat down tight, adjusted it front to back, and followed him.

They crossed to the dead-house and went inside. An old cow barn that had long since lost whatever paint it had had, it stood doorless and quiet and the light did not penetrate far within. The silver wood was paler yet by moonlight, crosshatched by the shadows of trees, and the sound of busy insects trickled out with a ticking buzz that spoke of time passing and of slow decay. Through some miracle of chemistry or climate, or perhaps owing to the gentle reek of his new clothes, Abel could not smell the corpses laid out in lines but could see them in their pathetic exposure, a pale string of bare feet that stretched back into the dark.

"What is it we're doin' here, Noé?"

"You reckon you'd take the oath?"

"What?"

"With me here. Right now. You reckon you can give your word not to take up arms against the Union no more?"

Abel shrugged and looked at him. "Well, hell, I don't see why not," he answered. "Your man Grant finished it up, so there ain't much point holding out."

"Just like that? You ain't much of a rebel, as I understand them."

"My parents are buried in New York," said Abel. "North Carolina is just a place I happened to be when all this mess got started."

Noé stared at him for a long moment, his dark face inscrutable in the tangle of shadows. Then he snorted, grinned, and said: "I wondered. You don't sound like a proper cracker."

"That don't mean I don't agree with the Cause."

"Do you?"

Abel shrugged again. He could feel the black soldier's eyes on him, could sense the set of his face sharpened with studied judgment. "Lincoln, he says we won't never be shut of each other," Noé finally said. "That we can't never be, so we mustn't be enemies. That's what he said: we mustn't be enemies. But you ain't no friend of mine, and I can't not hate you."

"All right."

Noé took a great, deep breath and exhaled with a long sigh. "If I was an officer, if I had me rank and a Bible, would you take the oath from me, Abel?"

"I would."

"All right, then," said Noé. "That's good enough."

A warm, salt-laden wind set the poplars to creaking. Catkins fell all around with soft little thuds, and Abel brushed several from the crown of his hat, smelling their gentle, sticky perfume on his fingertips. He rubbed his elbow and dug little troughs in the dust with his new brogans. Presently the wind fell away, and sound manifested from the sandy road that ran flat and white under the moon to the edge of the trees. And out of the trees the wagon resolved from the dark, aggregating from the shadows board by pale board with that ancient, repetitious stamp-creak-and-jangle common to all such equipage.

"We'll part company now," said Noé as the wagon swung around. "These men will take you with them after they're loaded up." Abel did not recognize either teamster. The driver, a spectacularly bearded man whose sad eyes Abel could pick out even in that starry dark, nodded while his companion, younger, also bearded, also melancholic, simply swung down from the jockeybox and unlatched the bedgate without comment.

"Noé," said Abel, nodding and touching the brim of his hat as the soldier strode off into the darkness.

After a moment, he returned to stand looking at Abel from a little patch of moonlight that lit his face with a soft, silvery light. He took a deep breath, released it, then reached down deep into a trouser pocket, removed a few pieces of paper money, and gave them to Abel.

"You might could use that in the days to come," said Noé.

Abel opened his mouth to thank him, then closed it, swallowed, and said, "Hey Noé?"

The soldier turned from the edge of the poplars. Pale flowers fell and caught the moonlight as they tumbled. "What?"

"What's the date, anyway?"

"April twelfth," he said, his voice falling off with distance. "Wednesday."

Abel nodded. "And where's that bottom rail now?" he called out to the dark, and from the dark came Noé's voice, soft with the suggestion of laughter: "Still up top."

The drivers were a Greek father and son from Ohio whose English was spotty at best and who were given to vast, deep silences. They lit two hurricane lamps, hung one from a nail set into the overtall brake lever, and set the other on the ground within the barn, its yellow light turning the dead men's darkening soles darker still.

The night was cool and the wind was fine and the pair worked without their scarves, moving with brisk and orderly composure. Abel made to help them but they waved him off, preferring to treat with each corpse themselves. By necessity, they heaved the bodies into the bed one by one, and when they'd four in a row, the son clambered in among them to straighten legs as best he could, to fold arms across chests, and to unbend necks from positions sad and horrible. The Greeks had blankets with them, some of proper wool and some of thin linen that they'd soaked in the bay—Abel could smell cold salt and bladder wrack rising from dark folds—and one of these they draped over the first layer of corpses, then settled a second layer of bodies upon that. And then another blanket and a third layer in an ever-deepening stratum. One of the last bodies they pitched into the wagon Abel recognized as the johnny from the cot across the aisle, his face in death become softened, slack, pitiable. Abel looked away as the Greeks shook the blanket over him and tied the load off.

They mounted the wagon, and the father gathered up the reins. There were still a dozen or more bodies in the dead-house behind them, and at least as many more would join them before the wagon returned mid-morning. Like players in some ancient tragedy, they looked down at Abel standing in the cool dark.

"You are . . . a Lincoln man?" the driver asked.

"I don't reckon I got a choice in the matter no more," said Abel, swinging himself up beside them. And when the driver cocked his head and looked to his son for translation, he quickly added, "Yes. I am a Lincoln man. Through and through."

The wagon followed the sandy track until it became a proper road, then left it and doglegged west upon another road before turning toward the capital. The sun rose and the day stood fine and clear and cool. They passed through little hamlets where celebrations of Lee's surrender were still in evidence. In Leonardstown, they saw six Union soldiers passed out before the doors of a depot half filled with crates of shoes, hardtack, and overcoats. Off the beaten track and not expecting much in the way of official traffic, they'd mounded up great heaps of straw for their comfort and stacked emptied flasks, bottles, and mugs in little cairns at their feet. In Bryantown, their passage disturbed streamers and curls of confetti in Union colors that had washed up in the lee of storefronts and parked wagons, and the surface of the road was scorched by the blasts of fireworks. In both towns, folk who were awake ceased whatever business they were about, uncovered their heads, and lowered their eyes as the dead-house wagon trundled past.

Abel left the Greeks at a bleak and nameless crossroads west of Nottingham. He stepped down from the moving wagon as it swung slowly about to take the south-running road, and the teamsters watched him without comment before easing the wagon to a halt. A discussion ensued between father and son that entailed much gesticulation and sharp tones. Their ancient, inflected tongue, coupled with the morning birdsong and the crisping of leafed-out trees beneath a springtime wind, put Abel in the mind of other mornings in other lands in eons long, long gone. After a few moments, the father having obviously won the argument, the younger Greek stepped off the wagon and gave Abel two dimes, pressing them to Abel's palm with fingers whose nails were raggedly chewed to the quick. He removed his hat to thank the lad, but the boy turned back to the wagon, and without a word father and son ferried their cargo southward toward some distant necropolis.

Abel went on up the road. Amidst the easy green hills and swampy woods outside Upper Marlborough, he came upon a sutler in checkered pants and lime green waistcoat taking his ease in the shade of his wagon. Abel bought from him a pair of socks, a double length of twine to lace his shoes with, a pair of raddled brown wool pants that had the benefit of not having a soldier's stripe, a little wedge of cheese, a fist of bread, and, on impulse, one thin cigar. The sutler looked at the paper and the coin in his hand after Abel paid him and, with a smile and a waggle of his eyebrows, gave back half.

Abel went on up the road. He had the expectation of violence against his person if it was thought he was an escaped prisoner, so out of sight of the sutler and with no traffic visible, he stepped into the trees to change his trousers. It was watery country, and he found himself beside a little creek running sluggish and dark between drooping trees. Water skippers by the dozen plied the surface tension of the sulky run, maneuvering between leaves floating curled and upended like green Chinese junks. Abel removed his shoes and changed his pants, then stripped off his shirt and splashed his face. He lifted palms of water to his hair until it was soaked, then clawed out the tangles, washed his feet, and dried himself on the shoddy pants, redressed, and went on.

By and by, he found blown up into the grass at roadside a number of sheets of oyster-colored butcher's paper of the sort used to pack firearms. Sitting down, Abel selected one, then crumpled and folded and snugged it down into the floor of his right shoe. When he stood again, he saw a broadside amidst the packing papers and picked it up. A Special Printing from the *Washington Star*, with Lincoln's Second Inaugural printed thereupon. Abel sat again, reading the words that Noé had tried to explain to him. A rider cantered down the road toward Bryantown, paused to look him over where he sat, and rode on when Abel did not look up. Two men on lunch break from the sawmill south of town came along and nodded the afternoon to him, but he did not reply, and they went on their way. Abel sat a long time in the grass, reading and rereading, and when he'd finished he folded the paper carefully, empaneling the words so that in his breastpocket they'd lie near his heart just so.

★   ★   ★

Three days later, as fine a Saturday as he had ever known, he was in an outdoor café in Millersville north of the capital enjoying the first cup of real coffee he'd had in three years when a great cry of anguish spilled from the telegraph office at the end of the street. People looked up from their concerns as the news traveled along, drawing after it a palpable bubble of grief. Abel set his cup down on the saucer and waited for it to wash over him, and when it did, he took a great, deep breath as though he'd been dunked in cold water. Setting a three-cent piece down on the table near the saucer, he stood, put on his hat, and followed the other folk heading toward the office.

A week later, he was camped on the outskirts of Baltimore, where a blond girl in a passing wagon tossed him an apple. When he moved on, it was along the Northern Central Railroad as it wound its way north towards Harrisburg. Abel walked the rails. He'd wandered for a week, just walking and getting reacquainted with freedom. He did not know where to go.

At some point, he crossed into Pennsylvania. Small groups of people had begun to collect where the rails crossed roads and near little woebegone shacks. A dark stain of cloud spread northward from the direction of the capital, and a wind disturbed the heads of blooming flowers. Nights prior, the moon had risen red.

Abel left the tracks for a little patch of wood and settled down for the night. The wind gathered itself and the trees creaked. The rails nearby crossed a dusty road, white and filmy in the dark, and at the crossing waited a family of blacks standing quietly. Abel rubbed absently at his ruined elbow as was fast becoming his custom and sipped from his canteen, cool water tasting of brass and stone.

A single engine came along the tracks, a long chain of white smoke spreading from its belled stack. A machine shape, moving swiftly down the line; the fast, transitory image of the conductor standing ramrod straight, then gone. The smoke slowly lifted through the dark. The waiting blacks began to sing the Battle Hymn, slow, soft, and mournfully. One of the women wept and one of the children held up a little Union flag and all the men uncovered their heads.

Not long after came another engine, going slower, pulling seven cars all draped in black crepe, the engine itself festooned with pale garlands. The train came along, side rods pale silver, steam from the balloon stack falling away in heaps. An iron mechanism low upon the land, stirring wind into the hayfields and the trees where Abel sat watching. And then it was gone, fading in echo and vanished from the night.

Abel went down to the tracks where the blacks still stood. They'd lit lanterns now to guide them home, and by that soft, yellowy light Abel saw their wet faces dumb with misery. They looked up at him as he approached.

"Evenin'," he said. He tried a smile on for size, but it was cramped and uncomfortable so he let it go. Tilting his head in the direction of the vanished train, he asked, "Was that . . . ?"

They eyed him wonderingly. One of the women opened her mouth to speak, but then her face collapsed and she buried it in her palms, weeping bitterly against tough, dry skin. The man beside her slipped an arm around her shoulders and nodded. "Yes," he said softly. "That was the Lincum train. They takin' him home."

Abel knelt in the dust of the road to touch the dark, smooth rail where it was still warm from the lonesome train's passing. He tried to understand how he felt, and the woman who'd been weeping sniffed deeply, breathing through her mouth in the way that people suffering will do, and finally asked, "Was you a Lincum man?"

Off beyond the farthest trees, the line curved back around and straightened again, and Abel could see the lights of the train re-

ceding, dwindling down to yellow pinpricks coruscating against dark curtains of remote trees before finally disappearing with distance and with time. He took a deep breath. "I was," he said softly. "I always was." And all the while he wished, desperately, that it were true.

# ELEVEN

## *The Forest Behind, the One Ahead*

*1899*

IN THE GRAY damp of early morning they came along the road between dark trees. Walking together, moving slowly with the muddy
road sucking audibly at the floors of their shoes. As though the earth
or something in the earth was wanting them. Walking single file with
the Haida leading, rifle cradled in his arms, his cheeks wet with mist.
And Willis stumbled along after, his mangled face bare and damp. His
demolished hand was wrapped in filthy rags, and the flies harassed
him even at this early hour, even in this cool wet.

A decade of wandering without purpose they'd had already, a decade more they could reasonably foresee if they were of a mind to
contemplate it. Railroading in the cold north wilderness—hammering
spikes into frozen soil and living in a thin-walled tent. Eating stale
bread, onions, and hot broth. Returning to the shelter one evening,
they found it vanished, carried away by the cold, cold wind as though
it had never been, and so they left off that work, turned south for

warmer climes. Willis carried only the clothes he wore, a skinning knife and a small cameo wherein rode the blurry, faded image of a woman he said had once been his sister.

The Haida carried the rifle.

They did not reach the States. A rape at Barkerville. Petty thievery gone bad, and a stagecoach with all hands dead save one at a thickly wooded crossroads between settlements. When the Haida cut the throat of a young girl at Soda Creek, they fled north to the Great Land and lost themselves in Juneau amidst the disheveled throngs of hungry gold seekers.

They worked two seasons at the Treadwell Mine on Douglas Island, where neither lost fingers, before moving on to Nome, where they spaded up beach sand near a river that flowed into the sea. A season spent shoveling sand into rockers before the Haida turned up a nugget. It was no Wonder but it was big as a big man's thumbnail and kept them warm and in drink and women through the winter. They used the last of the stake to buy a team of dogs with the idea of running mail and medicine, but the Haida killed a man the same week a local whore accused Willis of things too vile to utter, so they went south again.

Within a month they were killing the dogs for food, and by the time they reached Iditarod they had but one big male left. They fought him, won, and worked their way about that land fighting dogs. Finally they found themselves on the northern beaches of Washington State, south of Makah Territory, with a wolf-dog they'd bought from the Indians there.

Now they walked as they'd been doing for days and years, and when the morning finished bleeding dim light and dull color into the landscape, the Haida stopped.

Wheezing, Willis drew up beside him. His destroyed hand was slung up with an old piece of rag, and he looked up at the big Indian as if he'd speak. The Haida shook his head and gripped the rifle. Setting stock to shoulder, he fired into the trees.

A six-point buck came crashing from the green tangle and onto the road, where it fell, plowing little furrows into the mud. The Haida nodded, and Willis came forward to crouch beside the deer. Its eyes wide and brown and soft and not yet dead, it pawed the mud and tried to rise but fell back again. The little man reached out and fingered its antlers and the deer tried to lift its head again but could not.

When the Haida came up beside him and touched his shoulder, Willis stood. They turned from the deer where it lay panting in the mud and dying. They walked on up the road.

As he walked up into the mountains, Abel followed the course of the Little Sugar Creek as it ran down from the peaks where alders leaned over the rushing water to stir eddies into the current. Leaves of orange and red and yellow and brown and every other color swirled madly past him in clusters and long chains like a strange, bright parade. From time to time, he knelt to cup his hand into the creek. The water was cold and milky with rock flour. The dog drank beside him, staying close as he traveled through the forest. Such proximity was not its custom, and Abel chided the dog, and for its part the dog looked at him with tired brown eyes and plodded slowly along. They followed the creek into the hills rising green and brown and powdered already with early snows. Fat clouds, brimful with more snow, swung up against the hard faces of the mountains beyond and scattered silently.

The day after leaving the Makerses he thought of the long train ride ahead of him. Envisioning Port Angeles and wondering what work he'd find in town to pay his fare east, he did not think beyond that to the journey afterward or himself making it. He walked the day long, thinking these quiet thoughts, and when Abel reached for his haversack he could not find it.

Swearing, he stood and stared back the way he'd come and wondered if he'd left the sack behind when he stopped for his lunch. It was too far back to retrieve and would have been plundered by animals at any rate, so that first night and much of the next day neither he nor the dog took food. And when the dog glowered at him, Abel shook his finger at it and told it hush.

So late in the afternoon, when the dog flushed a hare from the brush beside a foam-cluttered creek pool, Abel raised the rifle and fired. That night, he built a fire on the slim bank and took out his knife, cut away the hare's head and long feet and buried them, then cut open the stomach, scooped entrails into his palm, and fed them to the dog. It gulped and licked and Abel watched it with a frown. "Did you even taste it?" he asked. The dog blinked tiredly and watched as Abel stripped the hide from the carcass and skewered the meat on a branch, then squatted by the fire with his breath steaming into the cold. Tiny dollops of fat bubbled up then slid sizzling into the coals, attended by tiny yellow flames that jumped and shivered. He watched what stars there were through the canopy. How they sparkled there, so cold, so remote. He ate the meat off the point of his knife while the dog watched him intently. "Shut up," he said. "You had yours."

Abel chewed as though he had a grudge against the meat and stared into the fire. The meat was tough and dry, and after a while he leaned his face over the creek to drink. The dog watched as he passed his sleeve over his mouth. "Old cuss," Abel muttered as he tossed it the rest of his meal and lay down.

That night came a windstorm that set the trees to clashing. Sometime near dawn the wind calmed and Abel woke to hear the wolf howling from the hills above. The dog stood stiffly, its tattered ears cocked. "Don't pay him no mind," Abel told it, patting the ground beside him, and the dog hobbled over and with small groans settled in with its chin resting on the old man's chest.

In the morning, Abel rose and sat to watch the creek run down the hill. A little sluggish here but still running quick at the center, as though in anticipation of a journey ending. After a while, he stood and shouldered his rifle, picked up his walking stick, gave a heavy sigh, and left the creek to follow a trail that led up into the snowy hills.

The dog lay beside the dregs of the fire for a time after. Its eyes open, it did not raise its head from the floor of the earth, but you could tell it was listening carefully to the old man as he went through the woods. After a while, the dog stood stiffly and followed.

The night Abel left, Glenn and Ellen Makers made love in the bedroom of the cabin while outside trees shuddered and swayed and clashed under the blunt touch of the wind. In the morning, Glenn rose early as was his custom and walked the long hill down to the road to the blowdown blocking the lane. When he returned, Ellen was still sleeping, so he gathered the crosscut and the kerosene, the axe, and the maul and, carrying the tools yokewise across his shoulders, walked back down the lane.

He bucked the tree first, feeling his tired, cramped muscles loosen as he went along—using the crosscut on the thick branches and lopping off the smaller with easy strokes of the axe. It was cool and damp but the morning was fine and he warmed with the work and the work was good. He rubbed kerosene on the teeth when they gummed with pitch and took a break after an hour to eat a soft apple he'd slipped into his pocket. Chewing, he watched the squirrels cavort in the branches, and when he'd finished his breakfast he tossed the core off into the brush for their delight. He had just begun to section the trunk, was in the midst of pushing the old saw forward and drawing it back again, watching pale flakes of sawdust go spiraling down onto the dark mud, when they came out of the mist.

He skinned the gloves from his hands. Wiping sweat from his face with a red rag plucked from his back pocket, he stood waiting, watching them on the road where they came slowly though the fog.

They were insubstantial in the gray mist, like weary, lonesome ghosts, and the trees to either side shed a gray haze that parted slug-gishly before them and closed again behind. And when they saw him, they stopped and stood staring until the smaller of them said with a wet, terrible voice, "Well, lookit here."

Glenn breathed and his breath steamed and parted, blown back past both his shoulders by a soft, cool breeze that disturbed the mist but did not break it. Nodding, he told them good morning and the larger of the two cocked his head. "You see an old fella come this way?" asked the Indian. "Maybe a few days ago? Maybe had him a dog with him?"

Glenn sniffed and pursed his lips. He glanced to the axe where it lay propped and looked back at them. "No," he said. "I've not seen anyone come along."

"You sure? Think about it now. We're lookin' for this fellow."

Glenn nodded. He was stepping toward the axe when the smaller man said, "Hey, Joe, you reckon he kept that little old mud shark? She was a sweet peach."

Glenn Makers blinked. Between the emotion and the act came a brightness, shading off into degrees of red. He came leaping over the branches of the fallen tree.

At the end of the lane in the cabin above, Ellen Makers woke to gunfire.

Ellen dressed quickly in the dim, bruise-colored light, then hurried to the gun cabinet. Her hands trembled, and when she finally man-aged the clasp, she scooped the rifle up and broke it open. With the slightest insuck of breath, she pressed the pad of her finger into the empty chamber as though her eyes had tricked her. Grit and oil and the acrid stink of old powder.

Outside were wind sounds and creaking trees; no animals called and there was no birdsong. Ellen turned and set the gun on the table that still yet bore pale white streaks of flour from her pie-making.

Pressed into the tight grain, they stood in stark contrast to the dark wood. The apples still left in the bowl jumped and rattled, and one fell from the table to roll across the floor.

She went frantically about, throwing open cupboards and upending drawers, looking for the little green paper box of shells. After a few moments of this, she stopped in the center of the room. The gun cabinet stood half open and with the box on the top shelf. She could not think how she'd missed it. Pushing the hair from her face, Ellen went forward, but a sound from outside drew her attention to the window where she saw them coming into the yard.

She knew they would come again, one day. They had as much told her so that night when the small one went at her while the Indian watched. She squeezed shut her eyes, took a deep, steadying breath, opened them. Her hand was on the shells when the front door came open and Willis walked in.

When he saw her he knew what she was about and with a snarl shoved her back and sent the shells scattering madly across the board floor. And then his hand was fisted in her hair and he flung her against the hearth where the fire had died down to but a few live coals and the stones had cooled.

Ellen cried out with the pain of it and dropped the rifle. Willis kicked it across the floor as the Haida appeared in the doorway. The big man filled the frame and blocked the light as though he sucked brightness from the air and his body or his heart gave back dark and his eyes were cold. Willis crouched and wrapped his hand in her hair again and she lay beneath him limp as he raked her face across the hearthstones. She felt one of her front teeth break at the gum line while another snagged and bristled apart like an old broom.

He pulled her back against himself then threw her forward again. Her forehead had come open and blood stung her eyes and the side of her face went numb. Willis bent her head back and put his face close. She smelled the stink of his ill-healed mouth, his unwashed body, and could feel him against her thigh where he pressed himself.

From the doorway, the Haida watched. "Where did that old man get to?" he asked her. It was the first time she'd heard him speak. "That old soldier?"

Willis knotted up her hair, and she cried out and told them. The Haida looked up to the foothills where they rose greenly toward the close, blue mountains. And when he asked her, she gave him directions as to the better, faster route. She did not know why she did this save from fear, but as Willis giggled softly against her ear with the fingers of his good hand twisting and pinching at her, she told him Abel had used an older trail and that the Haida could cut him off if he hurried, if he hiked through the night, if he left right now. The Indian nodded and looked at Willis. "You hear all that?" he asked.

The little man licked his horrid lips and craned his face into her hair as though to better get the scent of her. "I heard it," he said.

"Well," said the Indian as he moved off into the yard. "You finish and don't take too long catchin' up. I ain't waitin'on you."

Beside her, Willis made a sound—a wet sound of longing coupled with a mindless delight. Ellen turned and closed her eyes. She spit away a fragment of tooth and felt the other, frayed and chipped as it was, saw against the inside of her lip. He whispered against her ear but she could not tell the words for the mangling of his mouth, only his intent. He let go her hair to fumble with his belt and she kept her eyes shut as he went fishing around beneath her skirt. And when she opened them again she saw the poker lying athwart the firedog where Glenn had left it the night before and she thought of her husband and knew rage.

Ellen felt cold air on her thighs and his reeking breath warm and close as he pressed against her. He began to wheeze and his hips shimmied about as he struggled with his trousers. She took a breath and with a cry lunged for the poker, wrapped a fist around it, and with another cry swung it around, laying him open from temple to chin with the barb.

Willis crabbed back, shrieking, one good hand covering his newly bloodied face, and went thrashing about, his trousers bunched around his knees. Ellen stood and snatched up the rifle. She plucked a shell from the floor, broke open the gun, loaded it, and shut it again. Willis blubbered wetly his fear, but she was stone. She put the barrel between his legs and pulled the trigger.

The body twitched and kicked and shuddered for a while before finally giving in. During that time, Ellen drew up a chair, set the rifle across her knees, and, as she reloaded, watched Willis go about his dying. A rank stink, like rancid fat thrown on flames, filled the room. After a while, she stood and went out into the yard, but there was no sign of the Haida though she could feel him watching from somewhere on the trail above. She stood motionless for some time before finally going to the stable and hitching Emerson to the wagon. Then, with rifle set stock-down on the seat beside her, she drove down the lane to fetch Glenn.

When she saw the half-bucked tree, saw a section of gnarled gray bark and the mud close by all splashed with blood, she cried out and stepped from the trees. And when she saw Glenn where he lay, the rifle fell from her inarticulate hands. Ellen sank to her knees with her skirts belling out around her wide and bright against the dark earth and her hands covering her ruined face.

But then he moaned and she cried out and went to him.

Ellen crouched beside her husband, her thin white hands fluttering over him like two doves as she spoke his name, shouting to him as though she'd call him back from the dark place he was bound. After a time, his eyes opened, and his eyes showed her the pain of it.

"All right?" he finally whispered, his voice thick with hurt. When she began to weep, he put out his hand out to touch her cheek, then drew it back and closed his eyes.

In the end, it took the better part of an hour to get him back to the cabin. Once there, she stripped away his bloody shirt and his trousers where his bladder had voided. And when he was swaddled in blankets and resting beside the rekindled hearthfire, he said her name and began to weep with quiet, little-boy gasps that broke her heart but brought no moisture to his face. She touched the top of his head with her palms and told him hush.

She stayed beside him for a long time with her hand lightly touching him here and there as though to assure herself of his presence, of the still-strong heart beating within him. She watched him sleep. She watched the fire in the hearth. The day ended. She put more wood on the fire and went out onto the porch. She looked up the slopes, where the mountains were lost to clouds. A cold wind blew down from the heights, and she thought of the snow high on the slopes where it fell unceasingly. She thought of the Haida on the Marmot Pass Trail and the little trapper's shack below the saddle of the mountain. Ellen's hands ached upon the rifle. The cold would keep Willis's body and she was thankful for that, for she had not the time for burying or burning.

Swearing softly Abel's name, she went back inside, found Glenn sleeping peacefully, then went into their bedroom to change out of her dress.

As he walked, Abel Truman wondered if he would ever escape the sound of water. All his life it had followed him, dripping and gurgling and spattering like a whispered curse, a muttered reproach. For twenty years he had lived a meager life beside waters, and when he felt he'd had enough, he walked into the sea and the sea cast him back. Now Abel turned away from waters altogether and walked into the hills.

But as he went through the forest, it rained. He looked, frowning, at the sky. Rain fell in gray sheets that sometimes seemed to cease, but when he looked, he saw it never did. The forest was dark with rain, and the old man grumbled as he walked.

In the middle of the day, he came upon a talus slope that lay in a wide apron of scattered stone across his path. Muttering soft curses, Abel crouched in the shade of a boulder to rest and consider things. From the myriad crannies of the rockfall, pikas chirped nervously, and the dog, when it caught up to him, settled slowly and stiffly down beside him, ignoring the rock rabbits and closing its eyes. After a time, Abel began to slowly scrabble up among the stones.

For its part, the dog got slowly to its feet and set out after him. It did not go far, for the path over the rocks was difficult. For a short time it paced back and forth at the base of the slope, whining softly and pawing at the stones. When the old man did not turn, it began a furious barking and only ceased and sat again when he stopped and came back down through the rocks.

"What?" Abel asked. "What is it?"

The dog panted as Abel's fingers went exploring down its flanks and legs and when he felt a small, hard mass nestled deep in the dog's groin, he sat back. His lips moved around the lower half of his face, and he turned his head. Rain spattered against the stones. After a time, Abel reached and took the dog's head in his hand and pressed his forehead to its temple. If he spoke, his words were for the dog alone. Finally, sniffing and nodding, Abel stood and looked around again.

"All right," he said. "All right then. We'll spend the night back in the trees, but so help me God, we're going up in the morning, and I will leave you behind if you don't come along."

Abel was sick the night long, and when he did sleep, he dreamed dreams of running. The grass beneath his heels green and fragrant, bent by wind, and you could hear the wind rustling and moving in the grass and you could hear the officers shouting and the sounds of artillery crashing somewhere on the left near where the line was anchored on the woods and then trees across the field burst with fire and smoke and metal filled the air but no one fell as the long blue line pressed forward and Abel dreamed this dream and others like it and then he woke.

In the morning, the old man made his slow, painful way up the rockfall. The sun was but a rumor and the air was darkly cold. He staggered a little with the dog slung yokewise over his shoulders. Abel felt its tail working steadily against his side and turned to look it in the face. It panted happily. "You goddamn well better not be grinning," he muttered. "I ain't yet figured out how you talk me into this shit."

By late morning, they left the crumbling, loose stone to walk be- tween black trees that grew twisting along the top of the slope, and presently they crossed into snow. What rocks lay about shimmered with frost. Abel lifted his face to sniff the sudden, metallic freeze and set the dog down.

About the top of the slope, wind-stunted scrub pine canted from the snow fixed precisely to their shadows, while before them lay a wide meadow leveling off under the snow before climbing again into the trees. Dark clouds heaped at the eastern rim of the sky. He watched for a while the dog driving its muzzle into the powder, hunt- ing for scents and coming up again bearded whitely. A few flakes fell and melted on the backs of the old man's hands—both the crippled and the strong.

Abel and the dog moved across the meadow. The snow was deep and powdery, shelled by a thin crust of ice. The dog's breath appeared and vanished as it loped slowly ahead—as though the cold agreed with it. For a moment or two, Abel stood watching it—a lovely, redblonde blur suddenly fast upon the flowing, milk-white ground, its lean musculature rippled in constant motion flank and shoulder, its mouth a joyous red slant. Bounding through the snow, jumping up, coming down, turning back again to snip after its own tail, then running madly first one direction then another. Abel watched the dog at play in the snow and he smiled widely that it should leave its sickness behind if even for a moment and laughed out loud with a pure delight he'd not felt for a long while.

A random frieze of animal tracks crossed the meadow—designless and wild and from which Abel could tell but little of the creatures that made them, their habits, the directions of their homes. The trees ahead, where the land sloped up again into the mountains that now stood white and blue and close, stood feathered with fresh snow and silent. Abel's boots made bright crunching sounds as he walked.

He heard running water and, cutting to the left, found a little tributary of the Little Sugar Creek whetting the edge before the sudden upward surge of forest. The snow nearby was mud-smeared, and the water ran impossibly black between its banks. Abel looked at himself in the current; he stared for a long time at his dark, watery twin, then spat into its face and knelt.

He rinsed his mouth with cold water. Beside him, the dog lapped bitingly as Abel examined the little handprints of squirrels and marmot where they'd come to drink and the split ovals of deer pressed parenthetical into the mud. As though they'd record their passage through the wilderness for those who could decipher such scripture. Abel read and frowned.

He looked about, then kneeled again near one particular set. Whistling softly his amazement, he spaced its depth and width with his palm. He looked at the dog. "That's an elk," he told it. "Goddamn big. Old too."

Abel sniffed and looked about. "Funny thing," he said softly.

"Funny, funny thing." He looked to where the tracks crossed the stream and disappeared into the forest. "Where in hell is he goin'?" Abel wondered aloud as he crossed over the water and into the trees.

A whiskey jack flickered between the trunks like a shard of shadow falling through the light and more chattered from above and the sound of water faded behind him. Abel saw a sprig of green vanilla leaf sprouting through the snow beside a moss-bound nurse log and moved the soft fronds aside to pluck a delicate scallop of chanterelle. It smelled of apricots and tasted of chalk and rubber, but he was hungry and so chewed thoughtfully, wishing for his haversack. Abel looked for the dog but it was still down in the meadow so he ate the rest of the mushroom himself. He could see the passage of the elk through the trees, was already beginning to visualize it— the way it moved, its path upmountain—and after a time he threw the thick stem to the side and followed.

From time to time, Abel stooped to touch the track with two fingers. He knew it was a bull from the size of its print, the way its back hooves cleft and the tiny indentations of its dewclaws in the snow, and by the way it left its droppings in a trail, not clumped tidily in the fashion of a doe. Abel tracked it the rest of the day, leaving the trail sometimes, walking parallel to it, then cutting back to find the tracks once more. When he crouched he could see them where they ran between the trees and when he stood they disappeared into the snow—a trick of light, shadow, and snowfall. A phantom elk that went before him and he its spectral hunter. The dog watched him at this business. "I might could call him if I wanted to. Maybe," said Abel. "But I don't know what in hell he thinks he's doin'." He stared at the dog and rubbed his palm up and down across the prickly whiskers that had sprouted across his jaw. Abel winced when he brushed against the cut and shook his head.

The sky darkened with evening and with clouds the color of gunmetal. Snow shed fitfully down between the trees, and the tracks followed the slope as it rose. The old man paused and grimaced and put out his hand to grip a thin slide alder growing slanted from the snow. He propped the walking stick into the snow and clutched at the little tree, struggling to stay on his feet. Of a sudden, his face was cold, tingling. He felt heat rushing into his chest like steam, scalding his throat until he finally leaned to vomit. Swearing and panting, he fell to his hand and knees, then slid a short ways down the slope. After he'd come to a stop, Abel lay on his back, staring at the dark sky, and when the spell had passed, he rubbed handfuls of snow over his face. After a while, he sat up with his legs pointing downhill. "Well," he said quietly. "Well, shit." The dog walked three tight circles and lay down in the snow.

The old man sniffed and spat a little blood. The tincture of sickness spread across his tongue. He began coughing and the dog raised its head while he leaned over to try and better breathe. Rolling onto his knees, he sat in the snow with little white ropes of saliva depending from his lips. He looked at the dog when it whined and clawed the snow nearby. "You just be still," he told it.

Finally, the old man took a deep breath and reached for his rifle. He held it in his hand. It was old, the metal silvered by the wear of twenty years, its stock held together by baling wire. The barrel was speckled with snow, for the snow had begun to fall again. Abel let his fingers trail along it, feeling tiny grooves and nicks, the crack in the action from all the times he'd dropped it upon the beach stones. He stroked the palmsmoothed stock and looked at the places the wire had bled rust into the wood. He'd carried a weapon for a long time, his whole life it seemed. A life that had the appearance of beginning at Manassas. As though wife and child and home, all the fine times that had come before, had been a dream or something like a dream. But he could remember the cradle and the buttercups, warm sweet rolls and rain falling into the lake and the sound of his wife's skirts whispering across the floorboards, breathless with misery.

The old man looked up. Such remembering was hard on him. The dog lay in the snow a few feet away. Snow fell around them and the old man smelled woodsmoke on the air. "You stay out of it now," he told the dog, who raised an eyebrow without lifting its head from its paws.

Abel spat to the side, looked at the color of it upon the snow, and looked away again. He levered the rifle and turned it about, but his left hand was too clumsy and twisted up to hold it to the angle he wanted and his right arm was not long enough to reach the trigger. Abel swore and stood and stamped his feet in the snow and threw down his hat. When he stood, the dog stood with him, and he told it to sit down and shut up.

He spent a few moments just standing quiet in the snow with the dog, then scowled and looked about and sniffed the air. Woodsmoke. He watched the sky uphill where it was darkening with evening and saw a faint taper of smoke rising over the trees. Cursing softly, he stood, slung the rifle over his shoulder, and retrieved his walking stick. The dog stood, its tongue hanging out the side of its mouth while its breath steamed. "You just shut up," said Abel he started up the slope again.

He heard it bugle, loud and shrill—a lonesome haunt ghosting through the wood, the echo of its call hung in the quiet snowfall. Abel came out onto a broad, flat plain and listened to the elk. The plain stretched before him, bordered by snow-salted trees sparkling under the risen moon. Sloping talus fields reared northward. Glittering slabs of mountain rock stood veined darkly with ice. The moon shined out from a gap in the clouds to light the world blue and silver. He thought he saw the elk across the plain—a shadow, moving slowly into the trees—and he listened until the echo of its call had finally faded and the sound of the wind whispering atop the snow came back to the fill the void so left.

267

Abel stared at the snow as he walked, and the dog came along slowly behind him. It was as he was telling it what a good dog it was that he caught the scent of woodsmoke again. Squinting ahead through the falling snow, he found a light burning weakly in the window of a tiny shack near where the elk had crossed into the forest.

Abel stood staring at the teardrop flame fluttering behind thin windowglass. For all his age, his eyes were good, and he saw the single window was warped and scalloped with ice and he saw a small pile of split wood stacked against one wall and a tin stovepipe pushing out at an angle from the steeply pitched roof. A small mound of dark snow, purple with shadow, lay near the front door, and another mound lay near the trees beyond.

Abel sniffed and spat. He tasted sick in his mouth and looked down at the dog. "I know it," Abel said. "I reckon I'm hungrier'n you anyway, since I've been carryin' your ass. Meaner too. By a long ways." He nodded to the shack. "We'll go on over there and see if it's them Chinese."

Abel bid the dog stay, then set out. The stars came out in their thousands around the risen moon. Brightly cold and glittering like points of ice. Abel sighed when he heard the dog stagger up and limp along behind him. The sound of them walking through the virgin snow swept past on the wind and faded against the trees where they stood dark and quiet.

Abel heard nothing from the shack as he approached. He crouched fifty feet from the door and clucked his tongue and the dog lay down in the snow while he bent his head to listen. But for the wind blowing and chaffing the snow, there was no sound. And then came a thick, clotted cough. The heavy sound of bootsteps on the flooring within. The coughing went on hot and rattling and small and petulant. Abel heard a man's voice rise up and the sudden, sharp, fleshy smack of skin on skin. And then the man's voice again, lower

now and speaking soothingly as one might to an injured animal—reassuring and grave and decided and sad.

Abel stood, and behind him the dog also stood. When he moved the dog moved and together they approached the cabin then stopped when the door opened. The Haida stood slumped in the doorframe, glaring out at the night.

He staggered through the cold toward the woodpile but stopped when he heard the dog's low growl and spun back, slipping and falling. He fell across the threshold with his trousers caked with white and he swore mightily. The dog kept growling and the Haida fumbled about and Abel heard soft weeping from within the cabin, louder now with the door open, followed by the same weak, pitiful coughing. The Haida finally managed to stand and raise the rifle he'd been groping about for. He stood in the door, backlit by the sputtering candleflame, and pointed the gun out at the dark.

"Here now!" shouted Abel to the dog. The dog paced back through the snow and settled near Abel's leg, growling still. The Haida's gun barrel dipped and came back up.

"That you, old soldier?" called the Haida.

"It is," said Abel, trying to imagine, to see beforehand, the sequence of actions it would take to shoot and kill the Indian where he stood. "You go lightly now," said Abel. "Just passin' by and saw your light."

"Well, you just step on into this light so I can see you, or by God, I'll shoot you where you stand."

Abel went forward with his hands open and the Haida put the gun on him as he entered the weak light spilling slantwise from the door. "Ease up now," said Abel. "Ease up."

The Haida eyes were dark and recessed and they were bright with pain. His wide forehead was raked open and there was a filthy rag, spotted darkly, wound around his throat. The hands that held

269

the gun were nicked and deeply cut, as were his arms. The Indian wore an old pair of trousers that did not fit him well and that had about them that shiny luminescence that comes to fabric only after days and weeks of constant wear. His shirt was linen-thin and shapeless, splitting at the shoulders, while his ragged sleeves fluttered and snapped in the dark wind. He looked Abel up and down, then licked his dry lips. "Where's your bag, old soldier? You got food?"

Abel pursed his lips and shook his head. "Not a lick," he said. His eyes darted about, trying to see into the cabin. "Where's your partner?" he asked.

The Indian covered his long face with a hand and laughed into his palm. "He stopped to have him a visit with that little mud shark down yonder. I don't claim to know how it all worked out, but I heard gunshots and he ain't caught up with me yet so I reckon I've got a pretty good idea."

Abel breathed. His breath disappeared on the wind and he moved the twisted fingers of his left hand to try and flex the cold from them. The wind scraped against the snow, skittering loose crystals across the frozen crust. "You son of a bitch," he finally said, stepping forward.

The Haida's gun came up to press against Abel's chest, and even with his coat protecting him he could feel its cold mouth upon him. The dog stood and began barking viciously. Its front legs were braced, its head thrust forward, and its hackles stood along its back. It closed in on the Haida with short little steps. "You call it off," snarled the Indian. "You call it off or I'll shoot you so you ain't killed, then make you watch me kill it."

Abel shouted down the dog as the Haida sniffed and winced as though with some great inner pain. "I hate a dog," he said. "Always have. Even after everything. All that other . . . that was Willis's idea."

"I don't care."

The Haida blinked and sniffed again and looked at Abel. "That dog's sick," he said. "You can see it. Dog like that ain't no good to nobody. What you ought to do is shoot him."

"He's all right."

"What are you doing up here, old man?"

"Tracking an elk come this way."

"Shit. Elk don't come upmountain in winter. 'Less they're fixin' on dying. Shit, wolves've probably got it by now anyhow." The Haida winced and looked about, at the shadowy, snow-feathered slopes and the darker downward plunge of the slope across the plain. "There's a wolf about, old man," he said quietly, looking around. "The one we lost. Out there. Right now."

Abel shrugged. "You didn't hear that elk hollering? He come by not a hundred feet from your door."

"I been sleeping. Tryin' to sleep." The Haida ran a hand down his long face and looked up again to the close, dark mountains. "Elk, hey?"

"That's right."

"And you been trackin' him. Just up and decided that was what you was goin' to do."

"That's right."

"You figure you can bring him down with that old thing?"

Abel looked at the rifle he'd dropped and shrugged.

The coughing inside the shack began again. The Haida scowled and said, "You stay right there," then went into the shack and shut the door. He came back a moment later with a length of rope. Abel wondered why he had not used the opportunity of the closed door to ready his rifle but had no answer for himself.

The Haida handed him the rope. "You tie that thing up and come inside. I want to show you something." He leaned and spat. "And you leave the goddamn gun."

Abel took up the rope and made a slipknot to snug about the dog's neck. It growled quietly. "I know it," Abel told it. There was an old hitching post near the door, and he bent to tie the rope off.

"You make it short enough it don't dig up the Chinaman," said the Haida from the door. He jerked his chin to the dark mound frozen to the floor of the snow nearby.

Abel looked at him, and the Indian shrugged. "He wasn't as neighborly as he could've been when I come up yesterday." The Haida coughed wetly into his palm and grimaced.

The Haida went into the cabin. Abel could see the man through the ice on the thin window as he moved, blurred and twisted as a funhouse mirror. Swearing softly to himself, Abel propped his gun against the wall, took a breath, and stepped inside.

The Indian sat on the edge of a filthy, broken-down bed against the far wall near the stove. He held his skinning knife to the throat of a child who lay limply across his lap, her face gray with cold and drawn with hunger. On the bed behind them lay a dead woman, the girl's mother perhaps, half covered with a thin, stained blanket. Abel closed his eyes and took a breath, receiving on his flesh like a woman's soft touch the faint warmth of the fire rattling in the stove. He'd been cold for long enough that the sudden, thin heat set his fingers itching. Abel cleared his throat and looked at the Haida. "Don't you do it," he said.

The Haida pursed his lips. The girl's eyes were closed, but Abel could tell her life by the rise and fall of her chest. The Indian rested the blade against her bare throat and looked at Abel. "They was in quite a state when I come crost 'em," he said. "Lord knows how long they been up here. Stuck. Just plumb stuck." He nodded toward one wall to indicate the snow-bound plain outside. "Horse wandered off, wagon busted to shit, and them already out of food." He sniffed and scowled.

"What did you do to them?"

The Haida shrugged. "Not much, really," he said. "The man, well, he pulled on me so I was obliged to defend myself." He flashed a smile that held within its margins not a trace of mirth. "And this one here was sickly and looked about half starved anyway," he said, nodding to the thin gray corpse of the woman behind him. "She passed this morning. So that just leaves the little one." He dandled the girl on his knee, and she moaned softly. "And I don't believe she's long for this world either." He looked at Abel and smiled. With a quick move of his hand, he drew a thin, thin line along the girl's cheek with the point of the blade. "But she's sweet as a peach, ain't she? Like a china doll." He grinned again and chuckled. "China doll," he said. "That's funny."

"You son of a bitch."

The Haida shrugged.

The girl was perhaps seven years old and impossibly thin. Even through the stained folds of her tattered dress, he could see the crude angles of her limbs, the sharp points of her elbows and knees. Perhaps the first dark blush of frostbite at her fingers, toes, and earlobes. And he started when she opened her eyes, for they were milky as though thickening with cold.

Abel blinked and swallowed painfully. "She got a name?" he finally asked.

"Hell, I don't know," said the Haida. "This one"—he nudged the girl's dead mother, and the corpse trembled stiffly in the bed while the girl moaned and squeezed shut her eyes—"this one called her all kinds of things, but I couldn't make much sense of it." He blinked as though concentrating. "Shit, it don't matter none anyway."

Abel ignored him and slowly, painfully, crouched until he was at the girl's eye level. "Hey there?" he called softly across the room, and the girl opened her eyes and blinked. Abel held her eyes and said, "Don't you worry, honey. We'll figure something out."

Abel stood panting, his eyes heavy and warm in their sockets. The close warmth of the shack set his throat to itching, and he steeled himself, but no cough came.

"What are you goin' to do?" he asked the Haida.

The Indian pursed his lips, shifted a little, and hissed with the pain of it. Abel watched the way he held himself, the way he moved and breathed and blinked and sweated. Abel lifted his chin and said, "That Chinaman put a little metal into you."

The Haida scowled. "Little fucker," he said. "Shit. I told you he wasn't none too friendly when I came up."

"Gut?" asked Abel.

The Haida's lips drew back from his teeth.

Abel snorted. "You're a dead man."

The Haida stared reflectively into the middle distance. "Maybe so, maybe so," he said, nodding. "But I'll tell you what, this little peach is goin' with me." He settled the flat of his blade back against the girl's throat and she whimpered softly and closed her eyes.

Abel put his hand up, fingers spread. "Why?" he asked.

The Haida shrugged. "'Cause I can," he said.

"Goddamn it!" shouted Abel. He took off his hat and threw it on the floor, then picked it up again, holding it awkwardly between his hands. "All right," he said, taking a breath. "All right. Suppose . . . Suppose I get you down off this mountain. Get you back down to . . . that little farm. I'd do that."

The Haida's eyes narrowed. "Would you?"

Abel tucked his upper lip inside his lower and nodded. "You let me get that girl down off this hill, and I would. If your partner ain't shown up yet, there's no one else coming."

"I'm not afraid of dyin', old man. You?"

Abel snorted. "You got no idea, son."

The Haida looked him in the eye. "You're a liar," he said, and wrapped one fist into the girl's hair. Abel shouted, and outside the dog began to bark. The Haida grinned and lifted his chin. "You go on and get that elk you was hunting," he said. "Bring me back a little meat, and we'll talk about what all else you'll do for me."

"You're crazier'n a loon if you think I'm goin' to leave her alone here with you."

The Haida shrugged. The girl's throat was stretched across his knee and he tapped the point of the blade against the hollow above her breastbone. "I've seen folk die all kinds of ways," he said. "But I ain't yet seen nobody just bleed themselves to death. That'd be something new to see." He glanced around the cabin and shrugged again. "I burned the chairs, but you go on ahead and settle down on a piece of floor. We can watch her together."

"You son of a bitch."

"What are you goin' to do, old soldier?"

Abel scowled, clenching and unclenching his good hand. His crippled arm ached to the bone, and he was tired. His chest rattled, and after a few moments he ducked his head to catch the girl's eye. She blinked her hurt, gelid eyes, and her dry lips cracked open. "You wait here for me, honey," Abel told her. "You wait here, I'm coming back." He straightened and looked at the Haida. "You hear that?" he asked, turning to the door and going out again, into the night and the cold.

The dog struggled up to meet him, and Abel nodded and spoke to it and spent a few minutes going from the woodpile to the front door, making a small pyramid of firewood there that would be easy for the Haida to reach. The Indian's image trembled through the windowglass. Then Abel freed the dog and together they started slowly off across the plain with the wind blowing all around them, making the yet-unfrozen snow hiss like something deadly.

Abel heard the shack door creak open as he walked into the trees where the mountain began in earnest. He heard the Haida's voice, mixed in with the sound of the wind and the sound of the new snow that fell sizzling to the frozen crust. It was a small thing in all the world, that sound, and Abel paid it no mind.

He slept that night propped against a massive blowdown he judged as old before the coming of Columbus. He slept with the dog in his lap and the thin, torn blanket wrapped tightly about both of them. His hands shook, nor he could not stop them. His breath came clattering from his lips as though his very lungs were ashiver. The dog lay without moving, only opening its eyes now and again to gaze upon Abel Truman's face where his tears left thin trails of ice curling down his cheeks to pearl in his whiskers.

The dawn they woke to was still dark. White clouds hovered silently, and the mountains stood black and close. Neither man nor dog cast a shadow. As though their shadows abandoned them in the night, they walked shadowless and pale as lost spirits on the wander.

The old soldier raised his rifle a dozen times before noon, sighting clusters of branches that resembled antlers, bare twists of slide alder that he mistook for the curve of a muscled haunch. Each time, he'd still himself, crouch, and squint down the sight, then lower the barrel with slow disgust. The dog watched, mouth open and weary, as Abel leaned and spat and cursed. "I suppose you could do better?" he asked it.

It was early afternoon when he heard it bugle again. A long, drawn-out wail that hung in the chill, white air. He heard wild, savage barking, and the dog began to tremble and whine. Abel hushed it and cocked his head, sucking at a loosened tooth until he tasted blood. After a time, he cursed and started on again.

The scat, when he came upon it, was still warm. Behind him, the dog stopped abruptly, hackles raised. Abel broke the rifle, checked the shell, and suddenly thought of David Abernathy swearing clumsily and fumbling with his gun while Yankee bullets chewed up the pines of the West Wood all around them. The old soldier grinned and moved slowly up the slope.

The trees gave way to the back of a steep ridge that fell before him in a confusion of frost-coated stones as though something great and beastly had raked the back half of the hill raw. The day was clear and sunny on this side of the pass, and the old man could see across miles of snowy foothills down into the rolling green of the Puget Sound. He saw the blue of the inland waterways, cold with the sun bright upon their faces, and he saw distant smoke rising from stacks at Port Angeles. And he could see far to the east, where night was already darkening the Cascades, folding Mount Rainier in shadow while a round white moon rose behind. The gun was heavy in his hand, and he squeezed the stock to feel the baling wire bite into his palm like a comfort. Abel began to tremble. He closed his eyes a moment to imagine the smell of the town-smoke, to hear the trains running fast and metallic eastward toward home. Another ocean and another coast. Tilting his head, he sniffed the cold, blue mountain air, then looked down the ridge and softly swore.

The wolf harried the elk through the scrub pine and the boulders fallen from the mountain's shoulder. Huge. Dark about the face, with silver-gray fur running to dark again at the tips. A chest broad as a man's two hands. A dark shape low to the ground, moving like water over stones. It was silent as it ran, and it leapt with forelegs splayed, popping its jaws with its hackles rising between its shoulders. For its part, the elk ran, throwing powder into the air and swinging about its great, antlered head. The wolf, alone, had no chance to bring it down, but hunger, desperation, instinct, drove it on, and the elk ran and the wolf ran until the dark forest closed around them and they vanished.

Abel swore and spat. He swore and spat and sat down hard in the snow with his legs before him. The old man took great, deep breaths and his eyes were closed, his gray hair damp. The dog limped up beside him and lay down near his thigh. It whined softly and pawed at his trousers and Abel stared at it a long moment, seeing how it was and feeling something break apart within him.

As snow began to fall once more, he looked at the mountains. To his left and right, the peaks disappeared behind the snowfall and the air trembled with cold. He knew the signs. A day, maybe two, and the pass would be unreachable from either side and the cold would go bitter. Before him, he could still see down across the Sound where lights had come on in the towns to sparkle there, cold, remote, and now forever unreachable. "Goddamn it, Buster, but we got close," he murmured.

The snow ticked softly as it fell. Like a myriad of clocks in a quiet library, it spoke of age and memory and endings. Abel sniffed and spat. He set the barrel of the rifle to the side of the dog's head. "God-damn you anyway," he said tenderly. The dog's tail brushed through the snow. It rolled its eyes to look at him and opened its mouth.

An hour later, the old man made his slow, painful way down through the trees, trying to follow his own tracks back to the plain before they filled with snow and disappeared. Throughout the day, the sun had pressed cups into the snow, and now these all filled with shadow so there appeared to be innumerable dark pools all about him. He limped steadily, carrying the dog yokewise across his shoulders. Its tail worked weakly against him, and he turned to look it in the eye. It blinked at him and opened its mouth. "Don't you be looking at me like that," he muttered. "And don't you go getting used to this me-carryin-you shit neither."

Ellen Makers followed thin game trails that paralleled the main track as she went slowly up the mountain. Bruised, hurt and sick with worry and regret over leaving Glenn behind, she raised her rifle clumsily at every small sound crackling from the dark woods and waited with motionless dread until she was sure whatever she heard was not made by man. After years of living in a fluttery shade of fear, she had never been so afraid before.

She walked the day long and on into the first dark of the evening when shadows fell in great black panes from the canopy and robbed all color from the world. And then she crouched in the brush between the trail and the track and tried hard to hear him if he was close. She could not and he was not, yet still she waited and feared the outcome of her wait.

She made no fire that night and the night was long. Ellen wrapped a blanket around her shoulders and every few moments she reached through the dark to touch the rifle where she'd leaned it. Things moved in the forest. Crackling, bestial noises all out of agreement with the creatures making them; Ellen imagined bears and cougars and saw by pale moonlight the furtive silhouettes of rock rabbits and deer stepping about on wire-thin legs. Time and again, with quick, panicked breath, she raised the rifle to point it at the Haida come to her in the night shapeshifted in the way she'd always heard his folk could. And each time, as she set the gun down once more, she silently cursed Abel and herself and fixed in her mind the image of the big Indian crouching in the tent, stroking the rifle barrel as though it was his member and watching as Willis did things to her.

She slept but fitfully, and once when she woke the moon had run to dark and the sky had clouded. Her breath haloed her and the fallen pine needles crackled urgently with gathering frost. The world smelled quick and icy, and after a time it began to snow. Ellen could see it falling through the trees onto the wagon track that led to the pass, salting the mud and whitening the puddles where they'd skinned themselves with ice. Breathing against her hard palms, she rubbed them together, then pulled on a pair of Glenn's working gloves. After a while, she slept again.

And early in the morning she heard a wolf cry from the high slopes.

A single wolf that sang to the moon though there was no moon to sing to. And this was not singing. Its call went on and on, rolling down the slopes and into the valley where the trees thinned near the coast until the wind caught the sound and swept it to sea and it was gone as though it had never been.

When it was light enough to travel, Ellen ate a little bread and cheese. She stood and stretched, then went into the trees to make her toilet, dug a trough through the snow to the soil below with her heel to cover what she left behind, then rolled her blanket and slung it soldier-style, as she'd seen Abel do. She looked around her little camping place once, then twice, then walked up the trail toward Marmot Pass, where she figured she'd find one or the other of them.

It was night again when Abel came back onto the plain. The wind gouged designs into the snow, and the dark little shack upon the apron of white was dark within as well. He watched from just without the treeline with the dog across his shoulders but could not see the candle flame that had quivered in the window before. The thin scent of woodsmoke still flavored the wind. After a while, Abel grunted and started forward.

He set the dog in the snow before the shack. It pawed the crust and lifted its head to seek the old man's eyes. Abel bent over it and spoke and stroked its brow and its fine, soft cheek and ran his hand through the fur along its flank. The dog lay its head on the snow. The old man could see the shape of its death in its eyes and took a great, shuddery breath, but fell quickly quiet to hear the sound of the girl sobbing from within the shack.

Abel stood quickly and winced for the sudden pain of it. He stared at the door and wondered what he should do.

Swallowing and wincing, he gripped the rifle and stepped forward as quietly as the snow would let him. He went to the door. The wind picked up and blew against it, rattling and moving the old, rotten boards, and from its motion Abel could tell it was unlatched. Behind him the dog whined and struggled in the snow. He put his palm on the door and pushed it open.

The Haida sat spraddle-legged before the hearth, where only two coals still lived. He'd ruptured sometime in the night but the blood had barely soaked his clothing before freezing. Abel sniffed. A wave of nausea broke over him and he reached out with the bar- rel of the rifle to touch the Indian's shoulder. He did not move and no breath played from his lips. His eyes were closed and his raven- hair fell cold and stiff down his long face. The big Indian had a length of filmy, pale blue lace, as of a bride's garter, wrapped around one hand as though he meant it to be the last thing he'd see before dying.

Abel looked at the lace, then looked at the Indian. "No," he said. "You had too much badness in you to be comforted like that." And setting the rifle down, Abel worked the lace from the Indian's cold fingers and tossed it in the hearth where it lay smoking a moment before tiny yellow flames came dancing up along the tatting to throw about a shivering light.

Abel watched it burn, then stood and dragged the Indian's body outside. The moon went behind a cloud and it was fully dark. Snow fell. The snow raced over the plain on the wind as the wind rose once more. His clothing snapped and popped. He trembled and swal- lowed, could taste blood in his mouth, and swallowed again.

Abel walked to the dog and knelt beside it where it lay dead in the snow. He brushed snow from its face, then sat and pulled its head onto his lap. He told it what a good dog it had been and spoke softly, telling it things. Abel closed his eyes and said its name and rocked it back and forth in the cold and the falling snow. Save the wind, the only other sound was the ticking of the snow falling like soft laugh- ter, like lost time.

After a while, Abel stood and went into the cabin to tend to the girl, to build the little fire up, to take care of what he could and let go the rest.

The man who smelled of dogs and leaves and sweat returned. Jane Dao-ming remembered hearing him outside with the dog and then, after he came in, how quiet he was. A leaf-colored blur that moved across the floorboards and soon heat came from the hearth. And then a dragging sound and the old man's soft curses. And then he came back again and sat on the edge of the bed to help her dress. Speaking to her all the while, with a voice meant to be soothing but pitched all wrong for such work. The old man made small, sharp sounds when he came upon the places the Indian had put the knife on her and his voice was thick when he asked her name and thick again when he repeated it back slowly and carefully.

He asked could she see him. She felt the air disturbed before her face and realized he moved his hand there so told him yes. The man made a doubtful sound, then described for her his actions: how he was building up the fire and how that was all they needed, a good, strong fire. And the more he spoke the more tired and pale his voice became. And when Dao-ming's leg brushed against her mother's cold, dead arm in the bed beside her, she began sobbing.

The man who smelled of leaves and dogs sat beside her on the bed while she wept. He held her hand and stroked her hair and let her carry on without comment. And when she finished, he asked if she was hungry. She told him yes and then began to weep because of that particular, sharp, and constant pain. The old man did not move for a long time. Finally, he took a deep breath and stood.

She heard him go outside and he was out in the snow a long time before coming back. He rummaged noisily around the shack and soon she smelled meat cooking. When it was finished, he fed her carefully and the meat was stringy and tough but very sweet. It made her cry again to taste it and the old man told her try and sleep because in the morning they'd be leaving.

After the girl was asleep, Abel went outside to gather the last of the firewood. It didn't take many trips to exhaust the woodpile, and when he finished Abel stood in the center of the shack and watched the girl sleep. "What the hell are you goin' to do?" he said quietly, making fists with his strong right hand.

There was a sudden, burning itch high in the back of his throat, and he staggered outside to cough and retch into the snow. When he was finished, Abel went to the dog and carefully lifted it. It was very light. When a single tooth clicked like dumb stone against his thumbnail he thought his heart would break, and he could not look at the place on its thigh where he'd used his knife.

Morning found him sitting on the floor of the shack with the dog's head cradled in his lap. There was a small smile on his cracked, bloodied lips and his fingers turned ceaseless circles through the soft fur behind the dog's ear. When sunlight touched his face, he carefully eased the dog to the floor and went outside.

He found Dao-ming's father buried by snow and grimaced when he saw what the cold had done to him. Going back into the shack, Abel woke the girl and sat her on the floor so she faced the fire, then carefully eased the thin, stained sheet out from under her mother and took it outside.

There were no tools about the shack, so Abel had to use the butt of his rifle to lever the man's body from the ice. And in the end the stock broke and the baling wire cut his hand. He stood looking at the ruined rifle. Then he leaned, spat, and wrapped the man in the sheet and carried him inside and laid him on the bed with his wife and covered both of them with the blanket.

The girl sat on the floor where he'd left her, her blind face tilted toward the fire where it crackled in a yellow dance upon the firewood.

One hand rested on the dead dog's cheek and her face was wholly wet. He said her name and she stood to face him. Abel told her they were going and she held out her arms to him in the way he'd always imagined his own daughter would have. Sniffing wetly, he wrapped her in an extra blanket from the bed and leaned to lift her onto his left hip. Abel's crippled arm fit snugly around her as she set her arms about his neck and he knew that even though he might weaken, the arm would not. Nor would it bend from its crook so she would not fall from his grasp. Abel looked at his old, ruined arm where it fit around her and held her as though made for that purpose. "Well, imagine that," he murmured, rocking this way and that to test his grip. "Well, my Lord in heaven."

The fire burned brightly in the stove as Abel took a final look around. He looked down at the dog where it lay. "Goddamn you anyway, Buster," Abel said softly, and he kicked over the stove and stood to watch a moment as the flames spread like water.

Afterward, they stood together to watch the shack burn, the girl with her half-blind face turned toward the heat. Abel smelled the sweetness of her childish breath and thought of green grass and springtime, of horses and things running wild with joy. He took a breath and turned to start across the bright, snowbound plain.

At the tree line, Abel sat heavily down, wheezing with his breath burning in his chest. "All right," he panted. "All right now." He struggled to his feet and went weaving through the snow between the trees. Behind them, the burning shack threw a pillar of smoke into the sky.

"Am I too heavy?" asked Dao-ming, her accent thick, but her English clear.

"Naw," Abel panted. "No, I'm just too damn old." He glanced at her face and by the daylight could see the damage the cold had done to her dark eyes. Two pale stains rimmed by blood. Her feet were frostbitten, as were her hands and nose, and while Abel had wrapped her for warmth as best he could, he knew there was no way she could walk on her own. Swallowing, he staggered on, the breath rattling out of him. "It's just a march," he said. "Only a march." And he struggled on through the snow, down the slope between the trees.

They walked the day long and into the evening. They walked until the light was such that Abel could no longer be sure of their direction, and then they stopped in a small clearing where the trees stood windrucked in strange, tortured shapes like some wrongful orchard.

The girl was sobbing now. Her hands and feet were swollen red and hard. And the night, for the child, was long and cold. Abel did what he could: built up a tiny fire that constantly blew out, opened his coat and held her tiny, cold body against his own. And he spoke to her. He spoke all night long but did not know if she heard. Abel knew no stories to tell a child so instead described for her the stars and the planets in the heavens above. How his father would take him those long ago years to the hill south of their home where they would listen to the singing from the Negro church near the pine woods and look up at the stars. The pale ribbon of the Milky Way. Proud Orion in his glittering belt. The majestic ruin of the harvest moon and far, distant Mars that stirred men's blood to warring. He described for her the Leonids and pointed out four stars that fell for them that night. At intervals a wolf howled from the slopes above, lonely and long and wild and sad. And sometime that morning, well before the sun rose to pale the dark, Abel Truman rose with her from the snow and carried her onward.

As they went along, he described for the child's blind eyes the look of the snow in the forest and the characteristics of the trees around them. He told her how to make a tea from certain types of moss and how the sun pressed cups into the snow on the upper slopes. He recited all the hidden colors of the gray ocean and how it looked on summer evenings when warm winds blew and the stars lay reflected forever across its surface—as though there were two skies and no earth—and he described the mornings, too, when the fog lay close upon the waves and spilled from the forest so it seemed you were at the bottom of a great, warm cauldron. All these things and more, he told the child as they went along.

Abel walked until his feet went numb and he began to stumble. He spoke until his voice was croaking. And once, late in the day, Abel Truman raised his strong right hand before himself as though to push something back, away. He bent to lace his boots tighter and ate handfuls of snow to cool his throat. And he went on.

He told the girl of things he'd seen in his life—his soldiering days and the good people he'd known. He told her the story of the Wilderness where he fell and of Hypatia, who saved him there. He spoke to her of Glenn and Ellen Makers, and as night fell once more, Abel looked for stars above the canopy but saw only dark clouds. After a while, the snow began to fall again and steadily. A cold wind shifted. He carried her on, down the mountainside, through the dark trees.

Ellen Makers went slowly up the mountain through the snow. She held the rifle tightly crosswise and smelled the smoke long before she saw the column standing over the trees in the place she knew the trapper's shack to be. She stood watching it a moment, then rubbed the damp from beneath her nose and went on.

The track gave out onto a broad, snowy plain ringed by ice-veined mountain rock, and on the far side of the plain lay the smoldering ruins of the shack. Ellen crossed to it and stood warming herself beside the embers, wondering what to do. There were wolf tracks round about, and off to one side a dark mound upon the snow. She walked to it and took a fast breath to recognize the Haida laying there. She stood for some time thinking about things and trying to decide how to feel. It was not as she thought it would be, and she was fretful, her stomach knotted up with worry. She tried for some time to piece together a picture of the events by the clues left behind, but her skill for such unriddling was wanting and the day grew long and the embers cooled.

Eventually, the sun set and moon came out and by its high, blue light she saw a set of footprints leading into trees that stood silently and dark where the slope plunged valleyward again. A wolf howled close by, and Ellen jumped. After a moment, she turned to follow the trail down.

By morning, it had clouded over and begun to snow again. It fell thickly and fast, filling the steps behind her and painting the white world whiter still. The tracks she followed weaved ever downward through the trees and Ellen worried that she'd lose them to the snow. Late in the morning, she found where they'd camped and realized another set of tracks there. Smaller, as of a child's feet shuffling through the snow, they disappeared after a very short distance. "He's carrying someone," said Ellen. She took her gloves off, and as she crouched to touch two fingers to Abel's bootprint, a wolf stepped out of the forest.

The rifle was cold and heavy in her bare hands, and she had no way to know how long the wolf had been watching her before it came out of the trees. Dark about the face, the wolf was speckled with snow. Ellen could see the dog in it; in the folds of its ears and in its eyes, which gave glimpse to the workings of its innermost heart. She saw the collar it wore: crude and dull and handmade. The wolf stood without moving, watching her with its mouth open and its breath fogging the cold.

Ellen swallowed and brought the rifle quickly to her shoulder. As she sighted down the barrel the wolf lay down in the snow. She blinked and the wolf rolled over and stood, crusted in powder and beautiful amidst the snow-feathered trees.

Ellen held the rifle on it. She squinted down the barrel in the way

Glenn had taught her and stood that way, watching the wolf without moving, for a long time. It turned and paced, and as it did she saw again the dull gleam of metal about its throat. And when she lowered the rifle, it barked once and ran off, disappearing into the trees and the falling snow.

When she walked to the place it had been, she heard it bark again and looked to see it waiting for her farther down the slope. Ellen looked around. She wore a scarf tucked into her coat, and she took this off and tied it around her head and face for the warmth of it, then nodded. "All right," she said. "Show me."

She followed it the rest of the morning, through the trees and down the slope, and the walking was hard in the deepening snow. The air grew colder the farther down she went, and she could hear the wolf ahead of her, panting and crunching through the snow. Every now and again came great cracking sounds as branches, over-heavy with snow, came crashing down. Other than the wolf, there was no wildlife round about—only the soft tick of falling snow, the branches cracking like gunshots, and the ancient trees creaking cease-lessly like the speech of old men remembering other places, other times. There was no wind now, and the snow fell straight to earth, a hazy, pale scrim that made of the cold forest a phantom wonderland terrible in its beauty.

She was thinking of Glenn as she stumbled along, worrying for him, imagining the line of their life together, and seeing them in their age—quiet, a bit sad, but strong in their love. When a clump of snow slid from the branches and struck her shoulder, Ellen stopped. She could no longer hear the wolf, and when she looked, she saw its tracks veering away from the course it had followed all day to cut back up the slope between the trees and gone. As she stood wondering what to do, she heard the child sobbing from the trees ahead.

Ellen skinned the gloves from her hands. Taking a deep breath, she started slowly forward. She'd not gone fifty paces before finding

Abel Truman where he lay propped against the thick trunk of an old spruce.

He looked up at her, his face a frozen map that showed her the byways of his cares. Abel's coat was wrapped around a bundle held fast in the crippled crook of his left arm, and the cold had been at him, darkening with frostbite the tips of his ears and his fingers and his nose, and his lips were a shade of blue.

She threw the rifle down and knelt beside the old man. For all his manifold hurts, his eyes were bright, and when he opened his mouth his voice was hard to bear. "Lizzy," he whispered. "My 'Lizbet." Abel raised his hand to touch the side of Ellen's face where the scarf covered it, and she took his hand in her own, then hissed to feel the cold in it. "Oh, I missed you." He smiled a terrible smile. "God damn girl," he panted. "But I missed you so."

Ellen said his name and shook her head and the bundle he held made a sound. Abel swallowed and looked to it, then back to her. "It's our Jane," he said, blinking. "I went out . . . went out and brung her back."

With shaking hands, Ellen worked open his frozen coat and saw the child and saw how it was with her in the dark cold. "Oh, my God," she breathed, touching the girl's face to feel the heat at her cheek.

Abel made a sound, blinked fast as though coming awake, turning back from some place he was bound. "Ellen," he breathed. "Good . . . Her folks was killed up above . . . You go on, take her." And when she leaned to lift the child, she had to work to free her from Abel's crippled grip.

He leaned forward and pressed a little charm, a white cross carved of bone or something like bone, into Ellen's hand. He worked his lips about. "For the girl," he whispered, his tongue licking out over his lips. He closed his eyes, and when he opened them once more to look at her, she could tell he was far away and moving farther.

"You see?" he whispered. "You see, Hypatia? I told you I'd bring you along."

Abel closed his eyes. He was running. The grass was green with spring and fragrant, knee-high and cushioning his steps. And there was sun and a warm wind blew. Men called to him from the trees just atop the rise. He ran. He ran to them.

In the end, it took Ellen the rest of that day and all the next to get back down the mountain with the both of them. She made a crude travois from branches and strips torn from her scarf and laid Abel upon it. She held the child tightly, still wrapped in the old man's coat, for she cried out whenever Ellen tried to take her from it. The frame kept coming apart, so their progress was slow and wearying, and when they finally reached Makers' Acres, Glenn, looking thin and sickly, was waiting on the porch. They held each other a long moment, and then he helped her as best he could to get them all inside, where there was a fire and warmth.

They lay Abel and the girl together in the back room, covered them with blankets, stoked the fire, and left open the door so the heat would circulate. They stripped them from their frozen clothes and covered them again naked with blankets. When she saw what had become of the old man, Ellen turned away, and Glenn bid her leave the room while he tended them.

She stood near the hearth to watch the fire. Snow fell against the roof and the wind blew past the chimney, and for a moment, she fancied she heard the wolf howling from the hills above. Ellen went about the room touching dust from shelves that bore no dust upon them. The old, sweet smell of apples lingered.

Her frozen clothes were thawing, turning wet, and she began to feel cold. A dark stain of blood marked the hearthstones, and she ran her tongue over her broken teeth, then stared out the window, where the night was clearing. Glittering points of stars appeared, and she reckoned at least some should be falling. But none did. Instead, the moon came out to hammer the fallen snow silver and blue.

At some point Glenn came and sat down across from her. He looked wearier than she had ever seen him, and his unwounded hand trembled on the table when he laid it down. Ellen watched it there a moment before settling her own into it. It was warm and it was strong and when she looked at him the questions in her eyes were easy for him to read.

"She won't get her eyes back, I don't think." He shrugged and shook his head at the pity of it. "I think she can still see a little, or maybe just sometimes, but I'd be surprised if it lasts." He shrugged again. "If we're lucky, she'll keep most of her fingers . . . a few of her toes."

"He said her parents were dead. Killed."

Glenn pursed his lips. "Well," he said. "There'll be time enough for sorting all that out."

Ellen nodded. She traced the flour-whitened wood grain as though she'd conjure a primer from the tabletop. Setting her lips together over her broken teeth, she looked out the window to the stars where they glittered as only stars can on snowy nights in the dark of the wilderness. "Abel?" she asked.

"Dead," said Glenn.

# A Note on the Author

Lance Weller has published short fiction in several literary journals. He won *Glimmer Train*'s Short Story Award for New Writers and was nominated for a Pushcart Prize. This is his first novel. He lives in Gig Harbor, Washington, with his wife and several dogs.